Jennie blushed. She did that a lot. Travis liked it.

He moved closer, flattening his palms against the cab of the truck so that his arms encased her. He looked into her eyes. Looked at her lips. Gave her a second to figure out what was coming.

Ohmygod, she thought. *Oh—my—God!*

He lifted her off the ground, one arm around her waist. Her face was on a level with his; he kissed her slowly, caught her lip between his teeth and sucked on her flesh, and—and—

He kissed the place where her neck and shoulder joined.

It was magic.

Her eyes closed; the world went away.

And when he asked her to go home with him she gave him the only logical answer—because, after all, she was nothing if not logical.

She said, "Yes."

THE WILDE BROTHERS

Wilde by name, unashamedly wild by nature!

They work hard, but you can be damned sure they play even harder! For as long as any of them could remember, they've always loved the same things: Danger…and beautiful women.

They gladly took up the call to serve their country, but duty, honour and pride are words that mask the scars of a true warrior. Now, one by one, the brothers return to their family ranch in Texas.

Can their hearts be tamed in the place they once called home?

Meet the deliciously sexy **Wilde Brothers** in this sizzling and utterly unmissable new family dynasty by much-loved author Sandra Marton!

In August you met

THE DANGEROUS JACOB WILDE

In December were you able to resist

THE RUTHLESS CALEB WILDE?

This month meet

THE MERCILESS TRAVIS WILDE

THE MERCILESS TRAVIS WILDE

BY
SANDRA MARTON

MILLS & BOON

First published in Great Britain 2013
by Mills & Boon, an imprint of Harlequin (UK) Limited.
Harlequin (UK) Limited, Eton House, 18-24 Paradise Road,
Richmond, Surrey TW9 1SR

© Sandra Marton 2013

ISBN: 978 0 263 91006 3

Harlequin (UK) policy is to use papers that are natural, renewable and recyclable products and made from wood grown in sustainable forests. The logging and manufacturing process conform to the legal environmental regulations of the country of origin.

Printed and bound by
CPI Group (UK) Ltd, Croydon, CR0 4YY

Sandra Marton wrote her first novel while she was still in primary school. Her doting parents told her she'd be a writer some day, and Sandra believed them. In secondary school and college she wrote dark poetry nobody but her boyfriend understood—though, looking back, she suspects he was just being kind. As a wife and mother she wrote murky short stories in what little spare time she could manage, but not even her boyfriend-turned-husband could pretend to understand those. Sandra tried her hand at other things, among them teaching and serving on the Board of Education in her home town, but the dream of becoming a writer was always in her heart.

At last Sandra realised she wanted to write books about what all women hope to find: love with that one special man, love that's rich with fire and passion, love that lasts for ever. She wrote a novel, her very first, and sold it to Mills & Boon® Modern™ Romance. Since then she's written more than sixty books, all of them featuring sexy, gorgeous, larger-than-life heroes. A four-time RITA® award finalist, she's also received five *RT Book Reviews* magazine awards, and has been honoured with *RT*'s Career Achievement Award for Series Romance. Sandra lives with her very own sexy, gorgeous, larger-than-life hero in a sun-filled house on a quiet country lane in the north-eastern United States.

Recent titles by the same author:

THE RUTHLESS CALEB WILDE
  (The Wilde Brothers)
THE DANGEROUS JACOB WILDE
  (The Wilde Brothers)
SHEIKH WITHOUT A HEART

Did you know these are also available as eBooks?
Visit www.millsandboon.co.uk

CHAPTER ONE

FOR AS LONG as Travis Wilde could remember, Friday nights had belonged to his brothers and him.

They'd started setting those evenings aside way back in high school. Nobody had made a formal announcement. Nobody had said, "Hey, how about we make Friday evenings ours?"

It had just happened, was all, and over the ensuing years, it had become an unspoken tradition.

The Wildes got together on Fridays, no matter what.

Always.

Okay.

Maybe not always.

One of them might be away on business, Caleb on one coast or the other, dealing with a client in some complicated case of corporate law; Jacob in South America or Spain, buying horses for his own ranch or for *El Sueño*, the family spread; Travis meeting with investors anywhere from Dallas to Singapore.

And there'd been times one or more of the Wildes had been ass-deep in some bug-infested foreign hellhole, trying to stay alive in whatever war needed the best combat helicopter pilot, secret agency spook, or jet jockey the U.S. of A. could provide.

There'd even been times a woman got in the way.

Travis lifted a bottle of beer to his lips.

That didn't happen often.

Women were wonderful and mysterious creatures, but brothers were, well, they were brothers. You shared the same blood, the same memories.

That made for something special.

The bottom line was that barring the end of the world and the appearance of the Four Horsemen of the Apocalypse, if it was Friday night, if the Wildes were within reasonable distance of each other, they'd find a bar where the brews were cold, the steaks rare, the music an upbeat blend of Willie Nelson and Bruce Springsteen, and they'd settle in for a couple of hours of relaxation.

This place didn't quite meet that description.

It wasn't where the Wildes had planned on going tonight but then, as it had turned out, Travis was the only Wilde who'd been up for getting together at all.

The original plan had been to meet at a bar they knew and liked, maybe half a dozen blocks from his office, a quiet place with deep booths, good music on the speakers, half a dozen varieties of locally-brewed beer on tap and by the bottle, and steaks the size of Texas sizzling on an open grill.

That plan had changed, and Travis had ended up in here by accident.

Once he knew he would be on his own, he'd driven around for a while, finally got thirsty and hungry, stopped at the first place he saw.

This one.

No deep booths. No Willy or Bruce. No locally-brewed beer. No grill and no steaks.

Instead, there were half a dozen beat-up looking tables and chairs. The kind of music that made your brain go numb, blasting from the speakers. A couple of brands of beer. Burgers oozing grease, served up from a kitchen in the back.

The best thing about the place was the bar itself, a long

stretch of zinc that either spoke of earlier, better days or of dreams that had never quite materialized.

Travis had pretty much known what he'd find as soon as he pulled into the parking lot, saw the dented pickups with their rusted fenders, the half a dozen Harleys parked together like a pack of coyotes.

He'd also known what he wouldn't find.

Friendly faces. Babes that looked as if they'd just stepped out of the latest Neiman Marcus catalogue. A dartboard on one wall, photos of local sports guys on another. St. Ambrose beer and rare steaks.

Not a great place for a stranger who was alone but if a man knew how to keep to himself, which years spent on not-always-friendly foreign soil had definitely taught him to do, he could at least grab something to eat before heading home.

He'd gotten some looks when he walked through the door. That figured. He was an unknown in a place where people almost certainly knew each other or at least recognized each other.

Physically, at least, he blended in.

He was tall. Six foot three in his bare feet, lean and muscled, the result of years riding and breaking horses growing up on *El Sueño,* the family's half-million acre ranch a couple of hours from Dallas. High school and college football had honed him to a tough edge, and Air Force training had done the rest.

At thirty-four, he worked out every morning in the gym in his Turtle Creek condo and he still rode most weekends, played pickup games of touch football with his brothers…

Correction, he thought glumly.

He used to play touch football with Caleb and Jacob, but they didn't have much time for that anymore.

Which was one of the reasons he was in this bar tonight. His brothers didn't have much time for anything anymore and, dammit, no, he wasn't feeling sorry for himself—he was a grown man, after all.

What he was, was mourning the loss of a way of life.

Travis tilted the bottle of Bud to his lips, took a long swallow and stared at his reflection in the fly-specked mirror behind the bar.

Bachelorhood. Freedom. No responsibility to or for anyone but yourself.

Yes, his brothers were giving life on the other side of that line a try and God knew, he wished them all the best but, though he'd never say it to them, he had a bad feeling how that would end up.

Love was an ephemeral emotion. Here today, gone tomorrow. Lip service, at best.

How his brothers had missed that life-lesson was beyond him.

He, at least, had not.

Which brought him straight back to what had been the old Friday night routine of steaks, beer…

And the one kind of bond you could count on.

The bond between brothers.

He'd experienced it growing up with Jake and Caleb, at college when he played football, in the Air Force, first in weeks of grueling training, then in that small, elite circle of men who flew fighter jets.

Male bonding, was the trendy media term for it, but you didn't need fancy words to describe the link of trust you could forge with a brother, whether by blood or by fate.

That was what those Friday nights had been about.

Sitting around, talking about nothing in particular—the safety the Cowboys had just signed. The wobbly fate of the Texas Rangers. Poker, a game they all liked and at which Travis was an expert. Which was more of an icon, Jake's vintage Thunderbird or Travis's '74 Stingray 'Vette, and was there any reasonable explanation for Caleb driving that disgustingly new Lamborghini?

And, naturally, they'd talked about women.

Except, the Wildes didn't talk about women anymore.

Travis sighed, raised the bottle again and drank.

Caleb and Jake. His brothers.

Married.

It still seemed impossible but it was true. So was what went with it.

He'd spoken with each of his brothers as recently as yesterday, reminded them—and when, in the past, had they needed reminding?—that Friday was coming up and they'd be meeting at seven at that bar near his office.

"Absolutely," Caleb had said.

"See you then," Jake had told him.

And here he was. The Lone Ranger.

The worst of it was, he wasn't really surprised.

No reflection on his sisters-in-law.

Travis was crazy about both Addison and Sage, loved them as much as he loved his own three sisters, but why deny it?

Marriage—commitment—changed everything.

"I can't make it tonight, Trav," Caleb had said when he'd phoned in midafternoon. We have Lamaze."

"Who?"

"It's not a who, it's a what. Lamaze. You know. Childbirth class. It's usually on Thursday but the instructor had to cancel so it's tonight, instead."

Childbirth class. His brother, the tough corporate legal eagle? The one-time spook? Childbirth class?

"Travis?" Caleb had said. "You there?"

"I'm here," he'd said briskly. "Lamaze. Right. Well, have fun."

"Lamaze isn't about fun, dude."

"I bet."

"You'll find out someday."

"Bite your tongue."

Caleb had laughed. "Remember that housekeeper we had right after Mom died? The one who used to say, *First comes love, then comes marriage...*"

Thinking back to the conversation, Travis shuddered.

Why would any of that ever apply to him?

Even if—big "if"—even if marriage worked, it changed a man.

Besides, love was just a nice word for sex, and why be modest?

He already had all the sex a man could handle, without any of the accompanying complications.

No "*I love you and I'll wait for you,*" which turned out to mean "*I'll wait a couple of months before I get into bed with somebody else.*"

Been there, done that, his first overseas tour.

Truth was, once he'd moved past the anger, it hadn't meant much. He'd been young; love had been an illusion.

And he should have known better, anyway, growing up in a home where your mother got sick and died and your father was too busy saving the world to come home and be with her or his sons...

And, dammit, what was with his mood tonight?

Travis looked up, caught the bartender's eye and signaled for another beer.

The guy nodded. "Comin' up."

Jake's phone call had followed on the heels of Caleb's.

"Hey," he'd said.

"Hey," Travis had replied, which didn't so much mark him as a master of brilliant dialogue as it suggested he knew what was coming.

"So," Jake had said, clearing his throat, "about getting together tonight—"

"You can't make it."

"Yes. I mean, no. I can't."

"Because?"

"Well, it turns out Addison made an appointment for us to meet with—with this guy."

"What guy?"

"Just a guy. About the work we've been doing, you know, remodeling the house."

"I thought that was your department. The extension, the extra bathrooms, the new kitchen—"

"It is. This guy does—he does other stuff."

"Such as?"

"Jeez, don't you ever give up? Such as recommending things."

"Things?"

"Wallpaper," Jake had all but snarled. "Okay? The guy's bringing over ten million wallpaper samples and Adoré told me about it days ago but I forgot and it's too late to—"

"Yeah. Okay. No problem," Travis had said because what right did he have to embarrass his war-hero brother more than he'd already embarrassed himself? The proof was right there, in Jake using his supposedly-unknown-to-the-rest-of-humanity pet name for his wife.

"Next week," Jake had said. "Right?"

Right, Travis thought, oh, yeah, right.

By next week, Caleb would be enrolled in Baby Burping 101 and Jake would be staring at fabric swatches, or whatever you called squares of cotton or velvet.

Domesticity was right up there with Lamaze.

Nothing he wanted to try.

Not ever.

He liked his life just the way it was, thank you very much. There was a big world out there, and he'd seen most of it—but not all. He still had places to go, things to do…

Things that might get the taste of war and death out of his mouth.

People talked about cleansing your palette between wine

tastings but nobody talked about cleansing your soul after piloting a jet into combat missions…

And, damn, what was he doing?

A flea-bitten bar in the wrong part of town absolutely was not the place for foolish indulgence in cheap philosophy.

Travis finished his beer.

Without being asked, the bartender opened a bottle, put it in front of him.

"Thanks."

"Haven't seen you in here before."

Travis shrugged. "First time for everything."

"You want somethin' to eat before the kitchen closes?"

"Sure. A steak, medium-rare."

"Your money, but the burgers are better."

"Fine. A burger. Medium-rare."

"Fries okay?"

"Fries are fine."

"Comin' right up."

Travis tilted the bottle to his lips.

A couple of weeks ago, his brothers had asked him what was doing with him. Was he feeling a little off lately?

"You're the ones who're off," he'd said with a quick smile. "Married. Living by the rules."

"Sometimes, rules are what a man needs," Jake had said.

"Yeah," Caleb had added. "You know, it might be time to reassess your life."

Reassess his life?

He liked his life just fine, thank you very much.

He needed precisely what he had. Life in the fast lane. Work hard. Play hard.

Nothing wrong with that.

It was how he'd always been.

His brothers, too, though war had changed them. Jake had, still was, battling through PTSD. Caleb carried a wariness inside him that would probably never go away.

Not him.

Sure, there were times he woke up, heart pounding, re-membering stuff a man didn't want to remember, but a day at his office, taking a chance on a new stock offering and clearing millions as a result, a night in bed with a new, spec-tacular woman who was as uninterested in settling down as he was, and he was fine again.

Maybe that was the problem.

There hadn't been a woman lately.

And, now that he thought about it, what was with that? He wasn't into celibacy any more than he was into domes-ticity and yet, it had been days, hell, weeks since he'd been with a woman...

"Burger, medium-rare, with fries," the bartender said, slid-ing a huge plate across the bar.

Travis looked at the burger. It was the size of a Frisbee and burned to a crisp.

Good thing he wasn't really hungry, he thought, and he picked up a fry and took a bite.

The place was crowding up. Almost all the stools were taken at the bar; the same for the tables. The clientele, if you could call it that, was mostly male. Big. Tough-looking. Lots of facial hair, lots of tattoos.

Some of them looked him over.

Travis didn't hesitate to look back.

He'd been in enough places like this one, not just in Texas but in some nasty spots in eastern Europe and Asia, to know that you never flinched from eye contact.

It worked, especially because he didn't look like a week-end cowboy out for a night among the natives.

Aside from his height and build, which had come to him courtesy of Viking, Roman, Comanche and Kiowa ancestors, it helped that he'd given up his day-at-the-office custom-made Brioni suit for a well-worn gray T-shirt, equally well-worn jeans and a pair of Roper boots he'd had for years but then, why would any guy wear a suit and everything that went with it when he could be comfortable in jeans?

The clothes, the boots, his physical build, even his coloring—ink-black hair, courtesy of his Indian forebears, deep green eyes, thanks to his pillage-rape-and-romp European ancestors—all combined to make him look like, well, like what he was, a guy who wouldn't look for trouble but damned well wouldn't walk away from it if it came his way.

"A gorgeous, sexy, bad boy," one mistress had called him.

It had embarrassed the hell out of him—at least, that was what he'd claimed—but, hey, could a man fight his DNA?

The blood of generations of warriors pulsed in his veins, as it did in the veins of his brothers. Their father, the general, had raised them on tales of valor and courage and, in situations where it was necessary, the usefulness of an attitude that said don't-screw-with-me if you're smart.

It was a message men understood and generally respected, though there was almost always some jerk who thought it didn't apply to him.

That was fine.

It was equally fine that women understood it, too, and reacted to it in ways that meant he rarely spent a night alone, except by choice...

"Hi, honey."

Last time he'd checked, the barstool to his left had been empty. Not anymore. A blonde was perched on it, smiling as if she'd just found an unexpected gift under a Christmas tree.

Uh-oh.

She was surely a gift, too. For someone.

But that someone wasn't him.

To put it kindly, she wasn't his type.

Big hair that looked as if it had been shellacked into submission. Makeup she probably had to remove with a trowel. Tight cotton T-shirt, her boobs resting on a muffin-top of flesh forced up by too-tight jeans.

All that was bad enough.

What made it worse was that he knew the unspoken etiquette in a place like this.

A lady made a move on you, you were supposed to be flattered. Otherwise, you risked offending her—

Her, and the neighborhood *aficionados* who'd suddenly shifted their attention his way.

"Hello," he said with forced politeness, and then gave all his attention to his plate.

"You're new here."

Travis took a bite of hamburger, chewed as if chewing were the most important thing in his life.

"I'm Bev."

He nodded. Kept chewing.

She leaned in close, wedged one of her 40 Double D's against his arm.

"You got a name, cowboy?"

Now what? This was not a good situation. Whatever he did, short of taking Bev's clear invitation to heart, would almost surely lead to trouble.

She'd be insulted, her pals would think they had to ride to the rescue...

Maybe honesty, polite and up-front, was the best policy.

Travis took a paper napkin from its metal holder, blotted his lips and turned toward her.

"Listen, Bev," he said, not unkindly, "I'm not interested, okay?" Her face reddened and he thought, *hell, I'm not doing this right.* "I mean, you're a—a good-looking woman but I'm—I'm meeting somebody."

"Really?" Bev said coldly. "You want me to believe you're waitin' for your date?"

"Exactly. She'll be here any—"

"You're waitin' for your date, and you're eatin' without her?"

The guy on the other side of Bev was leaning toward them.

He was the size of a small mountain and from the look in his tiny eyes, he was hot and ready for a Friday night fight.

Slowly, carefully, Travis put down the burger and the napkin.

The Mountain outweighed him by fifty pounds, easy, and the hand wrapped around the bottle he was holding was the size of a ham.

No problem. Travis had taken on bigger men and come through just fine. If anything, it added to the kick.

Yes, but the Mountain has friends here. Many. And you, dude, are all by your lonesome.

The Voice of Reason.

Despite what his brothers sometimes said about him, Travis had been known not just to hear that voice but to listen to it.

But Bev was going on and on about no-good, scumbag liars and her diatribe had drawn the attention of several of the Mountain's pals. Every last one of them looked happy to come to her aid by performing an act of chivalry that would surely involve beating the outsider—him—into a bloody mass of barely-breathing flesh.

Not good, said the Voice of Reason.

The bloody part was okay. He'd been there before.

But there was a problem.

He had a meeting in Frankfurt Monday morning, a huge deal he'd been working on for months, and he had the not-very-surprising feeling that the board of directors at the ultraconservative, three-hundred-year-old firm of Bernhardt, Bernhardt and Stutz would not look kindly on a financial expert who showed up with a couple of black eyes, a dinged jaw and, for all he knew, one or two missing teeth.

It would not impress them at all if he explained that he'd done his fair share of damage. More than his fair share, because he surely would manage that.

Dammit, where were a man's brothers when he needed them?

"The lady's talkin' to you." The Mountain was leaning past Bev. God, his breath stank. "What's the matter? You got a hearin' problem or something, pretty boy?"

Conversation died out. People smiled.

Travis felt the first, heady pump of adrenaline.

"My name," he said carefully, "is not 'pretty boy.'"

"His name is not pretty boy," The Mountain mimicked.

Bev, sporting a delighted smile, slid from her stool. Maybe he'd misjudged her purpose. Maybe setting up a fight had been her real job.

Either way, Travis saw his choices narrowing down, and rapidly.

Bev's defender got to his feet.

"You're making a mistake," Travis said quietly.

The Mountain snorted.

Travis nodded, took a last swig of beer, said a mental "goodbye" to Monday's meeting and stood up.

"Outside," he said, "in the parking lot? Or right here?"

"Here," a voice growled.

Three men had joined the Mountain. Travis smiled. The next five minutes might be the end of him.

Yeah, but they'd also be fun, especially considering his weird state of mind tonight.

"Fine," he said. "Sounds good to me."

Those words, the commitment to the inevitable, finalized things, sent his adrenaline not just pumping but racing. He hadn't been in a down-and-dirty bar brawl in a very long time. Not since Manila, or maybe Kandahar.

Yes, Kandahar, his last mission, death all around him...

Suddenly, pounding the Mountain into pulp seemed a fine idea, never mind that deal in Frankfurt.

Besides, nothing short of a miracle could save him now...

The door to the street swung open.

For some reason Travis would never later be able to explain, the enraptured audience watching him and the Mountain turned toward it.

A blast of hot Texas air swept in.

So did a tall, beautiful, sexy-looking, straight-out-of-the-Neiman-Marcus-catalogue blonde.

Silence. Complete silence.

Everybody looked at Neiman Marcus.

Neiman Marcus looked at them.

And blanched.

"Well, lookee there," somebody said.

Lookee, indeed, Travis thought.

Sanity returned.

There she was. His salvation.

"Finally," he said, his tone bright and cheerful. "My date."

Before anyone could say a word, he started toward the blonde and the door with the confidence of a man holding all four aces in a game of high stakes poker.

She tilted her head back as he got closer. She was tall, especially in sexy, nosebleed-high stilettos, but she still had to do that to look up at him.

He liked it.

It was a nice touch.

"Your what?" she said, or would have said, but he couldn't afford to let things go that far.

"Baby," he purred, "what took you so long?"

Her eyes widened. "Excuse me?"

Travis grinned.

"Only if you ask real nice," he said, and before she could react, he drew her into his arms, brought her tightly against him and covered her mouth with his.

CHAPTER TWO

AN HOUR BEFORE she walked into Travis Wilde's life, Jennie Cooper had been sitting in her ancient Civic, having a stern talk with herself.

By then, it had been close to nine o'clock, the evening wasn't getting any younger, and she still hadn't put her plan into action.

Ridiculous, of course.

She was a woman with a mission.

She was looking for a bar.

Really, how difficult could it be to find a bar in a city like Dallas?

Very.

Well, "very" if you were searching for just the right kind of bar.

Dallas was a big, sprawling town, and she'd driven through so many parts of it that she'd lost count.

She'd started with Richardson and though there were loads of bars in that area, it would have been foolish, better still, foolhardy to choose one of them.

It was too near the university campus.

So she'd headed for the Arts District, mostly because she knew it, if visiting a couple of galleries on a rainy Sunday qualified as "knowing" a place—after eight months, she was still learning about her new city—but as soon as she got there, she'd realized it, too, was a bad choice.

The Arts District was trendy, which meant she'd feel out of place. A laugh, really, considering that she was going to feel out of place no matter where she went tonight, but it was also a neighborhood that surely would be popular with university faculty.

Running into someone who knew her would be disaster.

That was when Jennie had pulled to the curb, put her wheezing Civic in neutral and told herself to think fast, before her plan fell apart.

What other parts of Dallas were there?

Turtle Creek.

She knew it only by reputation, and that it was home to lots of young, successful, rich professionals.

Well, she'd thought with what might have been a choked laugh, she was young, anyway.

Rich? Not on a teaching assistant's stipend. Successful? Not in Turtle Creek terms, where the word surely referred to attorneys and doctors, financial gurus and industrialists.

What kind of small talk could she make with a man who was all those things, assuming such a man would look twice at her?

Assuming there'd be any small talk because, really, that wasn't what tonight was all about.

The realization sent a bolt of terror zinging along her nerve endings.

Jennie fought against it.

She wasn't scared.

Certainly not.

She was—she was anxious, and who wouldn't be? She'd spent weeks and weeks, planning this—this event.

She wasn't going to add to that anxiety by going to a bar in a place like Turtle Creek on a Friday night when—when singles mingled.

When singles hook up, Genevieve baby, her always-until-now-oh-so-logical alter ego had suddenly whispered.

"They mingle," Jennie had muttered. "And my name is not—"

Except, it was. For tonight. She'd decided that the same time she'd hatched this plan.

Good. You remembered. You're Genevieve. And you're trying to pretty things up. Tonight is not about mingling, it is about—

Jennie had stopped listening.

Still, there was truth to it.

Nobody could pretty this up.

Her plan was basic.

Find a bar. Go inside. Order a drink. Find a man she liked, flirt with him…

Forget the metaphors.

What she wanted was to find a man she liked enough to take home to bed.

Her teeth chattered.

"Stop it," she said sharply.

She was a grown woman. Twenty-four years old just last Sunday. That she had never slept with a man was disgraceful. It was worse than that.

It was unbelievable.

And the old Stones song lied.

Time wasn't on her side, which was why she was going to remedy that failing tonight.

"Happy birthday to me," she said, under her breath, and her teeth did the castanet thing again, which was ridiculous.

She had thought about this for a long time, examined the concept from every possible angle.

This was right. It was logical. It was appropriate.

It was how things had to be done.

No romance. This wasn't about romance.

No attachment. That part wasn't even worth analyzing.

She didn't have time for attachment, or emotion, or anything but the experience.

That was what this was all about.

It was research. It was learning something you'd only read about.

It was no different from what she'd done in the past, driving from New Hampshire to New York before she wrote her senior paper so that she could experience what had once been the narrow streets where Stanton Coit had established a settlement house for immigrants long before there were such things as social workers, or the trip she'd planned to see the Jane Addams Hull-House Museum in Chicago...

Her throat constricted.

Never mind all that.

Her days of academic research would soon be meaningless.

What she needed now was reality research, and if there wasn't such a branch of study, there should be.

And she was wasting precious time.

Jennie checked both rearview mirrors, put on her signal light and pulled away from the curb.

She headed south.

After a while, the streets began to change.

They grew narrower. Darker. The houses were smaller, crammed together as if huddled against a starless Texas night.

The one good thing was that there were lots of bars.

Lots and lots of bars.

She drove past them all.

Of course, she did.

None passed muster.

One didn't have enough vehicles parked outside.

One had too many.

One had the wrong kind.

Jennie's alter-ego gave an impolite snort. Jennie couldn't blame her. That made three out of three.

What was she, Goldilocks?

Okay. The very next bar would be The One. In caps. Definitely, The One.

She'd park, check her hair, her makeup—she'd never used this much makeup before and, ten to one, it was smeared...

BAR.

Her heart thumped.

There it was. Straight ahead. A bar called, appropriately enough, **BAR**. Well, no. That wasn't its name—she was pretty sure of that—it was simply a description, like a sign saying "liquor" outside a liquor store, or one that said "motel" outside a motel, or...

For God's sake, Genevieve, it's a bar!

She slowed the car, turned on her signal light, checked the mirrors, waited patiently for an approaching vehicle a block away to pass before she pulled into the parking lot.

It was crowded.

The last available empty space was between a shiny black behemoth of a truck and a battered red van.

She pulled between them, opened her door, checked the faded white lines, saw that she hadn't managed to center her car, shut the door, backed up carefully, shifted, pulled forward, checked again, backed up, checked one last time, saw she'd finally parked properly and shut off the engine.

Tick, tick, tick it said, and finally went silent.

Too silent.

She could hear her heart thudding.

Stop it!

Quickly, she opened her consignment-shop Dior purse, rummaged inside it, found her compact and flipped it open.

She'd spent twenty minutes this afternoon at Neiman Marcus, nervously wandering around among the endless cosmetic counters before she'd finally chosen one mostly because the clerk behind it looked a shade less unapproachable than the others.

"How may I help you, miss?" she'd said. "Foundation? Blusher? Eyebrows? Eyes? Lips? Hair? Skin?"

Translation: *Sweetie, you need work!*

But her smile had been pleasant and Jennie had taken a deep breath and said, "Do you do makeovers?"

Almost an hour later, the clerk—she was, she'd said, a cosmetician—put a big mirror in her hands and said, "Take a look."

Jennie had looked.

Nobody she knew looked back.

Who was this person with the long, loose blond waves framing her face? When had her pale lashes become curly and dark? And that pouting pink mouth, those cheekbones...

Cheekbones?

"Wow," she'd said softly.

The cosmetician had grinned.

"Wow, indeed. Your guy is gonna melt when he sees you tonight."

"No. I mean, that's just the point. I don't have—"

"So," the cosmetician had chirped, "what do we want to purchase?"

"Purchase?" Jennie had said, staring at the lineup of vials, bottles and tubes, the sprays, salves and brushes, even an instruction sheet about how to replicate the magic transformation. Her gaze had flown to the woman. "I can't possibly..." She'd swallowed hard, pointed to a tube of thirty-dollar mascara and said, "I'll take that."

Nobody was happy. Not the cosmetics wizard. Not Jennie, whose last mascara purchase had cost her six bucks at the supermarket.

Had all that time and money been worth it?

It was time to find out.

Even in the badly lit parking lot, her mirror assured her that she looked different.

It also assured her that she was wearing a mask.

Well, a disguise. Which was good.

It made her feel as if she was what she'd been trained to be, a researcher. An observer. An academic who would spend the next hours in a different kind of academia than she was accustomed to.

Jennie snapped the compact shut and put it back in her purse.

Which was why she was parked outside this place with the blinking neon sign.

Upscale? No. The lot was full of pickup trucks. She knew by now that pickup trucks were Texas the same way four-wheel drives were New England, but most of these were old. There were motorcycles, too.

Weren't motorcycles supposed to be sexy?

And there were lots of lighted beer signs in the window.

Downscale? Well, as compared to what? True, something about the place didn't seem appealing.

It's a bar, the dry voice inside her muttered. *What are you, a scout for* Better Homes and Gardens*?*

Still, was this a good choice? She'd worked up logical criteria.

A: Choose a place that drew singles. She knew what happened in singles bars. Well, she'd heard what happened, anyway—that they were where people went for uninhibited fun, drinking, dancing…and other things.

B: Do what she was going to do before summer changed to autumn.

C: Actually, it had not occurred to her there might be a part C. But there was.

Do Not Prevaricate.

And she was prevaricating.

She put away her compact. Opened the door. Stepped from the car. Shut the door. Locked it. Opened her purse. Put her keys inside. Closed the purse. Hung the thin strap over the shoulder of her equally thin-strapped emerald-green silk dress, bought from the same consignment shop as the purse, the Neiman Marcus tag still inside.

Assuming you could call something that stopped at midthigh a dress.

She knew it was.

Girls on campus wore dresses this length.

You're not a girl on campus, Jennie. And even when you were, back in New Hampshire, you never wore anything that looked like this.

And maybe if she had, she wouldn't be doing this tonight. She wouldn't have to be looking for answers to questions that needed answers, questions she was running out of time to ask...

"Stop," she whispered.

It was time to get moving.

She took a breath, then started walking toward the entrance to the bar, stumbling a little in the sky-high heels she'd also bought at the consignment shop.

She was properly turned out, from head to toe, to lure the kind of man she wanted into her bed. Somebody tall. Broad-shouldered. A long, lean, buff body. Dark hair, dark eyes, a gorgeous face because if you were going to lose your virginity to a stranger, if this was going to be your One and Only sexual experience, Jennie thought as she put her hand on the door to the bar and pushed it open, if this was going to be It, you wanted the man to be...

Was that music?

It was loud. Very loud. What was it? She had no idea. Telling Tchaikovsky from Mozart was one thing. Telling rock from rock was another.

She caught her bottom lip between her teeth.

Maybe she was making a mistake.

Yes, the place was far from the university. She wouldn't see anyone she knew, but what about the rest? Was it a singles bar? Or was it—what did people call them? A tavern? A neighborhood place where people came to drink?

Such a dark street. Such an unprepossessing building. That neon sign, even the asphalt because now that she'd seen it, close-up, she could see that it was cracked…

That's enough!

She'd talked herself out of a dozen other possibilities. She was not talking herself out of this one.

Chin up, back straight—okay, one last hand smoothing her hair, one last tug at her dress and she really should have chosen one that covered her thighs…

Jennie reached for the door, yanked it open…

And stepped into a sensory explosion.

The music pulsed off the walls, vibrated through the floor.

The smell was awful. Yeasty, kind of like rising bread dough but not as pleasant, and under it, the smell of things frying in grease.

And the noise! People shouting over the music. What sounded like hundreds of them. Not really; there weren't hundreds of people at the long bar, at the handful of tables, but there were lots of them…And they were mostly male.

Some were wearing leather.

Maybe she'd made a mistake. Wandered into a gay…

No. These guys weren't gay. They were—they were unattractive. Lots of facial hair. Lots of tattoos. Lots of big bellies overhanging stained jeans.

There were a few women, but that didn't help. The women were—big. Big hair. Big boobs. Big everything.

People were looking at her.

Indeed they are, Genevieve. That's what people do, when a woman all dressed up walks into a place like this.

Oh, God. Even her alter-ego thought she'd made a mistake!

Her heart leaped into her throat. She wanted to turn around and go right out the door.

But it was too late.

A man was walking toward her.

Not walking. Sauntering, was more accurate, his long stride slow and easy, more than a match for his lazy smile.

Her breath caught.

His eyes were dark. His hair was the color of rich, dark coffee. It was thick, and longer than a man's hair should be, longer, anyway, than the way men in her world wore it, and she had the swift, almost overwhelming desire to bury her hands in it.

Plus, he was tall.

Tall and long and lean and muscled.

You could almost sense the hard delineation of muscle in his wide shoulders and arms and chest, and—and she was almost certain he had a—what did you call it? A six-pack, that was it. A six-pack right there, in his middle.

A middle that led down to—down to his lower middle.

To more muscle, a different kind of muscle, hidden behind faded denim…

Her cheeks burned.

Her gaze flew up again, over, what, all six foot two, six foot three of him. Flew up over worn boots, jeans that fit his long legs and narrow hips like a second skin, a T-shirt that clung to his torso.

Their eyes met.

Tall as she was, especially in the stilettos, she had to look up for that to happen.

He smiled.

Her mouth went dry. He was, in a word, gorgeous.

"Baby," he said in a husky voice. "What took you so long?"

Huh?

Nobody knew she'd been coming here tonight. She hadn't even known it herself, until she'd pulled into the parking lot.

"Excuse me?"

His smile became a grin. Could grins be sexy and hot? Oh yes. Yes, they could.

"Only if you ask real nice," he said, and then, without any warning, she was in his arms and his mouth was on hers.

CHAPTER THREE

TRAVIS LIKED WOMEN.

In bed, of course. Sex was one of life's great pleasures. But he liked them in other ways, too.

Their scent. Their softness. Those Mona Lisa smiles that could keep a man guessing for hours, even days.

And all the things that were part of sex…

He could never have enough of those.

He knew, from years of locker-room talk, that some men saw kissing as nothing but a distraction from the main event.

Not him.

Kissing was something that deserved plenty of time. He loved exploring a woman's taste, the silken texture of her lips, the feel of them as they parted to the demand of his.

Women liked it, too.

Enough of them had mingled their sighs with his, melted in his arms, parted their lips to the silken thrust of his tongue to convince him—why not be honest?—that he was a man skilled at the act.

Tonight, none of that mattered.

The blonde was attractive—the ruse wouldn't work if she weren't—but there was nothing personal involved.

Kissing her was a means to an end, a way to get him out of a confrontation in a Dallas dive to a boardroom in Frankfurt without looking as if he'd gone ten rounds in a bar exactly like this one.

The key to success? He'd known he'd have to move fast, take her by surprise, kiss her hard enough to silence any protest.

With luck, she'd go along with the game.

Far more exotic things happened in bars everywhere than a man stealing a kiss.

Besides, a woman who looked like this, who walked into a place like this, wasn't naive.

For all he knew, she was out slumming.

A kiss from a stranger might be just the turn-on she wanted.

And if she protested, he'd play to his audience, pretend it was all about her being ticked off at him for some imagined lover's slight.

Either way, he wasn't going to give her, or them, a lot of time to think about it.

He'd kiss her, then hustle her outside where he could explain it had all been a game and either thank her for her cooperation or apologize for what he'd done…or maybe, just maybe, she'd laugh and what the hell, the night was still young.

Bottom line?

Kissing her was all he had to work with, so he flashed his best smile, the one that never failed to thaw a woman's defenses, reached out, put his arms around her, gathered her in…

Her eyes widened. She slapped both hands against his chest.

"What do you think you're doing?"

Travis showed her.

He captured her lips with his.

For nothing longer than a second, he thought he was home

free. Sure, she stiffened against him, said *"Mmmff"* or something close to it, but he could work with that.

The problem?

She went crazy in his arms.

It would have done his ego good to think she'd gone crazy
with pleasure.

But she hadn't.

She went crazy the way he'd once seen his sister Em do
when she'd bent down to pick up what she'd thought was a
compact and found herself, instead, with a handful of ta-
rantula.

The blonde in his arms jerked against him. Pounded his
shoulders with her fists. Said that *"Mmmff"* thing again and
again and again…

Somebody laughed.

Somebody said, "What the hell's he doin'?"

Somebody else said, "Damned if ah know."

What Travis knew was that this was not good.

"I'm not trying to hurt you," he snarled, his mouth a breath
from Blondie's.

"Mmmff!"

She struggled harder. Lifted her foot. Put one of those stiletto heels into his instep and it was a damn good thing he
was wearing boots.

He put his lips to her ear.

"Lady. Listen to what I'm saying. I'm not—"

Big mistake.

"Help," she yelled, or would have yelled—he could see her
lips forming the sound of that "h"—so, really, what choice
did he have?

He kissed her again.

This time, her knee came up.

He felt it coming, twisted to avoid it, then hung on to her
for dear life.

The crowd hooted.

Jeez, was he going to be the night's entertainment?

"Lady sure do seem happy to see you, cowboy," the Mountain shouted.

Everybody roared with laughter.

Okay.

This called for a different approach.

Travis thrust one hand into Blondie's hair, clamped the other at the base of her spine, tilted her backward over his arm just enough to keep her off balance and brushed his lips over hers.

Once. Twice. Three times, each time ignoring that angry *Mmmff.*

"Don't fight me," he whispered between kisses. "Just make this look real and I swear, I'll let you go."

No *mmmff* that time. Nothing but a little sighing sound…

And the softest, most delicate whisper of her breath.

"Good girl," Travis murmured, and he changed the angle of his mouth on hers…

God, she tasted sweet.

Slowly he drew her erect. Put both hands into her hair. Kissed her a little harder.

She tasted like sunshine on a soft June morning, smelled like wildflowers after a summer rain.

His arms went around her; he gathered her against the hardness of his body, felt the softness of her breasts and belly against him.

The crowd cheered.

Travis barely heard them.

He was lost in what was happening, the feel of the woman in his arms, the race of her heart against his.

An urgency he'd never felt before raced through him.

He was on fire.

So was she.

She was trembling. Whimpering. She was—

Sweet Lord.

The truth hit. Hard. She wasn't on fire for him, she was terrified.

She hadn't acquiesced to his kisses, she'd stopped fighting them.

What kind of SOB did this to a woman? Scared the life out of her, and all to save his own sorry ass?

All at once, the trip to Frankfurt lost its meaning. He was a financial wizard but what he really was, was a gambler. He'd lost money before; he'd lose it again.

Millions were on the line.

So what?

When had winning become so important he'd use someone—not just "someone" but a woman—to make sure the dice rolled the way he wanted?

He lifted his head. Looked down into the face of the woman in his arms.

His gut twisted.

Her skin was pale, the color all but completely drained away. Her breathing was swift; he could see the rapid pulse fluttering in her throat. Her eyes—her eyes, he knew, would haunt him forever. They were beautiful eyes, but now they had turned dark with fear.

"Oh, honey," he said softly.

She shook her head. "Don't," she said in a tiny whisper. "Please. Don't—"

He kissed her again, but lightly, tenderly, his lips barely moving against hers.

"I'm sorry," he said. "I never meant to frighten you."

There was a whisper of sound behind him. He was giving the game away. Screw it. Screw whatever would happen next. All he wanted was to get that look of fear off the blonde's lovely face.

"Lovely" didn't come close.

That cloud of silken hair. The dark blue eyes. The soft, rosy mouth.

She was still shaking.

No way was he going to let that continue.

"I'm not going to hurt you," he said. "I never intended to hurt you." Her face registered disbelief, and Travis shook his head. "It's the truth, honey. This was never about you. Not the way you think." He framed her face with his hands, raised it just a little so he was looking directly into her eyes. "I ran into a problem. With some people here."

"Damn right," the Mountain growled.

Travis heard him hawk up a glob of spit, heard it hit the floor.

The blonde looked past his shoulder, her eyes widening. She looked at Travis again. Two slender parallel lines appeared between her eyebrows.

"See, I told them I was waiting for my date—"

"Thass what he said," one of the Mountain's pals said. "But we knew he was lyin'—an' we know what to do with liars."

A loud rumble of assent greeted the proclamation.

The blonde's gaze swept past Travis again. Her eyes filled with comprehension.

"And then," Travis said, ignoring the interruption, "then, the door opened and you walked in. One look and I knew that you were right for me, that you were perfect, that you were—"

"The woman you'd been waiting for," the blonde said, very softly.

He smiled, a little sadly because there was no question how this was going down. The only thing he needed to do now was get her safely out of here because however she'd come to be at this bar tonight, she was definitely in the wrong place at the wrong time.

"Exactly right, honey. You were just the woman I'd have waited for, and—"

The blonde put her finger over his lips.

"Of course I was," she said, her voice louder now, loud enough to carry to the men behind Travis. "How foolish of

you to think that I wasn't going to keep our date, just because
I showed up a bit late."

This time, Travis was the one whose eyes widened.

"What?"

"I was angry, I admit. That quarrel we had last week?
About—about me thinking you'd been with another woman?"
She smiled. "I know I was wrong. You wouldn't cheat on
me, not ever."

For mercy's sake, man, say something!

"Uh—uh, no. I mean, you're right. I wouldn't. Cheat on
you. Ever."

She nodded.

"But I couldn't just admit that." Another smile, this one
half-vixen, half-innocent. "It's against all the precepts of
male-female genetically-transmitted courtship behavior."

The what?

"So I decided to keep you waiting tonight. Let you cool
your heels a little, kind of wonder if I was going to show up."
Another smile, this one so hot and sexy Travis felt his knees
go weak. "And you did wonder, didn't you? About me and
how I'd deal with our date this evening."

Travis tried to answer. Nothing happened. He cleared his
throat and tried again.

"Yes. Right. I surely did. Wonder, I mean, about how you'd
deal with our—"

"And you reacted to perfection! Every single DNA-coded
response was in evidence. Machismo. Dominance. Aggression. Even an attempt at territorial marking."

*Territorial marking. Wasn't that about male dogs peeing
on trees?*

"I am so pleased," she said, "that you've proved the tenets
of my paper."

"Your paper."

"Oh, yes, exactly! The way you reacted on seeing me, the
way you dealt with my less-than-warm greeting…"

There was a hum behind him. Whispers. Snorts. Laughter.
It was, without question, time to move on.

Travis nodded. "That's great. It's terrific. But I really think
we should discuss the rest of it out—"

"Why, sugar," the blonde all but purred, "don't tell me
you're upset by learning you've helped my research!"

Not just laughter, but a couple of deep guffaws greeted
that pronouncement.

Definitely time, Travis thought, holding his smile as he
took the blonde by the elbow and marched her to the door.

Halfway there, Jennie's alter-ego snickered.

Should have quit while you were ahead, Genevieve, it said.

Indeed, Jennie thought. She should have.

The stranger who'd kissed her was hurrying her toward
the door.

Maybe she'd taken this a bit too far.

She had, if the look on the man's face was any indication.

His eyes were cool. Slate-cool, and a little scary. His
mouth—she knew all about his mouth, the warmth of it, the
possessive feel of it, the taste—his mouth was curved in what
was surely a phony smile, and he was hustling her along at
breakneck speed.

Still, he'd deserved that last little jibe.

Saving him from being torn apart by that bunch of—of
stone-age savages was one thing, but she couldn't just let him
get away with what he'd done.

He'd scared the life half out of her, grabbing her, kissing
her, dragging her up against his body.

And, yes, she'd come out tonight for—for that knowledge
of men, of kisses, of hard bodies but she'd wanted it done on
her own terms, at her own pace, with her doing the choosing
of the man who'd—who'd complete her research.

A man in a suit. A successful executive, someone who

could be trusted to be gentle with a woman. Not a—a rough-and-ready cowboy in boots and a T-shirt and faded jeans.

Stop complaining. You wanted gorgeous, and gorgeous is what he is.

Yes. But still—

"Y'all come back soon," a voice called.

A roar of laughter followed the words.

She felt the cowboy stiffen beside her. His fingers dug into her elbow hard enough to make her gasp.

"Hey," she said indignantly, "hey—"

He flung the door open, stepped outside, but he didn't let go of her. Instead he frog-marched her through the parking lot to the enormous black pickup parked next to her Civic.

"Mister. I am not—"

"Are you okay?"

Jennie blinked. There was concern in his voice, and it wasn't what she'd expected.

"No. Yes. I guess…"

"That was a close call. You were doin' fine, until the end." He grinned. "Had to zing me a little, right? Not that I blame you."

"You? Blame *me*?" Indignation colored her voice. "Listen, mister—"

"Truth is, we probably got out just in time."

So much for indignation, which didn't stand a chance against confusion.

"In time for what?" Jennie said. "What was going on back there?"

"It's kind of complicated." The cowboy smiled. This time, that smile was real. "Thanks for digging me out of a deep, dark hole."

"Well, well, you're welcome. I guess. I just don't understand what—"

"It's not worth going into. It was a mix-up, was all."

He smiled again. Jennie's heart leaped. Did he have any idea how devastatingly sexy that smile was?

She told herself to say something. Anything. Gawking at him wasn't terribly sophisticated. But then, what would he know about sophistication? The boots, the jeans, the hard muscles...

Everything about him was hard.

The muscled chest. The taut abdominals. The—the male part of him that she'd felt press against her belly just before he'd stopped kissing her...

That's the girl, her alter ego said.

Jennie swallowed dryly.

Her brain was going in half a dozen directions at once.

"You—you really had no right to—to just walk up to me and...and—"

"—and kiss you?"

She felt herself blush.

"Yes. Exactly. Even in the most highly sexualized primitive cultures, there's a certain decorum involved in expressing desire..."

His smile tilted.

"Is there," he said.

It wasn't a question—it was a statement. And the way he was looking at her...

She took a quick step back.

Or she would have taken a quick step back, but the shiny black truck was right behind her.

"The point is," she said, trying to focus on why she was angry at him, "you shouldn't have done what you did."

"Kissed you, without so much as a 'hello.'"

"Right. Precisely. The proper protocol, prior to intimacy—"

Jennie stopped in mid-sentence. She sounded like an idiot. Even her alter-ego had crept away in embarrassment.

"Never mind," she said quickly. "It's late. And I—"

"Travis," he said. "Travis Wilde."

She stared at him. "Pardon me?"

He smiled. Again. And her heart jumped again.

"My name." His voice had gone low and husky. "I'm introducing myself. That would have been the proper protocol, wouldn't it?"

"Well, yes, but—"

"And your name is…?"

"Oh."

She swallowed hard. Again. She was not good at this. At male-female banter. At any of it.

"I could call you Blondie." He reached out, caught a strand of her hair between his fingers, smoothed its silken length. "Or Neiman Marcus."

"What?" Jennie looked down at herself. "Is the dress tag show—"

"That's how you look," he said softly. "As if you just stepped out of their catalogue. Their Christmas catalogue, the one that always has the prettiest things in it."

Her knees were going to buckle.

His voice was like a caress.

His eyes were like hot coals.

He was—he was just what she'd been looking for, hoping for—

"But I'd rather call you by your real name, if you'll tell it to me."

"It's Jen…It's Genevieve," she whispered. "My name is Genevieve."

"Well, Genevieve, you did a foolish thing tonight."

God, she could feel herself blushing again!

"Listen here, Mr. Wills—"

"Wilde. Travis Wilde."

"Listen here, Mr. Wilde. I only let you kiss me after I realized you were going to get killed if I didn't!"

He chuckled.

Even his chuckle was sexy.

"I was talking about you going into that bar in the first place."

"Oh."

"Oh, for sure. You have any idea what kind of bunch you were dealing with back there?"

"I—I—" Jennie sighed. "No."

"I didn't think so. But it's lucky for me you walked in."

"It certainly is," she said, lifting her chin. "Or you'd be just another stain on that already-stained floor."

He grinned. "Yeah, but a happy stain."

"That's so typical! Men and their need to assert power through dominance—"

"Men and their need to save their tails, honey. Ordinarily I wouldn't have bothered, but I have something going down Monday, and the last thing I need is to show up lookin' like the winner of a bare-knuckles fight."

"You couldn't have won. There were too many of them."

"Of course I could have won," he said, so easily that she knew he meant it.

A little tremor went through her.

She'd come out tonight in search of a man. And she'd found one. But he was—he was more than she'd anticipated.

More than handsome.

More than sexy.

More than macho.

And more than everything you'd want in bed, her alter-ego purred.

Jennie tried to step back again.

"Well," she said brightly, "it's been—it's been interesting, Mr. Wilde. Now, if you don't mind—"

"About those protocols," he said, his voice low, his tone husky, "have we met them all?"

"The what?"

"The protocols. The ones needed before any kind of intimacy."

The woman named Genevieve blushed.

Again.

She did that, a lot.

Travis liked it.

Would her face and breasts turn that same shade of soft pink during sex? Would her eyes lock on his the way they were now, dark and wide but filled with passion instead confusion?

Crazy as it was, the fate of the world seemed to hinge on learning the answer.

"Because if we've met those protocols," he said, moving closer, flattening his palms against the cab of the truck so that his arms encased her, "I'd like to take the next step."

"What next—what next—"

He looked into her eyes. Looked at her lips. Gave her a second to figure out what was coming.

"No," she whispered.

"Yes," he said, and in what seemed like slow motion, he lowered his head to hers and took her mouth.

Her lips parted. His tongue slipped between them. Her heart banged into her throat. The taste of him, the feel of him inside her mouth…

Ohmygod, she thought, *oh—my—God!*

He groaned.

His arms went around her.

Hers rose and wound around his neck.

She pressed herself against him. And gasped.

He was hard as a rock.

She wanted to rub against him. Wanted to move her hips against his. Wanted to—to—

He lifted her off the ground, one arm around her waist, the other just below her backside. Her face was on a level with his; he kissed her slowly, caught her bottom lip between his teeth and sucked on her flesh, and—and—

A dazzling jolt of pure desire shot through her, the same as it had for one amazing moment in the bar, when her fear and indignation had given way to something very, very different. Something she'd refused to admit, even to herself.

"Wait," she whispered, but he didn't and she didn't want him to wait, didn't want anything to wait even though this wasn't going according to plan.

He set her down, slowly, on her feet.

Don't stop, she thought.

He didn't.

He put his hands on her.

On her hips, bringing her, hard, against his erection.

On her breasts, oh, on her breasts, his thumbs dancing with tantalizing slowness over her nipples.

"What," she whispered breathlessly, "what are you doing?"

His laugh was low and husky and so filled with sexual promise that she almost moaned.

"What does it feel like I'm doing?"

She swallowed dryly. "It feels like—like you're making love to me."

"Good." He kissed her throat. "Because that's exactly what I am doing, Genevieve. What I want to go on doing."

He kissed the place where her neck and shoulder joined.

It was magic.

Her eyes closed; the world went away.

And when he asked her to go home with him, she gave him the only logical answer because, after all, she was nothing if not logical.

She said, "Yes."

CHAPTER FOUR

THE 'VETTE WOULD have been faster but Travis was driving his pickup tonight and the GMC Denali, modified to his specifications, was as fast as anything on the road that was street-legal.

Besides, his condo was only half an hour away.

Still, that half an hour seemed like an eternity.

Travis was having a tough time keeping his hands off the woman seated beside him.

Why wouldn't he?

He was in the prime of life, a sexually active, heterosexual male, and their meeting had been just unusual enough to have an edge of excitement.

Still, there was something almost primal in his hunger for her—for Genevieve—and he knew it.

He'd come close to taking her against the truck, right there in the parking lot.

There was something to be said for spur-of-the-moment sex in unexpected places but sex outside a bar filled with a bunch of what might charitably be called yahoos wasn't high on the list.

Besides, he wanted more than quick relief.

He wanted...

Who knew what he wanted tonight?

Had he gone into that bar looking for trouble?

As a boy, football had been an outlet for the anger he'd sometimes felt at his father for spending more time with the young men who served under him than with his own sons, even after their mother's death.

In Afghanistan, once he'd figured out that he was fighting in a war governed by politics and not morality, he'd taken to long, punishing runs across the hot desert sand.

So, tonight, was he angry at his brothers for abandoning him? For the changes in his life…

Hell.

What kind of thoughts were those to have when a beautiful woman was with him, a woman whose feel and taste promised paradise?

Maybe he was wrong. Maybe what he needed was quick relief, that moment when you sank into a woman's softness and heat…

Dammit.

He kept thinking like this, things would be over before they got started.

Ahead, a traffic light went from green to amber. He stepped down even harder on the gas and shot through the intersection before the light changed again.

Only another couple of blocks to go.

Genevieve was quiet. In fact, she hadn't said a word since they'd gotten into the Denali.

He glanced at her. She was sitting up very straight in the leather bucket seat, eyes straight ahead, hands folded in her lap.

Hands that were trembling.

Was she having second thoughts?

"Hey," he said softly.

She looked at him, then away. He reached over, put his hand over hers. Her skin was icy.

Was she frightened? It didn't seem possible, not after the

way she'd responded to him in the parking lot, but he'd lived long enough to know that anything was possible.

He wrapped his hand around hers, held on until her fingers unknotted and he could bring her hand to rest under his on the gearshift.

"We're almost there."

She nodded. And caught her bottom lip between her teeth. His body tightened at the sight.

"I live in Turtle Creek. Near Lee Park."

She didn't answer. Why would she? What was he, a Realtor taking a client to see a property? If only she'd say something...

And how come he was taking her to his bed?

He wasn't big on taking his lovers home with him. Not that this woman was going to be his lover but...

Why was he making this so complicated?

Travis cleared his throat.

"Did you—would you like to stop first? For a drink? For something to eat?"

She stared at him. Why wouldn't she? He knew, she knew, what was going to happen next and in the middle of all that, he was going to, what, stop at a diner?

Maybe.

He flashed a quick smile.

"It just hit me, we blew past the 'hello, how are you' formalities. So, if you'd like to stop at a restaurant—"

She moistened her lips with the tip of her tongue. His body tightened in response.

"No."

Her voice was low, but her answer was clear.

She wanted him as much as he wanted her.

It was a good thing his place was directly ahead.

He slowed the truck. Hit the button that opened the garage doors. Drove inside. Hit the button that closed the doors...

And thought, to hell with waiting, undid his seat belt, reached over and undid hers and drew her into his arms.

"Genevieve," he said, and he lifted her face to his. Her lips parted, and he kissed her.

It was like the parking lot all over again.

The kiss, the feel of her mouth under his, made his blood pound.

He couldn't remember ever feeling a hunger this deep.

At first, he thought it wasn't the same for her. She didn't move, didn't respond—until suddenly she made a soft little sound in the back of her throat and opened her mouth to his.

Now, he thought.

Right now. Right here. Get this out of the way so he could take her to bed without wondering if he could make it that far, but even in his fevered state, he knew the logistics—the cramped space—made it impossible.

Still, he had to touch her. Intimately.

Her skirt barely covered her thighs and he slid his hand under it, over the warmth of her skin.

She gasped.

"Wait," she whispered, but he couldn't wait, he had to at least do this, God, yes, do this, put his hand between her thighs, lay his palm over her silk thong...

She gave a sweet, breathless cry.

"Travis."

It was the first time she'd spoken his name.

The way she said it, the sudden hot dampness that soaked the thong, almost undid him.

He kissed her again, his tongue sweeping into her mouth. She moaned, dug her hands into his hair and he shoved the thong aside, stroked her, stroked her...

She made high, incoherent little cries.

He could feel his muscles tensing.

If he didn't stop now, it would be too late.

One last quick kiss. Then he stepped from the truck, went

to the passenger side and gathered her into his arms, capturing her mouth with his as he carried her to the private elevator that led to his penthouse.

He set her on her feet, swiped his keycard. The doors opened, then whisked shut, and he clasped her face between his hands.

"Don't be afraid," he said gruffly, though he didn't know what had made him say it. She hadn't been shy about admitting she wanted to go to bed with him.

Still, there was something about her, a hesitancy…

"I'm not afraid," Jennie whispered.

But it was a lie.

Almost as bad a lie as not telling him why she wanted to be with him.

All right.

It wasn't a lie.

What he made her feel had nothing to do with what she'd planned to do tonight.

Well, it did, but not as—as quite a research project.

That was how she'd thought of it from the beginning. That was how she'd intended it, how she'd planned it.

How would he react if he knew that?

More to the point, how would he react if he knew all the rest? If he knew she had never been with a man before…

And almost certainly would never be with one again?

And yet—and yet, all of that had somehow slipped away.

What mattered was how he kissed her, touched her. The way he was kissing her now. The way his erection pressed into her belly.

He felt huge.

Would she be able to—to accommodate him?

She had read scholarly articles, she had seen films. Academic films—sociology majors and psychology majors, grad psych students, often sat through hours of that stuff.

Most people had no idea how graphic those films could be.

But nothing had prepared her for this.

The feel of his aroused sex against her. The promise of all that masculine power. The insistent demand of it.

His mouth was on her breasts now. He nipped lightly at her nipples through the silk of her dress and they hardened into pebbles.

Her breasts ached.

There was an ache low, low in her belly, too.

And she was wet. Wet and hot.

She whimpered as he pushed down the bodice of the dress; his lips closed around one nipple but the silk of her bra was between her flesh and his mouth. The feel of his lips and teeth on her wasn't enough.

It was too much.

How could it be both?

He clasped her shoulders. Turned her, gently so that her back was to him. Her hair had come undone and he nuzzled it aside, kissed the nape of her neck, nipped the flesh, soothed the small, sweet torment with a stroke of his tongue.

She heard the hiss of her zipper.

"Wait," she gasped, "someone might—"

"It's a private elevator," he said in that rough, sexy, gravel-and-velvet whisper. We're all alone."

Jennie trembled.

All alone, she thought, as her dress slid down her hips and pooled at her feet.

All alone, she thought, as he kissed his way down her spine.

All alone, she thought, as he slowly turned her to him in her black lace bra. Black silk thong. Black, thigh-high stockings. Red stiletto heels.

His gaze moved over her. Slowly, so slowly it made her skin tingle. She felt that tingle in her breasts, her pelvis, her legs.

His eyes lifted. Met hers.

What she saw in those dark depths made her knees go weak.

Her hands came up. One fluttered to her breasts. The other went to the apex of her thighs. Slowly he reached out, caught her wrists, brought her hands to his mouth and kissed the palms.

"Don't hide from me, Genevieve," he said thickly. "Let me see you. You're beautiful. So incredibly beautiful…"

He released one of her wrists. Ran his hand lightly over her, from her lips to throat to her breasts, from her breasts to her belly, her belly to the vee of her thighs, his eyes never leaving hers.

"Travis," she said in an unsteady whisper.

"Yes," he said, "that's right. It's me, touching you. Me, wanting you." His eyes were almost black with hunger as he reached around her, undid her bra, let it drop to the floor. "Beautiful," he whispered, and then his mouth was on her flesh, her breasts, her nipples.

She was coming apart, coming apart, as she sobbed his name again.

"Genevieve. Spread your legs for me."

The words, the way he said them, sent an arrow of longing through her.

"Baby. Spread your legs."

Was it a request? Or was it a command? Either way, it was impossible.

She couldn't. No. She couldn't…

He kissed her again.

Heart pounding, she did what he'd asked.

He said something, low and hot with urgency. She couldn't understand the words but the look on his face told her everything she needed to know.

Still, she wasn't prepared for what happened next, the way he cupped her, the way it felt to know that the heat burning between her legs was now burning his palm.

A high, pealing sob of almost unbearable pleasure broke

from her throat. She swayed. He scooped her into his arms just as the elevator stopped and the doors opened, and she buried her face in the hard curve where his throat and shoulder joined, inhaling the scents of sex, soap and man.

She'd never understood that thing about women liking the smell of male sweat. She knew some of them did, it was a well-researched fact, but it had never made sense until now as she drew the masculine scent of him inside her with every breath.

He carried her through an enormous living room. Light filtered through tall windows, illuminated low furniture, high ceilings, burnished wood floors.

Ahead, a glass and steel staircase angled toward the next level.

He climbed it with her still in his arms, his gait steady, his heart beating against hers. He paused on the landing, kissed her and whispered her name.

Moments later, they were in another enormous room.

His bedroom, with the bed—big, wide, covered with black and white pillows—centered under a star-filled skylight.

He carried her to the bed, stopped beside it and put her down slowly, very slowly, her body sliding against his.

He kissed her.

Sweet, light whispers of his lips on hers that gradually grew deep and hungry until her head was tilted back, her face was raised to his, his hands were deep in the tumble of her hair as he held her.

They were both gasping for air, their breath mingling.

But she was almost naked and he wasn't. It made her feel...

She pulled back.

"What, baby?" he said.

"You haven't—you haven't taken off—"

"No. Not yet." His slow smile raised the temperature a thousand degrees. "I like having you undressed while I'm still wearing my clothes."

The truth was, she liked it, too.

There was something exciting about it.

He kissed her eyes, her mouth. When he swept his fingers over her nipples, she shimmered with heat. When his mouth followed the path his fingers had taken, she moaned.

Why hadn't someone told her this was how it felt, to have a man suck on your breasts? To know that he wanted you and to want him in return with such hot need that it made you breathless?

She heard herself whimper when he drew back.

"It's all right," he whispered, and it was all right because now he was peeling away the narrow strip of silk that secured her thong, working it slowly, slowly down her hips. Her legs.

"Hold on to me," he said gruffly.

She put her hands on his shoulders. He drew the thong to her ankles.

"Lift your foot," he said.

She did.

She would do anything he asked, anything, anything...

Jennie cried out.

But not this!

His mouth, at the delicate curls that guarded her womanhood. His fingers, gently opening her to him. His tongue, licking, teasing...

She wanted to push him away.

Instead, she tangled her fingers in his hair. Her head fell back. She moaned. Something was happening to her. She was trembling. She was coming apart.

The orgasm took her by surprise.

She screamed. Screamed again. Started to fall, but he caught her and took her down to the bed with him.

"Now," she heard herself plead, "please, Travis, please, please, please..."

He tore off his clothes, fumbled open the drawer in the low table beside the bed and took out a foil packet.

She had one quick glimpse of him naked as he tore the packet open.

He was beautiful, all that tanned skin stretched over layers of hard muscle.

And his sex.

She'd been right. He was big. So big.

She felt a moment of trepidation as he rolled the condom on.

"Genevieve."

She blinked, lifted her eyes to his.

He kissed her. Clasped her hands. Brought them high above her head.

And entered her.

At first, she watched his face.

The darkness of his eyes. The tightening of the skin over his cheekbones. The way his lips drew back from his teeth.

Her vision blurred.

She stopped watching.

Started feeling.

And, dear Lord, nothing had ever felt like this.

He was filling her. Moving deeper and deeper into her. She was drowning, drowning in ecstasy, everything in her centered on the feel of him filling her.

Her fingers wove through his.

There was so much of him. Even when she thought she had taken all of him, she hadn't. There was more of him.

More. More.

She gave an inadvertent gasp at a sudden flicker of pain.

He went completely still.

Her eyes flew open. Sweat glistened on his muscled shoulders, his chest, his arms.

"Genevieve?"

She saw the disbelief in his eyes. He was going to stop, she was sure of it, and she couldn't let that happen.

"Genevieve," he groaned, "goddammit, why didn't you—"

She lifted herself to him and impaled herself on his erection.

For a heartbeat, the world stood still.

Then Travis plunged deep, deeper still.

Jennie cried out as a wave of sensation swept her up, lifted her higher than the night, than the stars.

He collapsed against her. She started to put her arms around him but the second she touched him, he jerked away and sat up.

Her throat tightened. Automatically she clutched the duvet to her chin and sat up, too.

"Travis?" She cleared her throat. "Listen, I—I know you didn't expect—"

"Why didn't you tell me?"

"Why would I tell you?" she said in genuine confusion. "It's not exactly a conversation starter."

"I'd have done things differently." He hesitated. "Dammit, I might not have done anything at all. No man wants to be responsible for—for—"

"Is that what's worrying you? It shouldn't. I wanted this to happen. To, you know, lose my, uh, my—"

Ridiculous, that after all of this, she couldn't say the word. But he could.

"Your virginity." He looked at her, his expression unreadable. "Wait a minute. Are you saying you planned this?"

Warning bells rang. Something in the way he'd said that…

Travis grabbed her by the shoulders.

"You did, didn't you?"

She drew her bottom lip between her teeth.

His eyes narrowed.

"So, what was I? The lottery winner?"

"You were—you were a good choice. A very good choice," she said quickly, but she saw his mouth thin.

"A very good choice," he said in a soft, ominous voice.

"Why? Did I meet some kind of criteria? Some—some list of protocols in a textbook?"

"No," she said, and added the first stupid thing that came to mind. "I mean, the protocols I drew up were strictly my own…"

He rolled away, got to his feet.

"Get dressed," he said, his tone not just flat but cold as he grabbed his discarded jeans from the floor and yanked them on.

"Would you just listen to—"

She was talking to an empty room.

Jennie began to shake.

Maybe she hadn't handled this very well but she'd never imagined the man who completed her research would react this way. Weren't men happy to deflower virgins? All the data said they were.

And what did that matter now?

What counted was getting out of here.

She dressed quickly but then, how long could it take to put on a thong and a pair of shoes? Travis Wilde had never gotten around to taking off her stockings.

The very thought sent a rush of humiliation through her bones.

Everything else—her bra, her dress, her purse—was still in the elevator.

She wanted to weep but no way was she going to let that happen.

His shirt was still on the floor.

She snatched it up, dragged it over her head. It fell to the bottom of her buttocks. That left her with the tops of her stockings showing but it would have to do.

She went down the stairs as rapidly as the miserable stiletto heels would permit. The lights were on. She hated their bright luminescence but at least she could see where she was going.

The man who'd taken her virginity was standing at the

far end of the big living room, in front of the open doors of his private elevator. His dark hair was mussed; an overhead spot highlighted the planes and angles of his hard body. He was wearing only his jeans; he'd zipped the fly but he hadn't closed the top button.

He was a gorgeous sight—

As if that mattered.

Her chin came up.

She stalked toward him, hoping she wouldn't ruin her exit by stumbling in the damned shoes.

"Your clothes," he said.

Her face heated. Her dress, her purse, her bra were in the hand he extended toward her. She snatched everything from him, pulled the dress on over the shirt because no way was she going to take it off and let him see her breasts again, and stuffed the bra into her purse, though it barely fit.

She started past him again. His arm shot out and barred her way.

"Excuse me," she said coldly.

"I phoned down. The concierge will have a taxi waiting."

"I can call a taxi by myself."

"Don't be a fool. And take this. It should cover the fare."

She looked at the bills in his hand, then at him.

"I do not want your money, Mr. Wilde."

"Take it."

Jennie shoved his hand aside. "Are you deaf? I said—"

"Did you think this little escapade would be fun? Picking up a stranger. Turning him on. Getting him to take what it's obvious you haven't been able to get rid of in the usual way?"

"I am not going to have this conversation. Just step aside, please."

Travis grabbed her wrist.

"You damned well *are* going to have this conversation! What in hell were you thinking?"

"You want to discuss this?" Jennie said, glaring at him.

"Fine. Let's set the record straight. I did not pick you up. You picked me up."

"Like hell I did ! All I wanted—"

"All you wanted was to use me to save your precious self from getting beaten to a pulp! And I was kind enough to oblige."

"You did a lot more than that, lady."

"You're right. I make the sad mistake of letting you—of letting you seduce me!"

He laughed. Laughed! Jennie balled her hands into fists.

"*I* seduced *you*? You were all over me, baby. What happened tonight was an act of charity on my part. I mean, even without knowing you were a virgin, I knew you were in desperate need of a good—"

Jennie slapped his face.

"You're an unmitigated bastard," she said, her voice trembling.

"And you're a little fool," Travis snarled. "You're just lucky you didn't end up in bed with a—a serial killer!"

"Bad enough I ended up in bed with a—a man who— who doesn't know the first thing about—about sex and how to please a wo—"

Travis hauled her into his arms and kissed her.

She fought. She struggled. He caught her wrists in one hand, dragged her arms behind her and went on kissing her and kissing her until she moaned and her lips clung to his...

That was when he let go of her.

She stared at him, at the arrogant little smile curving his mouth, the I-told-you-so look in his eyes.

She wanted to say something pithy and clever, but her head felt as empty as her heart. The best she could manage was to spin away and stumble into the elevator.

The doors shut.

As soon as they did, she yanked down the straps of her dress, peeled off his T-shirt and dumped it on the floor. Seconds later, she emerged in a marble lobby the size of an airplane hangar. She marched through it, ignored the concierge calling after her, the taxi waiting at the curb. She wanted nothing, absolutely nothing, from Travis Wilde.

It was hotter than blazes, even at this late hour. She walked for endless blocks, sweated through the dress, took off her shoes and carried them because surely women's feet were not meant for four-inch heels.

She knew she must look awful. Cabs slowed when she hailed them, then sped away.

At last, one pulled to the curb.

The driver stared as she climbed in, but she didn't give a damn.

She was heading home, and Travis Wilde was exactly what he'd been intended to be.

An experience.

And if these last months had taught her anything, she thought grimly, as the cab rushed into the night, it was that not all experiences were good ones.

Alone in his condo, Travis paced like a caged tiger.

What kind of woman saw sex as research? What kind of woman thought she could use a man to rid herself of something she no longer wanted, and get away with it?

All those moans when she lay in his arms. The little cries of passion. Part of a plan…

Or real?

Real, judging by the way she'd responded to that last, furious kiss.

Yeah, but so what?

If he hadn't walked over to her in that bar, if someone else had, she'd have ended up in another guy's bed.

His jaw tightened.

And?

What did it matter? Why would he give a crap who Blondie slept with? Who took her virginity?

Who could make her tremble in his arms?

"You're an idiot, Wilde," he snarled.

A furious idiot, and the anger tucked away deep inside him, anger at a world that always seemed determined to prove he was unable to control it despite everything he tried, blazed hot and high.

He wanted to go back to that bar.

He knew the yahoos would be happy to see him, that he and they would step out into the night and trade blows until the darkness receded.

But he was Travis Wilde.

He was a man, not a yahoo. He *was* in control of his life, of himself, of his emotions.

And there was that trip coming up Monday. Not just for himself but for his clients, who had put their trust, and their millions, in his care.

He owed them better, although God only knew what he owed himself.

So he went, instead, to the workout room on the lower level of his penthouse. He ran miles on his treadmill, worked out on the Nautilus, lifted free weights until the sweat poured from his body.

Two hours later, exhausted, he showered, fell into bed and then into a dreamless sleep.

CHAPTER FIVE

TRAVIS'S WEEK PASSED quickly.

Three days in Frankfurt and a last-minute, two-day stop-over in London.

Success in each place, agreements negotiated and concluded. He felt great about it—victory was always sweet—but something was missing.

He couldn't get the woman out of his head.

And it made no sense.

Yes, the sex had been good. Great, when you came down to it. Not because she'd been a virgin but because she'd been—she'd been so sweet. So honest...

Except, she was neither of those things.

Not really.

Sweet? A woman who walked into a bar, looking for a hookup?

Honest? A woman who let a man find out she was a virgin when it was too late to change his mind?

And he would have changed it.

Of course, he would.

A man didn't want the responsibility of taking a woman's innocence...

Her wonderful innocence.

And, hell, what was that all about? He was not, never had

been one of those smug fools who thought a guy was entitled to bed everything in sight, but a woman should live like a nun.

Apparently, Genevieve had.

Until last Friday night.

And then she'd given herself to a man.

To him.

Except, he could have been anybody. That she'd walked into that bar at the right moment had been pure chance.

She hadn't chosen him, she'd stumbled across him.

"Stop it," he muttered, as he sat in the comfort of his private jet, flying high above the Atlantic.

The world was filled with women, beautiful, available women.

What he needed was to call one of them, take her for drinks and dinner.

Good plan.

But it could wait until he was home.

There was no rush.

It was Friday again, they'd land in a few hours, and he could think of half a dozen women who'd drop any plans to spend an evening with him.

Hey, if a man couldn't be honest with himself, who could he be honest with?

Still, he didn't reach for his cell phone when he got to his condo.

He was travel-weary; even the comfort of a private jet didn't make up for things like time zone changes. So he undressed, showered, put on a pair of old gym shorts, opened a chilled Deep Ellum IPA and took it out to the terrace, where he sank down in a lounger.

It was the kind of day Dallas rarely saw in midsummer: warm but not hot, no humidity, the sun shining from the kind of perfect blue sky he'd always associated with home.

Funny.

He'd flown fighters through equally blue skies, under the kiss of an equally hot sun, in places that were just unpronounceable names on a map to most people but those skies, that sun, had always seemed alien, as if he'd gone to sleep at home one night and awakened the next morning in a world that made no sense.

Travis lifted the bottle of ale to his lips and took a long, cooling swallow.

He knew that his brothers, who had also served their country, felt the same.

The wars of the last couple of decades had been very different from the ones their father had talked about when they were growing up.

The old man was a general. Four stars, all rules, regs, spit and polish. He'd raised them on tales of heroism that went back centuries—*"The blood of valiant warriors flows in your veins, gentlemen,"* he'd say—and on stories of their more recent ancestors, men who'd battled their way across the Western plains and settled in what eventually had become Texas, where they'd founded *El Sueño*, the family ranch—if you could call a half a million acre kingdom a "ranch."

Problem was, their father's stories didn't seem to apply to the realities of the twenty-first century, but at least they'd all come home again, if not quite the same way they'd left.

Jake had been wounded in battle, Caleb had been scarred by the dark machinations of an agency nobody talked about.

He'd got off lucky.

No wounds. No scars…

Suddenly he thought back a few years, to a woman he'd dated for a while after he'd come home.

Actually she'd been a shrink with enough initials after her name to fill out the alphabet.

She'd said he had a problem.

He couldn't connect emotionally, she said, and even though she'd sounded angry, she'd sighed and kissed him, and told him she could hear her internal clock ticking and it was time she found a man who wasn't just willing to take risks skydiving and flying and doing who in hell knew what else, it was time to find one ready to risk everything by committing to a relationship.

Travis took another mouthful of ale.

Then she told him she knew he couldn't help it, that he almost surely had PTSD.

But he didn't.

He hadn't bothered telling her that.

After all, she was a shrink and painfully certain that she knew all there was to know about the human psyche but the simple truth was, he'd come through two wars—Afghanistan and Iraq—just fine. No physical injuries, no Post Traumatic Stress Disorder.

A few bad dreams, maybe.

Okay, maybe nightmares, was more like it.

But he'd survive them.

He'd survived nightmares just as bad, the ones that had almost drowned him in despair when he was little and his mother left him.

Travis frowned.

Hell.

She hadn't left him. She'd died. Not her fault. Not anybody's fault. And he'd come through it, gathered himself up, moved on.

One thing a man learned in life.

It wasn't smart to become dependent on another human being.

To get emotionally involved, the way he'd done last week, with Blondie…

"Dammit," he said.

He hadn't gotten involved. Neither had she. Wasn't that the point? That she'd picked him to take her to bed instead of wanting him to do it…

And why was he wasting time, thinking about her? Why was she still in his head at all?

Travis finished the ale, got to his feet and headed inside.

He didn't need a date.

He needed a reality check, and what could be better for that than a couple of hours spent with his brothers?

He made a three-way call, got Jake and Caleb talking. After a couple of minutes of bull, he pointed out that it was Friday night.

"I always told you he was brilliant," Jake said solemnly.

"Yeah," Caleb said. "I bet he even knows the month and the year."

Travis ignored the horseplay.

"So are you two up for it? Can you get away for the evening?"

"Get away?" Caleb snorted. "Of course." And then he must have covered the phone because they heard him say, in a muffled voice, "Honey? You okay with me spending some time tonight with Trav and Jake?"

Travis snickered. Jake didn't. He just said getting together sounded good to him.

"You don't want to check with Addison?" Travis said blandly.

"Why would I?" Jake said, bristling, and then he cleared his throat and said Addison was meeting with her book club tonight anyway, so—

"So," Travis said, reminded once again, as if he needed reminding, of yet another reason why "commitment" was never going to be a word in his vocabulary, "where do you want to meet?"

Jake named a couple of places. Caleb said why didn't they try someplace different? A client had told him good things about a new place that had opened in the Arts District.

"Local beers, good wine list, great steaks, music up front

but booths in the back where, he says, you can actually hear yourself carry on a conversation."

"Won't it be overrun by university types?" Jake said. "You know, alfalfa sprouts, folk music, T-shirts that read, *Schopenhauer Was Right*?"

His brothers chuckled.

"Not if my client likes the place," Caleb said. "His brand of philosophy leans more toward Charlie Brown than Schopenhauer."

They all laughed. Then Jake said, "Okay. Let's try it. Eight? That okay?"

It was perfect, Travis assured them, and he found himself whistling as he headed for the shower.

Jake got there before the others.

He snagged a booth with a crisp fifty dollar bill and when he saw Travis come through the door, he got to his feet and signaled.

"Caleb's client got it wrong," he said. "If it were winter, the amount of tweed in this place would keep us warm straight through until spring."

"Yeah," Travis said, "I noticed. There's some kind of party up front, lots of skinny guys with beards and women with hair under their arms."

Jake laughed. "You always did have a way with words, but what the hell, we're here. And I just saw a platter of rib-eyes go by."

"Always knew you understood the basics," Travis said solemnly. He cocked his head. "Married life agrees with you, buddy. It's made you less ugly, anyway."

Jake grinned and they exchanged quick bear hugs.

"A fine compliment, coming from you, considering everybody says we look like two peas in a pod."

"Three peas," Caleb said, as he joined them. More quick

embraces, a few jabs in the shoulder, and then the brothers slid into the booth.

"How'd the trip to Germany go?"

"Great. I closed one hell of a deal."

"Perfect," Jake told Caleb. "He's handsome, like us. And modest, too. What a guy."

"And your love life?" Caleb said. "How's that going?"

Travis looked at him.

"What's that supposed to mean?"

Caleb raised an eyebrow.

"It means," he said with deliberate care, "how's your love life going?"

"It's going fine."

Jake laughed. "Hey, man. It's not a trick question. Our ladies are certain to ask."

Travis let out a long breath.

"Yeah. Okay. Sorry. I guess I'm still jet-lagged."

"Nobody special yet?"

"No," Travis said evenly. "But you know what I think about this line of questioning?" He sat forward, eyes narrowed. "I think—"

"What *I* think," Caleb said lazily, "is that we'd better decide what we're having, 'cause here comes our waitress."

Their orders were identical.

Porterhouse steaks, baked potatoes with butter, sour cream and chives.

"And an extra-large basket of fried onion rings," Travis said.

"Of course," Jake said, his lips twitching. "Every meal should include a vegetable."

Two beers, an ale for Travis.

The waitress brought those right away, along with a bowl of cashews.

They all dug in, drank, munched, talked about guy stuff.

Travis started to relax.

Why had he reacted so negatively to a simple question? It didn't make sense.

Talk helped.

Everyday stuff. Baseball, still going strong. Football, coming up soon. Jake's progress in remodeling the house and sprawling ranch that adjoined *El Sueño*. Caleb and his wife's search for a house and land of their own, and the news that ten thousand acres in Wilde's Crossing had just come on the market.

Their steaks arrived. They ordered more drinks. And just when Travis had almost decided he was home free, his brothers exchanged a look, laid their knives and forks on their plates and Caleb said, "Something bothering you, Trav?"

Travis forced a smile.

"Not a thing. Something bothering *you*, Caleb"

"Hey," Caleb said lightly, "watch yourself." He waggled his eyebrows. "I'm a trained interrogator, remember?"

Travis laughed, just as he was supposed to do. He thought about playing dumb, tossing back a look of complete innocence and saying he had no idea what they were talking about, but you didn't grow up with two guys who knew everything about you and lie to their faces.

Besides, until this moment, he hadn't realized how much last Friday night—correction, his reaction to last Friday night—was gnawing at him.

Still, he didn't have to tell them all the details.

So he shrugged, put down his knife and fork, too, blotted his mouth with his napkin and said, "I met a woman."

"He met a woman," Caleb said to Jake.

"Wow. Amazing. Our brother, the hotshot hedge fund manager, met a woman. So much for avoiding that question about his love life."

"I didn't avoid anything," Travis said tersely. "This has nothing to with love. And I have nothing to do with hedge funds. I run an investment firm—and why were you talking about me as if I'm not here?"

"Because the last time you were involved with a woman and wouldn't talk about her was when you had that thing going with Suzy Franklin."

Travis sat back, folded his arms over his chest.

"I was in fifth grade. And I wasn't 'involved' any more than I'm 'involved' now."

"He protests too much," Jake said.

"What did I just say about that 'he's not here' routine? And I'm not protesting. There's nothing to protest." He'd meant to make it all sound light but one glance at his brothers and he knew it hadn't worked. He took a breath, let it out and leaned over the table. "Look, it was nothing. See, I was minding my business in this place way downtown…"

"What were you doing downtown?"

"Actually, it was your fault. Your faults. Can you say 'faults'? Because it was. It was last Friday night, you guys couldn't make it, and…"

What the hell.

He told the story.

Most of it.

Some of it.

Finally, he got to the part he was still having trouble with.

"…and," he said, "then the door opened, this woman walked in and she was, ah, she was attractive."

"You mean, she was hot."

A muscle knotted in Travis's jaw.

"You could say that, yeah."

"And?"

"And, I figured if I could convince the drooling yahoos at the bar that I'd been waiting for her to show up, everything would be fine."

"Drooling yahoos," Caleb said dryly.

funds. I run an investment firm—and why were you talking about me as if I'm not here?"

"Because the last time you were involved with a woman and wouldn't talk about her was when you had that thing going with Suzy Franklin."

Travis sat back, folded his arms over his chest.

"I was in fifth grade. And I wasn't 'involved' any more than I'm 'involved' now."

"He protests too much," Jake said.

"What did I just say about that 'he's not here' routine? And I'm not protesting. There's nothing to protest." He'd meant to make it all sound light but one glance at his brothers and he knew it hadn't worked. He took a breath, let it out and leaned over the table. "Look, it was nothing. See, I was minding my business in this place way downtown…"

"What were you doing downtown?"

"Actually, it was your fault. Your faults. Can you say 'faults'? Because it was. It was last Friday night, you guys couldn't make it, and…"

What the hell.

He told the story.

Most of it.

Some of it.

Finally, he got to the part he was still having trouble with.

"…and," he said, "then the door opened, this woman walked in and she was, ah, she was attractive."

"You mean, she was hot."

A muscle knotted in Travis's jaw.

"You could say that, yeah."

"And?"

"And, I figured if I could convince the drooling yahoos at the bar that I'd been waiting for her to show up, everything would be fine."

"Drooling yahoos," Caleb said dryly.

"What did I say? He has a way with words," Jake said, just as dryly.

"You want to hear this or not?"

"We wouldn't miss it. Go on. A hot babe came strutting through the door—"

"She didn't 'strut,'" Travis said, a little sharply. "And she was—she was good-looking. Not hot. Not the way you're making it…" His words trailed away. His brothers were looking at him as if he'd lost his mind.

Dammit, he thought, and he cleared his throat.

"So, anyway, I, ah, I approached her. I told her I had a problem and asked her for her help. And, after a little, uh, a little persuasion, she agreed."

"Persuasion?"

"What'd you do? Talk her into a coma?"

Travis was silent for a long, long minute. Then he sighed.

"I kissed her," he said in a low voice because, hell, maybe if he talked about it he'd stop thinking about it.

About Genevieve.

Caleb stared at him. "And she went along with it?"

"Yeah."

"Aha." Jacob grinned. "Not just a hot babe. A hot babe looking for a night's diversion."

Travis looked at his brother through narrowed eyes.

"I told you, it's wrong to call her that."

Jake held up his hands. "Okay. Sorry. A lady looking for a night's—"

"She'd walked into the wrong place, that's all," Travis said tightly.

"So, you weren't just looking for her to get you out of there in one piece, you were going to protect her."

"Yes. No. Dammit!" Travis sat back, wrapped his hands around his half-empty mug of ale. "Look, let's drop it, okay? I got into a stupid situation, and that's the end of it."

"Yeah, but I don't see how this played out," Caleb said.

"This jerk and his friends were on you because they figured you'd been hitting on his woman. You said no, you were waiting for your date. This babe—sorry. This woman walked in—"

"She had a name," Travis said, in a dangerously quiet voice. "Genevieve."

Jake waggled his eyebrows. "Wow. Not just good-looking but French."

"Better and better," Caleb said.

Travis opened his mouth, then quickly shut it. All at once he didn't want to talk about last Friday night, not when it would involve giving away details that suddenly seemed far too personal.

"Never mind."

"Never mind? Bro, you can't leave us hanging. We're married men. Happily married, I hasten to add, but still, there's no harm in living vicariously."

"And it was just getting interesting. There you were, in this dive and, wham, a woman walks in, you kiss her, she's warm and willing…and what? You took her home? Went to her place? Or maybe—"

"Enough," Travis snapped.

His tone was cold, hard and flat. His brothers stared at him, then exchanged a quick glance. *What in hell?* that glance said, but they both knew that the line between asking questions and expecting answers had been crossed.

"Right," Jake said, after a few seconds. He cleared his throat. "So, ah, so did I tell you guys about the dude with the fabric samples? Man, I swear, he doesn't speak in any language I ever heard before. Batiste. Bouclé. Brocade. And that's just in the *B*'s…"

Caleb forced a laugh.

Jake kept talking and, finally, Travis forced a laugh, too. The waitress came by. They asked for refills on their drinks, talked some more…

And Travis, who had come out tonight for the express purpose of getting a woman he hardly knew, except in the most basic sense of the word, out of his head now realized he couldn't think about anything except her.

He held up his end of the conversation. More or less. An occasional comment, a laugh when it was expected, but he wasn't really there.

He was in his penthouse, Genevieve in his arms, her responses to his caresses, his kisses, his deep, incredible possession of her so honest, so passionate, so thrilling…until he'd ruined it, ruined everything by reacting like a selfish, stupid kid…

"Travis?"

He wanted to see her again.

Just—just to tell her he'd been wrong, that he shouldn't have said—

"Trav?"

He blinked. Focused his gaze on his brothers. They were staring at him, concern etched into their faces.

"Jet lag," he said with forced good humor. "What I need is coffee. A gallon of it, black and strong and…"

His words trailed off.

His heart thudded.

"Travis? You okay?"

The place had gotten crowded with people.

The bunch at the university party up front was still there. If anything, it had grown larger.

Two women, surely from that group, had just walked by. Save-the-Something T-shirts. Real jeans. Leather sandals.

One woman had dark hair.

One had light hair.

The one with the light hair was stumbling. The other was supporting her. Arm around her waist, face a mix of concern and irritation.

"Travis? Man, what's the matter?"

"Nothing," he said, as the women disappeared into the rear bathroom.

It had to be nothing.

The woman who'd been stumbling had looked just like Genevieve. Exactly like her.

Well, not exactly.

Her hair was that same golden color but it wasn't loose, it hung down her back in a long ponytail.

And, of course, she wasn't wearing a dress the size of a handkerchief, or shoes with heels high enough to give a man hot dreams.

So it wasn't her.

It couldn't be her.

It was ridiculous even to think it was her...

The bathroom door swung open. The two women stepped through it.

Travis got to his feet.

"Travis," Caleb said sharply, "what's going on?"

Hell. It *was* her. Genevieve. Her face was drained of color and she had her hand pressed to her belly.

"For crissakes, Gen," the second woman said loudly, "nobody gets sick on two margaritas!"

Travis dug out his wallet, tossed some bills on the table.

"I have to go," he said, his eyes never leaving Genevieve.

"Go where? Dammit, man, talk to us!"

"I'll call you later," Travis said. "Don't worry, everything's fine."

"The hell it is," Jake said.

He started to rise but Caleb, who'd turned to watch Travis, grabbed his arm.

"Let him go."

"Go where? Man, what's happening?"

"Look."

Jake looked.

Travis had reached the women. He said something to them. The one with dark hair gave him a quizzical look.

"You mean, with you?" she said.

Travis's response was loud and clear.

"Absolutely with me," he said, his tone no longer that of a guy who lived for the moment but, instead, that of the tough, take-no-prisoners fighter pilot he'd once been.

"Fine with me," the brunette said. She let go of the blonde, who swayed like a sapling in a Texas dust-storm as Travis scooped her off her feet.

"Whoa," Caleb said.

"Whoa, is right," Jake said, because after a couple of seconds of struggle, the blonde blinked hard, looked up at their brother and said, "Travis?"

"The one and only," Travis said grimly.

She looped her arms around his neck and buried her face against his throat. And he, jaw set, eyes hard as obsidian, carried her straight through the room and out the door.

CHAPTER SIX

TRAVIS WAS DRIVING his 'Vette tonight, not his truck. He'd parked it a short way down the street.

He hadn't thought about it, one way or the other—until he walked out of the bar with Genevieve in his arms.

Now he figured that having to walk a couple of minutes to get to the car was probably a good thing.

It would give him time to cool down.

He was beyond angry.

What in hell was in this woman's head?

Didn't she have any sense of reason? Walking into that bar last week, dressed to raise the blood pressure of every man breathing, and now, this. Drinking herself damned near senseless.

He didn't like rules, didn't believe in worrying much over what social pundits liked or disliked, but he did have opinions—and one of them was that a woman out of control was not a pretty sight.

As for drunks…

He didn't like drunks in general but when a woman went that route…

His sisters would say he was being sexist. Maybe he was, but that was how he felt.

And what if Genevieve hadn't got sick? What would have come next? Would she have let some guy pick her up, take her home? Touch her? Kiss her? Ease her thighs apart, bury himself in all that honeyed sweetness?

So much for calming down. If anything, his anger ratcheted up a notch.

A couple walking toward them laughed.

"Very romantic," the woman said.

Travis glowered. If only they knew the truth. This was as far from "romantic" as a man could get—and it was stupid.

What he was doing was stupid.

He wasn't Genevieve's keeper.

He should have left her with her pals. She was their problem, not his.

It wasn't too late; he could turn around, take her back to where he'd found her…

Genevieve moaned softly.

Yeah, but she was sick. Drunk, sure. But sick drunk made for a dangerous situation.

Two margaritas, her friend had said.

Hardly enough to get sick on, but she was. The moans. The way she'd clutched her belly. Even the way she'd let him all but kidnap her said everything he needed to know.

She was sick. And she needed—

She needed him.

He'd known it when he heard her whisper his name, when she gave herself over to him, buried her face against his throat.

She felt soft and feminine in his arms. And that sense that she trusted him. Needed him…

He tried not to think about that, or the way it made him feel.

It was a lot safer to concentrate on his anger.

"Damned fool woman," he muttered.

"I'm sorry," she said in a shaky whisper.

He hadn't meant her to hear him, but maybe it was a good thing that she had.

"Yeah," he said coldly, "right. I'm sure you are. Somebody

should have told you that what comes after the booze is never as much fun as the partying that precedes it.

She shook her head. Her hair slipped like silk across his jaw.

"I meant that I'm sorry for this. Not your problem."

"Damned right," he growled.

Jennie expected nothing more.

She knew he wouldn't say she didn't have to apologize, that he was only glad he'd been there to help her…

Genevieve Cooper, are you truly crazy?

It was her alter-ego talking, but Jennie refused to listen. She wasn't Genevieve, not anymore.

Plus, she knew what Travis Wilde was like. Hadn't she learned all she needed to know last week?

Besides, he had every right to be harsh and judgmental. He thought she was drunk. How could he possibly know the truth, that what she really was, was incredibly stupid?

No alcohol with these pills, Jennifer, the doctor had said.

Sure. But what did doctors know? Not much, as the last months had surely proved.

But the righteous Travis Wilde had no way of knowing that, and she wasn't about to enlighten him.

She'd decided, from the beginning, to keep her own counsel, which was a fancy way of saying it was her life and what was happening to her was her business, and she didn't want anybody involved in it.

Her parents were gone. She had no brothers or sisters. The last thing she wanted were strangers, offering phony sympathy. She'd had her fill of that from well-meaning hospital volunteers. Or therapy groups, where everybody thought they had problems until they heard hers.

She'd even tried private counseling, and what a joke that had become when the shrink had broken protocol, reached out and hugged her.

Protocol.

There it was again, the same stupid word that had fallen from her lips last week, after a simple decision to—to take her research to another level had led her into this man's arms, into letting herself feel like a woman instead of a—a creature drowning in a sea of test tubes and lab notes.

And what a mistake that had turned out to be.

Her car was just ahead. Thank goodness. Another minute and she would never have to see Travis Wilde again.

Jennie gathered all her strength, told herself it was vital that she not sound as awful as she felt.

"The tan Civic," she said. "It's mine." He didn't answer, didn't even slow down. "Mr. Wilde. I said, that tan car…"

"I heard you."

"Then put me—"

"You can get it tomorrow, when you're up to driving."

"I have already had the pleasure of retrieving my car, thanks to you. I have no intention of doing it again."

"I don't think you want to argue over the reasons you had to leave your car, last week or this."

He was right. She didn't. What she had to do was exert control.

"I am perfectly capable of driving my own car."

Sick as she was, she was pleased to have achieved what she thought was a determined tone.

Perhaps not.

He laughed, though it was not a pretty sound.

"And pigs can fly." He set her on her feet, held her steady with one arm around her waist while he dug out his keys and opened the 'Vette's door. "Get in."

"Where's Brenda? Brenda can—"

"Brenda's still partying with the rest of your pals. Go on. Get in."

"No. I absolutely refuse to have you—"

He muttered something short and graphic, scooped her

up again and put her into the passenger seat. Then he closed the door, went to the driver's side and got behind the wheel.

"Seat belt," he said sharply.

"Really, I don't—"

He reached across her, grabbed the end of belt and brought it over her body. His hand brushed over her breasts. She thought of what it would be like if he really touched her, not in passion but in an offer of comfort.

"Comfort" was not in his game plan.

She could tell by the way he fastened the latch, his motions brisk and efficient.

"What's your address?"

"I don't need your help, Mr. Wilde."

"Yes," he snarled, "you do. And it's a little late for formality, isn't it? I wasn't 'Mr. Wilde' when you were in my bed."

A wave of hot color rose in her face.

Nice, Travis told himself, a truly nice touch. She didn't deserve to be coddled but she was sick and he'd taken it upon himself to see her safely home.

Besides, he had no right to judge her.

She'd walked into a bar, looking for a hookup?

Her business, not his.

She drank to excess?

Her business again, absolutely not his.

There wasn't any reason to make things worse than they already were, especially when his real anger had just reversed itself and gone from her as its target to himself.

Touching her breasts had been inadvertent.

And his body had not clenched with desire.

Desire, even with her like this, he would have understood. What he'd felt instead, the overwhelming need to take her in his arms and comfort her, was the last thing he'd expected.

He didn't understand it.

Didn't want to understand it.

What he wanted to do was get her to her apartment and then get the hell out of her life.

Whatever life that was.

Who was this woman? Everything about her confused him, even the way she looked...Entirely different than last week.

Far as he could tell, she didn't have a touch of makeup on her face. Her hair was pulled back. She had on a cotton blouse. Sleeveless, simple, buttons all the way down the front. It was tan, pretty much the same color as her box-on-wheels automobile. And she was wearing jeans. Plain, no-name denim, not the torn kind that cost hundreds of bucks just so the wearer could look like somebody who actually worked for a living. Her feet were encased in flat leather sandals.

Nothing with the kind of heel that made a man play sexual fantasies in his head.

Not that she needed to dress the part of temptress.

She was beautiful just as she was, and even knowing she seemed woefully short on logic and maybe on morals didn't change the fact that he still wanted to hold her close and tell her he'd take care of her...

He hated himself for it.

Jaw set, he fastened his seat belt and started the engine. The Corvette roared to life.

"I'm still waiting for you to tell me where you live."

"This is ridiculous." She reached for the door handle. "I'll go back and get Brenda. She can—"

"No. She can't. I'm driving you home and it's not up for discussion. Now, what's your address?"

Jennie closed her eyes.

If only she hadn't let Brenda talk her into going out with most of the department to celebrate Peter Haley finally nailing his doctorate.

"Come on," Brenda had said. "You've been mopey all week. A couple of hours away from the books will make you feel better."

Maybe it would, she'd thought. So she'd gone with them.

And she hadn't even ordered the margarita.

Peter had, and everybody had looked at her when it arrived.

She knew why. It was because she never drank, not even that staple of university life—beer.

Don't you drink, Jen? someone always said. Or, *Good for you! I've heard that these 12 step programs are hard to stick with.*

Either way, there was no good rejoinder.

She was tired of people looking at her, of always being the one who ordered a Diet Coke.

One sip of the pale blue margarita, she'd thought. What harm could one sip do?

It had tasted lovely.

And it had *felt* lovely. Not the alcohol. What had been lovely was that, for the first time in months, she felt normal.

To hell with it, she'd thought, and she'd gulped down half of it—half, not two full drinks as Brenda had claimed.

And yes, for a couple of minutes she'd felt good.

And she was desperate to feel good.

To stop thinking about what lay ahead, and what it would be like.

To stop thinking about last week, and how she'd made a fool of herself with this very man.

This man who was every bit as gorgeous and as arrogant as she'd remembered.

The truth was, she remembered too much.

The feel of his hands on her. The way he kissed. And wasn't that pitiful? That all of that should still be with her? That a man who was such an unmitigated bastard could be such an accomplished lover that a week later, despite the fact that she despised him, that she couldn't afford to waste precious time on such nonsensical stuff, the sight of him could still make her heart start to race?

If only he hadn't been in the bar tonight…

"Are we going to sit here all night?" her unwanted rescuer said. "Because we will, unless you give me your address."

He would do it, Jennie knew. The best thing to do was give in, let him drive her home and know she would never have to deal with him again.

"I live near the university," she said in weary resignation. "Farrier Drive. It's a couple of miles past—"

"I can find it," he said.

She had no doubt that he could.

Besides, she had other things to think about.

Like not throwing up again, until she was alone—but, oh, dear God, that wasn't going to work out...

"Stop the car," she gasped.

He glanced at her, then swerved across two lanes of traffic to the curb. She had barely undone her seat belt when he was out of the car and at her side.

"Easy," he said, as he helped her onto the sidewalk.

A cramp pinched her belly and she groaned, leaned over and vomited although the truth was, mostly, she just gagged and made terrible sounds because there was really nothing left in her belly, but that didn't make things any less horrible, especially because Travis Wilde, world-class rat, stood behind her as if he weren't a rat at all, holding her shoulders and steadying her.

Done, she trembled like a leaf.

"Don't move," he said in a low voice.

She felt him lift one hand from her, then the other, as he slipped off his dark gray sports jacket, then wrapped it around her.

She wanted to tell him she didn't need it—it had to be ninety degrees tonight—but the truth was, she was ice-cold.

"Thank you," she said in a choked whisper.

He turned her toward him, took a pristine white handkerchief from his pocket. She reached for it, but she was shaking too hard to grasp it.

"Let me," he said.

She could hardly meet his eyes as he gently wiped her mouth, afraid of the censure she'd see in his gaze.

"Hey," he said softly. He put his fingers under her chin and raised her face to his, and what she saw in his eyes was compassion.

It made her want to lean forward and rest her head against his chest, but she knew better than to do that.

He was being kind. Not what she'd expected from him. And the last thing she needed. Too much kindness and she'd fall apart.

"I'm—I'm okay."

He nodded. "You will be. Getting all that booze out of your system helps."

"It isn't the tequila," she heard herself say, and could have bitten off her tongue, but he didn't pick up on it.

Instead, he smiled.

"It never is. And if it makes you feel any better, I'm not a novice at this. Heck, I have three sisters, all younger than I am, and I remember helping them clean up after a party."

It wasn't true.

He'd never had to do anything like that for Em or Lissa or Jaimie. If they'd gotten themselves plastered—and now that he thought about it, he figured the odds were good they each must have, at least once in their teen years—they'd covered for each other.

He, Jake and Caleb had covered for each other, too.

Genevieve had nobody to turn to.

Nobody but him.

The thought put a little twist in his gut.

Her face was pale; the elastic thing, whatever women called it, around her ponytail had come loose and strands of pale blond hair were in her eyes.

He tucked the strands behind her ears.

"Okay now?" he said quietly.

She nodded.

He steadied her with one hand, reached into the 'Vette, opened the console, took out a small bottle of water. He opened it; she held out her hand but she was still trembling.

"Here," he said, bringing the bottle to her lips.

She tilted her head back. Drank. Rinsed her mouth, then spat out the water.

"Thank you."

"Finish it."

"I really don't want—"

"Water will make you feel better."

He tilted the bottle to her lips again; she put her hand over his so she could lift it higher. His skin was warm, the feel of his fingers under hers reassuring.

"Good girl," he said, and she, a lifelong advocate for women's rights, felt herself glow under the words of what any self-respecting feminist would call sexist praise.

He capped the empty bottle, tossed it into the back of the car.

"Want to stay here, get a little more fresh air?"

"No. I feel much better."

"Are you sure?"

She couldn't bear the way he was looking at her, his eyes warm not only with compassion but with sympathy. She couldn't tolerate anything close to pity; it was the reason she'd left New England and come here, where nobody knew her.

And now there was this man who had suddenly turned sweet and generous and kind...

"I'm sure." She stood a little straighter. "Look, I know you're afraid I'm going to get sick in your car—"

"I'm not worried about the car."

"Of course you are. Why else would you give a damn?"

Good. That cold glare was in his eye again.

"You have one hell of an opinion of me."

"It only matches your opinion of me."

He opened his mouth, closed it again.

"Okay," he said, after a minute, "how about a truce?"

Her eyes met his. She shrugged.

"Fine."

He smiled. "Lots of enthusiasm in that word, Genevieve."

She stood straighter.

"My name isn't Genevieve." She took a deep breath. What did it matter what he called her? And yet, somehow, it did. "My name is Jennifer. Jennie."

He raised one dark eyebrow. "Why the pseudonym?"

"It wasn't a pseudonym."

The corner of his lips twitched.

"What else would you call using a phony name?"

She considered not answering, but she owed him some kind of honesty, even if it was only the smallest bit.

"I used a different name because—because that wasn't me last Friday night, okay? That—that creature who got all dressed up and headed into that bar. I wasn't that woman who—who went home with a strange man and—and—"

She felt her eyes fill with tears, and wasn't that pathetic? She looked away from him, or would have, but he caught her face in his hands and wiped away her tears with his thumbs.

"You weren't a creature. You were a beautiful woman. Brave, too."

His voice was soft. She didn't want softness, dammit. She wanted him to be the callous bastard she'd pegged him for.

She didn't want to like him.

She didn't want to need him.

She couldn't need anybody.

Not now. Not ever. Not—

"Baby," he said, not just softly but gently. It was too much, and she had to deal with it.

"And my name certainly isn't 'baby,' either." She jerked free of his hands. "So if you think a—a ration of Texas sweet-talk is going to make me dumb enough to sleep with you again—"

He let go of her, fast. So much for declaring a truce.

"Your mama should have taught you that it's polite to wait until you're asked." His eyes narrowed to icy slits. "Do us both a favor, *Genevieve*. Get back in the car so I can take you home and know we'll never have the misfortune to see each other again."

His comment had been no nastier than hers, but it hurt. She wanted to zing back a clever response, then walk away, but her brain was foggy, they were miles from her apartment—and she knew damned well that on this particular night, walking home wasn't an option.

"An excellent plan, Mr. Wilde," she said coldly. "And thanks again for reminding me that you are, indeed, a callous, pluperfect rat."

It wasn't much, but it was the best she could do.

She swung away. A sharp pain lanced through her head; the earth tilted. She gave it a couple of seconds until things steadied. Then she got into the car.

He got in on his side, slammed the door hard enough to make her jump.

The car flew into the night, and Jennie prayed that the pain in her head wouldn't get so bad that it would make her weep.

Neither of them said anything more until Travis turned onto her street, and into the garden apartment complex in which she lived.

The pain in her head had eased off. A minor miracle, but it wouldn't last. She needed to take a pill before it returned.

"Which building?" he said.

"You can stop at the corner."

"I can stop in front of your door. Which building?"

"You don't have to—"

"You're right, I don't. But I will. For the last time, which building?"

God, he was impossible. Maybe some women liked to be bossed around but she wasn't one of them. Still, if it got her home faster…

"That one," she said. "At the corner."

He drove to the end of the block, then into the driveway that led behind the building.

"What are you doing?"

He didn't answer but then, he didn't have to. What he was doing was obvious.

He was pulling into a slot in the small parking area.

"I'm seeing you to your door," he said brusquely.

"That is absolutely not—"

She was talking to the air. He was out of the car, already opening her door.

Jennie rolled her eyes and stepped outside.

"Do you always ignore people's wishes, Mr. Wilde?"

"Only when their wishes don't make sense, Miss…?"

"Cooper," she snapped.

"Only when their wishes don't make sense, Miss Cooper. Twenty minutes ago, you were tossing your cookies."

"That's a horrible phrase!"

"It isn't as bad as the act itself."

They were walking toward the back entrance to her two-story building. He tried to take her arm; she shook him off.

It was a stupid thing to do, considering that it was dark—one of the lights over the door had burned out—and the lot had potholes big enough to swallow you whole.

Inevitably she stumbled.

Just as inevitably, he caught her, put his arm around her waist.

"I don't need—"

"I'll be the judge of that."

"Dammit, Wilde—"

"Great," he said tightly. "No more 'mister.' At least we'll be on a less formal basis before you go facedown out here."

"I hate to spoil that lovely image but it won't happen. I'm much better now, thank you very much, and you've brought me to my door, so—"

"Keys."

"What is wrong with you? I just said—"

"I'm taking you to your apartment. Keys."

He held out his free hand, snapped his fingers—and was rewarded with the sight of her chin lifting and her eyes narrowing.

Damned if she didn't look like she wanted to slug him.

He fought against a smile.

No matter what, you had to admire her spirit. All dressed up for a night on the town, dressed down for a night with friends, sick or not, Jennie Cooper was one interesting woman.

She held the keys up by two fingers, gave him a four-letter smile and dropped them in his palm.

This time, what he fought back was a burst of laughter.

She had more than spirit; she had resiliency.

For some crazy reason, he wanted to kiss her, and that was patently ridiculous. Instead he did the only safe thing: turned his back to her and unlocked the door.

It opened on the kind of hallway he suspected was endemic to cheap student housing everywhere. A narrow corridor, dim lighting, closed doors.

Nothing unusual.

Still, a caution born of years spent on not-necessarily-friendly territory half a world away made him move forward and enter the hall first. A quick but efficient glance revealed nothing more threatening than a moth batting against an overhead light at the foot of a staircase.

He turned, ready to signal her past him, but she was already moving.

Her body brushed his.

His breath nearly stopped. And unless he'd forgotten how to read women, so did hers.

Electricity filled the space between them.

He knew what he wanted to do.

Take Jennie in his arms. Kiss her. Touch her. She'd let him do it, too. He knew it as surely as he knew what that look in her eyes meant…

How many bad ideas could a man have in one night?

He took a step back.

"Okay," he said briskly. "Which apartment?"

He wanted her to say it was on the second floor. Then he'd have the excuse to hold her in his arms again, but she swallowed hard, dragged her gaze from his and nodded toward the nearest door.

They walked to it. The same key opened the door, and they stepped inside.

The place was like all the off-campus housing complexes he'd visited back in his university days.

Small. Institutionally-furnished. Nothing to define it as Jennie's, except for a small plush animal sitting in a corner of the sofa.

It was a dog with long, floppy ears. One long, floppy ear, anyway. The other was pretty much gone, as was most of a faded red bow around its neck.

It was the kind of sentimental keepsake his sisters—well, Emily, anyway—were big on. Somehow, he hadn't expected Jennie to harbor such attachments.

"A silly thing."

Travis turned around. Jennie was standing a few feet away, eyes fixed on him.

"The dog," she said. "I don't know why I keep it."

"It's not silly to keep something you love."

"I don't love it. Why would anybody love a beat-up old toy?"

Their eyes met.

She cleared her throat.

"I need to—to—"

She gestured toward what he figured was the bathroom.

"Yes. Sure." He cleared his throat. "I'll wait."

"No. I mean, you don't have to…"

"I'll wait," he said.

She nodded.

Safely inside the bathroom, the door closed and locked, Jennie stared at herself in the mirror.

She looked awful.

Not that it mattered.

Travis had performed a rescue mission; what she looked like was unimportant.

She peed. Washed her face. Brushed her teeth. Took a pill for her headache, just in case it returned.

Then she took a few deep breaths, let them out, opened the door and went back into the living room.

He was standing beside the window.

Say something, she told herself, say anything!

"Great view of the parking lot, huh?" she said briskly.

He turned around.

"Yeah." A quick smile. "Well. Are you going to be okay?"

"I'll be fine."

"Because if you still feel sick—"

"Travis? What I said before, about it not being the tequila… It's the truth. I—I wasn't drunk."

She spoke the words in a rush, even as she chastised herself for having said them.

"Look, I didn't mean to…I shouldn't have set myself up as judge and jury. You drank too much. So what? Believe me, I've done the same—"

"It was a reaction to medication."

"Medication?"

He looked startled. Jennie's heart thudded. He couldn't

be more startled than she was but somehow, it had become important that he not think worse of her than he already did.

"You mean, an allergic thing?"

She took a deep breath.

"Not exactly. I get—I get headaches." That was certainly true enough. "I take something for them and—and the doctor warned me it wouldn't mix well with liquor but—but—"

"But, you forgot."

She hadn't forgotten. She'd just thought, *What the hell is the difference?*

Life was closing down so quickly…

But she couldn't tell him that.

"Something like that," she said, trying for a carefree smile.

He smiled, too. Her heartbeat quickened. She'd almost forgotten how devastating his smile was: charming, flirtatious, sexy…and all Travis Wilde.

"Well," he said, "after what happened tonight, you won't forget next time."

They both laughed politely—but nothing in their eyes was polite. The way he was looking at her, the way she was looking at him…

She turned away and walked to the door.

He followed.

She looked at him, held out her hand. He took it.

His touch sent a wave of longing through her.

"Anyway—anyway, thanks for taking me home."

"No," he said, "thank *you*."

"For what?"

"For tolerating me being such an ass."

"You weren't. I mean, you had every reason to think I was just plain drunk."

"Even so, I had no right to judge you." His hand tightened around hers; he moved closer. "As for last week—"

"Really," she said quickly, "there's no need to—"

"There's every need. You gave me a gift beyond measure that night."

She felt her face flame with color.

"No. I understand. I burdened you with—"

"You *honored* me." His voice was rough, so sexy she could hardly breathe. "No woman's ever given me such an incredible gift before."

He meant it. She could see it in his eyes, hear it in his words. It made her want to explain…at least, to explain as much as she could.

"Travis," she said softly, "I know I made it sound as if—as if you—as if what we did—was just something that I'd planned could happen with anybody. But—but—"

"But what?"

The rest was hard to say. To admit. She didn't want to embarrass him. Or embarrass herself. But he had the right to hear it.

She took a deep breath.

"But one step inside that bar and I knew I'd never go through with it. And then—and then—"

His eyes darkened.

"And then?"

"And then I saw you."

"You were a miracle, coming through that door," he said softly. "I told myself the miracle was that you could save my sorry tail…" He cupped her face with his hands. "But the truth is, the miracle was that you were so beautiful. And that I wanted you the second I saw you."

Her smile, her sigh, told him everything he'd spent the past week needing to know.

"Truly?" she said, all the innocence in the world in the one, softly-spoken word.

"Truly," he said. "I never wanted a woman the way I wanted you."

"What we did," she whispered, "it was—it was—"

"Incredible," he whispered back, putting his arms around her, bending his head to hers, nuzzling her hair away from her temple. "I thought about you every single minute since that night."

"Did you?" she said, her voice trembling.

"Every waking moment." He smiled. "Every sleeping moment, too." His smile tilted. "I dreamed about you."

Was he saying that to make her feel better, or did he mean it?

Stop analyzing, was the last thing her alter-ego said, before she sent it packing and moved fully into his embrace.

She could feel the hard, quick race of his heart.

"I—I dreamed about you, too."

He cupped her face. Lifted it to his.

"I don't want to leave you," he said gruffly.

Jennie took a deep, deep breath.

"Then don't," she whispered.

Travis kissed her. She kissed him back. He groaned, kissed her again, hard and deep.

Then he reached past her, and closed the door.

CHAPTER SEVEN

HE WASN'T GOING to make love to her.

What kind of man took advantage of a woman when she didn't feel well?

He just—he just wanted to hold her.

Be with her.

Kiss her, just a little. Like this. God, yes, like this. Kisses that made her tremble in his arms.

And he wanted to touch her.

Not in a way that demanded anything of her. Asked anything of her.

He only wanted to feel the softness of her hair as it slid through his fingers, the warmth of her skin under the stroke of his hand.

But with her lips clinging to his, parting to his, with her body pressed to his, wanting was rapidly giving way to the heady rush of need.

For the first time in his life, Travis saw the difference between the two.

He was a man who prided himself on self-control, even in sex. Especially in sex. Only a fool let his emotions carry him away with a woman.

But it was different with her.

With Jennie.

He couldn't get his thoughts together. Couldn't focus on anything but her taste, her heat, her sweet moans.

He tried.

He clasped her shoulders. Drew back, just a little. Looked down into her lovely, innocent face.

"Honey." His voice was hoarse; he cleared his throat but it didn't help. "Jennie. We don't have to do anything more than—"

She rose to him, put her hands into his hair, silenced him with a kiss.

"Are you telling me you don't want me?" she whispered.

Travis took her hand, placed it over his racing heart, then brought it down, down, down to the fullness straining the fabric of his fly.

"What do you think?" he said thickly.

She gave a soft, incredibly sexy laugh.

"I think you need to take me into the bedroom. Behind you, through that door."

He lifted her into his arms, carried her into a room that was hardly big enough to contain a chest of drawers. A nightstand.

And twin beds.

He almost laughed. Whatever he'd expected, it hadn't been this.

"It could be worse," Jennie said, as if she knew what he was thinking. He looked down at her, saw that her lips were curved. "The bedroom in my last place had bunk beds."

He did laugh, then; she did, too. But when he felt the brush of her breasts and belly against him as he lowered her slowly to her feet, their laughter faded.

Her eyes were filled with need.

Filled with him.

Desire, sharp and hot, still burned within him.

But so was something else.

He wanted to—to take care of her. Protect her.

He wanted to be the lover he had not been that first time. The lover she deserved.

He kissed her. Gently. Framed her face with his big hands.

"I'm going to undress you," he said softly. "And lie down with you in my arms. We don't have to do anything more than that tonight."

When she parted her lips to answer him, he silenced her with a kiss.

Then, slowly, his eyes fixed to hers, he began undoing the buttons of her blouse.

Normally, he was fine with buttons. Small, round bits of plastic; how difficult could opening them be, especially for a guy who'd been undressing women since the age of sixteen?

Very difficult.

His fingers seemed too big. Clumsy. He found himself concentrating, hard, on every miserable one of what seemed like an endless line of tiny plastic rounds that marched down her blouse.

She made a little sound.

He looked up.

"What?" he said, a little gruffly.

"Nothing. I mean—I mean—I can't—" Her hands closed over his. "Tear the blouse, if you have to. Just—just touch me…"

On a deep, long groan, he did what she'd asked and tore the delicate fabric in two.

Then he drew back.

Not a lot. Just enough so that his eyes could take delight from the delicate beauty he'd uncovered.

Creamy shoulders. The rise of rounded breasts above a simple, white cotton bra. A tiny, heart-shaped birthmark just below the hollow of her throat.

How could he not have noticed that last time?

How could he not have noticed how sweet, how innocent she was?

He kissed the heart.

Kissed the delicate curve of flesh rising above the bra.

Kissed the center of each cup, where the faint pucker of fabric hinted at the nipples that awaited the touch of his tongue.

Jennie made a sound that tore straight through him.

"Travis," she whispered, and he knew that no one had ever said his name with as much tenderness.

He reached for the clasp on her jeans.

Undid it.

Took hold of the zipper tab.

Drew it down.

Slowly he eased the jeans down her legs.

Such long, endless legs.

She was trembling.

Hell, so was he.

He slipped off her shoes, one at a time. Looked at her. Like this, barefoot, wearing the simplest bra and panties, she was a woman a man would ache to possess.

And, God, yes, he ached. For her.

"You're beautiful," he said softly.

Color swept into her face.

"I want to be," she said. "For you."

That was what he wanted, too. That her beauty, her unique self, be only for him.

"Aren't you—aren't you going to touch me?"

Her words were a magnificent torment. He wanted to do exactly that, wanted it more than anything…

He was drawn as tight as a bow.

He could see the pulse beating just beneath the tiny heart-shaped birthmark.

"Is that what you want?"

"Yes. Oh, yes."

"Take my hand," he said in a gravel-rough voice. "Show me where you want me to touch you."

He held his hand out to her. She stared at it. At him. He forced himself not to move.

It seemed an eternity but, at last, she took his hand. Brought it to her cheek. To her throat.

Her lips.

Parted them, and sucked one of his fingers into her mouth.

A low moan rose in his throat.

He was going to come. Sweet Lord, he was going to come...

He drew a harsh breath. Focused on her. Felt the pounding in his veins ease.

"Where else shall I touch you?" he said in a choked whisper.

Her eyes locked with his. She brought his hand down her throat.

To her breast.

Travis closed his eyes. Cupped his hand around the sweet weight, felt the push of the cotton-covered nipple into his palm.

"And—and here," she whispered, as she drew his hand over her ribs, over her belly...

And stopped.

She couldn't go any farther.

What she was doing was beyond anything she'd ever imagined doing with a man.

Letting him touch her so intimately.

Guiding his hand over her body.

Watching his face as she did it, seeing his tanned skin seem to tighten over the bones beneath it.

"Jennie."

She blinked.

His eyes had narrowed and glittered like shards of obsidian in the night.

"Don't stop," he said. "Show me what you want."

She took a breath. Took another.

"I want your hand here," she whispered, and she shifted her weight, brought his palm between her thighs, placed it against the part of her that throbbed with need for him.

He said something, low and fierce and shockingly primal.

She was hot and wet, and he couldn't wait, couldn't hold back, couldn't...

"Travis," she sobbed, "please, please..."

He reached for his jacket, prayed there were some forgotten condoms in the interior pocket. Yes. Thank God, there were two slim packets.

"Jennie," he whispered, "beautiful Jennie."

Somehow, he tore off his clothes. Fumbled with her bra, got the clasp undone, tried to deal with her panties, cursed and, instead, ripped them from her.

She was moving against him, her body hot against his, her mouth open and wet and seeking on his.

All his thoughts about doing this slowly, gently, never mind maybe not doing it at all, vanished like smoke on a windy morning.

The bed was a million miles away.

The wall was much closer.

"Hold on to me," he said as he lifted her. "Your arms around my neck. Your legs around my waist..."

She screamed his name as he thrust into her.

He went still; was he hurting her?

"Don't stop," she said, "don't-stop-don't-stop-don't-stop—"

He took her mouth with his. And moved inside her. Hard. Fast. She screamed as she came and still he went deeper, deeper, so deep that when the triumphal cry of his completion escaped his throat, the world spun away.

* * *

Somehow, they made it to the bed.

He put her down, kissed her, found his way to the bathroom and disposed of the condom.

The mattress was narrow; she made room for him but he gathered her to him, held her so she was draped over him, and the fact that there wasn't really room for two people in her bed didn't matter because he was never going to let go of her.

He was going to hold her like this until the end of time.

"Travis."

"Mmm?"

"I'm too heavy…"

He laughed.

So did Jennie.

It was a lovely feeling, all that rock-hard male muscle vibrating with laughter beneath her.

The scientist in her had never thought that people would laugh when they made love.

The woman in her was thrilled by the realization.

"Seriously. You can't be comforta—"

"You know," he said, "when I was a kid, I had this old blanket that I absolutely adored."

She folded her hands on his chest, propped her chin on them and gave him a wary look.

"And?"

"And," he said, his expression dead-serious, "I couldn't go to sleep unless I had it draped on top of me."

It took all her effort to keep a straight face.

"Nice. Very nice. So, I remind you of an old blanket?"

He grinned.

"Does it help if I say it was a comforter, not a blanket?"

Jennie sank her teeth lightly into his shoulder. He gave a mock yelp.

"Hey. That was a compliment."

"Telling a woman she reminds you of a blanket, even if you call it a comforter, is *not* a compliment, Mr. Wilde."

"I didn't tell it to a woman, I told it to you." His grin faded. "Only to you, Jennie. Because you're the only woman I want in my arms."

"That's lovely," she said softly. "Because you're the only man I want in mine."

He kissed her. Kissed her again. She could feel him hardening against her and then he kissed her one last time and gently moved out from under her.

"Don't go," she said, before she could call back the plea, but it was okay, saying it, letting him know how much she wanted him, it was fine because he kissed her again and told her, against her lips, that he wasn't going anywhere except to get another condom.

"Why would I ever leave you?" he said when he came back to her and rolled her beneath him.

"Travis." His name trembled on her lips. "Oh, Travis..."

"Jennie," he whispered, and then he was inside her.

She awoke to middle-of-the-night darkness, and to confusion.

She was in her bed—there was no mistaking the lumpy mattress—but she wasn't alone.

She was lying on her side, head pillowed on a hard shoulder. An equally hard arm and leg were flung possessively over her body.

For a split second, her brain froze.

And then it all came back.

Travis, taking her out of that bar. His anger and then his concern. His toughness and then his tenderness.

His lovemaking.

His amazing, incredible, glorious lovemaking.

I should get up, she thought. *Do whatever it is a woman does when she awakens with a man beside her.*

What *did* you do in those circumstances?

You left the bed. And, what? Did you do just the basics? A bathroom visit? Fix your hair? Put on some makeup? Get dressed. Oh, absolutely. Get dressed, for sure. Get out of the bedroom, give the man some space.

All of that made sense.

Except, she really didn't want to move.

It was—well, it was lovely, just lying here, Travis's shoulder serving as her pillow, his arm and leg over her.

He was so warm. So solid.

So wonderfully real.

Sex wasn't what you read about in textbooks. It wasn't what you saw in psych counseling videos. It was—it was—

It was Travis.

He stirred in his sleep; his arm tightened around her and he drew her closer.

And this. Waking in a man's arms. The feeling of him caring about you, protecting you.

Who would have dreamed that, too, was part of sex?

Research. That was what she'd called her plan to learn what sex was like, because calling it anything else had seemed ugly—but there was no pretending this was research any longer.

This was about him. Travis Wilde. A man she'd picked up in a bar, who was now her lover.

For a heartbeat, surely no more than that, Jennie gave in to the luxury of letting herself think of him that way. As her lover…

Pain knifed behind her eye, a brutal reminder of the truth and of where that truth would inevitably take her.

She clamped her lips together, biting back the cry that rose in her throat, but there was no stopping the pain. It was red-hot; it was ice-cold. It was worse than it had ever been.

She knew what would happen next. The chills. The shaking. The bits of her vision going gray.

She couldn't let that happen, not while Travis was here.

She bit her lips hard, anything to keep the agony at bay, to let her get away without waking him. She moved quickly, carefully, slipped out from under the shelter of his arm and leg.

He stirred again, mumbled something. She held her breath until he was quiet. Then she rose to her feet, stumbling a little, recovering fast, gritting her teeth against the agonizing throbbing inside her skull.

She wanted to find her robe but there was no time to look for it with the room buried in the blackness of night. The last month, she'd slept with a night-light, a foolish talisman against the dark that was coming for her, but it gave her comfort. She slept with the one-eared toy dog, too; for foolishly sentimental reasons, she'd kept it all through her teen years. It had ended up being the one remnant of a time she'd been whole and well.

Tonight, of course, there was no light. And no toy dog.

Travis had been her talisman. Her comfort.

Carefully, she made her way to the bathroom. She eased the door shut behind her, felt for the shelf over the sink, danced her fingers along it, searching for the little bottle of tablets.

She didn't touch the light switch.

She knew, from experience, that it would hurt her eyes. Besides, it would seep under the door and wake—

Her hand swept over the collection of tiny vials and containers.

"No," she whispered, but it was too late. All of them fell, tumbling into the sink, the sound as loud and clear as if she'd come in here to play the cymbals.

The door flew open. The switch on the wall beside her clicked on; bright light flooded the bathroom.

She flung her arm over her eyes.

"Jennie," Travis said sharply, his voice rough with sleep. "Baby, are you all right?"

"Yes. Yes, I'm fine."

Travis stared at her.

Fine?

He'd been thrown from horses just learning the feel of
a man's weight; he'd been ejected from a plane about to go
down under enemy fire. He'd been hauled through a public
square by a squad of goons determined to make an example
of the Yankee pilot who represented everything they despised.

He understood what "fine" meant when it was spoken
through tight lips from a face white with pain.

"The hell you are," he growled.

Gently, he clasped her shoulders, then sat her on the closed
toilet seat. There was a mess of pill bottles in the sink, plastic, probably, but he checked her face, her hands, her body
for blood.

Satisfied that she wasn't hurt, he clasped her wrist to draw
her arm from her eyes…

"Don't!"

Her voice was high and sharp.

His heartbeat tripped into double-time. So much for her
not being hurt.

"What is it?"

"Nothing. I told you, I'm—"

Travis cursed, gently drew her arm down.

Her eyes were tightly closed.

Okay.

No blood. No cuts. No bruises. But she was paper-white,
and shaking, and when he asked her to open her eyes so he
could check them, she hissed out a long, low "noooo."

"Jen," he said, squatting down before her, "you have to
talk to me. What happened? I woke up, you were gone and
then I heard a crash—"

"I—I had a headache." Her voice seemed weak; it sent a
chill down his spine. "So I came in here to get—to get something for it."

"Why didn't you put on the light? Why won't you let me see your eyes?"

"I didn't think I'd need the light. I mean, I know where everything is. And my eyes…"

A soft moan broke from her throat.

Travis cursed himself for being an ass.

She was hurting; she'd probably scared herself half to death and instead of helping her, he was asking her a bunch of dumb questions.

"Okay, baby. I get it. You have another headache, like the one you had earlier. And the light…"

The light.

Of course.

A former P.A. had suffered from migraines; she'd told him about the unbearable pain, the way exposure to light made the pain worse.

It was clear that Jennie had the same problem, and that she was having a bad attack.

He rose, switched off the light. He'd turned on the bed-side lamp; its soft glow, coming through the open door, was enough for him to see by.

"Don't move," he said in a voice that commanded as much as it comforted.

Quickly, he scooped everything out of the sink—the vials and containers had all stayed closed—carried the stuff into the bedroom and dumped it on the dresser.

There were lots of labels; none of them bore names that were familiar.

"Which of these pills were you looking for?" he said.

Jennie told him.

He found the correct vial, shook a tablet into his hand and went back to her.

"One second, baby."

There was a white plastic cup on the sink. He filled it with water and squatted before her again.

"Open," he said as he brought the pill to her lips.

"I can—"

"Did I ever tell you I was a Boy Scout in my misguided youth?"

Her lips curved in a semblance of a smile.

"Come on. Take the pill. Good girl. Now a drink of water…"

He returned the cup to the sink. Took a neatly-folded face cloth from the towel bar and ran it under cold water from the tap, wrung it out and went back to her.

Her eyes were still closed, her face still pale. He took her hand, turned it up and placed the cool, damp cloth in her palm.

"Lay that over your eyes, honey."

"Travis. You don't have to—"

"'On my honor,'" he said solemnly, "'as a Scout…' You want me to go back on those words?"

She gave a soft, tentative laugh. His heart leaped with joy.

"You? A Boy Scout?"

"Well, no. My brothers and I had our own thing going." *Talk,* he told himself, as he saw color begin coming back into her face, *talk and keep talking, let her hang on to the sound of your voice and maybe it'll help drive away the pain.* "Besides, Mr. Rottweiler, the troop leader, hated us."

"His name was not Mr. Rottweiler!"

Good. Excellent. She was listening to him, concentrating on his stupid jokes. The pill, the compress, were working.

"How come you're so smart, Blondie? His name was Botwilder. Close enough, we figured."

"And he hated you?"

"Yeah, well, see, we'd tipped over his outhouse…"

The breath hissed between her teeth. Travis felt his gut knot; he reached for her, lifted her carefully into his arms. She wound her arms around his neck, buried her face against his throat.

"Nobody has outhouses anymore," she said drowsily.

"Ah, but the Rottweiler did," Travis said briskly as he carried her into the bedroom. "He made his wife and his nineteen kids use it."

Another soft, sweet laugh. Another wish to pump his fist in the air.

"Not nineteen," she said, and yawned.

"Okay. Not nineteen. Eighteen."

He switched off the table lamp. Dawn was breaking—the light in the room was a pale gray.

Gently he lay her down on the narrow bed.

His heart turned over.

She was naked and beautiful, but what he saw, as he drew the duvet over her, was her amazing combination of strength and vulnerability.

"Travis," she whispered.

"I'm here, Jen."

"Thank…"

And then, she was asleep.

He watched her for a minute. Then he whispered, "Okay," reached for his clothes…

Except, he wasn't going anywhere.

He wasn't leaving her.

She needed him.

An image shot into his head.

He, as a very little boy. Sick as hell with something kids get, a virus, a cold, whatever. Waking in the middle of the night, wanting the comfort of a pair of loving arms to hold him, then realizing there were no loving arms, not anymore.

His mom had died, and his father was away saving the world.

Travis dropped the clothes. Pulled back the duvet, climbed into the narrow bed.

Would taking Jennie in his embrace wake her?

He didn't have to decide.

She sighed in her sleep, rolled toward him, burrowed into him as if they had always slept together like this.

He wrapped her in his arms.

Kissed her forehead.

And fell into a deep, dreamless sleep.

CHAPTER EIGHT

SUNLIGHT BLAZED AGAINST Travis's eyelids.

He groaned, rolled onto his belly...

And almost fell off the bed.

His eyes flew open; his brain took survey. Narrow room Narrow bed. Narrow window. What the hell...?

Then, he remembered.

Jennie. Bringing her home. Making love to her, how incredible it had been.

And hours later, she'd been so ill. That migraine...

"Jennie," he said, as he shot to his feet.

He'd stayed the night to take care of her. Some job he'd done! He hadn't heard her leave the bed. Leave him. Where was she? Was she hurting?

He started for the door.

Dammit, he was naked.

"Clothes," he muttered, looking around the room for the stuff he'd discarded like a wild man last night.

There. On the dresser. A neatly folded stack of all his things.

He grabbed only his khakis, pulled them on, zipped them but didn't bother with the top button, went in search of her...

And found her in the minuscule kitchen, standing with her back to him. Her hair was loose; she had on some kind of oversize T-shirt. Her long legs were bare, as were her feet.

She looked bed-rumpled. Sex-rumpled. And he wanted, more than anything, to sweep her into his arms, take her back to bed.

That he wanted her so with such intensity, even after all the times he'd had her last night, made his words sound gruff.

"Dammit," he growled, "where'd you go?"

She spun toward him. She had a mug in her hand; a dark liquid—coffee, by the welcome smell that permeated the room—sloshed over the rim.

"Travis! You startled—"

He crossed the floor in three quick steps and pulled her into his arms. The coffee sloshed again, this time onto his toes. The stuff was hot, but he didn't care.

"I thought something had happened to you."

"No. I'm fine. I just thought coffee would be a good—"

He kissed her.

She tasted of coffee, cream and sugar.

There'd been times he'd started mornings in Paris with Champagne, in Seville with hot chocolate. But he'd never begun the day with a sweeter flavor on his tongue than the taste of Jennie's mouth.

When he finally lifted his head, her eyes were bright, her lips softly swollen.

"I missed you," he said, before he could think. "Waking up alone wasn't what I had in mind."

She smiled. And blushed.

He loved that blush. It was sexy and innocent at the same time, and made him wonder if he was the first man who'd spent the night with her in his arms.

Just because he was the first man who'd made love to her didn't mean she hadn't done other things with other men.

Hell. Where was he going with that line of thought? He kept reminding himself that he wasn't old-fashioned about women and sex…

Except, it seemed as if he was. About this woman, anyway, and about having sex with her.

About making love with her.

About staying the night in her bed and, come to think of it, how often had he done something like that? Truth was, he could probably count the number of times on the fingers of one hand.

Women tended to get the wrong idea when you spent the night. They read more into it than it deserved.

The way to keep expectations reasonable was to avoid certain trip wires.

Spending the entire night in your lover's bed was one sure trip wire—and why was he thinking of Jennie as his lover? He'd spent two nights with her. That hardly made them "lovers."

Suddenly, the kitchen seemed even smaller than it actually was.

He let go of her, cleared his throat and moved past her to a shelf above the stove where coffee mugs hung from little hooks.

"Great idea," he said briskly. "Making coffee, I mean."

He could feel her looking at him as he filled the mug and added a dollop of cream.

"Yes," she said, after a couple of seconds. "I'm no good at all until I get my morning dose of caffeine."

"Mmm. Same here." There was a teaspoon on the counter. He picked it up, stirred his coffee—but how long could a man take to stir coffee? "So," he said, even more briskly, "you're an early riser, huh?"

"You don't have to do this."

Her voice was low. Something in it made him wince.

"Hey," he said, "why would I turn down a cup of—"

"You don't have to stay. Really. It isn't necessary. I mean, what you did last night—taking care of me, tending to me—that was—it was much, much more than—"

"You were sick."

"Yes. But that doesn't mean—"

He put down the mug and turned toward her. Forget bed-rumpled. Forget sexy. She looked small and fragile and all at once, he hated himself for being such a selfish, unfeeling bastard.

"Come here," he said gruffly, although he was already moving toward her, his arms open.

She went straight into his embrace.

"I'm sorry," she said unsteadily. "I'm not very good at this. I guess I'm not good at it at all. I don't know what I'm supposed to say after—after—"

Travis put his hand under her chin and raised her face to his.

"How about, 'Good morning, Travis. Are you as glad to see me as I am to see you?'"

Her eyes searched his, and then she gave a tremulous smile.

"Are you? Glad to see me? Because—because really, if you just want to leave—"

He silenced her with a kiss.

"Confession time," he said softly. "I'm not sure of what to say, either. I don't—I don't usually..." He cleared his throat. "Spending the entire night in a bed that isn't my own isn't something I've done very often."

He watched her trying to make sense of what he'd said, saw her eyes widen when she did.

"Oh," she said.

And blushed.

God Almighty, that blush!

"Well," she said quickly, "you were—you were kind to do it. I mean, to stay because I—"

"I stayed because I hated the thought of leaving you."

Her lips curved in a smile. What could he possibly do except kiss that smile? And kiss it again, when she sighed, put her hands on his chest and rose toward him.

He wanted to undress her.

Touch her.

Kiss her everywhere.

But she'd been so sick last night…She needed coffee. Food. Not sex.

Except, he didn't want sex.

He wanted to make love to her…

Travis clasped her shoulders, ended the kiss, flashed a quick smile.

"Okay," he said, yes, briskly, and if there was a word that went beyond "briskly," he needed it now. "Time for breakfast."

Her lashes rose. There was a blurred, dreamy look in her eyes.

"To hell with breakfast," he growled, and he drew her against him and kissed her again and again, each kiss deeper, more demanding than the last until she was clinging to him for support, leaning into him, her hands twisted in his hair. "I want you," he said against her mouth.

"That's good," she whispered. "Because I want you, too."

His body, already hard, felt as if it might be turning to stone.

"Your headache…"

She gave a sexy little laugh.

"What headache?" she said, and he swung her into his arms and took her back to bed.

A couple of hours later, they were in his car, on their way to breakfast.

Well, to brunch.

When she'd said she couldn't go with him, that she had to go get her car, he'd phoned the mechanic who worked with him on his 'Vette when it needed something, and asked him to stop by for her car keys.

She'd stayed in the bedroom when the guy showed up but she'd heard Travis describe her old, if honorable, vehicle.

"A tan two-door?" she'd heard the guy say with disbelief, and Travis had said, in solemn tones, that spending half an hour driving it would be good for the guy's soul.

He'd come back to her, still chuckling.

Just remembering it made her smile.

Now she glanced at him from under the curve of her lashes.

They'd completely missed the hours when most people had breakfast.

Instead, they'd spent the time in each other's arms.

And it had been wonderful.

At one point, when she'd sobbed his name and begged him to end the beautiful torment, he'd clasped her wrists, drawn her arms over her head, said—in a sexy growl that had only added to her excitement—that he was never going to end it, that he was going to keep her where she was, on the edge of that high, high precipice…

Even thinking about it made her a little breathless.

Was sex like this for everyone?

She knew it wasn't.

The books said sex was different for all couples but she'd have known that anyway, because sex with Travis was—it was—

Really, there weren't words to describe it.

She'd gone looking for sex.

For the experience of it, because—because time was closing down around her and she couldn't let that happen without knowing what life had not yet shown her, because sex was supposed to be such a powerful part of your existence.

But she had not expected this.

The passion? The excitement? The clinical physiology of orgasm?

Yes, yes, and yes.

But the reality was…

Beyond description. Especially the wonder of those last

few minutes when you felt—you felt as if you were drowning in sensation.

And the rest.

The way you reacted to the sound of your lover's voice. His strength. His tenderness. The feel of his body under your hand, its taste on your mouth.

There was more. Much more, and some of it didn't have a thing to do with sex. Like Travis's smile, or his easy laughter.

Even the way he took control of things.

Of her.

She'd always thought that kind of behavior was male arrogance and, yes, her lover had an arrogance to him, but it wasn't born out of pride or ego or aggression, it was born of the innate ability to lead.

Jennie glanced at him again.

Added to all that, he was beautiful.

She loved watching him.

He did everything with self-assurance. He even drove that way, as he was right now, his attention on the road, his hand light on the steering wheel, the other on the gearshift…

On her hand, lying just beneath his.

What if she hadn't stopped at that awful bar a week ago? What if Travis hadn't been there? What if she hadn't gone along with the game he'd initiated?

What if she'd let fearless Genevieve morph back into cautious Jennie, the Jennie who had not understood how quickly life could change?

Most of all…

Most of all, what if the years still stretched ahead of her, bright and golden in their clarity? What if she was like everyone else, able to reach out and take what she wanted without having to stop and remind herself that she had no right to do so?

Anger flared within her.

And she couldn't afford that anger.

It was too devastating. Too crippling. It stole what little remained of moments and hours and days that might still be filled with happiness.

She'd learned that the hard way.

One minute, you were looking into a future of clear skies and bright promise...and the next, clouds had covered the sun and the future was looking at you, sneering, saying, *Okay, lady, here I am, this is the way it's really gonna be, and what are you gonna to do about it?*

Crumple, had been her first reaction.

But then her alter-ego, for lack of a better term—and what better term would someone who'd taken that double major in psychology and sociology come up with—her alter-ego had said, *Dammit, stand up and fight!*

It didn't change the end game, but it changed the way you got there, head bowed or head high...

"Hey."

They'd pulled to the curb outside a restaurant. Travis was watching her, his dark eyes narrowed.

"Hey yourself," she said, with what she hoped was a smile.

"Are you all right?"

"I'm fine!" she said brightly. Too brightly, perhaps, going by the intensity of his gaze.

"Tell me the truth, honey. Is that migraine back?"

"No. I'm good. Really."

He looked at her for a long minute. Then he flashed that sexy smile, the one that seemed to melt her bones.

"Except when you're bad," he said huskily, "and you're perfect, either way."

She blushed.

He grinned.

"I love the way you do that."

"Do what?"

"The way you blush." He undid his seat belt, leaned in,

undid hers and took her lips in a soft, sweet kiss. "It's one hell of a turn-on."

She blushed even harder. This time, his smile was wicked.

"Keep that up, we're not going to get into the restaurant."

He was right. They wouldn't. If he smiled that way again, kissed her again…

"Jennie," he said in a low voice, because what she was thinking was probably right in her eyes.

What she was feeling was probably only a heartbeat behind, and she couldn't let him see that because it was impossibly out of the question, it was not what he'd signed on for and, oh God, it was far, far more than she'd ever even considered…

"You going to feed me, Wilde?" she said, reaching for the door handle, laughing in a way that she hoped didn't sound as phony to him as it did to her. "Or let me swoon away from hunger right here, in your car, with everybody in Dallas walking by?"

"The only swooning I want you doing is the kind that happens when I take you in my arms," he said.

But he wasn't laughing.

Neither was she.

They stared at each other for what seemed an eternity.

Then Travis cleared his throat, stepped out of the car and the world began spinning again.

She ordered yogurt and fresh fruit.

He ordered pancakes, bacon and eggs.

"The menu says they use only certified humane, free-range eggs," she said, after the waitress had brought them orange juice.

Travis raised an eyebrow.

"And that's good, right?"

She nodded. "Absolutely. Did you ever see any of the documentaries about how chickens are raised?"

"No," he said quickly. From the look on her face, he was happy that he hadn't.

"Back home—"

"Where's that?"

"New Hampshire."

"Ah. Thought I heard a touch of New England in that accent of yours."

She wrinkled her nose.

"You're the one with the accent, cowboy, not me."

He grinned. "Anyway, back home…?"

"I spent part of a summer working at an egg farm." Her smile faded; a little shudder went through her. "'Farm' turned out to be the wrong way to describe it. It was an eye opener."

He'd never thought about it before. Now he did.

"Yes," he said, "I'll bet."

Their meal arrived, her bowl of yogurt heaped with big, shiny strawberries. He watched as she plucked one from the heap, brought it to her lips and bit into it.

Crimson juice ran down her chin. She got to it, fast, with her napkin.

He thought about how he could have got to it faster, with his tongue.

Not a good thing to think about, in a public place.

"So," he said quickly shifting a little in the leather booth, "is that why you're such an early riser?" She looked at him blankly and why wouldn't she? Talk about non sequiturs… but it was the best he could do on the spur of the moment. "You were up with the sun this morning."

"Oh." She smiled. "It has nothing to do with chickens. It's academia." Her smile became a chuckle at the look on his face. "I have three early classes a week. I'm a T.A. A teaching—"

"A teaching assistant."

"Uh-huh. It's a grad course. The Psychology of Male-Female Relationship Patterns."

Travis nodded. Male-female relationships. He could almost feel his appetite fading.

"Must be—"

"Deadly dull."

His eyebrows rose. She laughed.

"I know I shouldn't say that but it is." She brought the tea-spoon to her mouth. "And what do you…" Her face pinkened.

"What?" he said, his eyes on the spoon, imagining what the coolness of the yogurt would be like in the warmth of her mouth.

"I only just realized…I don't know anything about you."

"You know everything about me," he said in a low voice. "Everything that matters."

"No. Seriously. If you and I—"

"Honey." His gaze went from the spoonful of creamy yo-gurt to her rosy lips. "Save me here, will you? Put that yo-gurt in your mouth so I can stop working up a sweat thinking about it."

"Thinking…?"

Man, what a mistake to have told her that. She was blush-ing again. He'd made love to her enough to know her chest and breasts turned that same rose-petal pink when she had an orgasm, when his lovemaking caused her orgasm…

"Do it fast," he said hoarsely.

She put the spoon down.

"Travis. Don't look at me like that."

"Like what?"

"Like—like—" She caught her bottom lip between her teeth. "Tell me—tell me about yourself."

He grinned. "Change in conversation, huh?"

"Absolutely. Come on. Tell me about Travis Wilde."

"There's not much to tell."

Jennie rolled her eyes. "You don't really think I'll fall for that, 'shucks, ma'am, ah'm jest a plain cowboy' stuff, do you?"

He burst out laughing.

"Talk about accents…Is that how guys in Texas sound?"

"Some of them." She smiled. "But not you. Were you born here?"

"You mean, am I an honest-to-God Texan?" He put his knife and fork across his plate, pushed it aside, reached for his coffee. "I am. I was born here. Well, not here. Not in Dallas. I was born in Wilde's Crossing?"

"A town with your name?"

"Wildes have been in Texas a long time, honey. You listen to my old man tell the story, we've been here ever since Thor the Hammer wrecked his longship on the Corpus Christi bar."

Jennie grinned. "No, he didn't."

He grinned back. "Okay. Maybe not, but yeah, we go back a bit."

"Are you ranchers?"

Amazing, he thought. He knew every inch of this woman's luscious body, she knew his, and yet, they were only just having this conversation.

"We have a place in Wilde's Crossing. *El Sueño*."

"The Dream."

Somehow or other, that she knew what the words meant pleased him.

"Yes. Do you know Spanish?"

"I had two years of it in high school."

"Ah."

"Plus two years of German. My father said, if I was going into science, it was a good idea to know German."

Travis cocked his head. "'The Psychology of Male-Female Relationship Patterns' is science?"

"Yes. No. I mean, there's this whole controversy, whether psych and sociology are sciences or not…" She made a face. "Travis Wilde. You're trying to change the subject."

He sat back, sighed, drank some coffee.

"Okay. I was born in Wilde's Crossing. I grew up on *El*

Sueño. I liked ranching well enough but math always fascinated me..."

He paused. Math? How come he was telling her that? Women had made it clear that "math" wasn't sexy. Being a finance guy, an investor, was.

"Math," she said. "If only I'd known you in high school." She smiled. "I'd have flunked calculus if it hadn't been for Mary Jane Baxter."

Travis tried not to smile. She was full of information, his Jennie; all you had to do was find the right button and out it came.

"Mary Jane Baxter?"

"A girl I knew. See, we did a trade. I coached her in English Lit. She coached me in Calc."

"Sounds like a good deal all around."

"It was." She sat back in the booth. "But you're not a math teacher. Not with that car and condo."

"No. Well, for a while I was in the Air Force."

"Really?"

He nodded. "I flew planes. Jets." Her eyes widened. "Fighter jets," he added, watching her face.

Hell, he was boasting. He knew the effect that bit of news had on women; if their eyes glazed over at the thought of a guy doing math, they positively glowed on hearing a guy was a jet jockey—and wasn't that pathetic? That he wanted to impress her?

"Did you serve in the war?"

He nodded, all his boasting forgotten.

"Yeah."

"That must have been hard. Seeing things. Doing things..."

Her voice was low. Her eyes said she understood that flying a fighter jet in battle left a man with memories that weren't entirely pleasant.

"Yeah. Sometimes, it was."

"But other times, it must have been wonderful."

He smiled. It occurred to him that it was a long time since he'd thought about that part of it.

"What's it like? To soar over the world?"

"Well," he said...

And he told her.

About the sense of freedom. The joy. About the sight of the earth, far below. About the first time he'd taken the controls from his instructor.

"It wasn't a fighter jet, it was a crop duster. See, I loved planes, even when I was a kid. And this guy used to work for us—"

"For *El Sueño*."

She'd remembered the name of the place he still thought of as home. For some reason, that pleased him.

"Exactly. He taught me to fly, and then I worked like crazy all one summer on another ranch, earning enough money so I could pay for real lessons..." He paused. "I'm talking too much."

"No. Oh, no! I love hearing about you as a little boy. I can almost picture you, boots, jeans, a cowboy hat—"

Travis laughed.

"Bumps, bruises and dirt. That was me. My brothers, too. Our mom used to say we were the reason Johnson & Johnson made Band-Aids..."

His words trailed away.

He'd told Jennie more about himself in ten minutes than he'd ever told anyone in a lifetime.

"It must be nice to have brothers."

He cleared his throat.

"Don't let them hear me admit it," he said with the kind of grin that made it clear he was joking, "but they're great guys."

"Did they go into the Air Force, too?"

"Caleb went into some government agency he can only tell you about if he kills you after." She laughed; he took her hand and brought it to his lips. "Jake went into the Army. He flew combat helicopters." His smile tilted. "He was wounded. Badly. And, for a while, he lost his way…" He paused. "I—I guess I kind of lost mine, too."

His own admission stunned him.

He had never said anything like that, not even to Jake or Caleb…but it was true.

He'd always been into risk: high stakes poker had given him the money to start his investment business, but the risks that came of being part of a war nobody could quite get their heads around had affected him.

Coming home and putting everything on the line—all his considerable winnings, his reputation, his mathematical ability—had been, in some dark, crazed way, a means of taking control of his life.

Risk everything, win everything.

All you had to be sure of was whether or not the risk was worth taking…

"Travis?"

Jennie's voice was soft.

All at once, he felt as if every risk he'd ever taken had been nothing compared to this…

"Yes." He cleared his throat, searched blindly for a way to change the subject. "Tell me about you."

"There's not a lot to tell," she said, lying so easily it terrified her. "As I said, I'm from New Hampshire. No brothers, no sisters. Not like you, with all those brothers—"

"Only two. And three sisters. Emily, Lissa and Jaimie. Well, half sisters, but we never think of them like that. Our mother died and our father married again. We lost her, too."

"It's hard, losing your parents." Jennie paused. "Mine died in a car crash when I was eighteen."

Travis wrapped both her hands in his.

"Leaving you alone?"

"Yes." She cleared her throat. "Tell me about your father."

There was more to her story; he was certain of it, but if she needed to change the subject, he'd let her.

"Ah." Travis waggled his eyebrows. "The old man is a four-star general."

"Oh, boy."

"Oh, boy, indeed. You can't imagine what it's like, growing up under the eye of somebody who thinks he's perfect."

Jennie smiled. "Actually, I can. Well, not exactly. My folks never said they were perfect—but they were. A pair of professors. Dad was a classicist. Mom was a medievalist. Brilliant, both of them. They had me late in life, so they were kind of overprotective." She sighed. "And when I said I wanted to go into psych and sociology—"

"I bet that went over about as well as when I said I was leaving the military to start my own investment firm."

"Exactly. I might as well have said I wanted to, I don't know, to play in a sandbox for the rest of my life."

"But you're happy, doing—" he grinned "—doing whatever it is you do."

Jennie laughed.

"I teach. Well, I will teach…"

Her smile, so lovely and wide, faded. Darkness filled her eyes.

"Honey? What is it?"

"Nothing," she said. "Nothing at all."

"Is it your headache? Is it back?"

"No." She blinked, smiled, but he could see tears glittering in her eyes. "I'm fine. Really. I'm absolutely fine."

He moved fast, leaned over the table, all but pulled her into his arms.

"Yes," he said gruffly, "you are," and when her tears began spilling down her cheeks, he took out his wallet, tossed a stack of bills on the table and did the only thing a man standing on the edge of a precipice could do.

He took her out of the restaurant, took her home to his place where he held her in his arms and made love to her until the tears she wept were tears of joy.

CHAPTER NINE

HE WANTED HER to spend the night with him.

She said that she couldn't.

"I have to go home," she said as she lay in his arms in a lounger on the terrace.

"It's almost midnight. That means it's almost Sunday, and Sunday's a day when nobody has to do anything."

She laughed. "You make that sound so logical."

"It *is* logical. Would a mathematician say anything that wasn't?"

"You're an investment banker, Travis Wilde. You play the stock market. What's logical about that?"

Travis clapped his hand to his heart.

"You wound me, madam."

Jennie laughed. "Seriously. I have to go home."

"Why?" he said, trying to make light of it because she had no way of knowing he hardly ever asked a woman to spend the night in his bed—and he was still amazed that having her do that was what he wanted. He kissed the tip of her nose. "Have to feed the cat?"

"I wish," she said, a little wistfully.

"You like cats, huh?"

"I like animals. But—"

"But?"

"But, I never had one. My mother said pets would make

a mess. And when I went away to college, you couldn't have pets in the dorm."

Travis thought of the big mutt he'd found wandering on campus his freshman year, and brought back to his dorm suite.

"Dogs are not allowed," the R.A. had said with authority.

"Right," Travis had replied…and moved the dog into his room for the rest of the semester, when he'd taken him home to *El Sueño*.

But Jennie wouldn't have done that.

She was a good girl, and good girls didn't break rules…

Except for the one about walking into a bar to pick up a guy and hand over your virginity.

Why? Why had she done something so out of character? Because now that he knew her, he could not imagine she would ever have done such a thing.

There had to be a reason.

She was keeping part of herself a secret. He knew it. And it worried him.

"Travis," she said softly, lifting her head from his shoulder and smiling at him. "You look so serious. What are you thinking?"

He smiled back at her.

"I'm trying to come up with some brilliantly creative reason that will convince you to stay."

She wanted to. Desperately. Hours had gone by since the headache and it might not return for even more hours. Still, if it did…

You need to keep your meds with you, Jennifer, the doctor had said, but carrying around a container of tablets and capsules would be a constant reminder of—of what was happening to her, and she wasn't ready for that.

Not yet

He brushed his lips lightly over hers.

"Now who's looking serious?"

Jennie forced a smile.

"I'm thinking."

"A dangerous habit—unless you're thinking of changing your mind about leaving me."

A swell of emotion rose inside her.

She didn't want to leave him. Not ever. How could you leave a man like this?

He kissed her, slid his hand under the shirt he'd given her to wear. She caught her breath as he stroked her nipples.

"Travis—"

"I'm just helping you come up with a reason to stay."

She laughed.

"You're a bad influence on me," she said, but it wasn't true. He was a wonderful influence. In all her life, she had never been this happy, felt so alive...

Tears welled swiftly, dangerously in her eyes. She tried to bury her face against him before he could see them but she wasn't quick enough.

"Sweetheart. What is it?"

"Allergies," she said brightly. "Nothing to worry about."

And, really, there was nothing to worry about, because what was the point? She couldn't change fate, couldn't change life...

Couldn't change what was happening in her heart, each time Travis kissed her or touched her or said her name.

"Stay with me," he said.

Do what your heart tells you, her alter-ego whispered.

And what it told her was to stay.

In the morning, when he staggered into the john, eyes half closed because it was Sunday and surely there was a law against fully waking up early on Sundays, Travis finished what he'd gone into the bathroom to do, flushed the toilet, washed his hands, reached for a face towel and came up, instead, with something small and silken.

His eyes flew open.

It was a pair of white panties.

Jennie's.

Evidently, she'd rinsed them last night and left them to dry.

Travis looked at them. So honest. So unsophisticated.

So Jennie.

A funny feeling swept over him.

Among the few women who'd ever spent the night, a couple had left things on the vanity. A compact. A lipstick. He wasn't an overly fastidious man but seeing those things in what was his space had irritated him no end.

Seeing Jennie's panties on his towel rack sent a warmth through his veins.

He liked seeing them there.

He liked seeing her in his bed.

And he was old enough, wise enough, to know that liking those things could be dangerous to a man's stability and sanity.

Okay. Time for her to leave. She'd stayed the night. They'd made love when they'd first gone to bed, then during the night.

He'd give her a cup of coffee, then drive her home. Phone her in a few days, ask her to dinner, to a movie, whatever.

It was a good plan, but it fell apart as soon as he went back into the bedroom and saw her.

She'd just come awake; her eyes were sleepy-looking, her hair was mussed, and when she saw him, she smiled.

"Good morning," she said softly.

Travis shook his head as he made his way to her.

"It isn't," he said solemnly, "because we haven't yet performed a vital morning ritual."

Her eyebrows rose. "What ritual?"

"This one," he said, and he took her in his arms and kissed her, and she returned his kiss with such tenderness that he could have sworn he felt his heart swell.

* * *

They spent the morning reading the papers, eating omelets Jennie made after she'd opened the fridge, rolled her eyes and finally unearthed half a dozen eggs, what remained of a pint of cream, four English muffins, a stick of butter and the biggest find of all, a chunk of still-usable Gruyère to add to the eggs.

There was other stuff, too: a bunch of little white cardboard containers Travis thought might have contained leftover take-out Tex-Mex.

"Unless it's take-out Chinese," he said apologetically.

"Hard to tell, I guess."

"Yuck," she said, dumping the containers in the trash.

"Hey," Travis said, his hand on his heart, "what can I tell you? Cooking isn't my thing."

Thankfully, it seemed that coffee was.

He had two pounds of Kona beans in the freezer, a grinder in the cupboard and a pot with more dials and buttons on it than Jennie had ever seen in her life.

She rolled her eyes again but admitted he got points for not completely destroying her faith in starting the day right.

Travis grinned, came up behind her, wrapped his arms around her and lightly bit the nape of her neck.

"I thought what we did a little while ago definitely started the day right."

"Behave yourself," she said sternly, but she leaned back against him and tilted her head up for a kiss.

After breakfast, they showered again. His shower was big enough for a dozen people, she said, and he gave a mock growl, took her in his arms and said he'd fight off anybody foolish enough to try to share the shower with them because she belonged strictly to him.

He meant the words as a joke.

But once he'd said them, he stopped smiling. Jennie did, too.

"Strictly to me," he said gruffly, and he made love to her against the glass wall, beneath the kiss of the warm spray.

He wanted to take her out.

Well, what he really wanted was to take her to bed, again, but he knew how much he'd love walking down a street with her beside him.

He thought about the things the women in his past had liked to do.

Did she want to go window-shopping? She wrinkled her nose. Stroll through a flea market? Another wrinkle of that cute little nose. How about a walk in the park? A drive?

She chewed on her lip.

"What?" he asked.

She hesitated. "I don't suppose…I mean, I heard a couple of other T.A.'s. talking…No. Never mind. It's silly. A drive would be—"

"Nothing's silly, if it'll make you happy." Travis took her hand and brought it to his lips. What did she want to do? Go to see some chick flick, probably. Well, fine. Not fun but he could surely survive—

"Six Flags," she blurted.

For a second or two, he was lost.

"Six flags of what?" He blinked. "You mean, the amusement park?"

She nodded. Her eyes were round and bright.

"Could we?"

Travis grinned, put his arm around her shoulders and gave her a loud, smacking kiss.

"A woman after my own heart!"

"Oh, my," Jennie kept saying, as they strolled through the park, hand in hand.

Everything made her squeal with delight. The grilled turkey legs. The funnel cakes. The giant hot dogs.

And the rides.

They drew her like a candy store drew kids.

"Can we watch?" she kept saying, and Travis would say sure, of course, and while she watched the rides and the riders, he watched her.

Was it possible this was all new for her?

"Honey?" he said as she stood, head tilted back, mouth forming a perfect "O," her fingernails digging into his hand as terrified people shrieked and screamed with delight while plummeting earthward on a parachute ride, "haven't you ever been to a place like this before?"

She shook her head, but her eyes stayed locked to the parachute tower.

"No."

"Little parks only? Okay. Maybe there isn't anything like this in New—"

"My parents didn't approve of amusement parks."

Her parents. The duo that had been upset because she hadn't wanted to be a doctor or a lawyer or an accountant.

"Well, how about local fairs? You know, Ferris wheels. Old-fashioned roller coasters."

Jennie shook her head.

"Not those, either. My parents were very protective, remember?"

"Aha," he said, trying to imagine how it must have been for her to grow up in such a closed-off world.

"They meant well," she said quickly, because his "aha" had dripped with meaning. "But they were always, you know, careful I didn't do anything that might be, you know, dangerous or, you know, risky, or—"

"What I know," Travis said gently, drawing her into the curve of his arm, "is that they wanted to protect you."

She nodded. "Exactly. But—but—"

"But," he said, smiling, trying to make light of what she'd missed, "life is short."

She looked up at him, her eyes suddenly dark with something he couldn't read.

"Yes. It is. And when I—when I realized that, I knew there were so many things I'd never done, that I wanted to know about…"

Like making love.

She didn't say it.

He did.

And when he did, she nodded.

"I wanted to know about sex," she said in a low voice. "But what I learned about was—was making love. And it wouldn't have been making love if I hadn't found—" Her words stumbled to a halt. "Oh, God! Travis. I didn't mean that the way it sounded. Please, I swear, I'm not trying to—"

He took her in his arms and kissed her.

It was either that or say something he couldn't imagine saying to a woman he'd met a week ago, something he'd never imagined saying to any woman ever, or at least not for maybe the next hundred years.

Something that made no sense, he told himself, but as she melted against him, he knew that nothing had made sense since the night she'd walked into that bar.

Nothing—except the sweet, sweet joy he felt, holding his Jennie in his arms.

After a while, he figured she was happy just looking at everything.

Logical.

For a girl who'd never so much as ridden a Ferris wheel, going on one of the park's big rides would surely be daunting. That was fine with him. Just being together made the day perfect—and when he saw her staring at somebody munching on one of those enormous turkey legs, he figured he knew a way to make her smile.

"Lunch," he said.

Jennie looked at him.

"You get your choice of gourmet treats, madam. A turkey leg. A hot dog—though you have to understand, they won't do 'em with the sophisticated panache of the Wilde Brothers—"

She laughed.

A good sign, because she'd been very quiet for the last twenty or thirty minutes.

"Or fried chicken. A hamburger. Pretty much any non-PC, artery-cloggin' goody your heart desires—"

"The roller coaster."

"Huh?"

"The wooden one. Where we were a little while ago. The one called Judge Something-Or-Other." Her eyes were shining. "Can we ride it?"

Travis hesitated. "Honey. You sure you want to start with something like that? There are easier rides to—"

Jennie bounced on her toes. The last time he'd seen somebody do that, it had been his sister Lissa, aged three or four, pleading for him to let her ride his horse instead of her pony.

He hadn't been able to say "no" then.

And he sure as hell couldn't say it now.

She loved riding that roller coaster.

She screamed and shrieked, and laughed with such joy that he forgot he'd given up nonsense like amusement parks a long time ago and laughed along with her.

"Again," she said when the ride ended.

They rode the coaster again.

And then they rode everything else, or damn near everything else, before Travis said, "Enough," took her in his arms for probably the hundredth time that day, kissed her and said it was time they took a break, ate something, drank something while he told himself he was being, yes, protective, but not the way her parents had been.

But he understood how they'd felt.

Someone as good and sweet as Jennie deserved to be protected.

"Okay," she said. And laughed. "Actually, I just realized—I'm starving! I could eat a horse!"

"Them's fightin' words, here in Texas," Travis said solemnly.

They ate tacos. Fried chicken. One of those turkey legs.

"It's from a brontosaurus, not a turkey," Jennie said, chomping into it.

Travis watched her eat and tried not to smile.

"More?" he said politely, after she'd finished the leg.

She thought about the giant hot dogs she'd seen, glistening on the grill. Then she remembered something Travis had said.

"What did you mean about the Wilde Brother's hot dogs?"

He laughed.

"When we were kids, Jacob, Caleb and I would cook up these feasts."

"Feasts? With hot dogs?"

"Have some faith, woman. Would we call it a feast if it only involved hot dogs? These were special. We fried 'em." He laughed at the expression on her face. "Actually, I did. Jake made the fried cheese sandwiches. Caleb was the marshmallow expert." Travis brought his thumb and index finger together. "Dee-lish-ee-oh-so!"

Jennie reached for a napkin.

"That did it. I'm full."

He grinned.

"Amazing. You should be popping out of your jeans by now." He held out his hand. "Come on. Let's get some lemonade."

They found a stand, bought huge plastic glasses of lemonade and found a quiet spot on a bench beneath a tree.

"So," Travis said, "what's your professional opinion of amusement parks, Dr. Cooper?"

Her smile, so bright during the past hours, seemed to dim a little.

"I don't have a doctorate yet."

"But you will."

She shrugged her shoulders. "You never know."

"Well, true. Life's unpredictable, but—"

"I had a wonderful time today!"

He smiled, reached for her hand.

"Me, too."

"All those rides…" Her eyes shone. "What do you call them? Thrill rides?"

"Right."

"Well, they're definitely thrilling. But basically, they're safe. I mean, the parks wouldn't have them if they weren't. Right?"

"Right," he said again, and wondered where the conversation was going because, clearly, there was something in the wind.

"What I mean is," she said slowly, "there's no real risk."

Travis grinned. "Got it. Nope. No real risk, so it's safe to tell your folks that— Oh. Honey. I'm sorry. I forgot."

"It's okay," she said softly. "That's the way life is. You're born, you die…"

She fell silent.

Travis thought he felt her hand tremble in his.

"Okay," he said briskly, "we're out of here. You've had enough sun and enough risk for the day."

"No. I mean, that's what I was saying. There really isn't any risk in taking these rides. It's wonderful," she added quickly. "I mean, I had more fun today…" She looked at him. "I never actually did anything risky."

Travis nodded. The conversation was on track again.

"But you have," she said. "Haven't you?"

"Well—"

"Did you ever go bungee jumping?"

"Yes. And it's not all it's cracked up to—"

"Back country skiing. Scuba diving. Rock climbing. Swimming with sharks."

"Jennie." His tone was harsh; he hadn't meant it to be. "Where are you going with this?"

"I want to try something risky."

A muscled knotted in his jaw.

"You already did. You got all dressed up, walked into a bar—"

Her face crumpled. She sprang to her feet.

He caught her by the wrist.

"I said it wrong, dammit. I didn't mean it the way you think." When she shook her head, he rose, too. "What I'm saying is that anything might have happened to you that night, anything at all. And the thought of something happening to you, something or someone hurting you…" Travis clasped her shoulders and turned her toward him. "Do you know how much you mean to me?" he said in a thick voice. "Do you have any idea how important you've become to me?"

She shook her head.

"You don't know me. We've only been together—"

"I know how long we've been together. But I know something else, as well." He looked deep into her eyes. "This— you and me—this isn't—it isn't just a man and a woman and—and sex—"

She shook her head and tried to turn away. He wouldn't let her.

"I'm saying it wrong, dammit. What I mean is—"

"I know what you mean. I—I feel it, too." Tears glittered like stars in her eyes. "I never meant for this to happen," she whispered. "That I'd find someone like you, that I'd find such happiness—"

He kissed her.

Gently. Only their lips met, as if touching her might shatter the moment.

And as he kissed her, he tasted the salt of her tears.

Something ran through him, an emotion so new, so rare that it stunned him, and with it came a question.

Could everything a man thought he wanted out of life completely shift in little more than a week?

Even asking the question was dangerous.

Travis put his arm around Jennie, held her to his side as they headed back to his car.

Dangerous, sure.

But as he'd learned years ago, you could say that about anything that was really worth doing. Or having.

Life was all about risk.

What he hadn't known was that, if a man was really lucky, he might just stumble across one special risk that had the power to change his life, forever.

CHAPTER TEN

ALMOST A MONTH later, on a gray, rainy morning, that was all he could think about.

Risks.

The kind he'd always taken.

Not the kind he was taking now.

He'd been a wild kid, the same as his brothers. But none of them had ever done anything cruel or stupid and—predictably—their streaks of wildness had eventually been channeled into positive stuff.

Jake, flying helicopters and now running *El Sueño* as well as his own ranch.

Caleb, taking the darker route into secret government service and now taking on law cases that drew headlines.

He, Travis, flying jets and then going into big-time finance.

Risky things, all. But still, with an edge of predictability to them.

Not anymore.

This wasn't predictable.

What he felt for Jennie.

What he believed she felt for him.

It made what had existed between him and the girl who'd written him that Dear John letter years ago, laughable.

She had never been a serious part of his life.

They'd come together as much because of his glamorous

status as a fighter pilot as her flashy looks. He'd never really looked ahead and envisioned her as part of his real life.

Jennie was already in his real life.

She wasn't just his lover, she was his friend.

Hell, she was his roommate.

Her toothbrush hung beside his.

They were—it still amazed him—they were living together, and they hadn't been apart for more than a few hours each day for the last three and a half weeks.

So, yes, this was a very different kind of risk.

It involved putting aside an entire way of life, one that was free of restraint or rules or obligations to anyone but himself.

It involved, he thought, staring out his office window on a rainy morning, something he'd never imagined himself doing.

Living with a woman.

It wasn't that he'd never considered it. The thought had certainly crossed his mind before, not often, but there'd been times it had, at the start of a relationship…

And, man, he'd always hated that word—relationship—but that was what this was, a relationship.

He and Jennie were living together.

And he loved it.

Coming home to her each night. Starting the day with her each morning.

He loved it.

Travis rose from his chair, tucked his hands into his trouser pockets and paced slowly around his office.

Talk about a shocker…

Until now, living with a woman had never gone beyond casual speculation.

The simple truth was, the excitement of an affair faded. The fun wore away. The prospect of spending all his time with one woman pretty much 24/7 lost its appeal.

It had never been the fault of any of his lovers.

It was just the way things were.

Man wasn't meant for monogamy. *He* wasn't, at any rate…

He paused at the floor-to-ceiling, wall-of-glass window, and stared out at the gray Dallas skyline.

Turned out, what he'd been meant for was Jennie.

They went to sleep in each other's arms and woke that same way. They ate together. Talked about mundane stuff like where to have dinner, complicated stuff like global warming. They went out, stayed in, listened to music, did all the things couples did and bachelors didn't…

And he loved it.

Especially coming home to her at night, when just seeing her smile, having her go into his arms, was more than enough to smooth whatever jagged edges the day might have left in its wake.

Jennie was living with him.

She had been, for almost a month.

The excitement? Still there. The fun? Of course. But there was more than that to it.

Being together was…He searched for the word.

It was joy.

The arrangement, for lack of a better word, had come about without plan.

It had started that Sunday when they'd gone to Six Flags.

They'd gone for a drive afterward.

Then they'd stopped for supper at a little Thai place he knew. The place was six tables big, with no pretensions at being anything but a Mom-and-Pop joint where the decor rated a zero but the food was Bangkok-perfect.

It turned out Thai food was new to Jennie.

How you could get through college and grad school without having Pad Thai or Tom Yum Goong was beyond him, but then he remembered those overly-protective parents who'd raised her to be cautious about everything, and he understood.

Sex. Roller coasters. Thai food.

He teased her, asked her if there was anything more he

was going to introduce her to and she looked at him in a way that was suddenly completely serious.

Then, she laughed and said if there were, she'd let him know.

If she were six decades older, he'd have said she was working on a bucket list.

She wasn't, of course.

She was simply a woman learning about life.

He'd ordered for them both. *Tom Kha Gai*. Red Curry. *Pad Thai*.

"Oh, my," she said, after she'd tasted the soup.

"As in, 'Oh, my, this is good'? Or, 'Oh, my, I don't like this at all!'"

"Are you kidding? It's amazing!"

She was what was amazing, he'd thought, watching her.

They ate from each other's plates and talked all through the meal, about Texas and New England, nothing special, and when they left the restaurant, he'd driven her to her apartment.

"I don't want to leave you," he'd said, at her door.

"I don't want that, either," she'd said softly. "Come in, just for a while."

He'd taken a deep breath.

"I have a better idea," he'd said, no planning, no preparation, but as he'd said the words, he'd known they were right. "Pack something for tomorrow. Come home with me."

She'd hesitated, long enough so his heart had almost stopped beating.

"I can't," she'd finally said.

"You can do anything that makes you happy," he'd said softly. "Unless being with me won't make you happy."

Silence.

Then she'd gone up on her toes and kissed him.

She'd packed a summer skirt. A T-shirt. Sandals. Underwear. Makeup, shampoo, what he thought of as girl stuff, though he knew better than actually to call it that.

A man didn't grow up with sisters without learning something.

Finally, she'd put her laptop computer in its case, added a couple of books and a stack of printed notes.

"Ready," she'd said, and again, without planning or analyzing it, he'd heard himself suggest she add a few more things to what she'd packed.

"You know, just in case you, ah, you decided to stay a few days…"

It had been one of those time-stands-still moments, he silent, she staring at him through wide eyes.

Then, with typical Jennie-directness, she'd said, very softly, "Are you asking me to live with you?"

With untypical directness, at least when it came to women, he'd said, "Yes."

She hadn't gone back to her place since that night, except when he'd driven her there so she could pick up more of her things.

He'd tried to take her shopping. At Neiman Marcus, of course, but she wouldn't let him.

She was independent, his Jennie, so he compensated by buying her gifts, then telling her, eyes wide with innocence, that whatever he'd bought was on sale and couldn't be returned.

He'd done it again last night, handed her a gift-wrapped small box at dinner at the Thai place that had become a favorite.

She'd opened the box, gasped at the gold bracelet and heart inside, and looked at him with shining eyes.

"Travis. I can't—"

"You have to," he'd said. "It's that damned no-returns policy."

Her lips had curved in a smile.

"I love it," she'd said. "Thank you."

"You're welcome," he'd said, and without warning, he'd

suddenly imagined her opening an even smaller box, one that held a diamond solitaire.

Their food had arrived at that moment, and they'd spent the rest of the meal talking.

Actually, he'd done most of the talking.

He'd found himself telling her about the ten thousand acres of land for sale in Wilde's Crossing, about how he was considering buying it.

"I love what I do," he'd said, "and I'll always go on doing it, but ranching is in my blood."

"Must be the Viking DNA," she'd said solemnly but with a little smile in her eyes, and he'd laughed and then, without planning to, he'd heard himself ask, very casually, how she felt about open spaces, about horses and dogs and kids, which were pretty much the staples of ranch life...

And realized he was holding his breath as he waited for her answer.

"I grew up watching old John Wayne movies," she'd finally said, in a small voice. "My father owned every one. And—and I used to think how wonderful if must be, to saddle a horse and ride and ride and ride without ever reaching the boundaries of your own land, and then to ride home to a house full of love and laughter, to the arms of a man you adored..."

Her voice had trembled. Her eyes had darkened. He'd reached for her hand.

He'd come within a heartbeat of saying that she could, if she married him, but a crowded restaurant wasn't where a man wanted to tell a woman he loved her.

Besides, the look on her face troubled him.

Something was wrong.

Jennie definitely had a secret, and it was not a good one.

He'd sensed it before, several times, but he'd never pushed her to reveal it because, back then, he'd still believed in separation. In independence. In being responsible for oneself and nobody else.

Not anymore.

She had a secret that made her unhappy and, by God, it was time he knew what it was so he could deal with it.

Had she been in jail? Was she on the run for a crime? Was somebody after her?

Impossible things, all of them, but there was a darkness haunting her, and she had yet to share it with him.

Didn't she realize that whatever it was, he would deal with it?

That he would go on loving her?

Because he did love her. He adored her.

And she loved him, too.

He could see it in her smile. In the way she curled into his arms at night and responded to his kisses in the morning. It was even in the way she said his name.

It was time to say the words.

Tonight, he was going to tell her that he loved her. And after she'd told him she loved him, too, he would ask her what was causing her such anguish.

Her headaches, painful as they were, never brought such sadness to her eyes, but her headaches seemed more frequent.

"Have you taken your medicine?" he'd say, and she'd say yes, she had, and then she'd change the subject.

Except, last night, a muffled sound had awakened him.

The place on the bed beside him was empty.

He'd risen quickly, gone into the bathroom, found her huddled on the closed toilet, trembling, her face white, teeth chattering.

Terror had torn at his gut.

"Sweetheart," he'd said, going down on his knees before her. "What is it?" No answer. He'd reached forward, swept her tangled hair back from her face. "Is it a headache?"

"Yes," she'd whispered.

"Did you take a pill?"

Another yes.

He'd risen to his feet.

"I'm calling my doctor," he'd said, and she'd grabbed his arm and gasped out, "No! I don't need a doctor!"

The hell she didn't.

But he hadn't wanted to upset her, so he'd scooped her into his arms, carried her to bed, brought her a cold pack—he'd started keeping them in the freezer—and held her in his arms until she'd fallen asleep.

Dammit, he thought now, as he sat down behind his desk again.

He'd been so caught up in thinking about how much he loved her, how he was going to tell her so, tonight, that he'd lost sight of what he should have done first thing this morning.

She didn't want to see his doctor? Okay. He couldn't force her to do it, but his physician was an old pal. He and Ben had gone to the same high school, played on the football team. They'd gone to the same university, taken some of the same undergrad courses before Ben went into medical school and Travis set his sights on aerospace engineering..

He'd go see Ben, tell him about Jennie, tell him the name of the meds she was taking and find out if there wasn't something a lot stronger and better.

No way could he go on watching the woman he loved suffer...

The woman he loved.

It felt so good to know that he loved her. To know he was going to tell her he loved her—

His cell phone rang.

He grabbed it, didn't take time to check the screen.

"Honey?"

"Sweetie," his brother Jake purred. "I didn't know you cared."

Travis sat back.

"Jacob. What's up?"

"From hot to cold in less than a minute. Travis, my man, you're breakin' my heart."

Travis laughed.

"Okay. Let's start again. Hey, Jake, great to hear from you. How're things going?"

"Tonight's what's going," Jake said. "I thought the three of us could get together at that place near Caleb's office."

"Yeah. Well, sorry, but—"

"Trav. You were the one accusing us of ditching the Friday night stuff but we got together last week and the week before, and you were the guy who was missing."

True. Very true. Travis rubbed his hand over his forehead.

"The thing is, I, ah, I have something going on…"

"Does it involve 'honey'?"

Jake's tone barely masked his laughter—and his curiosity.

Travis took a deep breath. What the hell, he decided, maybe it was time.

"Tell you what. I'll meet you guys there. I won't stay long. I…" Deep, deep breath. "I have to get home. To Jennie."

"To who?"

"Her name is Jennie," Travis said quietly. "And I guess it's time you guys knew about her."

Jake finally located his tongue, hanging somewhere in the vicinity of his chest.

"Sounds good," he said.

Then he hung up the phone, called Caleb and said, "You are never going to believe this but it looks like Travis is hooked."

"Hooked?"

"As in, he's coming by tonight."

"So?"

"He won't stay long. He has a woman waiting for him. At home."

There was a moment of silence. Then Caleb Wilde laughed.

"Uh-oh," he said.

Jake grinned. "Ain't that the truth?"

* * *

A few hours later, Travis paced the living room of his penthouse.

He'd gone home early.

Stupid thing to do.

Today was Jennie's late day at the university. She wouldn't be home for another half hour, which was more than enough time for him to have second-guessed himself a hundred times.

Telling Jake he'd meet him and Caleb tonight. What for? He was going to tell Jennie he loved her. He wouldn't want to leave her after that.

Okay.

Okay, no problem.

He'd take her with him. Introduce her to his brothers…

No. Forget that. He'd tell her he loved her. Then she'd tell him what it was that, when he least expected it, stole the joy from her smile.

Travis ran his hands through his hair.

Dumb thing to do, piling on so many heavy things for one eve—

The elevator hummed. Made the soft thump it always made when it stopped.

He swung toward it.

The doors opened.

Jennie stepped from the car.

"Sweetheart," he said…

And stopped.

God, the look on her face! It was one of such sorrow that he forgot everything, ran to her, took her in his arms and drew her into the room.

"Jen? What's wrong?"

"Nothing."

She was lying. He could see it. He could feel it, too. She was trembling.

He scooped her up. Carried her to a big leather chair. Sat down with her held tightly in his arms.

"Honey. Don't lock me out. I know there's something you're keeping from me—"

"I love you," she said. "I know I'm not supposed to tell you that but—"

He could have sworn he felt his heart take wing.

"Jennie. My beloved Jennie. I love you, too."

"See, I've studied the dynamics of—of—" For an instant, her eyes lit with happiness. "What did you say?"

"I said I adore you. I love you. I want to marry you. I want us to have kids, raise horses, do whatever makes you happy as we grow old together…"

A sob burst from her throat.

"No! I can't."

"Jennie—"

She shot to her feet.

"I can't marry you," she whispered.

"Of course you can."

She shook her head. "No. You don't understand. There's something I—something I haven't told you. I should have. I know I should have, but—"

Travis stood and gathered her into his arms.

"Whatever it is," he said softly, "we'll deal with it."

She made a little sound, something between a laugh and a sob.

"We can't deal with it."

"Of course we can. *I* can. Is it a legal problem? Caleb will help us. Is it something in your past? Whatever it is—"

"I'm sick."

"I know. The migraines. We'll take care of those, too. My doctor—"

"Travis." Jennie took a deep breath. Travis tried to draw her closer to him, but she kept a distance between them by flattening her hands against his chest. "I—I have—I have…"

She shut her eyes, then opened them again, and looked into the eyes of her lover. "I have a tumor," she whispered. "In my brain."

He stared at her while he tried to process her words.

"A tumor? But—"

"In my brain. And there is no 'but.' It's been there for months, and it's been growing." She drew a shallow, sharp breath. "My symptoms—"

"The headaches," he said hoarsely.

She nodded.

"Travis. I'm—I'm dying."

The room tilted. He thought he was going to pass out but he couldn't, he had to be strong for his Jennie.

Besides, it couldn't be true. He told her that she must have been misdiagnosed.

She got her briefcase. She had a file in it. Reports, scan results.

The diagnosis was accurate.

He told her how foolish it was to rely on tests from one hospital.

She spread the reports over the dining room table.

The tests had been repeated in three different major medical centers.

He stared at the papers. An icy hand seemed to close around his heart.

"Why didn't you tell me?" he finally said.

"I should have. I should have let you know the truth so that you wouldn't—you wouldn't have become involved with—"

He grabbed her. Silenced her with a kiss that tasted of terror and panic and desperation.

"I love you," he said. "I love you! Do you think knowing this—this thing is inside your head would have kept me from loving you?"

She wept.

He wanted to weep with her, but his brain was whirring. He needed a plan.

Minutes later, he had one.

"I know people in Germany. In the U.K. Hell, I know people all over the world. We'll fly to Europe—"

"Travis. My beloved Travis." Her voice broke as she looked up into his eyes. "It's all over. I've just come from my doctor. He says—"

Travis slammed his fist against the table.

"I don't give a good goddamn what your doctor says! I'm not going to let this happen. I refuse to let it happen. I love you, love you, love you—"

She rose on her toes. Kissed him. Kissed him again and again, until he responded.

"Make love to me," she pleaded. "Now. Make love to me—"

He took her there, in the living room, with passion, with tenderness, giving her all that he was.

She gave him all that she was in return.

At the end, she cried. And fell asleep in his arms.

He held her tightly to him, felt the beating of her heart, the warmth of her breath.

"I will not let you die," he said, his voice low and hard and fierce with determination. "I—will—not—let—it—happen!"

Finally, exhausted, he slept…

And dreamed.

Jennie was standing next to him. Leaning over him.

She was weeping.

"Goodbye, my love," she whispered, "goodbye."

Her lips brushed his forehead.

He stirred. Came awake…

And found himself alone.

"Jennie?" he said.

He went from room to room. There was no sign of her.

Panic beat leathery wings in his chest.

He called her on her cell phone.

She didn't answer.

He ran for his car. Drove to her apartment.

She wasn't there.

He checked her office on campus.

Nothing.

God, dear God, where was she?

He went back to his place, driving like a madman in case she'd somehow materialized somewhere in those empty rooms, but she hadn't.

Where could she have gone? Who would possibly know? That woman at the bar that night. Edna? Barbara? Brenda. That was it, but how in hell could he find a woman named Brenda in a city the size of Dallas?

"Think," he said aloud, "think!"

There had to be someone who'd know what she would do, where she would go…

Her doctor.

He would know.

But who was he? Where was his office? Dammit to hell, why didn't he have that information?

Maybe she had an address book. An appointment calendar. If she did, maybe the doctor's name and address would be in it.

Travis went through Jennie's things. Tore her stuff apart. Found no address book or appointment book or anything else.

Wait a minute. Would the medicines she took have the doctor's name on the bottles?

He knew where she kept the tablets. Some were in a little silver pill box she carried in her purse. The rest were in his medicine cabinet.

Yes. There they were, but the only thing on the labels were the unpronounceable names of the meds, and the name and phone number of the pharmacy that had filled the pre-scriptions.

There were a frightening number of prescriptions.

He phoned the pharmacy. Spoke his way up the chain of command but nobody would tell him the doctor's name or anything beyond the fact that the law protected a patient's privacy.

There had to be a way…

Travis pumped his fist in the air.

There was. His pal. Ben Steinberg. Surely he could get the name of Jennie's guy out of the pharmacy staff.

He thought about phoning, decided against it, got in his car and raced to Ben's office, caught him just as he was leaving.

"Ben. I have to see you."

"Travis? Are you sick?"

"No. My friend is sick. My friend…" Travis swallowed hard. "The woman I love gets these terrible headaches…"

"Ah." Ben smiled. "Well, tell her to phone my office and—"

"You don't understand."

Ben looked at him. "Man," he said quietly, "you look like hell." He hesitated. "Okay. Come into my office and fill me in."

Travis did.

When he finished, Ben's expression was grave.

"Did she say what kind of brain tumor it is?"

Travis shook his head.

"All she'd tell me was that she was—that she was—"

Ben nodded. "Yeah. Okay. You need to find her but I don't see what I—"

"If I find her doctor, maybe he can tell me where she's gone." Travis reached in his pocket, took out a vial of tablets, handed them to his friend. "I called her pharmacy. They won't give me the doctor's name. But they'll give it to you."

Ben nodded again. He thought about ethics, and patient confidentiality, and the fact that a woman named Jennifer Cooper had made it clear she didn't want the man who loved her to be with her as she died.

Mostly, though, he thought about the fear, the desperation in the eyes of an old friend.

Then he reached for the phone.

CHAPTER ELEVEN

IN THE END, finding Jennie's doctor didn't help.

Peter Kipling didn't know where she'd gone, either.

"I wouldn't break patient confidentiality if I actually knew," he said, "but I'd at least tell you she was safe."

But she wasn't safe.

His Jennie was desperate and alone, probably in excruciating pain, with a death sentence hanging over her.

Hours later, an exhausted Travis finally stumbled into the bar where he was supposed to have paid a pleasant visit to his brothers.

They saw him come through the door, signaled him to their booth...and turned grim-faced when they got a closer look at him. His face was gray, his hair was standing up in little tufts.

He looked like he'd aged a dozen years.

"What's happened?" Jake said sharply.

Travis looked at them.

"Are you sick?"

"No. I'm not sick. It's my Jennie who's sick."

His brothers exchanged looks. *His Jennie?*

"She's missing." Travis sank into the booth. "I've been looking for her for hours but I can't find her."

Caleb and Jake exchanged another look.

A lover's quarrel? Something more serious?

"Listen," Jake said slowly, "if she doesn't want to see you—"

"She's gone, Jacob. She's vanished."

"What do you mean, vanished?"

"Vanished," Travis said wearily. He put his elbows on the table, rubbed his hand over his eyes. "I can't find her anywhere."

Caleb's jaw tightened. "I have contacts," he said. "The police. Some private guys I'd trust with my—"

"You don't understand."

"No," Jake said gently, "we don't. How about explaining?"

Travis grabbed the beer bottle that stood in front of Jake. He took a long, thirsty swallow. Then he put it down, looked from the concerned face of one brother to the equally concerned face of the other, and did exactly that.

It took ten long minutes.

When he'd finished, his brothers were silent. It was the kind of silence that means nobody can think of anything useful to say.

Finally, Caleb cleared his throat.

"Telling you we're sorry won't cut it."

Jake nodded in agreement. "What we need is to do something that will help you. And your girl."

"Jennie," Travis said. "Her name is Jennie."

"Jennie. Of course." Caleb rubbed his forehead. "I need her full name. Her cell phone number. Her address. The department she's in at the university."

Travis shook his head.

"I told you," he said, his voice hoarse with exhaustion, "she's turned off her phone. She isn't at her apartment. I checked her office on campus. She's gone."

"I understand," Caleb said carefully. "Still, give me the info. Everything you know about her. Places she likes. People she knows. Where she's from."

"Yeah. Okay." Travis gave a sharp, sad laugh. "It's something to do, anyway."

Caleb took a small notebook and a pen from his pocket, shoved them both toward Travis.

"I want the name of her doctor. His phone numbers. And Ben's number. I haven't spoken to him in years."

Travis nodded as he jotted down the things Caleb had requested.

"Trav?"

Travis looked at Jake.

"When I was hospitalized in D.C., you know, after I was wounded…I got to know some of the other patients. One was this Special Forces guy. He had a—he had a brain tumor."

"Jennie's is inoperable. The tests—"

"Yeah. So was his." Jake paused. "But there was this neurosurgeon…His family brought him in as a consultant. The next week, they moved the Special Forces dude out of Walter Reed. I don't know where they took him, but a couple of months later, there he was, stopping by for a visit, and he looked like a new man."

"Jake. What's this have to do with—"

"Maybe nothing. Maybe everything. I have the guy's number. Why don't I give him a call?"

"Holden says the neurologist treating Jennie is the best in Dallas."

"I'm going to give my friend a call anyway, okay?"

Travis nodded. "Sure," he said, but his eyes were dull with discouragement.

Another silence. Then Caleb slapped the table top and rose to his feet.

"Okay. Let's get started."

Jake rose, too. So did Travis. He looked from one of his brothers to the other.

"I feel so useless…" His voice broke. "There must be something I can do."

"There is," Jake said briskly. "Go home. Eat something. Get some sleep. You need to stay strong, for Jennie. And stay put, just in case she comes looking for you."

"Hell. You're right. I never thought of..." He took a long breath, then exhaled it. "Call me. Both of you. Even if it's only to tell me you haven't come up with anything, okay? Just—just keep in touch."

The brothers embraced.

"Don't give up hope," Caleb said softly.

"Caleb's right," Jake said. "This is a long way from over."

"Yeah," Travis said, but they all knew he was lying.

It took Caleb less than two hours to find Jennie through his network of contacts.

He phoned Jake with the news as he drove to Travis's condo.

"She's on a flight to Boston, where she'll change planes for Manchester, New Hampshire."

"Excellent," Jake replied. "That'll put her within spitting distance of Boston Memorial."

"What's Boston Memorial?"

"A major hospital—and the place where that Special Forces guy tells me the world's most prominent neurosurgeon is running a hush-hush experimental program."

"Why do those words scare the crap out of me? Hush-hush. Experimental." Caleb, who was driving far too fast, swerved around a truck. "Even that phrase, 'the world's most prominent neurosurgeon...' According to who?"

"According to whom," Jake said, automatically correcting his brother's grammar which was, Caleb know, a really good sign that Jake was feeling upbeat, even hopeful. "According to my guy, and I believe him."

"Okay. But if it's so secretive, if it's experimental, how do we get Jennie into the program? There's no time to waste, Jacob. We all know that."

"She's already in," Jake said. "My guy called the Boston neurosurgeon, faxed him her medical file. He phoned me." Jake gave a little laugh. "Turns out, there are times it pays to be a wounded warrior with a shiny medal."

Caleb nodded, as if Jake could see him. He knew how his brother hated to talk about what had happened to him during the war, how he shunned all publicity about the medal he'd won. That he'd shared such a thing with a stranger, used it for leverage, was filled with meaning.

"Good job, man," he said softly.

Jake cleared his throat. "Hey, it's for Travis, right? And there are no guarantees."

"You mean," Caleb said, "anything could happen."

"I mean," Jake said bluntly, "that first the surgeon has to check Jennie out and agree to do the operation. And even then—"

"Right." Caleb hesitated. "Travis will have to know that."

"He'll know it. And he'll go for it. Hell, man, it's all we've got."

"Sure. But will she?"

"Good question," Jake said. "Only one way to find out."

"I'm on my way to Travis's place right now," Caleb said.

"Me, too. Meet you there in ten."

"In five."

Jake made a sound that approximated a laugh.

Maybe, just maybe, things were looking up.

They arrived at Travis's condo less than a minute apart.

They'd told him to shower. Eat. Rest. The only certainty was that he'd showered: his hair was still wet, and he'd changed his clothes.

Aside from that, he looked like a man who'd been pacing the floor and slowly going crazy.

The way he greeted them confirmed it.

"I cannot go on doing this," he said. "Just standing around here, my thumb up my—"

"Calm down."

"Calm down?" He spun toward Jake, eyes blazing. "The woman I love is out there alone, a—a monster consuming her brain, and the best you can do is tell me to—"

"I have one of the Wilde jets standing by."

Travis blinked. He looked at Caleb.

"You found her? How? Where? Is she okay? Did she ask for me?"

"One question at a time, Trav. I pulled some strings. Called in some favors. She's okay, she's on a plane heading for Boston, and she couldn't ask for you because she doesn't know we found her."

"Boston," Travis said. "She's going home. To New England." His face twisted. "Doesn't she know I'd want to be with her?"

Jake and Caleb glanced at each other in unspoken agreement that there was no sense in trying to answer that question.

Obviously Travis knew it, too.

"Okay," he said, "let's go after her. She's from New Hampshire. How will she get there? Has she rented a car?"

"She's changing planes in Boston. Actually she has two changes—"

"Which gives us time to get to Boston before she does."

Jake and Caleb looked at each other.

Travis's voice was stronger. He was taking command. It gave them hope he'd come through this, no matter how it ended.

"I love her," he said, his voice filled with certainty. "I won't let her face this alone."

"Yeah." Caleb laid his hand on Travis's shoulder. "There's something else."

"What?"

Jake cleared his throat.

"It's a long story," he said, "but it turns out there's an experimental program. A surgery to treat—what the hell do you call these things? Inoperable meningiomas."

"An oxymoron," Travis said angrily. "If the thing is inoperable, there can't be a surgery for it."

"I'm not a doctor, okay? Maybe I'm saying it wrong but the guy I knew at Walter Reed…I told you, it's a long story. The bottom line is that there's a surgeon—a team—doing this stuff."

The hope that suddenly glowed in Travis's eyes made both his brothers want to take him in their arms.

They didn't.

They knew Travis had to stay focused. And strong.

"First, they'd have to agree Jennie qualifies for the operation. And then," Jake said with brutal frankness, "it doesn't always work. Some patients die during the procedure. Some never come out of the anesthesia and end up on life support. Some survive but they're—they're damaged."

Travis gave a bitter laugh. "That's your good news?"

"What I said was, it doesn't always work. But when it does…" Jake drew a breath. "When it does, those patients resume normal lives."

"Oh, God," Travis whispered. "Oh God, Jennie…"

"Don't get your hopes too high," Caleb said bluntly. "This is one huge risk. Jennie will have to understand that."

"You don't know her. My Jennie never met a risk she wouldn't take." He glanced at his watch. "Why are we still standing here? We're wasting time."

Jake and Caleb nodded. They could hear the courage, the energy in their brother's voice.

"Go on," Jake said. "Pack while we get things going. Then we'll get the hell out of here."

Travis nodded, headed for his bedroom.

Jake and Caleb would buy what they needed in Boston.

Both men phoned their wives, offered quick explanations of what was going down.

"Tell Travis I love him," Jake's wife said.

"Tell Travis we're all with him," Caleb's wife said.

Two minutes later, the Wildes were on their way to the airport.

They reached Boston an hour before Jennie's plane was due, and stood at the gate, waiting.

Travis had never imagined time could move so slowly.

Whenever he looked at his watch, the hands were in the same place on the dial.

After the fifth or sixth time, he figured it was broken—except, Jake's watch read the same as his.

Jake said, "How about coffee?"

Caleb said, "How about a sandwich?"

Travis shook his head. All he wanted, all he needed, was to see Jennie.

They waited. And waited.

At last, a plane taxied to the gate. A disembodied voice announced the arrival of the flight Jennie had taken.

The ramp door opened.

The first of the disembarking passengers appeared. Most of them hurried into the terminal.

After that, nothing.

Travis's heart was racing.

Where was she? Was Caleb's information wrong?

His breath caught.

There she was.

Walking slowly, her face white, her eyes huge. He could almost feel the pain throbbing in her head.

He wanted to run to her, sweep her into his arms...

She saw him.

And froze.

He had not let himself think about this. About how she would react on seeing him. She had left him, after all.

"Jennie," he said, and opened his arms.

She sobbed his name, and flew into them.

He held her to his heart. Rocked her in his embrace. She lifted her face to his and he kissed her, kissed her again and again.

She was weeping. He was, too.

Behind them, Jacob and Caleb looked at each other, then turned away.

Their eyes were damp.

It was turning into one hell of a day.

Jake had taken a suite at a hotel in Boston.

Caleb had arranged for a limo.

They drove to the hotel in silence after a brief conversation, Travis saying, "Honey, these are my brothers, Jacob and Caleb," Jennie saying, "Hi," Jake and Caleb saying *Hi* in return.

Then she'd looked at Travis and asked him why his brothers were with him, how had he found her and where were they going?

Travis had considered everything he had to tell her.

Yes, but not here.

Instead, he'd drawn her closer to him—he hadn't let go of her since she'd gone into his arms—kissed her temple and said, "Will you trust me, sweetheart?"

Jennie knew there was only one possible answer, and she'd given it.

"Yes," she'd whispered, because what else could she tell the man she had already trusted with her heart?

The suite was spacious. A sitting room. Three bedrooms. Three bathrooms.

Caleb and Jake vanished into two of the bedrooms.

Travis led Jennie into the third.

She was wobbling. Her eyes glittered. He knew it was with pain.

He sat her down on the edge of the bed. Knelt and slipped off her shoes.

"Do you want to sleep for a while, honey?" he said softly.

She shook her head, winced when she did.

"No. I want you to tell me what's going on. Your brothers are with you. Why? And why are all of you behaving like you have a big secret?"

He sat down next to her and clasped her hand.

"I refuse to let you die," he said in a low, fierce voice.

"Travis. I know you want to deny the truth. For a long time so did I. But—"

He silenced her with a tender kiss.

"Listen to me, just for a minute. Will do you that?"

Jennie sighed. "Okay," she whispered, "but—"

"I tried to find you," he said. "When I couldn't, I turned to my brothers for help. Caleb located you." He smiled. "Sometimes, it's useful to have a former spy in the family. Jake—Jake did other things."

Her eyes searched his. "What other things?"

"Remember, I told you he'd been wounded in Afghanistan. Badly wounded. He was hospitalized at Walter Reed, and while he was there, he met somebody, another soldier who—who had a tumor. Inoperable, like yours. At least, they said it was inoperable."

Jennie tore her hand from his and got to her feet.

"No," she said. "No more! I've tried a dozen cures. Nothing worked." Her voice broke. "I can't do it again, Travis. Believing there's—there's some kind of—of medical miracle, only to find out that—that…"

Travis rose and stood before her.

"Jake's friend was accepted into an experimental program, right here at Boston Memorial."

Jennie turned away and clapped her hands over her ears. "I'm not listening!"

"Honey. Please. Hear me out."

"I've done it all. Tests. Shots. Drugs and more drugs. I've seen a thousand doctors. All of it led to one thing." She swung toward him, her mouth trembling. "I'm dying, Travis. It's why I did all those—those crazy things. Why I wanted to experience as much of life as I could. I knew, sooner or later, I'd have to accept what was coming."

"Jennie—"

"And I did. I accepted it. Until I fell in love with you."

She'd said the only words he'd ever wanted to hear.

"Leaving you was the hardest thing I ever did." Her eyes searched his for understanding. "I love you so much—"

"Then why did you run away from me?"

"Because I love you! Because I didn't want you to be there to see—to see what's going to happen to me. Because I didn't want you to look back years from now and—and remember me broken and lost and drained of life—"

Travis pulled her into his arms and kissed her.

"What gives you the right to make those decisions for me?" he said gruffly. "I *love* you, dammit! I adore you. I want to be with you whatever happens."

"Even to see me die?"

"Even that," he said, his voice breaking. "But you won't. I'm trying to tell you about this surgery—"

"No."

"Jennie. Don't say 'no' until you hear me out."

"How about *you* hearing *me* out?" She stood straight within his embrace, her eyes locked to his. "I've done everything they told me to do, everything they said would work. Nothing did. Nothing will. And—and I can't go through it again. The hope. The desperate, awful hope and then the letdown." She took a breath. "It's over. I'm dying and there's no way to stop it—unless you believe in miracles and I have to tell you, I don't."

Travis framed her face with his hands.

"What I believe in," he said, "is you. Your strength. Your courage. Your determination. Add in some damned good science, a surgeon who's found a way to save lives. Would you walk away from that?"

"It's useless, don't you see? Useless!"

"I thought you were the girl who believed in taking risks."

Tears were flowing down Jennie's face.

"You're not fighting fair."

"No. I'm not. Why would I, when it comes to wanting you with me forever?"

"You're merciless," she said, but her eyes, her voice, said otherwise.

Travis forced a smile.

"That's me. The merciless Travis Wilde. A man who won't give up his woman without a fight." He stroked his hand down her back. "I'll be there. With you. I'll be at your side the whole time. My love, my heart, all that I am will be with you."

Jennie bit her lip.

"Suppose—suppose I said yes. Do you know the odds of me coming through something experimental?"

"When we meet the surgeon, he'll tell us."

"And—and if I didn't come through, if I didn't survive, I wouldn't know the difference. But you would. I know you, Travis. You'd eat yourself alive for having had even the smallest part in this."

"I'll eat myself alive if I just let you leave me." His eyes darkened. "Fight for your life, honey. I'll fight for it with you. The doctors will do their part. We'll do ours. Just don't give up. I need you to be the girl who loves roller coasters, because that's the girl you really are."

Jennie didn't answer. He wondered if she'd really heard him, if she understood how much he adored her.

At long last, she laid her head against his shoulder.

"All right," she said quietly. "I'll meet with the surgeon."

Travis started to speak. She put her hand over his lips.

"I'll talk with him, but I can't promise more than that."

"Okay. That's good. It's fine. We'll talk to him."

"We?"

"Yes. Because we're one unit, honey. I'm you. You're me. Unless, of course, you don't want me to—"

She kissed him.

"Take me to bed," she said softly.

"Honey. You're so pale. And I know your head hurts."

"Take me to bed," she said. "Just hold me." Her voice trembled. "I need to feel your body warm and hard against mine."

He took her to bed. And held her.

And when she turned toward him, kissed him, stroked him to life, he made tender love to her.

She fell asleep.

Then he rose, dressed, went quietly into the sitting room where his brothers were waiting.

"Make the appointment," he said. "To meet with the doctor."

Jake smiled. "Already done. Tomorrow morning at 8:00 a.m." He went to Travis and held out his hand. "She's one hell of a woman," he said, and Travis, not trusting himself to speak, nodded as he shook Jake's hand, then Caleb's.

They were right.

His Jennie was one hell of a woman.

And if he needed proof, which he surely didn't, he got it the next morning when he and Jennie met with the surgeon.

She answered dozens of questions clearly and calmly.

Underwent endless tests, some of which looked like they'd been dreamed up by aliens.

At noon, the surgeon met with them again.

"Okay," he said briskly, "as far as we're concerned, it's a go."

Travis squeezed Jennie's hand.

"The odds on my making it through the operation?" she said.

"Fifty-fifty."

Travis winced but Jennie nodded.

"Thank you for being honest."

"No sense in anything else, Ms. Cooper. It's important you know as much of the truth as I know."

"And what about coming through but—but being a vegetable? What are the odds on that?"

"Honey," Travis said.

Jennie shushed him.

"I need to know," she said, "because I think I'm even more afraid of that than I am of dying. Doctor? What odds will you give me?"

"Better ones. Better, in your favor." The doctor smiled; then his smile faded. "But it's always a possibility."

Silence.

Jennie's face revealed nothing.

Travis, who had pushed her to get this far, hated himself for it. A fifty-fifty chance she would die. A slightly lower chance she'd survive with severe brain damage.

"No," he heard himself say. "No, honey, you can't—"

Jennie reached for his hand.

"When's the soonest we can do this?" she said. "Because now that I've decided to do it, I really don't want to sit around and wait."

"Actually," the doctor said gently, "we can't afford to wait. How does tomorrow morning at 6:00 a.m. sound, Jennie?"

Travis felt like a man standing at the edge of an abyss.

"Wait. We need to—to talk. Do some research—"

Jennie looked at him. "I want to do this," she said calmly. "And I need you to be strong for me."

She was right. They both had to be strong. And, suddenly, he knew exactly how they would get that strength.

"Marry me," he said.

Jennie's smile trembled. "If I can, when this is over—"

"Not then. Marry me now. Tonight."

"No. No! What if—"

"I love you," Travis said. "I'll always love you." He took her in his arms. "When you go into that operating room tomorrow, you're going in there as my wife."

Jennie cried. She laughed. She kissed the man she loved.

"Do I get a say in this, Mr. Wilde?"

"No. You don't." His eyes took on a suspicious glitter. "Get on the roller coaster, honey," he whispered. "Take this ride with me."

She kissed him.

And she said, "Yes."

CHAPTER TWELVE

AT FIVE MINUTES of eight that evening, the Wilde brothers gathered in the hospital's Serenity chapel.

It was a glass-walled room with a small fountain as its focal point. Water from the fountain ran over shiny black and gray stones, creating a peaceful sound. Slender ornamental trees provided a soothing touch of green.

Caleb and Jacob had been busy.

Caleb had come up with another old "contact" who'd located a judge powerful enough to arrange the waiver of the usual license requirements and to perform the ceremony.

Jake had somehow found a florist who'd miraculously arranged for dozens of white roses and white orchids to be delivered to the chapel in record time.

Travis wanted to tell his brothers what their thoughtfulness meant to him but he didn't trust himself to speak.

He didn't have to.

His brothers hugged him and made it clear they understood.

Promptly at eight, the chapel doors opened.

Jennie appeared, on the arm of her surgeon.

He wore a dark suit.

She wore a short white lace dress, courtesy of one the nurses who was part of the team that would be taking care of her. The dress was simple and beautiful.

As beautiful as the bride herself.

Travis stood straight and tall.

He smiled at her, and she smiled back.

And, in that instant, he knew he had been waiting for this woman, for this moment, his entire life.

Music began playing, an instrumental version of "And I Will Always Love You," courtesy of Jake's iPod.

Jennie's face lit.

Still on her doctor's arm, she started toward Travis. Her steps wobbled at the very end, and Travis stepped quickly forward and took her in his arms.

"I love you," he said softly, and she smiled again, her eyes glittering with happy tears.

The service was brief.

The judge spoke of love and commitment, joy and sorrow, of how love was life's one true constant.

When it was time to make their vows, Travis realized they didn't have rings...

Except, they did.

Jake and Caleb had thought of everything.

Jake handed him a plain gold band to put on Jennie's finger.

Caleb handed Jennie a matching band to put on Travis's finger.

It was time to speak their vows.

"I, Travis Wilde, take this woman, Jennifer Cooper..."

His voice was strong and sure.

Jennie looked into his eyes.

"I, Jennifer Cooper, take this man, Travis Wilde..."

She spoke softly, but her words were clear and certain.

A moment later, the judge smiled.

"By the rights vested in me by the State of Massachusetts," she said, "I now pronounce you husband and wife. Mr. Wilde—Travis—you may kiss your bride."

Travis cupped his wife's face in his big hands.

Both of them were smiling. Both of them had tears in their eyes.

"Mrs. Wilde," he said softly.

Jennie laughed. "Mr. Wilde."

"I love you," he said.

She put her arms around his neck. He lowered his head to hers.

And as they kissed, he knew that the words, *I love you,* could never be enough to tell her what she really meant to him.

Travis spent the night by his wife's side.

He'd brought her two wedding gifts.

Her beloved, one-eared plush dog, which he'd arranged to arrive by courier..

And a hand-written IOU, promising her a kitten.

She wept, kissed him, and they held each other close.

At a few minutes before six the next morning, the surgeon came by. He shook Travis's hand, gave Jennie a quick hug.

Moments later, an attendant wheeled Jennie from her room.

Travis went with the gurney as far as they'd let him, holding his wife's hand, smiling at her, telling her how much he adored her, that he'd see her very soon, that as she fell asleep, he wanted her to think about where she wanted to spend their honeymoon.

"New York," he said. "Or Paris or Rome, or anywhere you choose."

She was already a little groggy from medication; her voice was slurred but her words were deliberate.

"I want to go home," she said. "To your place in Dallas. That's home to me, it has been ever since we met."

"Right," he said brightly, "of course," he said, even more brightly because he was a heartbeat away from sobbing.

The gurney stopped.

There were massive doors ahead.

"Sorry, Mr. Wilde," one of the attendants said softly, "this is as far as you can go."

Travis bent over the gurney. He put his arms around Jennie as best he could and lifted her closer.

"Think of me," he whispered. "Think of us. Think about all the years ahead."

"I love you," she said. "I love you, love you, love you…"

The gurney started moving. The doors opened, then shut.

Travis stumbled back against the wall.

Long minutes later, he made his way slowly to the private waiting room the hospital had arranged for the Wildes.

His brothers were there.

"Trav," they said, and they drew him into their strong arms.

Time passed, but surely snails moved faster.

One minute. Two. An hour.

And, while the hands of the clock on the wall, the hands of the watch on Travis's wrist crawled forward, amazing things began to happen.

The door opened, and Emily and Jaimie walked into the waiting room.

Travis looked up, saw them and got to his feet.

"Travis," they said, and he opened his arms and they flew to him.

His sisters-in-law appeared a little while after that.

"Sage," he said hoarsely, "Addison…"

They kissed him, whispered words of encouragement.

God, he thought, *I am a lucky man!*

Lissa showed up next.

He knew she must have flown in from California on the red eye, that she probably hadn't slept, but her tear-shot smile and hugs were all a brother could ever want.

A couple of hours later, the door swung open again.

Travis rose slowly to his feet.

"Dad?"

General Wilde walked straight to his son.

"Travis," he said. He held out his hand. Travis reached for it but then his father cleared his throat, pulled back his hand and wrapped Travis in tight embrace.

"I got here as soon as I could."

Travis nodded. "I—I—"

"I hear your Jennie is quite a woman."

Travis tried to say yes, she was, but all that came out was a choked sound of joy.

Morning became afternoon, afternoon became evening.

Lights blazed on in the waiting room.

Darkness descended over the city.

The Wildes paced.

Talked in low voices.

Endlessly looked at the clock. At their watches.

Lissa, Sage and Emily left, came back with stacks of newspapers and magazines that went untouched.

Jaimie and Addison went out, returned with sandwiches, pastries and munchies.

Those went untouched, as well.

Jake disappeared, brought back a pizza.

Caleb vanished, showed up with two boxes of doughnuts.

"You have to eat," they all told Travis, but he didn't and neither did they.

Coffee, however, was a big success.

Everybody gulped it down.

After a while, by unspoken agreement, they stopped checking the time.

What was the point?

Time was either their friend—the surgery was taking so long because every step was going well—or it was their enemy—the surgery was taking so long because nothing about it was going well.

Every now and then, somebody in hospital green appeared in the doorway.

The first time, they all leaped to their feet, but it turned out the operating room team had simply sent someone to say that the surgery was progressing.

"How much longer?" Travis said.

He didn't get an answer.

The second time, he changed the question.

"How is my wife?" he asked.

The answer was still the same, but with an addendum.

The surgery was progressing, and the doctor would be down to see them when it was over.

Fourteen hours into what had become the longest day in the history of the universe, the neurosurgeon walked into the room.

He looked exhausted, and his expression was impossible to read.

The Wildes, almost as haggard-looking as he, sprang to their feet. Without plan or discussion, they gathered around Travis in a protective semicircle.

Travis opened his mouth, then shut it.

It was the general who finally spoke.

"My daughter-in-law?"

The surgeon nodded.

"She made it through," he said, his eyes on Travis.

Travis's knees buckled. Caleb and Jake, standing on either side of him, grasped him by the elbows.

"And?" Travis said hoarsely.

"The tumor's gone. We got it all."

Travis nodded.

"Is she…" He hesitated. "Is she all right? Was there any—was there any—"

"She's stable. Her vital signs are good. But…"

That "but" made all the Wildes stop breathing.

"But, we're not out of the woods until she regains consciousness."

Travis nodded again. It seemed all he was capable of doing.

"You mean, when the anesthesia wears off."

"She's unconscious, Travis. It isn't the anesthesia. It's her brain's reaction to the trauma of surgery." The doctor cleared his throat. "We just have to wait. I wish I could be more helpful but I can't."

Another nod.

"I understand," Travis said. He didn't, not really, but what was the sense in admitting it?

They had to wait. They just had to wait…

"I want to be with her."

"Travis," the doctor said, not unkindly, "the best thing you can do is go back to your hotel, eat something, get some sleep. We'll call you the second your wife—"

"I want to be with her," Travis said, in a tone that would not admit any argument.

The doctor sighed.

"She's in recovery. We'll let you know when she's in her room. You can see her then."

Two more hours dragged by.

Travis told everyone to go to the hotel.

"I'll phone," he said. "I promise."

"Not yet," Jaimie said softly, and the others echoed those words.

At last, a nurse appeared.

"Mrs. Wilde is in her room," she said. "Mr. Wilde, if you'd come with me…"

Travis rose slowly to his feet.

His brothers hugged him. His father patted his back. His sisters and sisters-in-law kissed him.

"I'll call you," he said.

And he followed the nurse out the door.

* * *

Jennie was sleeping.

He could almost believe that because of her peaceful expression.

But there were tubes everywhere. Her head was wrapped in layers and layers of gauze. She was hooked to a battery of machines.

"Sweetheart," Travis said.

"She can't hear you, Mr. Wilde," the nurse said gently.

Travis ignored her.

He drew a chair close to the bed, wrapped his hand around his wife's and said, "Baby, it's me. I'm here. And I love you."

The surgeon came by.

Checked the machines, the tubes. Gently lifted Jennie's eyelids, shone a light into her eyes.

"Well?" Travis said.

"Nothing's changed. And that's good. She's holding her own."

Travis nodded but it wasn't good. He wanted to hear that his wife was coming back to herself, back to him.

"You might want to get some sleep," the surgeon said. "In that lounge. Someone will wake you if—"

"I'm staying with my wife."

The doctor smiled.

"Of course."

The lights were bright.

A police siren was blaring.

Travis shot upright.

He'd fallen asleep bent forward, his head on the bed. It was daylight—that was the brightness in the room. And somewhere in the distance, a police car was racing toward its destination.

Jennie had not moved.

Travis could feel his cell phone vibrating.

He ignored it.

It stopped. Then it vibrated again.

He frowned, carefully let go of his wife's hand, got to his feet, took the phone from his pocket and walked to the windows.

Jake: "It's me, Trav. Anything?"

Travis shook his head, as if his brother could see him. "No."

Caleb: "What can we bring you? Some Danish? Bagels?"

"Nothing. Just—just wait at the hotel."

"Trav. You shouldn't be alone…"

"I'm not," Travis said gruffly. "I'm with my wife."

More time went by.

The Wilde bunch gathered in the private waiting room, same as the prior day.

Travis had no idea they were there.

They'd agreed they had to be there, for themselves if not for him, but they suspected that knowing they were there, worrying about them, would be a distraction that would not do him any good.

They spoke in hushed voices about everything, anything… and nothing, because they only topic on anyone's mind was Jennie Wilde and what the healing process would reveal.

Nobody wanted to take things further than that.

It was close to sundown.

Streetlights outside the hospital blinked on.

It was raining.

Inside the hospital, the corridor lights brightened.

Jennie still lay motionless with her husband seated beside her, clutching her hand.

He was talking to her, as he had been most of the last hours, babbling about whatever came into his head.

"Football season's coming," he said. "Do you like football? Did I ever tell you I played? I bet you'd be great at touch football. My brothers and I play sometime. My sisters, too, and Addison. Not Sage, 'cause she's pregnant. Did you know that? I'm going to be an uncle. Heck, you're going to be an aunt…"

His voice faded.

Jennie didn't move.

Despair was a wild thing, clawing for purchase in his chest.

"So," he said thickly, "are you one of those women who likes sports? No? Doesn't matter to me, sweetheart. I'll be happy for the chance to quarrel over the TV remote, you know, me clicking on a baseball game, you grabbing the remote and clicking on a couple of talking heads…"

Without warning, a sob broke from his throat.

"Jennie. Talk to me. Please, honey…"

He kissed her hand. Laid it gently on her chest. Got to his feet and walked to the window because he couldn't cry in front of her just in case she could hear or see or know or—

"…ice skate."

Travis spun around.

"Baby?"

"Always wanted to learn to ice skate," his Jennie said, her voice soft and fuzzy around the edges but, God, it was her voice, her voice…

He hurried to the bed. Wrapped his hand around hers.

"Jennie?"

Slowly, slowly, her lashes lifted.

"Jennie. Oh, God, Jennie!"

She turned her head. Her eyes were wide open, her gaze clear, her pupils focused directly on him.

"Travis?" She began to weep. "Is that really, really you?"

Travis sank onto the edge of the bed. Tears streamed down his face as he took his wife in his arms.

"It's me," he said. "I'm here, and so are you."

Her lips trembled, then curved in the most wonderful smile he had ever seen.

"Wasn't it a lovely wedding?" she whispered.

Travis laughed. He cried.

"It was perfect," he said.

He kissed her. She kissed him back.

Outside, the rain suddenly stopped, revealing the setting sun.

Soon, the moon would rise.

And the lives of Travis and Jennie Wilde would start all over again.

EPILOGUE

THE RESIDENTS OF Wilde's Crossing disagreed on lots of things.

Politics. Health care. The economy. Soybean futures.

Most of the arguing was genial, but it was still arguing.

People couldn't agree on everything...

Except on the party General John Hamilton Wilde threw a year later at *El Sueño*.

It was, they all said, the best party in the best town the state of Texas had ever seen.

A line of barbecue grills a mile long.

Well, maybe a slight exaggeration there but the point was, nobody could recall ever having seen so many grills in one place.

Tables groaning under the weight of salads and slaw, green beans and corn. Grits done a dozen different ways. Fried chicken. Biscuits. Cakes. Pies. Cookies.

More tables loaded with things to drink.

Punch. Wine. Beer. Ale. Good Texas whiskey. Coffee. Tea. Lemonade.

Nobody went thirsty.

A wooden dance floor had been laid behind the house. There was a band to play what Wilde's Crossing kids called oldies, another to play rock. There was a Mexican mariachi band. And inside the house, in the big, wood-paneled library, a string quartet played whatever it was that string quartets played, for the more sedate guests.

"Something for everyone," Travis said softly to his wife, as he held her in his arms behind a big cottonwood tree.

She smiled. His heart swelled. She had, without question, the most dazzling smile in the world.

"All I need is you," she said.

"I couldn't agree more," he said, smiling back at her.

She sighed. Laid her head against his shoulder.

"You have a wonderful family."

"It's your family, too, honey. And you're right. They're something special. Even the old man."

"Emily says he's changed."

Travis chuckled. "The understatement of the year."

"Well, look at all that's happened in that year," Jennie said. "Caleb and Sage had a baby."

"Uh-huh."

"Jake and Addison are pregnant."

"Right."

"And so are we."

"Exact..." Travis jerked back. "What?"

His wife laughed.

"We're having a baby," she said.

She watched the different emotions race through her husband's eyes. Shock. Joy. And, as she'd expected, a little touch of fear.

"It's fine," she said softly.

"You spoke with—"

"I called the doctor this morning. Yes. It's just the way he said, Travis. The tumor's completely gone. I'm okay. One hundred percent okay." She leaned back in his arms and smiled up at him. "So, we're pregnant. You're going to be a daddy."

Travis blinked.

"A daddy. I'm going to be a—"

He laughed. Whooped. Bent his beautiful wife back over his arm and kissed her breathless.

"I love you, Travis Wilde," she said against his lips.

"And I love you," he said. "With all my heart. And I always will."

Not terribly far away, within hearing distance but, thankfully, obscured by the branches of a giant oak, Emily, Lissa and Jaimie Wilde stood frozen in place.

They'd never intended to spy on their brother and sister-in-law; in fact, they hadn't even known Travis and Jennie were there.

They'd taken a stroll to get away from the party for a few minutes, to get away from, as Lissa had put it, "the busybody matchmakers."

"Every female over the age of twelve seems determined to marry us off," Emily had said, with a shudder.

"They seem to think it's time, now that the boys are married," Jaimie had agreed, with a matching shudder.

"Yeah," Lissa had said, "well, good for them. But I'm not looking for marriage."

"Not now," Em had said.

"Maybe not ever," Jaimie had added.

So, being trapped behind a tree, having to listen to their brother and his wife, had been, well, okay, it had been...

"Sweet," Lissa offered, as Travis and Jennie finally strolled away.

"We'll have to remember to look surprised when they announce that they're having a baby," Em pointed out.

"Definitely," Jaimie said. "And, really, I'm glad they're happy. All of them, you know? But—"

"But," Lissa said solemnly, "that isn't what I want."

"I don't, either."

"Same for me."

The sisters nodded. Then, because they were Wildes,

which meant they weren't just easy on the eyes, they were also smart, Em grinned and raised the bottle of Champagne she'd snatched for liquid sustenance from one of the party tables before they'd set off on their little walk.

Her sisters grinned, too. Lissa lifted her flute and Em's; Jaimie raised hers.

"To men," Em said, popping the Champagne cork with a flourish.

"Got to keep them where they belong," Lissa said, as Em filled the glasses.

"In bed. And around when you need something heavy lifted," Jaimie said.

"Aside from that," Em said, "give us the single life!"

The sisters laughed, cheered, slugged back the Champagne.

And thanked whatever gods might be watching for the freedom to be women, and not yet wives.

* * * * *

"Mr. Kazarov," she said, her voice a little too shrill, a little too brittle.

Roman *tsk*ed. "After all we were to each other, Caroline? Is this how you greet an old friend?"

"I wasn't aware we were friends," she said, remembering with a pang the way he'd looked at her that night when she'd informed him they couldn't see each other anymore. He'd just told her he loved her.

Roman shrugged. "Then we are certainly old acquaintances."

One eyebrow arched as his gaze slid down to where she clutched the wrap over her breasts. She'd worn a strapless black dress tonight, but she felt as if she were naked under the silk from the way his eyes took their time perusing her. Heat flared in her core. Unwelcome heat.

"Old *lovers*," Roman said as his eyes met hers again.

SCANDAL IN THE SPOTLIGHT

The truth is more shocking than the headlines!

Named and most definitely shamed,
these media darlings have learnt the hard way
that the press always loves a scandal!

Having a devastatingly gorgeous man on their arm
only adds fuel to the media frenzy. Especially when
the attraction between them burns hotter
and brighter than a paparazzo's flashbulb…

More books in the **Scandal in the Spotlight** miniseries
available in eBook:

GIRL BEHIND THE SCANDALOUS REPUTATION
by Michelle Conder

BACK IN THE HEADLINES
by Sharon Kendrick

NO MORE SWEET SURRENDER
by Caitlin Crews

Visit www.millsandboon.co.uk

A GAME WITH ONE WINNER

BY
LYNN RAYE HARRIS

First published in Great Britain 2013
by Mills & Boon, an imprint of Harlequin (UK) Limited.
Harlequin (UK) Limited, Eton House, 18-24 Paradise Road,
Richmond, Surrey TW9 1SR

© Lynn Raye Harris 2013

ISBN: 978 0 263 91006 3

Harlequin (UK) policy is to use papers that are natural, renewable
and recyclable products and made from wood grown in sustainable
forests. The logging and manufacturing process conform to the
legal environmental regulations of the country of origin.

Printed and bound in Spain
by Blackprint CPI, Barcelona

Lynn Raye Harris read her first Mills & Boon® romance when her grandmother carted home a box from a yard sale. She didn't know she wanted to be a writer then, but she definitely knew she wanted to marry a sheikh or a prince and live the glamorous life she read about in the pages. Instead, she married a military man and moved around the world. These days she makes her home in North Alabama, with her handsome husband and two crazy cats. Writing for Harlequin Mills & Boon® is a dream come true. You can visit her at www.lynnrayeharris.com

Recent titles by this same author:

REVELATIONS OF THE NIGHT BEFORE
UNNOTICED AND UNTOUCHED
MARRIAGE BEHIND THE FAÇADE

**Did you know these are also available as eBooks?
Visit www.millsandboon.co.uk**

For MPP

CHAPTER ONE

Russian Billionaire Rumored to Be Acquiring Troubled Department Store Chain

SHE WAS HERE. Roman Kazarov knew it as surely as he knew his own name, though he had not yet seen her. The woman at his side made a noise of frustration, a tiny little sound meant to draw his attention back to her. He flicked his gaze over her, and then away again.

Bored. The woman was beautiful, but he was bored. One night in her bed, and he was ready to move on.

Her fingers curled possessively around his arm. He resisted the urge to shake them off. He'd brought her here tonight on impulse. Because Caroline Sullivan-Wells would be here. Not that Caroline would care if he had a woman on his arm. No, she'd made it very clear five years ago that she didn't care about him in the least.

Had never cared.

Once, her rejection had cut him to the bone. Now, he felt nothing. Nothing but cold determination. He'd returned to New York a far different man than he'd left it five years ago.

A rich man. A ruthless man.

A man with a single goal.

Before the month was out, he would own Sullivan's, the luxury chain of department stores founded by her family.

It was the culmination of everything he'd worked so hard for, the symbolic cherry on top of the ice-cream sundae. He did not need Sullivan's, but he wanted it. Once, he'd been an acolyte at the feet of Frank Sullivan. And then he'd been unceremoniously tossed out, his work visa terminated, his dreams of providing a better life for his family back home in Russia shattered.

All he'd dared to do was fall in love with Caroline, but that one act had been the same as strapping on wings made of wax and flying too close to the sun. He'd fallen far and fast.

But now he was back. And there was nothing Caroline or her father could do about what he'd set in motion.

As if in answer to some hidden command, the crowd parted to reveal a woman standing on the other side of the room. She was deep in conversation. The glow from the Waterford chandelier overhead shone down in just such a way that it appeared to single her out, wreathing her golden-blond head and milky skin in a nimbus of pale light.

Roman's gut clenched. She was still beautiful, still ethereal. And she still affected him, which only served to anger him further. He had not expected it, this jolt of remembered lust and bittersweet joy. He stood there and willed the feeling away until he could look at her coldly, critically.

Yes, much better. That was what he wanted to feel—disgust. Hatred.

His jaw tightened. She chose that moment to look up, almost as if she'd sensed something was wrong, as if there was a disturbance in her well-ordered circle of friends. There was a crease in the smooth skin over her hazel eyes, as if she was annoyed at being interrupted.

But then she saw him. Her eyes widened, her pink lips dropping open. She put a hand to her chest, then thought better of it and dropped it to her side—but not before he saw how he affected her. For a long moment, neither of them looked away. She broke the contact first, saying something to the person she'd been talking to, before she turned and fled through a door behind her.

Roman stiffened. He should feel triumphant, yet he strangely felt as if she'd rejected him again. As if his world were about to come crashing down just as it had five years ago. But that was not possible, not any longer. *He* had the upper hand now. He was the victor, the conqueror.

And yet bitterness coiled inside him, twisting and writhing on the floor of his soul, reminding him of how far he'd fallen, and how hard. Reminding him of how much that fall had cost him before he'd been able to pull himself up again.

"Darling," the woman at his side said, drawing his attention from the door through which Caroline had disappeared, "can you fetch me a drink?"

Roman gazed down at her. She was pretty, spoiled, an actress with a face and body that usually drove men wild. She was used to commanding attention, to having her whims obeyed without question.

But what she saw in his face must have given her pause. She took a step back, her fingers sliding over the sleek fabric of his bespoke tuxedo. She was already calculating, already trying to recover from her mistake.

Too late.

"I do not fetch," he told her coolly. And then he reached into his breast pocket and pulled out his wallet. He took out five crisp one-hundred-dollar bills and pressed them into her hand. "Enjoy yourself for as long as you wish. When you are finished, take a cab home."

She reached for him as he turned. "You're leaving me?"

Her eyes were wide, her confidence in her beauty shaken. He would have felt sorry for her, except that he was certain loads of interested men would swarm around her as soon as he walked away. Roman took her hand from his sleeve, lifted it to his lips and pressed a kiss to the back of it. "It is not meant to be, *maya krasavitsa*. You will find another who deserves you."

And then he left her standing alone as he went in search of another woman. A woman who would not escape him this time.

Caroline took the elevator down to the first floor and hurried out to the sidewalk. Her heart hammered in her head, her throat, and she clutched her wrap to her body and tried to breathe evenly. *Roman.*

She blinked back the sudden tears that hovered, and gave the doorman a shaky smile when he asked if she'd like a taxi.

"Yes, please," she said, her voice a touch breathless from her flight. Of all the people to be in that room tonight. And yet she should have expected him, shouldn't she? She'd read that he was back in town. The newspapers couldn't seem to leave the subject of Roman Kazarov alone. Or his mission.

Caroline's fingers tightened on the silk wrap. It would be hopelessly wrinkled when she was done, but she hardly cared. She'd known she would have to see him again, but she hadn't expected it to happen quite yet. No, she'd expected to face him in a boardroom—and even that thought had been almost enough to make her lose her lunch at the time.

How could she face him again? How? One moment, one look from across the room, and she was a jittery wreck of raw emotion. He had always had that effect on her, but she was nevertheless stunned that he still did. After all this time. After everything.

"Caroline."

Her spine melted under the silken caress of her name on those lips she'd once loved so much. Once, but no more. She was a woman now, a woman who had made her choice. She'd do the same thing again, given the circumstances. She'd saved Sullivan's then; she would save it now, too.

No matter that Roman Kazarov and his multinational conglomerate had other ideas.

She turned with a smile on her lips. A smile that shook at the corners. She only hoped it was too dark for him to notice.

"Mr. Kazarov," she said, her voice a little too shrill, a little too brittle.

She needed to find her strength, her center—but she was off balance, her system still in shock from the surprise of seeing him in that room tonight.

Her heart took a slow tumble over the edge of the shelf on which it sat, falling into her belly, her toes. She felt hollow inside, so hollow, as she gazed up into those bright, ice-blue eyes of his. He was still incredibly handsome. Tall, broad-shouldered, with dark hair and the kind of chiseled features that made artists itch to pick up their palette knives and brushes.

Or made photographers snap-happy. Yes, she'd seen the photos of him since he'd burst onto the scene a little over two years ago. She still remembered the first time, when Jon had handed her the paper over breakfast and told her she needed to see who was featured there.

She'd nearly choked on her coffee. Her husband had reached for her hand and squeezed it. He was the only one who knew how devastating news of Roman would be to her. In the years that followed, she'd watched Roman's rise with trepidation, knowing in her gut that he would return one day.

Knowing that he would come for her.

Roman tsked. "After all we were to each other, Caroline? Is this how you greet an old friend?"

"I wasn't aware we were friends," she said, remembering with a pang the way he'd looked at her that night when she'd informed him they couldn't see each other anymore. He'd just told her he loved her. She'd wanted to say the same words back to him, but it had been impossible. So she'd lied. And he'd looked...stunned. Wounded. And then he'd looked angry.

Now, he looked as if he could care less. It disconcerted her. She was off balance, a mess inside. A churning, sick mess, and he looked cool, controlled. Calm.

But why was she a mess? She'd done what she'd had to do. She would do it again. She tilted her chin up. Yes, she'd done the right thing, no matter the personal cost. Two people's happiness had been nothing compared to the well-being of the countless people whose livelihoods had depended upon Sullivan's.

Roman shrugged. "Then we are certainly old acquaintances." One eyebrow arched as his gaze slid down to where she clutched the wrap over her breasts. She'd worn a strapless black dress tonight, but she felt as if she were naked under the silk, the way his eyes took their time perusing her. Heat flared in her core. Unwelcome heat. "Old *lovers*," Roman said, as his eyes met hers again.

She turned and stared across Fifth Avenue toward the park, her insides trembling. Traffic was jammed up, barely moving due to some unseen obstruction, and she knew her cab would be a long time in arriving. How would she endure this?

She'd hoped beyond hope that she would never see him again. It would be easier that way. Safer.

"You do not wish to be reminded?" Roman asked. "Or have you decided to pretend it never happened?"

"I know what happened." She would never forget. How could she when she had a daily reminder of the passion she'd once shared with this man? Panic threatened to claw its way into her throat at the thought, but she refused to let it. "But it was a long time ago."

"I was sorry to hear about your husband," he said then, and her stomach twisted into a painful knot.

Poor Jon. Poor, poor Jon. If anyone had deserved happiness, it had been him. "Thank you," she said, the lump in her throat making her words come out tight. Jon had been gone for over a year now, but it still had the power to slice into her when she thought of those last helpless months when the leukemia had ravaged his body. It was so unfair.

She dipped her head a moment, surreptitiously dashing away the tears threatening to spill down her cheeks. Jon had been her best friend in the world, her partner, and she missed him still. Thinking of Jon reminded her that she had to be as strong as he'd been when facing his illness.

Roman was a man, and men could be defeated. "It won't work," she said, her voice fiercer than she'd thought she could manage at that moment.

Roman cocked an eyebrow. So smooth. "What won't work, darling?"

A shiver chased down her spine. Once, he'd meant the endearment, and she'd loved the way his Russian accent slid across the words as he spoke. It was a caress before the caress. Now, however, he did it to torment her. The words were not a caress so much as a threat.

She turned and faced him head-on, tilting her head back to look him in the eye. He stood with his hands in his pockets, one corner of his beautiful mouth slanted up in a mocking grin.

Evil, heartless bastard. That was what he was now. What she had to think of him as. He wasn't here to do her any favors. He would not be merciful.

Especially if he discovered her secret.

"You won't soften me up, Roman," she said. "I know what you want and I plan to fight you."

He laughed. "I welcome it. Because you will not win. Not this time." His eyes narrowed as he studied her. "Funny, I would have never thought your father would step down and leave you in charge. I always thought they would carry him from his office someday."

A shard of cold fear dug into her belly, as it always did when someone mentioned her father these days. "People change," she said coolly.

And sometimes those changes were completely unexpected. A wave of love and sadness filled her at the thought of her father, sitting in his overstuffed chair by the window and staring at the lake beyond. Some days he recognized her. Most days he did not.

"In my experience they don't. Whatever was there at the start will continue to be there in the end." His gaze slid over her again, and her skin prickled. "People sometimes want you to think they've changed, in order to protect themselves, but I find it's never true."

"Then you must not know many people," she said. "We all change. No one stays the same."

"No, we don't. But whatever the essence was, that remains. If one is heartless, for instance, one doesn't suddenly grow a heart."

Caroline's skin glowed with heat. She knew he was speaking of her, speaking of that night when she'd thrown his love back in his face. She wanted to deny it, wanted to tell him the truth, but what good would it do? None whatsoever.

"Sometimes things are not as they seem," she said. "Appearances can be deceptive."

As soon as she said it, she knew it was the wrong thing to say. His icy eyes grew even frostier as he studied her. "I have no doubt you would know this."

Fury and sadness warred inside her. The only thing to do was to pretend not to understand his meaning. Caroline gave a superior sniff. "Nevertheless, Daddy has reevaluated his priorities. He's enjoying himself at his country estate these days. He worked hard for it, and he deserves it."

There was a lump in her throat. She gritted her teeth and turned to look hopefully for a taxi, willing herself not to cry as she did so. She wasn't ordinarily overcome with emotion, but thinking about her father's illness in the presence of this man she'd once loved was a bit overwhelming.

"I had no idea you were interested in taking over the business someday," Roman said, his tone more than a bit mocking. "I'd rather thought your interests lay elsewhere."

She whipped around to look at him. "Such as shopping and getting my nails done? That was never my plan."

It had been her parents' plan, however. It was simply not done for a Sullivan woman to work. They married well and spent their days doing charitable work, not dirtying their hands in the business. No matter that she'd wanted to learn the business, or that her father had indulged her a bit and let her intern there—because business experience would do her good in her charitable duties, he'd said over her mother's protests. Jon had always been the one intended to run the department store chain once her father retired.

Which Frank Sullivan would not have done anytime in the next twenty years had the choice not been taken from him. Now that Jon was dead, there was no one else but her. And she was good at what she did, damn it. She had to be.

"You've had a bad year," Roman said softly, and her heart clenched. Yes, she'd had a bad year. But she still had Sullivan's. More importantly, she had her son. And for him, she would do anything. Sullivan's would be his one day. She would make sure of it.

"It could always be worse," she said, not meeting Roman's hard gaze. She'd told herself repeatedly that things could always be worse just so she could get through the day—but she really didn't want to know how much worse. Losing a husband to cancer and a father to dementia was pretty damn bad in her book.

"It *is* worse," he said. "I'm here. I don't arrive on the scene until a company is struggling, Caroline. Until profits are squeezed tight and every month is a struggle to pay your suppliers just enough so they'll keep the shipments coming."

Caroline blinked. *The stores.* Of course he was talking about the stores. For a minute, she'd thought he was being sympathetic. But why would he be? She was the last person he'd ever show any compassion for.

And she could hardly blame him, could she? They hadn't exactly parted on the best of terms.

Though her heart ached, she feigned a laugh that was as light as the evening breeze. It tinkled gaily, as if she hadn't a care in the world, when in fact she felt the weight of her cares like an anvil yoked to her neck.

"Oh Roman, really. You've done quite well for yourself, but your information cannot always be correct. This time, you are wrong. Dead wrong. You won't get Sullivan's, no matter how you try." She waved a hand toward Fifth Avenue, encompassing the park, the horse-drawn carriage with its load of tourists passing by, and the logjam of cars and trucks packing the avenue. "Times have been bad everywhere, but look around you. This city is alive. These people are working, and they need the kind of goods Sullivan's provides. They want what we have. Our sales are up twenty percent this quarter. And it will only get better."

She *had* to believe that. Her father had made some bad decisions before anyone realized he was ill, and she was working her hardest to fix them. It wasn't easy, and she wasn't assured of success, but she wasn't ready to give up yet, either.

Roman smirked. Literally smirked. "Twenty percent in *one* store, Caroline. The majority of your stores are suffering. You should have sold off some of the less profitable branches, but you didn't. And now you are hurting."

He took a step toward her, closed the space between them until she could feel his heat. His power. She wanted to take a step back, to put distance between them, but she would not. She would never give an inch of ground to this man. She couldn't. She'd made her choice five years ago and she would stick by the rightness of it until the day she died.

"Thank you for your opinion, as unsolicited as it might have been," Caroline said tightly. The nerve of the man! Of course she'd thought of selling off a few of the stores, but when she'd tried, the offers hadn't exactly been forthcoming. It should have been done two years ago, but she hadn't been the one in charge then. By the time she'd taken the lead, the economy had tanked and no one wanted to buy a department store. She was doing the best she could with the resources she had.

"I've done my research," Roman said. "And I know the end is near for Sullivan's. If you wish to see it continue, you'll cooperate with me."

Caroline tilted her chin up again. She'd been strong for so long that it was as natural to her as breathing. She might have been young and naive five years ago, when she'd loved this man beyond the dictates of reason or sense, but no longer.

"Why on earth would I do that? Are you saying I should just trust you? Sign over Sullivan's and trust that you'll 'save' the stores that have been in my family for five generations?" She shook her head. "I'd be a fool if I did business that way. And I assure you I am no fool."

Miraculously, a taxi broke through the traffic and pulled to the curb then. The uniformed doorman drew open the door with a flourish. "Madam, your taxi."

Caroline turned without waiting for an answer and entered the cab. She was just about to tell the driver where to take her when Roman filled the frame of the open door.

"This is my taxi," she blurted as he shifted her over with a nudge of his hip.

"I'm going in the same direction." He settled in beside her and gave the driver an address in the financial district. Caroline wanted to splutter in outrage, but she forced herself to breathe evenly, calmly. Her heart was a trapped butterfly in her chest. She couldn't lead Roman to her door. She couldn't bear to have him know where she lived. If Ryan came outside for some reason…

No. Caroline gave the driver the address of a town house

in Greenwich Village. It wasn't *her* town house, but she could walk the two streets over to her own house once the cab was gone.

"How did you know we were going in the same direction?" she demanded as the taxi began to inch back into traffic.

He shrugged. "Because I'm in no hurry. Even if you went north, I could eventually go south again."

Caroline tucked her wrap over one shoulder. "That seems like a terrible waste of time."

"I hardly think so. I have you alone now."

Her heart thumped. Once, she would have been giddy to be alone with him for a long cab ride. She would have turned into his arms and tilted her head back for his kiss. Unwelcome heat bloomed in her cheeks, her belly. How many clandestine kisses had they shared in taxis such as this one?

Caroline didn't want to think about it. She slid as far away from him as she could get, and turned to stare out the window at the mass of humanity moving along the sidewalks. A young woman in a yellow dress caught her eye as she walked beneath a streetlamp, her arm looped into the man's beside her. When she threw her head back and laughed, Caroline felt a pang of envy. When was the last time she'd laughed so spontaneously?

Arrested by her laugh or her beauty, or some unidentifiable thing Caroline couldn't see, the man drew the girl into his arms. Caroline craned her neck as the taxi moved past, watched as the girl wrapped her arms around the man's neck and their lips met.

When she turned back, she could feel Roman's eyes on her in the darkened taxi.

"Ah, romance," he said, the words dripping with cynicism.

Caroline closed her eyes and swallowed. She bit her lip against the urge to say she was sorry for any pain she'd caused him. They'd said everything five years ago. It was too late now, and she wasn't the same person she'd been then.

"What do you want from me, Roman?" Her voice sounded strained to her own ears. If he noticed, he didn't comment.

"You know what I want. What I came here for."

She turned to look at him, and barely stopped herself from sucking in her breath at the sight of him all dark and moody beside her. After five years, was she still supposed to be this affected by his dark male beauty?

"You're wasting your time. Sullivan's isn't for sale at any price."

There was silence between them for a long moment. And then he burst into laughter. His voice was rich, deep and sexy, and a curl of heat wound through her at the sound.

"You will sell, Caroline. You will do it because you can't bear to see it cease to exist. Be stubborn—and watch when your suppliers cut off your line of credit, one by one. Watch as you have to close one store, and then another, and still you cannot fill your orders or keep your stores supplied with goods. Sullivan's is known for quality, for luxury. Will you cease to order the best, and settle for second best? Will you tell your customers they can no longer have the Russian caviar, the finest smoked salmon, the specialty cakes from Josette's, the designer handbags from Italy or the custom suits in the men's haberdashery?"

A shiver traveled up her spine, vibrated across her shoulder blades. Her stomach clenched hard. Yes, it was that bad. Yes, she'd been studying the list of her suppliers and wondering how she could cut corners and still keep the quality for which Sullivan's was known. The specialty food shop was hugely expensive—and yes, she'd thought of downsizing that department, of eliminating it in some markets.

She'd wanted to ask her father. She'd wanted to sit at his feet and ask him what he thought, just as she'd wanted to turn to Jon and ask him for his opinion. But they were unavailable, and she would not choke. She would make the hard choices. For Ryan. She would do it for Ryan.

Family was everything. It was all she had.

"I won't discuss this with you, Roman," she said, her voice as hard as she could make it. "You don't own Sullivan's yet. If I have anything to say about it, you won't ever get that chance."

"This is the thing you fail to understand, *solnyshko*. You have no say. It is as inevitable as a sunset."

"Nothing is inevitable. Not while I have my wits. I intend to fight you with everything I have. You will not win."

His smile was lethally cold. And dangerously attractive if the spike in her temperature was any indication.

"Ah, but I will. This time, Caroline, I get *my* way."

Her heart thumped. "And what's that supposed to mean? Surely you aren't still brooding over our brief affair. You can't mean to acquire Sullivan's simply to get revenge for past slights."

She said the words as if they were nothing, as if the mere idea were ridiculous, though her pulse skittered wildly in her wrists, her throat.

The corners of his mouth tightened, and her insides squeezed into a tight ball.

"Brooding? Hardly that, my dear. I've realized since that night that my…" he paused "…*feelings*…were not quite what I thought they were." His gaze dropped over her body, back up again. "I was enamored with you, this is true. But love? No."

It should not hurt to hear him say such a thing, but it did. She'd loved him so much, and she'd believed that he had loved her in return.

And now he was telling her he never had. That it was all an illusion. The knowledge hurt far more than she'd have thought possible five years after the fact.

"Then why are you here?" she asked tightly. "Why does Sullivan's matter to you? You own far more impressive department stores. You don't need mine."

His laugh was soft, mocking. "No, I don't need them." He

leaned toward her suddenly, his eyes gleaming in the light from the traffic. Her stomach clenched in reaction, though she hardly knew what she was reacting to.

"I *want* them," he growled. "And I want *you*."

CHAPTER TWO

Kazarov Ruthless in Business and Bed, Beauty Says

HE HADN'T INTENDED to go that far, but now that he had, it was interesting to watch her reaction. Her breath hitched in sharply, her hazel-green eyes widening. She dropped her lashes, shielding her eyes from his as she worked to control her expression.

Since the moment she'd spun toward him on the pavement, he'd been remembering what it had been like with her. It annoyed him greatly. He had his pick of women. The kind of women who took lush gorgeousness to an art form, while Caroline's beauty was less studied, less polished. Perhaps she was merely pretty, he decided. Not beautiful at all, but pretty.

But then she raised her lashes and speared him with those eyes, and he felt the jolt at gut level. She was an ice queen, and he wanted nothing more than to melt her frigid exterior. It angered him that he did. He'd had no intention whatsoever of touching her, yet here he was, threatening her with the prospect of once more becoming his mistress.

"Why?" she said, her voice laced with the same shock he felt at this turn of events.

Roman shrugged casually, though he felt anything but casual at the moment. "Perhaps I have not had enough of you," he said. "Or perhaps I want to humiliate you as you humiliated me."

She clutched her tiny evening purse in both hands. "You aren't that kind of man, Roman. You can't mean to force me into sleeping with you."

Savageness surged within him. And the bitter taste of memories he'd rather forget. "You have no idea what kind of man I am, *solnyshko*. You never did."

Her lip trembled, and it nearly undid him. But no, he had to remember how cold she was, how ruthless she had been when he'd laid his heart on the line and made a fool of himself over her. He'd trusted her. Believed her.

And she'd betrayed him.

Roman clenched his jaw tight. He'd fallen for her facade of sweet innocence—but it had been only a facade. He'd made the mistake of thinking that because he was the first man she'd given herself to, she felt more than she did.

I don't love you, Roman. How could I? I am a Sullivan, and you are just a man who works for my father.

He hadn't been good enough for Caroline Sullivan-Wells and her blue-blooded family. Forgetting that singular detail had been a mistake that had cost him dearly. Cost his family. When he'd been forced to leave the States, to return to Russia without a job or any money—because he'd sent most of it home in order to care for his mother—he'd lost much more than a woman he'd fancied himself in love with.

"I have a child, Roman. I don't have time for anyone in my life besides him."

Bitterness flooded him. Yes, she had a child. A son she'd had with Jon Wells, only months after she'd cut him from her life. She'd had no trouble moving on to the next man. Marrying the next man. Roman no longer cared that she had, but when he thought of what he'd been doing in those months after he'd left the States, the resentment nearly overwhelmed him.

His words came out hard. "I don't believe I said anything about a relationship."

Something flashed in her eyes then, something hard and cool—and something that spoke of panic shoved deep beneath the surface. His senses sharpened.

Interesting.

"I won't sleep with you, Roman. Do your worst to me, to Sullivan's, but you won't gain what you think you will."

Neither of them said anything for a long moment. And then, on impulse, he reached out and slid a finger along her cheek. The move clearly surprised her, but she didn't flinch. A bubble of satisfaction welled within him as her pupils dilated and her skin heated beneath his touch. She was not unaffected, no matter that she pretended to be.

"How do you know what I wish to gain, *solnyshko?*" he purred.

Caroline couldn't breathe properly. From the first second he'd touched her, sparks of sensation had been going off inside her like fireworks on the Fourth of July. Her body ached. Her limbs trembled. And liquid heat flooded her core without the slightest hesitation.

What was wrong with her?

Just because she hadn't actually had sex in forever was no reason to respond to this man. Other men had touched her, yet she'd felt nothing. She'd tried to date a couple of times after Jon's death, because everyone told her she should, and because she was so incredibly lonely without him in her life.

But each time her date leaned in to kiss her, she felt a wave of panic, not lust. The kisses were unremarkable, the touches not worth thinking about. She'd excused herself the first second she could, and she'd never accepted another invitation.

She was beginning to think she was meant to be alone, that she'd only experienced the passion she had because it had given her Ryan. Those days were long over.

Until now. Until the instant Roman had run his finger over her skin, she'd thought she was, for all intents and purposes, frozen inside.

"Why are you doing this?" she asked, her voice little more than a whisper. She didn't want to feel anything for him. Not now. It was too complicated, and she couldn't face the trouble it would cause her.

His ice-blue eyes were intent on hers, his presence overwhelming in the small space of the taxi. His gaze dropped to her lips, took a leisurely trip back up to meet her eyes.

"Why does anyone do anything?"

He was as she remembered, and yet he was different, too. Harder. More ruthless. In spite of what he'd said about not being in love with her, was it her fault that he'd changed? "I'm sorry, Roman," she said, despite her determination not to. "I didn't mean to hurt you."

His laugh stroked softly against her heightened nerves. "Hurt me? *Nyet,* my darling. You did not hurt me. Wounded my pride a bit, perhaps. But I quickly recovered, I assure you."

Caroline swallowed. She'd been devastated after that night, but she'd borne it all with quiet stoicism. Jon had been the only one who'd known what it had cost her to marry him.

She dropped her gaze to where she still clutched her purse in her hands. She'd done what had to be done. She'd been the only one who could. When Jon's parents had insisted on the match, when they'd threatened to sell their shares in Sullivan's and deliver majority control to a rival who would gut the stores and scatter their employees, Caroline had stepped up and done her duty. She'd saved the family legacy and thousands of jobs. It was something to be proud of. And she *was* proud, damn it.

Too proud to cower before this man.

She lifted her chin and met his hard gaze. She refused to

flinch from the naked anger she saw there. And the need. He let that show through for a moment, and it stunned her.

How could he still want her after all that had happened? After the horrible things she'd said in order to make him go away?

But he did. Worse, she realized that she wanted him, too. She wanted to lean in and kiss him, wanted to feel the hot press of his mouth against hers once more. She'd never felt so alive as when he'd kissed her.

But no, that was another time. She'd been younger, more carefree, and unaware of the profound sadness life could bring. She knew better now. If she kissed him—if she let herself fall into him—it would only hurt worse once she had to disengage again.

"I'm glad to hear it, Roman. We weren't right for each other. You know it as well as I."

He snorted. "You mean that you were too good for me. That Caroline Sullivan deserved someone far better than the son of a Russian laborer. The peasant blood that runs through my veins would sully your bloodline."

"I was young," she said, shame twisting inside her at the things she'd had to let him believe that night. But it had been the only way. She'd had to burn the bridge behind her or risk tiptoeing across it again. "And that was not precisely what I said."

"You didn't have to. I understood your meaning quite clearly."

Caroline took a deep breath. There was too much pain here, too many memories. Too many what-ifs. "I know you don't understand, but it was the only choice I had."

It wasn't an explanation, but it was more than she'd said five years ago.

He looked at her in disbelief. "You would dare to say such a thing? To suggest you had no choice in your actions that night? What sort of tale of woe do you intend to ply me with, Caroline?"

Before she could dredge up an answer, the taxi came to a stop and the driver announced over the tinny speaker that they'd arrived at the first destination. Caroline turned her head to stare blindly at the unfamiliar house, before she remembered that she'd purposely given the wrong address.

She drew in a calming breath and turned back to face the angry man beside her. "Good night, Roman."

"I'll walk you to the door," he said, his tone clipped, as she reached for the handle.

"No," she blurted. "I don't want that."

"Then I will wait until you are safely inside before leaving."

Caroline licked suddenly dry lips. "No, don't do that. It's fine. This neighborhood is quite safe. I sometimes take walks later than this just to clear my head."

It wasn't true—the walks, anyway—but she didn't want him to stay, since she couldn't enter the house they'd stopped in front of. She didn't even know who lived here. She knew her immediate neighbors on her street, but not those any farther afield.

Why had she panicked when he'd gotten into the taxi? Why hadn't she simply given her address instead of lying? Now she was caught like a fish on a hook, and he was watching her with more than a little curiosity in his gaze.

"I am not so coarse as to leave a lady on a darkened street. I insist."

He reached across her, intending to pull the handle. She reacted blindly, turning into him and pressing her mouth to his throat. The first touch was shocking. His skin was warm, his pulse a strong throb in his neck, and something soft and needy quivered to life in her core.

She didn't know what she was doing, except that she had to get him away from here before he figured out this wasn't where she lived. She'd wanted to distract him before he could ask questions, but she hadn't bargained on the feelings pulsing to life inside her. She felt as if she'd touched a hot iron. Logic dictated she pull away, but fear drove her onward. An irrational fear, certainly, but she was committed now.

Roman gripped her shoulders and pushed her back against the seat.

"What is this, Caroline? Moments ago, you proclaimed your intention not to sleep with me."

She sucked in a breath. Her body was still sizzling with heat and need from that single contact. What she said next wasn't precisely untrue in light of that fact. "I'm lonely, Roman. It's been a long time, and—and I miss having a man in my bed."

One dark eyebrow arched. "Really? How perfectly convenient."

She reached for him, tried to put her arms around his neck and pull him closer, so she could blot out the maddening voice in her head that screamed she'd lost her mind. She hadn't lost her mind, but she cared more about Ryan than she did herself. She would protect her child with every breath left in her body.

If she'd just given the correct address in the first place, she could've left Roman in the car. But she'd panicked, and if he found out she'd lied, he would wonder why. He would want to know what she was hiding.

Caroline choked on a silent laugh. God, she had so many things to hide, didn't she? Ryan, her father, the state of Sullivan's finances.

"Take me to your place," she said, her voice raw with emotion. She only hoped he would chalk it up to desire and not fear.

Roman still held her at arm's length, his dark gaze raking over her face as if he could ferret out all her secrets. She lifted her chin and stared back, willing him to believe her. And it wasn't so hard, really, since a part of her *did* want him.

A part she could not indulge, no matter the dangerous game she played.

Roman let her go and told the driver to continue to the address he'd given. Caroline slumped against the seat. She'd thought she would be relieved, but instead the tension in her body wound tighter. She kept expecting Roman to reach for her, to enfold her in his arms and take what she'd been offering.

But he didn't, and that disconcerted her. He should be trying to kiss her, not sitting beside her like a large, silent mountain.

Ten minutes later, the car stopped at another location, and Caroline's pulse spiked. She had to get away from him, had to go home and lock herself away in her bedroom while she processed everything that seeing him again had made her feel.

"I'm feeling a little unwell," she said, as Roman swiped a credit card through the reader. "Maybe I should go home, after all."

Roman didn't even look at her. "If you are unwell, then you must come up and let me get you something for your…"

"Head," she blurted. "I feel a migraine coming on."

"Pity," he replied, as he took the receipt the driver handed to him, and ushered her from the car before she could think of how to get him to leave without her.

"You'll just need to call another one," she said as he led her toward the glass doors of a tall building. "I really should get home. My child needs me."

"Funny you did not think of this when you were sitting in front of your doorstep."

"I—I was overwhelmed."

Roman punched in an entry code and the doors slid open. "By sudden desire for me, yes. I am very flattered." Except that he didn't sound flattered at all. He sounded bored. "Now come and take something for your head."

Caroline hesitated a moment, but where would she go if

she didn't go inside? This was the financial district at night, not Times Square. The taxis were fewer, the bustle much less. Did she want to stand on the street in an evening dress and frantically wave at taxis?

In the end, she entered the building, walking in silence beside the man she'd once loved, as he led her past a desk staffed with a security guard, and into a private elevator. The ride up was quick, and she was hardly surprised when the doors opened at the penthouse. Roman exited the elevator. She followed, her heart hammering as she stepped inside the masculine space.

A wall of windows lined the entire front of the apartment, looking out over the Manhattan skyline. The space was open from one end to the other, each area flowing into the next: the kitchen with its huge marble-topped island and stainless appliances, the dining room, the living room in which they stood, and onward toward the bedroom she could see through the open door to her right.

Roman left her standing in the living room. She heard the clink of glassware, and then liquid being poured. He returned a moment later with a glass of water and a bottle of aspirin.

"For your headache," he said, when she didn't move to take them from him.

"Oh, yes," she blurted. "Thanks."

She took the water and then Roman shook two aspirin into her hand. She popped them in her mouth and swallowed them down. She truly did have a headache, but it was due to stress and not a migraine.

Roman went and opened a sliding door to a large terrace. After a moment's hesitation, Caroline followed him outside. The night air was cool this high up, the breeze that ruffled her hair refreshing. She'd laid her small purse on a table inside, but she'd kept her wrap. She pulled it tighter and gazed out over the city.

"Is this yours?" she asked.

"*Da.* I bought it over a year ago."

Her insides twisted. "You've come to New York before?"

He'd walked the same streets she had? Gone into the shops? What if she'd rounded a corner one day, with Ryan holding her hand, and bumped into Roman? A chill that had nothing to do with the night air skated over her soul. She felt as if she should have known he was here somehow, but the truth was that she hadn't.

He turned to look at her, his eyes sparkling in the lights from the living room. "Of course. Did you think I would avoid it because you were here?"

She shook her head. "No, but I'm surprised I didn't hear of it before. The press does seem to follow you around."

She didn't purposely seek information about him, but even she could not avoid the checkout stand headlines when they blared something about the sexy Russian and his latest conquest, be it female, business or real estate.

He shrugged. "I am interesting to them because I came from nothing. If I returned to nothing, they would abandon me in a heartbeat."

He could never be nothing, this tall, enigmatic man who made her ache in ways she'd nearly forgotten.

"You've done well for yourself," she said, trying to keep the subject somewhat safe.

Except there was no safety with him.

"Yes," he said, his voice cool. "I know it must be a shock to you and your family. With enough polish, even the filthiest of mongrels can appear well-bred and sophisticated."

His words smarted. She had never thought him beneath her, though she'd let him believe that in the end. Her mother, however, had never approved of her infatuation with him. Both her parents had been nearly frantic with the thought that Caroline would not do her duty and save the stores, when Jon's parents had pushed for marriage.

She'd proved otherwise, but to this day her mother refused

to speak of Roman, though she surely knew that her grandson didn't resemble Jon Wells in the least.

"That was a long time ago," Caroline said quietly. "I'd rather not speak of it anymore."

He took a step toward her, closing the distance until she could feel the warmth emanating from his body. Her brain told her to run; her body told her to step into him. She was paralyzed with warring desires—but Roman was not.

He looped an arm around her waist casually, tugged her toward him until she was flush against his body. She shuddered with the burning memories the contact brought up. Flesh against flesh, hard against soft, heat and moisture and pleasure so intense she'd thought she would die.

"Do you wish to forget everything, Caroline? Have you forgotten this?"

His head dipped toward hers, and she closed her eyes, unable to turn away even if she'd wanted to. She didn't want to.

For one brief moment, she wanted to feel this sensation again. She wanted to feel the incredible heat of desire for a man—*this* man—burning her from the inside out. She wanted to feel like a woman one more time.

His mouth claimed hers almost savagely, his tongue sliding between her parted lips to duel with her own. Caroline's knees turned to liquid, until she was leaning into Roman and supporting herself with her hands gripping his strong arms.

He held her against him, his body responding to hers in ways that made her sigh with longing. He demanded everything in that kiss, and she gave it. She didn't know how to do anything else. Roman was the only man she'd ever burned for; shockingly, she still burned for him.

He threaded a hand in her hair and dragged her head back to give him better access. Caroline's hands slid along the opulent fabric of his tuxedo, wound around his neck, her body arching into his with abandon.

She was flung back through time to another moment, another kiss. The first time he'd ever kissed her, they'd been standing on a terrace like this one—only it had not belonged to him. It had been her family apartment on Fifth Avenue, and her parents were having a cocktail party. Roman, as her father's star employee in the accounting and marketing department, had been invited. He hadn't been a member of the upper crust, but he'd stood out in his tuxedo as if he'd been born to be there.

Caroline had never doubted his ability to fit into her world. She'd been flirting with him on and off for the last several weeks. She'd made a point to go through his department every time she'd gone to the Sullivan Group's headquarters.

That night, however, she'd seen a different side to Roman Kazarov. He'd been utterly breathtaking and totally in control. Smooth, suave, compelling. She'd known, watching him talk with one of her mother's society friends, that he was completely out of her league. She was the one who was not sophisticated enough for him.

And so she'd thrown herself at him when she'd found him alone on the terrace. To her surprise, he'd taken what she'd given. And asked for more. Their affair had been hot, passionate, and a little too out of control.

But oh, how exhilarating it had been!

Caroline tilted her hips into his, felt the overwhelming evidence of his arousal. Her knees were already liquid, but now her resolve was following into more flexible territory. Would it truly hurt to spend one more night with him? It had been so long, and she *was* lonely. That had not been a lie.

With a soft curse, Roman broke the kiss. He gripped her shoulders, held her at arm's length. His eyes were hotter than she'd yet seen them. Her stomach clenched, both in confusion and fear. A thread of disappointment wound its way through her as her limbs regained their strength.

"What is this all about, Caroline?" he demanded. "What are you trying to hide?"

CHAPTER THREE

Is the Sullivan Heiress Kazarov's Latest Squeeze?

HIS VOICE WAS harsh, hard, and she flinched from the coldness in it. A moment ago, he'd been kissing her as if nothing had ever gone wrong between them. And now he was back to hating her.

"I have no idea what you mean," she said coolly. In spite of his lethal appeal, she would not fold. She would do nothing except what she wanted to do. And she would win this battle in the end. That's all she cared about: winning.

Thank God he'd kissed her, she thought. Because now she knew she could survive it.

Roman let her go and shoved a hand through his hair. Her lips still tingled from his kiss, and her body still ached with want. It was disconcerting. She realized she was cold and turned to search for the wrap, which must have fallen when she'd gone into his arms. She found it and dragged it over her bare shoulders again, shoring up her resolve as she did so.

"You lied about your address," Roman said.

Her heart seemed to stop in her chest for the longest moment before kicking hard again. Of course he'd known she hadn't given the correct address. "I did. I admit it. But how did you know?"

"Because it is my business to know everything about the

people whose companies I intend to acquire." It was said without a trace of irony, as if it was the most ordinary thing in the world for him to know where she lived after all this time. To not only know, but to let her try and deceive him without once saying a word. It made her furious. And anxious.

"You could have said something," she told him tightly. "And saved me the trouble of continuing the lie."

"And miss this charming interlude? I think not. But tell me why you did it."

Caroline licked her lips. Ryan would be in bed by now, his little body tucked under his race car blankets. He would not come bounding out the door. Nor would he have if she'd let the driver take her home in the first place. She'd simply panicked at the thought, and look where it had gotten her. *Fool.*

She needed time to think. God knew she wasn't thinking very well at the moment. She'd been stressed and overworked these last few weeks. There was so much to do, so much to work out, if Sullivan's was to make their next loan payment to the bank. She should be at home, working on the projections before her meeting with the bank tomorrow, not sparring with this ruthless man.

Roman was watching her curiously. And she didn't kid herself that he was anything less than a threat. Under the curiosity lay a tiger waiting to pounce. One sign of weakness, one more mistake in judgment, and she would be toast.

"I lied because I was angry. I didn't want you taking me home." She sniffed. "It was quite a shock seeing you again, I admit. And then you got into the taxi with me, though you were not invited."

He looked dangerous. "That doesn't explain what happened next."

Caroline's face flamed. No, it certainly didn't explain the panic that had made her try to use the promise of sex to distract him. She lifted one shoulder in a careless shrug. Let him think the worst of her. She did not care. "It's not the first time I've thrown myself at you. Perhaps I was feeling nostalgic."

Roman snorted. "Of course. This explains everything."

"And on that note, I think I should go home now," she said, stiffening her spine and facing him with all the haughtiness she possessed. "Clearly, I made a mistake."

His eyes narrowed as he continued to study her. "*Da,* you should go." He strode past her and back inside, where he picked up her purse and handed it to her. Caroline gripped the clutch tightly, embarrassment and fury warring within her for dominance.

Once, he couldn't keep his hands off her. Once, she'd gloried in the knowledge that she could make this man burn for her. Now, he was throwing her out. Which was what she wanted, of course—and yet it pricked her pride, too. No longer was she irresistible to him.

As if to prove the point, Roman's gaze traveled insultingly slowly down her body before finding its way to her face again. "I find that, while you still have the ability to excite me, I'm not precisely moved to take you to my bed."

"What a relief," she snapped, though inside his words smarted. "Though I'm not stupid enough to presume you'll be changing your plans for Sullivan's, I am relieved to know they no longer include me in the bargain."

His laugh was low, deep, sexy, and it sent tiny waves of rebellious delight crashing through her.

"Oh, I still have plans for you, *solnyshko.* Just none for tonight."

Roman stood on the terrace once she'd gone, glass of Scotch in hand, and gazed out at the lights of Manhattan. Though he was on the top floor, he could still hear the sounds of traffic below—the screech of brakes, the sharp clarion of a siren. Somewhere in that traffic, Caroline rode toward her home in

Greenwich Village, her perfect blond hair smooth, her lipstick refreshed, her composure intact.

Nothing touched Caroline for long. He'd learned that five years ago. When she'd been in his arms, in his bed, their bodies entwined and straining together, she'd been completely and utterly his.

When they'd dressed again and he'd put her in a cab home—because she'd insisted she could not stay overnight and rouse her parents' curiosity—she'd left him completely behind, forgotten until the next time.

He, however, had lain awake thinking of her. Thinking of how he could make her his permanently. Such a fool he'd been.

Their affair had been brief, a matter of weeks only, but he'd fallen hard. And she had not fallen at all. He'd had a long time to think about why he'd done something so uncharacteristic. And what he'd decided, what he'd realized for the pitiful truth, was that she'd represented something golden and unattainable. He, Roman Kazarov, son of a violent, evil monster and a gentle woman who'd married down, before she'd realized she'd made a terrible mistake, had possessed the ultimate prize in his all-American golden girl.

He'd fallen for Caroline because she'd made him believe his circumstances didn't matter, that his worth had nothing to do with where he'd come from. And then, once he'd believed her, she'd yanked the rug out from under him.

Roman took a sip of the Scotch, let the liquid scour his throat on the way down. She'd made him forget what was most important in his life. He'd lost sight of his reason for being in America in the first place, and it had cost him dearly. His mother's last months were spent not in the lush nursing home he'd been paying for while he worked at Sullivan's, but in a run-down two-bedroom apartment where he and his brothers did their best to care for her as she slipped further and further into sickness.

He didn't blame Caroline for it; he blamed himself. Acquiring Sullivan's wouldn't bring his mother back from the grave, or change her last months of suffering, but he planned to do it anyway. To remind himself of the folly of allowing anything or anyone to come between him and his goals.

He thought of the kiss he and Caroline had shared tonight, and a tendril of heat slid through his groin. He *had* wanted her. But he'd be the one to decide where and when, not her. And it wouldn't be in his home, the way it had always been before. There'd been something about the way she would come to him, and then leave him replete in his own bed, that had made him feel the difference between their circumstances more acutely.

He'd been the hired help, the poor supplicant in the one-bedroom apartment, while she'd been the heiress breezing in and out of his life. Taking her pleasure and going back to her gilded existence. And to her proper fiancé, as he'd learned too late.

He'd known Jon Wells, though barely. He'd been a quiet man, perhaps even a bit shy. Not the kind to handle fiery Caroline. Roman remembered thinking that she'd been joking at first. Except she'd never laughed, never strayed from what she was saying.

I'm marrying Jon Wells.

But you love me, he'd said, his heart crumpling in ways he'd never thought possible.

It's been fun, Roman, but I don't love you. I never did.

He could still see her face, so wooden and haughty; still hear the words falling from her poisonous lips. Roman drained the Scotch and went back inside. There, he took out the dossier he'd had compiled on the Sullivan Group, and flipped to the section about Caroline.

There was a photo, and a brief information sheet with her statistics and address. There was also a photo of her son, Ryan Wells. Roman forced himself to study the picture, though it always made him feel edgy inside to look at the face of her child with another man.

The boy was blond, like Caroline, and his eyes were blue. Roman looked at the information sheet again. *Four years old.*

It jabbed him in the gut every time.

With a curse, he put the photos away and began to read about the Sullivan Group's latest problems with their loans. They'd taken on too much debt in an effort to staunch the flow of their losses. It wasn't working. Without an influx of cash—major cash—Sullivan's would be pushed to liquidate their assets in order to meet their obligations.

He should let it happen. He should walk away and let the place crumble into oblivion. But he couldn't. He wanted Sullivan's. He wanted every store in their possession—every cashmere sweater, every diamond, every pricey jar of caviar, every last bottle of exclusive champagne. Quite simply, he wanted it all.

But, mostly, he wanted to see the look on their aristocratic faces when he owned everything they'd once thought him not good enough for. He would be the one to destroy Sullivan's. And there would be nothing they could do to stop him.

They only needed a little more time. Just a little, and she could pull this off. Caroline sat in the conference room with her chief financial officer and waited for the financiers from Crawford International Bank to arrive. She'd come in early this morning to work on the projections, and she bit back a yawn as she refilled her coffee.

She hadn't slept well last night. No, she'd tossed and turned, thinking of that kiss with Roman. Thinking of every moment in the car with Roman, and then every moment in his apartment. It hurt to look at him. Physically hurt. He reminded her of everything she stood to lose. And everything she'd gained because of their affair five years ago.

Jon always used to tell her that everything would look

better in the morning, once she'd slept on it. At first he'd believed it, and she had, too, when they kept hoping the chemo would make a difference and save his life. Finally, she'd had to admit that the clarity of morning did nothing to erase the doubt and pain of the day before.

Oh, she never told Jon she'd stopped believing, but she suspected he had, too. Toward the end, he'd said it less and less. Caroline bent her head and swiped at a stray tear. She didn't have time to cry right now. She had to face the bank's financiers and convince them Sullivan's was on the right track to return to profitability and pay their loans. And then she had to deliver on that promise.

Easy peasy.

She waited anxiously while the clock ticked past the appointed hour. The doors didn't open and no one came to announce the arrival of anyone from the bank.

At half past the hour, the phone rang. Caroline snatched it up on the second ring.

"There's a call for you, Ms. Sullivan," her secretary said. "A Mr. Kazarov. Shall I put him through?"

Caroline's fingers flexed on the receiver. *No,* she wanted to shout. *Never!* But she knew, as surely as she knew her own name, that she had to take the call. Roman wasn't calling to discuss last night, nor was he calling to ask about her health. He was calling at precisely this moment for a reason.

A reason she dreaded.

"Rob, can you excuse me?" she said to her CFO. He nodded and rose to leave. Caroline instructed Maryanne to put the call through as she sat back in her chair and prepared for battle. She didn't know what Roman had done, or tried to do, but she wasn't accepting it lying down.

"*Dobroye Utro,* Caroline." Roman's smooth voice came over the line, and a shiver skated across her skin at the sound of the Russian vowels and consonants. Such a sexy voice, damn him. "I trust you slept well?"

"Perfectly well, thank you," she said coolly, though nothing could be further from the truth. "And you?"

"Like a baby," he said cheerfully, and she wanted to reach through the line and strangle him.

"I assume you're calling for a reason," she said irritably. "Or did you wish to ask me out on a date?"

Roman laughed, and she chided herself for the flood of warmth that dripped down her spine like hot honey. There was a time when his voice over the phone had filled her with illicit urges. She could spend hours on the phone with him then, and had. God knew what they'd found to talk about for so long.

"So impatient. This was always your problem, *solnyshko*. Haven't you ever heard that good things come to those who wait?"

"Really, Roman," she scoffed. "Have you taken to speaking in clichés now? Has your English deteriorated? Or perhaps you're just so busy gobbling up companies that you've become too lazy to be more creative."

"I have quite a creative mind, I assure you," he purred into the phone. A lightning bolt of desire shot through her. Her skin grew warm, her body tensing with a sexual ache that made her angry. It was just a voice, for God's sake!

"As fun as this is," Caroline said briskly, "you need to get to the point. I have an important meeting in five minutes."

"Actually, you don't," he said. "If you are waiting for the bankers, that is."

Fear fell over her like a heavy blanket, dousing the electricity stirring in her blood. She didn't need to ask how Roman knew about her meeting. It was clear he did know, so asking would be a waste of breath.

"I suppose you wish to tell me something," she said, cutting straight to it. "Shall I shave my head in preparation for the executioner's ax? Or did you have a slower, more painful death in mind?"

"So dramatic, Caroline," he chided her. "But that is part of your charm."

Caroline ground her teeth in frustration. "And your ruthlessness is yours," she said, so sweetly it made her teeth ache.

"Ah, you speak to me of ruthlessness? Interesting."

Caroline clicked her pen open and closed. Open and closed. "Why is that interesting? You've been traveling the globe for the past two years, collecting companies, and still you aren't satisfied. I'd call that ruthless."

"Perhaps not as ruthless as stomping on a man's heart," he said evenly. There was no hint of emotion in that voice, no warmth or coolness, and she shuddered involuntarily.

"As if you haven't made a second career of breaking women's hearts," she said, her pulse thrumming in her throat, her wrists.

"I learned from the best."

Caroline closed her eyes, willing herself to stay focused. He was trying to rattle her—and he was doing a good job. Since the moment she'd seen him last night at that party, she'd been on edge. Fear, stress, anger, regret—they all coiled together in a giant lead ball in her belly.

"Tell me what you want, Roman," she said. "Why are you calling me now, and how do you know my meeting is canceled?"

"I know because I canceled it."

Her stomach dropped into her toes. "*You* canceled it. And how did you manage that?" she asked, though she feared she had a good idea what he was about to say.

"There is no longer a need to discuss your loans with the bank, *solnyshko*."

"You bought the loans," she said, a lump forming in her throat. She'd known it was a possibility that someone could buy their debt, but her family had been dealing with Crawford International Bank for years. Her father and Leland Crawford had been golf buddies, and she'd had no reason to think he would ever consider selling the loans without first coming to them.

The last time she'd seen Leland, he'd assured her he was in their corner. He hadn't been happy with her father's sudden "retirement," though he did not know the reason behind it. No one did, other than her, her mother and Sullivan's board of directors.

And she intended to keep it that way. Her family didn't need the public scrutiny while their loved one suffered from a cruel disease that robbed him of his memory and his life. The board—some of whom had been sitting when she'd still been a little girl in a school uniform—supported her leadership. Leland knew that much, even if he didn't know the reason. That he would sell the loans without giving her a chance stunned her.

She closed her eyes and breathed deeply. What was done was done.

This was a setback, but it wasn't the end by any stretch.

"You bought the loans, but you haven't bought Sullivan's," she said fiercely. "We are not in default and you can't foreclose."

Roman laughed again, a soft chuckle that made the hairs on her arms prickle in response. "You are not in default *yet*."

Caroline gripped the phone. Hard. "We won't default. I promise you that."

"Very good, Caroline," he said. "Fight me. I like a challenge."

"Really? I would have thought you preferred your quarry to lie down and roll over before your overwhelming might."

"Oh, I like that too. But only when it's appropriate."

Caroline sucked in a breath. How did he manage to infuse such an innocuous statement with blistering sex appeal?

"I have to go now," she said tightly. "I have work to do."

"*Da*, you have much to do. And when you are finished for the day, you will join me for dinner."

"I think not," Caroline said, hot anger rising in her throat, flushing her skin with heat. "You bought the loans. You did not buy me."

"Think carefully, Caroline," he growled. "It wouldn't take much for your suppliers to cut off your line of credit. If that happens, you will surely default. And then I will own it all. You wouldn't want that, would you?"

"You would go that far?" she said bitterly. "You would interfere with our supply chain in order to win?"

"I think you already know the answer to your questions."

A moment later, the line went dead.

CHAPTER FOUR

Secret Tryst? Sullivan Heiress Spotted Entering Hotel

BLAKE MILLER THREW her a worried glance as she moved around her dressing room, searching for the right earrings to go with the pink Valentino sheath she'd chosen for the evening.

"Are you planning to tell him?" Blake asked.

Caroline yanked open a drawer and seized the pearl drop earrings she'd been looking for. She was absolutely furious. After her conversation with Roman, she'd had to change into her running gear and hit the company gym for an hour just so she would calm down.

It hadn't worked as well as she would have liked. She was worn-out, but still angry.

She'd had no intention of jumping to Roman's tune, but she'd finally realized that he had her right where he wanted her. She couldn't let him interfere with Sullivan's supply chain, not when she needed every trick at her disposal to make the loan payment on time.

She would go to dinner. But that did not mean she had to like it.

"Tell him what?" Caroline asked as she shoved one of the posts into her ear.

Blake frowned. "About Ryan."

Caroline jerked, her gaze shooting toward the door. But Ryan wasn't there, and she let out a sharp sigh.

"He's watching a cartoon with a sponge character," Blake said.

Caroline tried to smile, though she wanted to chew nails. But not because of Blake. She softened her tone. "You know very well what the name of the cartoon is. We've only had to watch it a gazillion times."

He shrugged. "I know. But I'm refusing to acknowledge I do in hopes I'll be able to forget those horrible songs."

"Good luck with that," she said. "I think they're imprinted in my memory forever."

She finished putting on her earrings and studied herself in the mirror. There were purple smudges beneath her eyes, and her cheekbones were looking a little sharp. She needed to work less and eat a little more often, but she'd been so stressed lately that sleep and eating were not her top priorities.

"Caroline." She turned toward Blake to find him watching her worriedly. "You didn't answer my question."

She closed her eyes. "I know." Then she came over and took his hands in hers. "I love you, Blake. You're the best thing that ever happened to Jon, and I love that you're a part of our lives. Without you, taking care of my little boy these days would be a lot harder."

Blake shrugged. His green eyes seemed to overflow with sadness for a moment, but then he sucked it in and gave her a smile. "I love you and Ryan, too. You've kept me sane these last months since Jon died." Blake squeezed her hands. "He wanted you to be happy, Caroline. He worried about you."

"I know."

"He regretted that he wasn't stronger when your parents insisted you marry."

"It wasn't his fault," Caroline said. "He was as trapped as I was."

She'd always suspected Jon was gay, but she hadn't really

known until he'd told her, after she'd confessed she was pregnant with another man's child. That was the moment they'd become coconspirators and partners in truth.

"But he cost you the man you loved, and he regretted that very much."

They'd talked often of what they should have done, but they'd both known they wouldn't have done anything differently. Jon's parents were ultraconservative, and they would have cut him off without a dime had he confessed his sexual orientation. They'd bought him a wife with their investment in Sullivan's, and once he was married and had a child on the way, they'd assumed everything was well and he was on the proper path.

But you couldn't buy off a cancer diagnosis.

"We both did what we had to do." She pulled in a deep breath. "And to answer your question, Jon is Ryan's father. It would be too confusing for Ryan if he suddenly had a new daddy."

"Ryan was so young when Jon died. He barely remembers him." Blake looked sad. "People often remarry after their spouse dies. Kids get new parents. I'm sure this man would understand the need to protect Ryan until he's old enough to know the truth."

Her heart was a cold lump in her chest at the idea of telling Roman he had a son after all this time. How would she do that? *Hey, Roman, about that last night we spent together before I told you I didn't want you in my life anymore...*

By the time she'd realized she was pregnant, several weeks later, Roman had disappeared from her life as if he'd never even existed. He'd left no forwarding address. She knew because she'd asked Jon to check with Human Resources.

Until two years ago, she'd had no idea what had become of him. By then it was too late to dredge up the past. She and Jon and Ryan were a family, and Roman was a man working his way through women and companies like a rocket blazing across the sky.

"I'm not marrying Roman Kazarov, Blake. Whatever we once had is dead and buried. He despises me now. And I'm not especially fond of him, either."

"He has a right to know about his child, don't you think?"

Caroline turned and grabbed her wrap. Her fingers shook as she put it around her shoulders and smoothed the fabric. "I think it's too late for that. I don't imagine he'd take the news well after all this time. And what if he tried to take Ryan away from me?" She shook her head as a wave of panic swelled inside her. "I can't risk that, Blake."

He sighed heavily. "I know, sweetie. I just wish there was a way."

"I don't think there is," she said with a touch of sadness. "He left before I knew I was pregnant. And then I married Jon. Whatever happened between us is in the past now. And it needs to stay there."

A few minutes later, the car Roman had sent for her arrived. Caroline kissed Ryan good-night, told him to be a good boy for Uncle Blake, and went out to get in the car. The air was warm tonight, but she pulled her wrap tighter and settled into the back seat of the limo. They didn't head south toward the financial district, as she'd expected, but north, toward Central Park. When the car finally stopped, it was in front of an exclusive hotel that faced the park.

Caroline went inside, expecting to find Roman waiting for her in the restaurant, but a uniformed attendant directed her to an elevator instead. She hesitated on the threshold, but then stepped inside. Whatever Roman was up to, it wasn't going to turn out the way he thought.

The elevator disgorged her at the entrance to an opulent suite. Soft music filled the area and a dining table sat near a gently flickering fire. A woman in a crisp uniform came forward and offered to take her wrap as Caroline walked into the room.

"Thank you," she murmured as she handed it over.

Roman sat at a desk nearby, a phone to his ear as he talked to someone in Russian. He didn't sound stressed. No, he laughed—and she almost hated him for it. How smug, how cool, how superior and in control.

He'd always been that way, except that he'd seemed to lose a tiny bit of that control whenever she'd walked into the room. And before long, she remembered, he'd lost the rest of it. Caroline shuddered with the memories that assailed her at that moment: hot skin, cool sheets, and the glorious perfection of his lovemaking.

Things she most definitely did *not* want to think about.

She accepted the glass of champagne someone handed her, and turned away from the man at the desk. She could see Ryan in him, and it disconcerted her. Last night, she'd been so rattled at seeing him again that she hadn't paid as much attention to the quirks of movement or the features that he'd given to his son.

Tonight, in just a few seconds of looking at him, it was all there. The slope of the nose, the blue eyes, the stray lock of hair that insisted on falling forward over his brow, and the way he raked it back again with an impatient hand. Her heart felt like a lead weight in her chest. She'd never thought to see Roman again when he'd left five years ago, and now he was here.

But what was she supposed to do? Confess everything to him and put her child in jeopardy? Would Roman try to take Ryan away from her? Or would he reject his son? Oddly, the thought of him rejecting her precious little boy was somehow worse than the thought of him wanting to take Ryan away.

Roman ended the call and stood, all lethal grace and sexiness in his dark trousers and deep crimson shirt. A suit jacket was slung over the back of a chair, a tie loosened and lying on top of it. He looked so graceful and cool under pressure, and she resented him for it. He had no idea what a maelstrom of emotion he was stirring up in her life. And, she suspected, he wouldn't care if he did.

No, strike that. He would care. He would congratulate himself on it.

"I am happy you could make it," he said in way of greeting.

Caroline stood tall in her platform pumps and cocked a hip as if she were bored. "I don't believe you gave me a choice," she said. "So here I am."

His eyes slid over her. "Yes, here you are."

His gaze felt like a caress, a sensual stroking of her nerves, and she took another sip of champagne to mask her discomfort. "Having your apartment fumigated?" she asked, glancing around the hotel suite with cool disdain.

Roman laughed. "Not at all." He took a glass of champagne from the waiter standing nearby with a tray, and held it high, studying the pale liquid, before taking a sip. "I don't entertain women in my home, sorry to say."

Icy blue eyes speared her with a coldness that made her shiver inside.

"How fascinating," she replied, maintaining her bored tone, though she was anything but. No, her heart thrummed and her skin prickled with heat beneath her dress. She only hoped that little beads of sweat weren't glistening across her brow.

"Yes, and it's all due to you, I might add."

She nearly choked on the champagne. "Me?"

He turned and flicked a hand toward one of the servers. The team melted away, disappearing through a door and leaving them alone in the room.

When Roman turned back to her, his eyes were a curious mixture of heat and coolness—and hatred. Caroline darted her tongue over her lower lip.

"I prefer to keep my affairs away from home these days," he said. "Her bed, her apartment, a hotel. You taught me that."

Caroline swallowed as she thought of all the times they'd made love in his bed, only for her to leave him at the end of it and go back home again. She'd been afraid of what her parents would think if she didn't come home. She'd annoyed him more than once with her refusal to spend the night. She'd hated leaving, but it had been necessary.

"I'm glad I was good for something then," she said evenly. What else could she say?

"You were good for a few things. You could be again."

"I won't be your mistress, Roman," she said firmly, refusing to pretend she didn't know what he was talking about. What he was insinuating.

"Really? Last night, as I recall, you practically begged me to take you to my bed."

Yes, she had. And though it had started out as an act, by the end of the night, when he'd kissed her on the terrace, she'd almost been ready to beg him for real.

"A mistake," she said. "One I won't be repeating."

Roman laughed again, and she found that the sound scraped over her nerve endings and left her trembling.

"This is far more interesting than I'd expected it would be," he said, as he came over and took her arm. Her entire body became attuned to that one spot that he touched, sizzling and aching and wanting more than she'd dared to want in five long years.

How could she be thinking like this when he was a threat to her? When she was absolutely furious with him?

She pulled her arm from his grasp and stepped out of his reach. He merely smiled and swept out his hand with a flourish, pointing to the table. "After you then."

Caroline went over and yanked out a chair. But Roman was there, ever the gentleman, pushing the chair in for her as she sat. Then he took a seat on the opposite side.

As if they had some kind of radar tuned to Roman, the waitstaff returned at that moment and served dinner, before disappearing again. There was red wine, rack of lamb, delicate new potatoes tossed in cream and butter, and grilled summer squash.

"Eat, Caroline," Roman said, as she hesitated to pick up her fork.

Her stomach was so twisted into knots that she wasn't sure she would be able to eat a bite, but after she tasted the first forkful, she nearly moaned with pleasure as the flavors exploded on her tongue. With the current state of affairs at Sullivan's, she'd been eating on the run for weeks—salads, half sandwiches, the occasional slice of pizza. A real meal, eaten leisurely, was heaven.

Or would be if she had a different dinner companion.

She looked up to find Roman watching her. She dropped the fork as if she'd been caught doing something she shouldn't, and glared at him.

He grinned. "We won't talk business yet," he said. "Enjoy the meal."

"It's fine," she told him, leaning back and crossing her arms over her chest. "Why waste time? The sooner we talk, the sooner I can go."

He lifted his wineglass and took a long sip before setting it down again. "You look as if you've done nothing but business for months. Eating is a pleasure, Caroline. It should be enjoyed, savored. Business will wait."

He cut into his food. She waited for him to say something else, but when he didn't, when he ate as if he was sitting there alone, she picked up the fork and took another bite of lamb. It was absolutely delicious—rosemary, thyme, salt, a hint of garlic, and the fresh flavor of the meat combined into the perfect sensory experience.

Yes, eating was a pleasure. Jon had been a great cook, so good that they'd never hired a chef until he'd gotten ill and needed specialized care. Even now she employed a personal chef, but mostly to feed Ryan something other than takeout. She often ate on the run, while multitasking, and couldn't remember the last time she'd sat down and enjoyed a meal simply for the food alone.

Her free time was spent with Ryan, not savoring meals.

"I don't see how you've managed to create an empire if you stop for leisurely meals three times a day," she said after a long silence. There was sarcasm in her tone, certainly—but also envy.

"Don't forget sex," he told her, his blue eyes suddenly sharp on hers. "I stopped for that, too."

A dull pain rolled through her at the thought of Roman with other women. *Ridiculous.* She knew he'd not been celibate over the last few years. There wasn't a tabloid alive that hadn't detailed his exploits with the various models, actresses, beauty queens and heiresses he dated.

"You are a man of many talents," she said, lifting her wineglass high. "I salute you."

He watched her drink, his gaze following the slide of her throat as she swallowed. A flood of heat rushed through her system, but whether it was due to the alcohol or him she wasn't quite certain.

"Does it make you feel good?" he asked, leaning back in his chair and studying her like a specimen under a microscope.

Caroline blinked. "What? The wine?"

"No. The rebellion."

She lifted her chin. "I have no idea what you're talking about. Rebellion? Against whom?" She laughed as she shook her head. "You are nothing to me, Roman. Why would I need to rebel against you? In fact, I find the entire notion insulting. I don't need your permission—or your approval—to be exactly who I am."

"How did Jon Wells ever handle you?" he murmured.

Ice crackled through her system then. "Do not speak of Jon," she said, her voice hard. "He has nothing to do with this."

Roman's gaze sharpened as he watched her. "You loved him."

"Of course I loved him! I married him, didn't I?" She didn't know why she said that last. It hadn't been necessary, or even a real reason for her marriage to Jon. Not that Roman knew that. The fire in his eyes banked momentarily before flaring again, fueled by fury and loathing.

Was this really how she wanted to deal with the man who owned her loans? Was it necessary to antagonize him, when he already had so many reasons to despise her?

Caroline folded her arms and willed her temper to subside. "Why are we sitting here pretending to have a civilized conversation, when we both know it's impossible?"

Roman looked so cool it irritated her. "Like it or not, *solnyshko,* I own your loans."

"And what dirty trick did you have to perform to get Leland to sell them to you, I wonder."

Roman's eyes glittered. "You are terribly reckless, aren't you?"

"I don't like to be controlled."

He laughed, the sound soft and somewhat menacing. "Is this how you would behave with Leland Crawford? Or any other bank manager who controlled your debt? Would you accuse them of trickery or be so openly hostile?"

"Leland wouldn't ask about my relationship with my husband," she retorted. "Nor would he imply I needed to sleep with him in order to save Sullivan's."

Roman looked utterly dangerous in that moment. "I've never implied that sleeping with me would save your precious stores. I said I wanted them. And you. That is not quite the same thing, is it?"

CHAPTER FIVE

Where Is Frank Sullivan? While Rome Burns,
He's Nowhere to Be Seen

HER PRETTY EYES went wide, but she lowered her lashes, hiding them from him before Roman could discern her thoughts. Oh, he knew she was angry. And frustrated. Perhaps it wasn't very nice of him, but he enjoyed it.

Since last night, when he'd kissed her, he hadn't been able to stop thinking about before, about all the nights when she'd burned up in his arms. She might be trying so hard to be an ice queen now, but he knew what lay under that cool facade. Heat, fire, incineration.

It angered him to be thinking this way about her, after everything she'd cost him, but perhaps it was poetic justice. This time, he would be the one to take—and the one to walk away unscathed. The more he thought about it, the more he liked the idea.

"I have a son," she said, her voice firm. "And as much fun as it is to play this game with you, I have to think of him first. I'm not going to be your mistress, Roman. Not for any price."

"Is that so?" He liked her fire, her defiance.

Her cheeks flushed as she stared at him. "If you were a decent man, you wouldn't even think such a thing."

He laughed. "I never said I was decent, Caroline." He

leaned forward then, spearing her with a glare. "But I am honest, which is more than you have ever been, *da?*"

She dropped her gaze for the barest of moments, her throat working. And then she was staring at him again, her chin up, her eyes flashing. "I can't change your opinion of me. I'm not going to try."

"That would be a fruitless endeavor," he said coolly. "Especially since you are not being honest now, either."

She looked as if he'd slapped her. Her mouth fell open as she drew back in her chair. She wrapped her fingers around the strand of pearls at her neck and worked them back and forth for several moments before she seemed to realize what she was doing. She dropped her hand to her lap and kept it there, her ice queen demeanor a bit tattered around the edges now.

"I have no idea what you're talking about," she said haughtily.

Her superiority made him want to lash out. "Regardless of what lies you tell yourself, you wanted me last night. Had I not been the one to put a halt to it, you would have begged me to make love to you."

Was that relief he saw in her eyes? Guilt? It was gone far too quickly for him to be sure. "You are much too full of yourself, Roman. I had a moment of weakness, but it wouldn't have gone anywhere."

"Shall we test this theory again?" he growled, a sharp feeling clawing through him. Not for the first time, the feeling she was hiding something prickled to life inside him.

Her eyes flashed. "Is this how you would treat any of the other business colleagues you invite for dinner?" She leaned forward suddenly, her expression fierce. "Would you try to force any other rival to sleep with you, or I am a special case?"

He'd forgotten how passionate she could be when anger

brightened her features. It made the ache in his groin sharper than ever. "I've never said I would force you, Caroline."

She blinked, her righteous indignation stonewalled for the barest moment. "Haven't you?"

He took a sip of wine, enjoyed the rich complexity of the rare vintage as it went down. He loved being able to afford whatever he wanted. He'd grown up with nothing, less than nothing, and he'd watched his parents fight over every little thing. He and his brothers had run wild, stealing food and clothing, fighting with other kids for recreation. Nothing had been easy in his life. Nothing had been handed to him on a silver platter the way it had been to her.

He'd never despised her for it. What he'd despised her for was making him feel, once more, like the son of a violent brute who could barely spell his own name, much less count the coins in his pocket.

When Roman had lost his work visa, he'd lost everything.

And he'd failed his mother, in the same way his father had done when he'd drunk his paycheck every week. There was never enough food, never enough money to pay the bills, yet she'd worked tirelessly to make sure her sons had what they needed. Roman thought of her wasting away in that tiny bed in the grungy apartment he'd had to move her to, and felt like breaking something.

"You have it wrong, Caroline," he told her matter-of-factly, shoving the boiling emotions—the frustration, horror and rage—down deep. "I want you, this is true. But it will be you who comes to me. You who cannot deny the passion still between us."

She made a choking sound. "You are beyond arrogant," she finally managed to say. "And if you expect me to fall into your bed simply because you exist, then you *are* deluded."

He shrugged with a casualness he did not feel. "Nevertheless, it is what will happen."

Because, in spite of her protests, she wanted him. He'd

known that from the moment he'd first touched her last night. And even if he hadn't been so attuned to a woman's signals, he could hardly have gotten it wrong when they'd kissed on the terrace.

That had been the kiss of a woman who *needed*.

Her eyes narrowed. "I'm going to enjoy this," she said, her voice hovering on the edge of ferocity. "Because I will never do what you expect me to do, Roman. You've placed your bet on the wrong pony this time."

He merely took another sip of wine. He did it because it infuriated her. "So you say, *solnyshko*. And yet, we will see…."

She dropped her gaze from his, and he knew she was working on her temper. Working to make sense of everything that had happened between them thus far. When she lifted her head again, he could see the determination there. The fire and grit.

He rather enjoyed the sharper edge to her personality. If she'd rolled over, if she'd cried and begged him to be merciful, he'd have had a harder time goading her.

She picked up her wineglass and took a delicate sip. "I suppose you'll want to discuss the projections," she said, as if the last several minutes of conversation had never happened. "We have exciting things planned at Sullivan's this quarter, and we'll make our next payment on time, I assure you."

"And what does your father think?"

She blinked at him. "My father is retired. He has no opinion about what's going on at Sullivan's."

Roman didn't believe her. Frank Sullivan might have retired and left Caroline in charge of the day-to-day operations of the company, but he was not the sort of man to fade into the background. That wasn't like the Frank Sullivan that Roman remembered. That man had been brilliant. And ruthless once his mind was made up.

"Surely he remains in an advisory capacity," Roman said.

"Your business is with me," Caroline replied firmly. "I

am the CEO of the Sullivan Group. My father is enjoying his retirement."

"And what will he say when Sullivan's defaults?"

Her eyes were hard. "We won't default."

Roman shrugged. "I think you will. I've put a lot of money into my research. I don't think it will be contradicted."

"Then why did you take the risk?" she demanded. "Why buy our loans when we won't make the payment? It will cost you a lot of money."

Roman leaned back in his chair. This was the part he loved. The part where he faced an adversary and let them know exactly how vulnerable they were. "I have a lot of money," he said smoothly, shrugging. "I can afford to lose some of it in order to get what I want. Besides, once you default, I will get my money back. Do you wish to know how?"

She looked fierce. Defiant. "Does it matter? You want to tell me, and I'm unlikely to run through the door before you can. Go ahead, say what you so desperately want to say."

He laughed. "I would hardly describe it as desperate. It is merely the truth, and whether you hear it now or later, you will hear it." He picked up his glass and studied the way the wine coated the fine crystal as he swirled it. A good vintage. "I'm going to sell Sullivan's, Caroline. Piece by piece."

Her color flared, but the only betrayal of her mood was the movement of her throat as she swallowed. "And how do you propose to do that? I don't think many companies are in a buying mood for department stores these days."

"Because you've tried to sell, haven't you?" She looked surprised, but he continued before she could speak. "Of course you have. Don't deny it. Just the more unprofitable stores, of course. And no one wanted them. But you were not looking in the right place. Nor were you considering how much the buildings or fixtures would bring if you were to liquidate all of the stores."

She blinked. "Liquidate? Sell the assets?" Her skin seemed

to pale in the firelight. "You'll take a loss. In today's real estate market, the property losses alone could be very high."

He shrugged. "Perhaps. And perhaps not. Regardless, I will make money in the end."

Her jaw tightened. "And that's what matters most, right?"

"But of course. What else is there?"

"Tradition," she said softly. "Family."

He snorted. "Sentimentality is not what will get you through this, Caroline. You have to be hard, ruthless, willing to do whatever it takes."

"Like you, right?" Her eyes glittered as she stared at him.

"Don't fool yourself, *solnyshko*. We are all ruthless when survival is at stake. Even you."

"I have a son, Roman. Sullivan's will be his one day. I intend to make that happen."

"Then you will have to be extremely ruthless to make it so, won't you?"

"I suppose I will." She said it like a vow, and Roman's blood thrilled to the challenge in her voice.

He raised his glass. "May the best man win."

"Or woman," she said, lifting her glass and clinking it against his.

Soon after, the waitstaff cleared the table and poured coffee. Caroline didn't look at him as she spooned sugar into her coffee and stirred. He could tell by her color that her temper was still high.

Her hair gleamed golden in the soft light from the fireplace, and the pearls at her ears bobbed delicately as she moved her head. He had a sudden urge to go to her side and pull the pins from her hair. He remembered it cascading over his hands like liquid gold, the light picking out strands that gleamed like fire as it fell through his fingers.

Someone set a plate in front of him, but he didn't look at it. Instead, he watched her. Her chin snapped up and their gazes caught.

"Blueberry cheesecake from Junior's," she said. "Was that on purpose?"

His groin ached. "It was your favorite, as I recall."

"I—" She swallowed, suddenly at a loss for words, and he knew she was remembering the same thing he was. The two of them sitting in bed, eating cheesecake from the box with one fork—and then she'd dipped her finger into the blueberry sauce and smeared it over his nipple.

The cake got ruined after that, along with his sheets, but he hadn't cared.

"You're an evil man, Roman Kazarov," she said, her voice hardening again. "You want me to remember what it was like between us. You want me to want it again."

Roman smiled coolly. "I never said I fight fair, *solnyshko.*"

No, he did not fight fair. Caroline sat at her desk the next day with the newspaper spread before her and wanted to strangle him.

Love Nest? Sullivan Heiress Spends Cozy Evening with Kazarov

There was a photo of her entering the building, and a speculative piece on what she and Roman had been up to for three hours, followed by a photo of her leaving. My God, they'd watched her go in and then they'd sat there until she'd left again.

And she'd bet every last share she owned in Sullivan's that Roman had known it would happen. Why else demand a private dinner? She was no stranger to media attention, but her life had been so sedate lately. Not only that, but she was perhaps also still experiencing a honeymoon period after Jon's death. So long as she was the grieving widow, she wasn't interesting to them.

Drop in a virile, handsome, notorious man, and she was suddenly newsworthy again.

Caroline crumpled the paper and dropped it in the trash.

She had a business to run and she wasn't about to let Roman interfere with that. No matter that he was too sexy for words, or that he fed her cheesecake with the sole aim of reminding her of that decadent night they'd once shared. As if she could have ever forgotten. No, she hadn't forgotten, but she'd been determined to pretend she had.

She'd failed spectacularly. Even now, she could see Roman lying against white sheets, his body smeared in blueberry sauce and cheesecake, his manhood rising up proudly while she bent to take him in her mouth and—

Her cell phone rang. She checked the display and then snatched it up, fury—and heat, damn him—pumping into her veins at the sight of his name.

"You think this is amusing, don't you?" she demanded without preamble.

"Hello to you as well," he said, his sexy voice strumming across her taut nerves like silk. "And you cannot allow them to get to you. Ignore it."

"How do you know what I'm talking about?" she demanded, suspicious that he didn't even ask what she meant.

"I have lived closely with the press for the past two years. There will always be stories, Caroline. The trick is not to care."

"Easy for you to say," she said. "And I've lived with them practically my whole life, except they didn't often find the need to humiliate me in their pages."

"Then you have been lucky."

"I get the feeling that's changed," she grumbled. "No thanks to you."

She focused on the computer screen in front of her, a spreadsheet and graphs showing the impossible figure she needed to generate in order to make the next loan payment, in two weeks' time. She'd been so positive she could do it, but now, with Roman in possession of the debt, she wasn't so sure. And that made her feel waspish.

"To what do I owe this unexpected pleasure?" she snapped, turning her chair from the depressing figures and facing the expansive Central Park view instead. It was sunny today, gorgeous, and she wished she was out in it, lying in the grass in the park with Ryan and Blake and a picnic blanket.

"So diplomatic, Caroline," Roman chided, whipping her back to reality with a thud. "When what you really want to do is tell me to go to hell."

"This is a professional relationship. Besides, as much as I'd like to say it, it won't do me any good. You'll still be here, digging into me like a very large and annoying thorn in my side."

He chuckled, and she found herself suppressing the sudden urge to smile. Ridiculous. There was nothing about Roman Kazarov that could make her smile.

"I intend to take a tour of your stores. I want you to accompany me."

He spoke as if it was the most normal thing in the world to say. Her heart tumbled to her toes before beginning to throb. "I can't leave New York, Roman."

He made a noise that sounded like a snort of derision. "You need to. If you narrow your focus to one store, or to a handful of stores in the metropolitan area, how will you correct what is wrong in the others? New York will not carry you, no matter what you believe."

"I know that," she said stiffly. "But I can't just take off. I have a child."

"He has a nanny, I presume?"

She thought of Blake, who had been her de facto nanny since Jon had died. They'd had a girl from Europe, but she'd left them shortly after Jon's death. Blake had seemed the natural replacement. He was an artist by trade, but he hadn't worked on anything in a very long time.

"Yes, but I won't leave my child for days on end just to gratify your urge to make me squirm."

There was silence on the other end for a long moment.

"Then bring him and the nanny along. You are a woman of means, Caroline. You can do this."

Yes, she could. But she didn't want to. She could think of nothing more terrifying than Roman and Ryan in the same room together. "You don't need *me*. I'll send someone with you."

He said something in Russian. His tone suggested it wasn't polite.

And then his voice came over the line again, hard and cool and oh so commanding in crisply accented English. "This is not a request, Caroline. You will go. I will send a car for you and the boy at five."

"I most certainly will *not*," she said, her heart hot with anger—and fear, she had to admit. Fear for her son. Fear for herself. It was a disaster waiting to happen. "As I've already told you, you bought the loans, not me. I'll send my CFO."

"Send your CFO and watch your supply lines begin to dry up."

"You're a heartless bastard," she replied, turning back to her spreadsheets. Her heart sank just a little bit more at what was written there.

She thought he chuckled softly. "Then we understand one another perfectly, don't we?"

CHAPTER SIX

*"I Can't Resist Him," Caro Says as Kazarov Whisks Her
Away for Romantic Weekend*

CAROLINE BOARDED THE Kazarov jet at precisely a quarter to
six. She'd sat in her chair after he'd hung up on her and considered her options. Oh, she'd been tempted to stay in New
York, regardless of what he said.

In the end, she'd decided to be ready when the car arrived,
no matter how furious she was with the autocratic man who'd
sent it. She wanted to save Sullivan's, so she had to make
tough decisions. Do tough things.

Just like always.

Blake and Ryan followed her onto the jet. Roman was
waiting for them in the main cabin. He gave only the slightest start at the sight of her nanny. But then he subsided back
into the smooth, suave man she knew him to be. Nothing
rattled Roman. Not for long anyway. And a male nanny was
not about to faze him, no matter that it probably wasn't what
he'd expected.

Ryan hugged Blake tight, his blue eyes wide as he took in
the gleaming interior of the corporate jet. Caroline's heart
was in her throat as Roman looked at her child for the first
time. *Their* child. She'd hoped Ryan would be asleep when

they arrived, and that Blake could carry him into another compartment and keep him there.

But her son had been wide-awake and asking a million questions. The questions had only subsided only when they'd left the car and stepped onto the tarmac. His eyes grew wider as Roman stood, and then Ryan turned his head and buried his face against Blake's shoulder. Caroline put her hand on his back and rubbed.

"It's okay, sweetie. Mr. Kazarov is a friend of Mommy's."

Hardly, but what else could she say?

"You can take him into that cabin back there," Roman said to Blake, his tone clipped. He refused to look at her and Ryan.

Blake's gaze strayed to hers, and she nodded. Once they were gone, she whirled on Roman.

"Do *not* treat Blake as if he's just the hired help. Ryan and I consider him family. Jon did, too."

Roman's eyes were hot. He looked…uncomfortable. It surprised her to see him so tense, but he quickly hid it beneath his polished demeanor.

"I apologize," he said smoothly. "I'm not accustomed to children."

She didn't quite know what to say to that. She hadn't expected such an admission. Or an apology. Which did not make him more reasonable, she reminded herself.

"This was your idea," she told him tightly. "You could have avoided the problem if you'd not insisted I accompany you."

"I am aware of it." He sat down in a plush leather club chair and resumed work on his computer. She stood there, fuming. He'd upended her life in the space of a couple of days—and then made her scramble today as she'd readied her family to travel—and he showed absolutely no remorse for it.

"Have a seat, Caroline," he said, without looking up. "We'll be airborne soon."

She stood her ground. "Where are we going?"

"Los Angeles." He looked up, studied her. "You object?"

"That store is doing well," she said. "I'd have expected you'd want to see one of the underperforming locations first."

"If things are going well in L.A., then perhaps you could determine which lessons might be applied to your other stores."

"You don't want to help me fix things, Roman. So why are we doing this?" She flung herself into a chair and crossed her legs. His gaze strayed over her bare calves, and she found herself leaning toward him, as if she wanted to encourage him.

She leaned back again, deliberately, and folded her arms. What was the matter with her?

His gaze met hers. "This is where you are wrong, *solnyshko*. I bought your debt, and therefore I am concerned about the company's welfare. If you lose money, I lose money."

"Rather defeats the purpose of taking us over, doesn't it? If we default on the loan, it's yours. If we pay up, you have nothing."

"Oh, I don't expect you to pay up. But I do expect to know where the profit is, and how I can turn things to my advantage once you default. I refuse to lose money, Caroline. It's not smart business to lose money."

No, it wasn't smart business. And Sullivan's had been losing money since her father had started to lose his sense of self. She'd done her best to turn things around, but she'd been at the helm for only six months. It took time. Time she didn't have.

She thought of her father and wanted to howl. The loss of his memory had been so subtle at first that they hadn't even recognized it. Forgetting which direction to turn when he left the building. Forgetting where his favorite café was located. Putting his keys in the refrigerator instead of in the bowl by the door.

But then one day he'd left the Fifth Avenue apartment for work—and been found wandering around Central Park hours later, disheveled and confused. He'd recognized her mother, but not her. Not at first, anyway.

"And here I thought you were going to sell it off piece by piece," she said, drawling out the words. "Do make up your mind, Roman."

His smile was as friendly as a hungry lion's. "I still need to know where the money is, darling," he said, his tone as condescending as her mother's after an evening spent hobnobbing at one of her society friends' art auctions.

Really, Caroline, the things that people will buy these days and hang on their walls. Appalling.

Caroline folded her arms and turned to stare out the window as the plane began to roll toward the runway. Within a few minutes, they were airborne, and she opened up her computer to get some work done. She'd just pulled up a spreadsheet when Ryan came bounding into the cabin. Blake was hot on his heels, looking exasperated and a little harried.

"Mommy, Mommy," Ryan cried.

"What is it, baby?" Caroline said, pushing her computer aside and wrapping her arms around her son as he hurled himself headlong into her.

"Sorry," Blake said. "He got away from me."

"It's fine," Caroline replied, hugging Ryan tight. She glanced over at Roman. He'd gone very still as he watched her and Ryan, and her heart climbed to dizzying heights. Would he see what she saw every time she looked at her son? What Blake saw, if the way his gaze kept moving between the boy and the man was any indication?

Caroline breathed in the sweet scent of her child and squeezed him to her. "What did you want, sweetheart?"

He bounced excitedly. "Are we going to see Grandma and Grandpa in Florida?"

Her stomach squeezed into a tight ball. Jon's parents. Oh, God. They weren't exactly on speaking terms anymore, but Ryan hadn't forgotten them. Jon had confessed on his death-bed that Ryan wasn't his. He'd insisted he had to tell the truth, and she'd understood.

Richard and Elaine hadn't taken the news very well, to say the least. They'd cut off all contact shortly after Jon died. Thankfully, they'd given their interest in Sullivan's to Jon long before then.

"No, sweetie, not this time. We're going to California with Mr. Kazarov."

Ryan turned wide eyes on Roman, as if just realizing he was there. Then he stuck his thumb in his mouth. It was a habit he was getting too old for, but she didn't correct him this time. Everything about this trip was disconcerting to him, so why add another layer of stress?

"Say hello to Mr. Kazarov," Caroline said. "This is his plane we're riding on."

"Hello," Ryan whispered, before turning his head into her shoulder again.

"Hello...Ryan," Roman said, his voice sounding tighter than she'd yet heard it.

Ryan turned to stare at Roman. This time, his blue eyes were intent, his brow wrinkled as he studied the man who'd fathered him. It took everything Caroline had not to fall apart then and there.

"Mommy, he talks funny," Ryan said in a whisper that was not a whisper.

"Mr. Kazarov is from Russia. It's a big country very far away. And I bet he thinks *we* are the ones who talk funny."

Ryan looked puzzled, as if he hadn't quite considered that possibility before. "Can your plane fly to Russia?" he asked.

Roman looked like a man who wanted to be anywhere but here. He was clearly out of his comfort zone, and Caroline started to intervene. But just like that, something shifted in his expression and he was suddenly back in his element again.

"It can," he said. "I have done this many times."

"Can we go to Russia?"

"Someday, perhaps," Roman said. "But not today."

"Maybe we can go see Grandma and Grandpa, too."

"Yes, perhaps."

"Sweetie," Caroline interjected. "Why don't you go with Blake and play with the toys we brought?"

"Will you come play, too?" he asked, his eyes so serious.

Guilt was a hot sting in her heart. She'd been so busy lately, and while Ryan had Blake, Blake was not a substitute for her. "Of course I will. But give me a few minutes to talk to Mr. Kazarov first, okay?"

Ryan nodded and then turned and blazed past Blake, on his way back to the other cabin. Once he and Blake were gone, Caroline looked over at Roman. He was watching her this time, his eyes steady and burning.

"I'm sorry," she said. "He's only four, and more than a little energetic."

Roman shrugged as if it were nothing. "This is to be expected." He paused a moment before speaking again. "He looks like you."

And you, she thought. God help her. But if she'd been worried he would see Ryan and know the truth, she'd just been proved wrong.

"He has his father's eyes," she said softly. Roman's expression hardened, and she felt as if her heart would burst. At that moment, the naked truth punched her with a force she couldn't ignore.

He deserves to know.

He had a *right* to know. And yet how would she tell him? She swallowed. "I'm sorry if he disturbed you just now."

"It's fine." Roman turned back to his computer and tapped a key. Then he was still for a long moment. "I'm not good with kids. I don't know what to say to them, or what they need."

Her throat ached. "They aren't that difficult to understand. Sometimes, it doesn't matter what you say, so long as you simply talk to them. You were a kid once, so think of that."

He swiveled toward her again, and she had to keep herself from recoiling at the look in his eyes. They were flat, dead of emotion. It stunned her, made her want to reach for him and ask him what had happened to put that kind of look on his face.

She did not. Instead, she clasped her hands together and willed herself not to move.

"My childhood was nothing to draw from in terms of how to treat children, believe me. My father was a drunk and a brute. We learned to stay hidden if we wanted to survive."

"Roman," she said, her eyes prickling with sudden tears. "I'm so sorry. No child deserves that."

His gaze was hard, bleak. She wondered what else he might say. Instead, he waved a hand in dismissal, as if he hadn't just said something devastating.

"Go, Caroline. Play with your son. Leave me to work in peace."

A car waited at the airport to take them straight to the Beverly Hills Hotel, where Roman had rented one of the presidential bungalows. It was a sumptuous space, with three bedrooms, a private pool and courtyard, a kitchen, and even an outdoor treadmill and shower. The bungalows were private, sequestered from the hotel in areas where other guests were not allowed. There were gardens, tropical plants and lush greenery that hid the bungalow from prying eyes. It was like having a home in the middle of L.A.

After making sure Blake and Ryan were settled for the evening, Roman insisted they go to Sullivan's now, incognito. It was late, but with the time change from New York, the store was still open for another hour. Caroline dressed in a pair of jeans and a silk tank top before putting on a dark blazer and jeweled gladiator sandals.

She met Roman in the great room, her breath catching at the sight of him in jeans and a dark T-shirt. He looked younger, more carefree, and her heart ached for the man she'd once loved. He used to make her laugh, she remembered. He was serious, but he was funny, too.

She hadn't once seen his funny side since he'd returned. It surprised her how much she longed for it. And how much she still ached over his revelation on the plane. She hadn't been able to stop thinking about him as a small child, cowering from the man who should have loved him instead of frightening him.

They took a rented sports car and drove down Sunset Boulevard. Traffic wasn't thick at this time of the evening, fortunately, though it was still somewhat heavy, and they arrived at the mall where Sullivan's was located in good time. Roman left the car with valet parking and they walked into the store together, a pair of anonymous shoppers on an evening outing.

The store was packed with people even at this hour, and Caroline felt a swell of something approximating pride and relief wash over her. Everything looked crisp and perfect. The salespeople were busy and efficient, and the store oozed the kind of upscale comfort Sullivan's was known for.

Roman went over and stood by the center railing, looking up and down the four levels of the store. People packed the escalators, carrying packages and bags, laughing and talking. It reminded her of everything she loved best about Sullivan's. She hadn't spent much time on the floor lately, because she was always in her office worrying over the figures, but she realized, standing here, that she needed to get into the stores more often.

They were in her blood, and it made her feel more alive than she had in a while to stand here and simply breathe in the atmosphere of happy shoppers and a thriving store.

"Let's go to the food shop," she said suddenly, feeling as if she was twelve again and her mother had told her she could have a treat. "I want something chocolate and scrumptious."

Roman didn't object, following as she led the way down

the escalator to the lowest level. The food area was full of
shoppers standing at the counters, purchasing the specialty
cheeses, the salads, the meat and fish and lobsters, and the
various delicacies Sullivan's was known for. The chocolate
counter was mobbed, but Caroline was determined. Finally,
she managed get to the front and order some truffles. The
staff moved efficiently, and though there was a small bit of
grumbling here and there, everyone got served in good time.

She and Roman cut through the crowd and made their
way back to the escalators. Caroline dug into the signature
gold-and-black bag and popped a truffle into her mouth as
they stepped onto the escalator to the men's department. "Oh
God, that's good," she said, her eyes closing as she chewed.

"Is it blueberry flavored?" he asked, and she snapped her
eyes open to find him staring at her.

"No," she said, swallowing. Then she held the bag out.
"Do you want to try?"

He reached in and took a piece, sliding it between his lips
and chewing oh so slowly. She couldn't seem to tear her gaze
from his mouth, from the lips that had once kissed every
inch of her body and brought her such unbelievable pleasure.

"I like it better when you feed it to me," he said, his voice
silky and hot all at once. "Like the blueberries."

She dropped her gaze away from his, suddenly self-con-
scious. It seemed as if the noise and commotion around them
had disappeared, as if it was suddenly just the two of them
alone in the middle of the vast store. "I liked that, too."

Oh God, had she really just said that? It wasn't what she'd
meant to say at all. She'd intended to say something along
the lines of how the past was the past, no matter how much
she'd enjoyed it. But with that one utterance, she'd proved he
was right when he'd said she still wanted him.

She did, but she wasn't sure how she felt about it. He was
both the instrument of her destruction and the instrument of
her greatest happiness.

She should be furious with him. Furious over his arrogance and autocratic ways. Furious over his threats to her business.

But right now, she couldn't seem to summon much fury. No, she remembered him on the plane, his expression stark as he'd told her in a few words that his childhood had been anything but happy.

She wanted to know that man, the one who ached. The one who was still human. The one she'd once loved.

He lifted his hand and pushed her hair away from her face, tucking it behind her ear. Her entire body focused on that one point of contact, as if lightning had been concentrated in his fingertips. Her blood hummed, her veins swelled and the very air around her seemed charged with electricity.

"Feed me the next piece," he told her, his eyes hot and bright. She hesitated but a moment, her heart thrumming a steady beat that threatened to make her dizzy. Then she dipped her fingers into the bag, withdrew a single piece of chocolate and pressed it between his lips, her fingers sliding into his mouth, over the silky heat of his tongue.

He sucked the chocolate from her fingers, his hot eyes never leaving hers. He'd moved closer to her—or she to him—until she could feel the heat of his body burning into her, though they did not touch anywhere else.

They reached the top of the escalator and she broke apart from him guiltily. Roman, however, took her hand and led her through the men's department to the dressing rooms. There was no one standing nearby, so he dragged her straight into the nearest one and closed the door.

The dressing room was big, but not too big, and the lighting was soft. There were mirrors on three walls, and she backed toward one, holding the bag of chocolate held against her chest. Roman grinned, his eyes bright, and she sucked in a breath as he advanced on her.

"What are you doing?" she squeaked.

"You know what I'm doing, Caroline. And you want me to do it."

Oh, she did. She definitely did.

Her nipples felt tight, and her breath shortened in her chest. Worse, her feminine core throbbed with the ache of sexual arousal. Her body didn't seem to realize there was too much water under the bridge, too much time and hurt between them. And her brain was beginning to think it didn't matter.

Roman backed her against a mirrored wall, one hand on either side of her head, creating a cage from which she knew she could escape if she wanted to.

She didn't want to.

"Do you have any idea how I've longed for this?" he said in a growl, his head so close to hers, his lips firm and sensual as he spoke.

She tilted her head back until it rested on the wall. Her mouth was near his. So near. "Tell me," she said breathlessly.

"You wish to talk?" he asked, moving forward again, his hips crowding into hers, his big body pinning hers to the wall. She could feel his hardness, the perfect leanness of his muscles as he pushed against her.

And then, because she knew there had to be more to it than that, she flexed her hips against his—and felt the hardness she'd wanted to feel all along. He made a sound in his throat that should have frightened her, but didn't. No, it only made the hunger in her body sharper.

She moved her head back and forth against the mirror, answering his question.

"I won't kiss you," he said, his eyes falling to the dip in her tank top, back up again. Hot eyes. Beautiful, ice blue eyes. "I won't touch you at all, Caroline."

"Roman." His name was a plea on her lips. She sounded like a stranger, and yet she was caught in the grip of this feeling. This need for him. It was as if the past didn't exist. As if nothing existed between them except the here and the now.

And right here, right now, she wanted him.

"Kiss me, *angel moy*," he whispered in a gravelly voice. "Touch me. It is the only way."

CHAPTER SEVEN

"They Were All Over Each Other," Man Says—Kazarov and Caro Spotted Cozying Up in L.A. Department Store

IT DIDN'T MATTER that she shouldn't do this, that her sensible side was telling her to stop right this instant, that it was too complicated and too dangerous. Her wild side wanted to taste Roman Kazarov again. Her wild side wanted to remember what it was like to want a man, to need a man, to lose what was left of her sanity over a man.

But not just any man. Only this one. It had always been only this one.

And so she stood on tiptoe and touched her tongue to his bottom lip. Just that, so light and delicate. He tasted like chocolate, sweet and dark and delicious. And like Roman, heat and power and sizzling electricity.

"More," he said, and she wrapped her arms around his neck, sank into him, arched her body into his.

And then she kissed him. It was light, tentative, searching.

Roman would have none of it. His hands shifted from caging her in to holding her face while he took her mouth with all the power and devastation she knew he was capable of.

This was not a kiss. It was a possession. A complete and total annihilation of her resistance. His tongue sought hers, demanded a response—and she gave it. She went wild with it, with the knowledge that she was in his arms once again, that she'd never wanted to be anywhere else.

On some level, she knew her response had only been made possible by what had happened on the plane earlier. By his fear and wariness of Ryan, and by his stark testimony that his childhood had been nothing approximating normal.

She hurt for Roman. It wasn't reason enough to give herself to him, she knew that, but she hardly needed reason when instinct and biology seemed to be enough. She had never, ever been able to resist Roman Kazarov. From the first, she'd wanted him with a violence she'd never felt in her young life.

And once she'd had him, once he'd been hers to possess again and again, the fire had only burned brighter and hotter.

Roman Kazarov was a fever in her blood, a virus she couldn't seem to shake.

His big hands speared into her hair, shaped her head as he held her for his kiss. She made a noise of frustration, of helplessness, as she tried to press herself closer to him. Her body arched into his, and his hands left her head and traveled down her spine, over her buttocks, testing the feel and weight of her as he pulled her into his groin.

He lifted her and she wrapped her legs around his waist, held on tight while he kissed her with all the devastating skill that she knew he possessed. She was wild, wanton, and she didn't care. All she wanted was to merge herself with him, to lose herself in him the way she once had.

He flexed his hips, and she shuddered as lightning streaked through her. Then he pressed her into the wall and, with devastating precision, moved against her most sensitive core until she was wild with need for him.

He was her ruin, her devastation. He was like a hot fire that threatened to burn her as he swept over her. Caroline wrapped her fists into his shirt and tugged it from his waistband.

She didn't want the barrier of clothing between them, didn't want anything but skin and heat and passion.

"Not here," he said, tearing his mouth from hers suddenly. "Not like this."

"I don't care," she gasped.

He set her away from him abruptly, though she nearly sobbed in protest. He held her at arm's length, though she tried to move into his embrace again. Before her body cooled, before she forgot this feeling. Before reality intruded.

His eyes looked almost as wild as she felt. It was a small comfort, but at least he was not unaffected. "You will care, *angel moy*. You will. Maybe not now, but tomorrow you would hate me for this."

She subsided in degrees against the wall, her palms pressed against the cool mirror, and wanted to cry in frustration. Her body throbbed, her nipples were tight little points in her bra, and her core ached with the need to have him inside her, driving them both to completion.

It had been too long. Far too long.

And she would lose her nerve by the time they got back to the bungalow. Ryan was there, and Blake, and she couldn't see herself letting go, knowing they were in the next room.

She wanted to sob in frustration, but only closed her eyes and breathed deeply, trying to regain her sense of self. It was good this had happened, she told herself. Good she knew her limits.

"I want to go now," she said.

He tipped her chin up, his gaze searching hers. What he saw there must have told him what she was feeling inside. He let her go and stepped back, away from her.

"So this ends here, *da?* You kiss me, want me, but you cannot admit it to yourself beyond this moment."

"It's not a good idea, Roman. For either of us."

"Why should this be? I want you. You want me. How is this a problem?"

She picked up the bag of chocolates she'd dropped, and clutched it to her chest as if it were a shield. "You know why it's a problem," she said, her throat closing over the words. "You hate me and—"

"I don't hate you," he said sharply.

It was her turn to gape. He swore and raked a hand through his hair, then turned and tucked his shirt in again. The color in his cheeks was high, the sharp blades of his cheekbones standing out in his starkly handsome face.

She wanted to go to him, wanted to pull his head down to hers and just hold him close. Forget, for a few moments, all the pain and heartbreak between them.

She wouldn't, though. She couldn't.

"I left you," she said. "I married another man."

He spun on her, his eyes blazing. "I know this. But in order to hate you, I would have had to love you first. I didn't, Caroline. I only thought I did."

It was a lie.

They zipped through the streets of Beverly Hills in silence, the only sound the roar of the engine as Roman whipped in and out of traffic. He'd told her he hadn't loved her, but it was a lie. He had loved her with everything he had in him. Which, God knew, wasn't much. No wonder she'd left him.

He'd returned to New York convinced he hated her. But when he'd held her in his arms tonight, he hadn't felt hatred. He'd felt lust and want and the urgent need to possess her. Hate had had no place in what he felt then.

Roman made the turn into the hotel and pulled up to the valet stand. Across the street, photographers milled, no doubt searching for the latest celebrity scandal. But he was just as good, so they soon came running over, cameras flashing and microphones at the ready, while he cursed himself for not using a more private entrance.

"Mr. Kazarov, is it true you're sleeping with Bambi Royale? What are you doing in L.A.? Any plans to buy up any stores here? Is Hall's vulnerable?"

Roman ignored them, going to Caroline's side and ushering her into the hotel. She said nothing, but kept her head down and hugged those damn chocolates close as if they were a prized possession.

Why had he stopped her back there? Why hadn't he let her rip his clothes off in the middle of that dressing room, with the public only a thin wall away? It wouldn't be the first time he'd had sex in a risky place.

He'd taken her into the dressing room because he'd needed to kiss her, needed to stoke the fires of her desire for him. He hadn't expected the flame to get out of control, though God knew he should have. If the past was anything to go by, he should have known they would burn hot the moment they touched.

Foolishly, he'd thought he had his desire for her under control. She was just a woman, after all, and he knew how to handle women. But the minute she'd kissed him, he'd gone up in smoke. A small, rational part of his brain had known he couldn't make love to her against the wall of a dressing room—but he'd wanted to.

God, how he'd wanted to.

She'd practically begged him to do it. But he wanted more than a hasty screw in a public place. He wanted to spread her out before him on a bed, like a banquet of delights that he had all the time in the world to sample.

They reached the bungalow and went inside. The house was quiet. She glanced at her watch, as if seeking a way out of an awkward situation.

"Blake has probably put Ryan to bed," she said. "I think I'm headed there, too."

All Roman had to do was kiss her. Step into her space, wrap his arms around her and bend her backward. She would fall, her resolve crumbling like a domino toppling over.

And yet that wasn't enough for him. He wanted more than her surrender. Needed more. But he recognized it would not happen tonight. There was too much between them now, too many raw feelings. She wanted escape; he could see that.

And perhaps it was best for them both. He had to deal with this aching in his chest, this feeling of rawness that had accompanied his outburst that he didn't hate her. He'd lived with the hatred for so long that its sudden absence left him reeling and unsure.

"This is a good idea," he said coolly. "In the morning, we'll go back to the store, only this time we'll announce ourselves."

He had to focus on business, because it was the one thing he understood right now. The only solid foundation beneath his feet.

She dipped her chin to her chest briefly, and then looked up again, her hazel eyes clouded. "That sounds perfect."

"Good night, Caroline," he said, before turning and walking toward his room.

"Good night," she replied, her voice soft and somewhat uncertain. He almost turned and went back to her. Almost, but not quite. He shut the door behind him and stood there for a long minute. But there was no soft tread on the floor, no knock on his door.

Roman swore softly before peeling his clothes off and climbing into bed alone.

Caroline didn't know what time it was when she finally gave up the pretense of sleep and flipped the covers back. Her heart had been racing for hours now, as if she'd drunk a vat of coffee right before bed. It wasn't caffeine, though. It was Roman.

She couldn't stop replaying every moment of the evening, from the second he'd asked her if the chocolates were blueberry flavored, until the minute he'd turned and walked away from her, only hours ago. She wanted a do-over. She wanted to be cool and aloof in answer to his query, and she most definitely didn't want to slide a piece of chocolate into his luscious mouth.

And she could really do without hot, almost-sex up against a mirror in one of her own department stores. What was the matter with her? Had she lost every last shred of self-respect she possessed? Was she really the kind of woman who abandoned herself in a public place for the sake of a man's touch?

She was very afraid she was, at least when that man was Roman.

Caroline pulled on a robe over her silk pajamas and went to the kitchen for a drink. The house was dark, quiet, the only sounds those of the air purifiers whirring softly in the night and the hum of the refrigerator. She grabbed a cool bottle of sparkling water and twisted off the cap. She stood there for a long while, thinking and sipping the water, until she heard a splash, as if someone was diving into the pool.

She padded over to the glass doors fronting the pool area and slid them open. A man cut through the water in smooth even strokes. *Roman.*

She stood for a long minute, watching the beautiful grace of his body as he swam, the bunch and stretch of muscles, the way his hands barely came out of the water before slicing back in again, propelling him forward like a machine.

He reached the end of the pool, and then disappeared beneath the surface, only to pop up again almost halfway to the other side. He swam for several lengths before he went under and didn't come back up again.

She waited, expecting him to surface, but nothing happened. Caroline's heart did a flip in her chest, and then she stumbled across the pool deck to the edge. Her water bottle—plastic, fortunately—fell to the deck with a crunch as she started to yank her robe off.

He split the surface right in front of her, and she bit back a scream of surprise.

"You scared the hell out of me!" she yelled, her heart hammering, her pulse throbbing hot.

Water rolled down his face. He dragged a hand over his hair, slicking it to his head as he stood in the center of the pool, completely unharmed and unflappable. Caroline wanted to throw something at him. If she'd still been holding the water bottle, she would have used that.

"I did not know you were there," he said smoothly.

"That's not much of an apology," she told him sharply. And then her mouth went dry as she watched fat drops of water slide down his chest and over the hard ridges of his abs, visible above the waterline.

"It wasn't intended to be one."

Caroline closed her eyes for a second. "I thought you were drowning."

"Then I thank you for caring," he said. "I would have thought you might believe it would solve all your problems if I were to disappear."

She started to deliver a sharp retort, but bit it back at the last second. "You're teasing me. That's not nice."

He shrugged and moved toward the edge of the pool where she stood. "Perhaps I am."

Her robe decided at that minute to stop clinging to her shoulders and puddle at her feet. She resisted the urge to snatch it up and cover her body. Not that she was indecent, but the thin silk of her pajamas felt so much more revealing in the middle of the night than her dresses did during the day.

"I was worried," she added unnecessarily. And then she huffed. "Do you have any idea the headache it would cause me were you to drown in my presence? I'm sure there are some who would claim I planned it."

Roman stood beneath her now. He tilted his head back to look up at her. "Then I will be sure not to drown in your presence."

"That is much appreciated," she said.

He grinned. "And now you may want to turn around. Unless you wish to see more of me than you bargained for."

Caroline's throat closed up. *Oh my.* "You're…naked?"

She hadn't noticed that. She'd been standing in the doorway, and he'd been moving too fast. She'd been thinking about the smooth beauty of his body in the water, not wondering if he happened to be wearing trunks. And then when she had come closer, he'd been beneath the surface. She hadn't yet realized…

Oh. My. Heavens.

"There didn't seem much point in putting on a swimsuit at three in the morning," he told her seriously.

It was suddenly too hot. Tiny beads of sweat formed between her breasts, and her nipples beaded tight against her silk top. Roman's gaze narrowed, and she reached up to fold her arms over her breasts. Let him think what he wanted. It was nothing to do with him, and everything to do with the heat and the breeze and—

Damn it, it *was* him. Caroline lifted her chin. "There are other people in this house," she said primly. "Any one of us might have come out here."

He actually laughed. "Because so many people like to swim at three in the morning. Not to mention the other occupants of this house, besides you, are male."

"Yes, well, one of them is very likely to find what you're displaying quite attractive. Just so you know."

"I'd guessed that already. I'd also guessed that he realizes I am far more attracted to you than to him."

Caroline sniffed. "That's no reason to run around naked, now is it?"

"I like being naked," he said, and her heart skipped a beat. "Surely you remember this?"

"I remember you're an exhibitionist," she said. It wasn't quite true, but she'd never seen anyone more comfortable in his own skin than Roman. "How could I forget?"

His lips curled in a smile. "How indeed? And if you don't wish to see the exhibition, then I suggest you turn around."

She meant to turn around. She planned to turn around. But it suddenly seemed so ridiculous to do so. As if she were a child whose mother had put a hand over her eyes to stop her from seeing something she wanted to see.

She cocked a hip in that bored manner she affected with

him when she wanted him to think she was so cool and controlled. "One can look without touching."

"Can one? Interesting."

Before she could answer, or rethink her show of bravado, he rose from the pool in a smooth, liquid move, like a water god rising from the sea.

And she didn't turn away. Water ran down his body in rivulets, over the hard muscles of his torso and abdomen, over his hip bones, down the trail of dark hair that ran from his belly button to his groin, and down the hard, strong legs that propelled him over to the chair where he picked up a towel and rubbed his head.

Caroline's breathing grew shallow. Hot need spiraled inside her belly, flowed into her limbs, melted in her core until she felt rubbery and unable to move. Oh, what a mistake she'd made in not turning around.

A huge, huge mistake.

He still hadn't moved to wrap the towel around his body. Instead, he dried off slowly, surely, each inch of him more perfect and beautiful than the last.

She was mesmerized. And she realized, standing there with her feet glued to the pool deck, that she hadn't seen a naked man in five long years. Not since the last time she'd seen Roman naked.

He turned and wrapped the towel around his hips, tucking it in until it lay right below his hip bones. And, oh, she wanted to press her mouth there, just there, right beside his hip. And then she wanted to lick her way across his hard abdomen, and down the happy trail to where his thick penis lay.

She would take him in her mouth, feel him grow impossibly hard against her tongue....

"Caroline." His voice was like a whip cracking in her ear.

"What?" she said sharply, her pulse thrumming in her wrists, her throat.

"Don't look at me like that unless you intend to do something about it."

"I have no idea what you mean," she said, bending to scoop up her robe. Except she was far too hot to put it back on, so she balled it up and held it at her side.

He only looked at her, with that superior smirk on his face. Caroline closed her eyes. Damn it, she was tired of pretending she didn't have needs. She wanted to stop being strong, and she wanted to go to him and run her fingers over that hot, smooth skin. She wanted to follow with her mouth, and she wanted to let him do every last thing to her that he wanted to do.

She knew from experience how amazing and formidable he was in bed, and she ached to know that kind of pleasure again.

What would it hurt? What *could* it hurt? They were here, in California, in a gorgeous private bungalow in the middle of the night. If she slept with him once, if she got him out of her system, there would be no need for a repeat.

Then she could concentrate on beating him at his own game.

"You're lying," he said softly when she opened her eyes again, moving toward her on silent, graceful feet. He stopped in front of her, so close but not quite close enough. A drop of water fell from his hair and landed on her silk pajama top, spreading outward over her nipple. Molding what she knew he could already see.

"I might be," she said softly, her gaze on his, her heart pumping hard at the heat in his eyes. "And what if I am?"

"Then do something about it, *solnyshko*. Take what you want."

CHAPTER EIGHT

Caro and Kazarov Setting Up Love Nest?

THE NIGHT WAS oddly silent as they stood facing each other, close enough to touch but neither moving to do so. Caroline's heart was a trapped bird in her chest. She was afraid, desperately afraid, that if she did this, if she moved toward him as she wanted, something would change.

That she would lose a part of herself, irrevocably, if she did. She'd worked hard to forget him—not that forgetting him had been possible. Perhaps, instead, she'd worked hard to put him behind her. Where he needed to be. If she let him back in now, then what?

"Once," she said. "Only this once."

She expected him to agree. She expected him to say *yes, absolutely, now drop the clothing.* What man wouldn't agree if it meant having sex?

But Roman stood there, silent and brooding, and shook his head slowly, deliberately, until a slow burn started in her belly and rose into her throat, her cheeks.

"Take what you want, Caroline. But understand that from now on, I shall also take what I want. As often as I want. There will be no hiding from what this is, not this time. You aren't going home at the end of the evening and pretending it didn't happen."

His words smarted. And yet she was still thinking about it. Still aching and needing. Wishing there was a way. *Could* she accept his conditions? There was no one to stop her this time, no one to tell her she couldn't have what she wanted.

"You drive a hard bargain," she said, her eyes fixed on his. "Perhaps an impossible bargain."

"Then walk away, my darling," he told her. "Go back to your bed and pleasure yourself, as I am sure you have had to do far too often."

She felt as if he'd slapped her. She thought of lying in her bed, alone, her hands running over her breasts, down her body, her fingers sliding to where she needed them most. It was too lonely, too clinical, to contemplate. Not when he was here, this hot, beautiful, dangerous man who had once known her body so well.

"I—I've not been with anyone in a long time," she told him. It was the truth, but not the whole truth. How could she admit she'd been with no one but him, ever? To admit it would not only make her pitiful in his eyes, it would also give away the truth of Ryan's parentage. And she couldn't do that just yet. Not until she was certain Roman wouldn't do something drastic.

"I understand," he said. "You are afraid. And yet, do I not know you, *solnyshko?* Do I not understand what it takes to make your body sing? Do you think that I could have forgotten this?"

She swallowed the tears that threatened to spill free. "Five years is a long time. And you've had many lovers since."

He put a finger under her chin, tilted her face up until one of those tears escaped and fell from the corner of her eye. "Not one of them was you."

"Don't say things like that, Roman," she chided, needing to bring this back to ground she understood. To less emotional ground. "I might start to think you care."

"I care about making love to you," he said. "Nothing more.

I won't lie to you, Caroline, and tell you this is something it isn't."

"I have no idea what makes you think I'd want more," she said, though her throat ached with emotion. "My, what an inflated opinion you have of yourself."

If she expected him to take offense, he didn't. He just kept watching her with those burning eyes. "Then what will it be? Pleasure? Or a lonely bed?"

She should choose the lonely bed. It was the safest option. And yet she was tired of the safe option. She'd been doing what was best for everyone except herself for a very long time. Though she couldn't say that Roman was best for her, he was at least a choice she could selfishly make. And she wanted him. Terribly.

The only one who would get hurt this time was her.

"Kiss me, Roman," she said, a shiver rolling over her. "Kiss me like you did earlier."

He snaked an arm around her body and tugged her close. And then he dipped his head and took her upturned mouth as if it were a delicacy for him alone. He licked, sucked, teased and tormented—and she knew he hadn't kissed her like this earlier. Not quite like this, with such heated intention. This was the kiss of a man who was in supreme control, a man who intended to strip her naked and take her body as if it had been made for his pleasure.

"Come," he said roughly, taking her hand and leading her into the house. "I have to wash off this chlorine."

He led her into the master bedroom, and then through the bath and outside to a shower that was surrounded by a tall wall but open to the night sky above. He shed the towel and turned on the taps. And then he dragged her under the water with him, fully clothed.

"Roman," she gasped as the cool water plastered her silk pajamas to her skin. Her nipples beaded tight, and his thumbs flicked over them while he fused his mouth to hers once more.

The water warmed, but she no longer cared that it had been cool. She was anything but cold as flames licked into her. Her hands were free to roam his body, free to caress and cup and feel. It didn't take her long to wrap her hands around him, around that hard, hot part of him she craved.

Roman groaned into her mouth, and she felt a surge of feminine power. For all his strength and hardness, all his ruthlessness, he couldn't remain unmoved here. Not when it was the two of them and nothing but skin and heat and explosive passion.

His hands went to the front of her shirt, and then he was yanking it apart, buttons flying—and she didn't care. He shoved the sodden mass off her shoulders. Her pajama bottoms soon followed, though she had to pull away and peel them off each leg before stepping into his embrace again.

Only she didn't want his hands on her yet. She wanted to make him wild with need, wanted to taste him again. She slipped from his grip like quicksilver and sank to her knees in front of him.

"No," he gasped—but she took him in her mouth before he could stop her. His entire body stiffened as he grabbed the shower wall. Water poured down over them both while she licked her tongue up and down his length. He was hot and hard and satiny—marble sheathed in silk.

"Caroline, *solnyshko, nyet,*" he said, as she wrapped a hand around him and squeezed.

But she wouldn't stop. The only way to do this, the only way she *could* do this, was to make him lose control first. Because she knew, if he had his way, she'd be writhing and sobbing and begging him for more.

This way, he was the one who begged. He was the one who needed and gasped and lost himself in her. She was relentless, licking and sucking him until he cried out, until his body jerked and he spilled inside her. She took him all, took everything he had to give, and then he shuddered before sinking to his knees and facing her there on the thick tiles.

"That wasn't the way it was supposed to happen," he said, his breath whooshing out of him as if he'd just run a marathon. Caroline went to him and pressed her body fully against his, wrapped her arms around his neck. She loved the sensation of her naked flesh against his naked flesh, of the heat and hardness and slippery feel of the water.

"I didn't realize there were any rules," she told him.

He laughed, the sound rusty and breathless. "If there were, you have just broken them all."

It didn't take Caroline long to realize that she hadn't won a thing by making him lose control first. No, if anything, she'd guaranteed her sensual torture at his hands. He began by soaping her body slowly, thoroughly, his clever fingers slicking over her breasts, her nipples, pinching them softly until she wanted to scream.

Until she was so sensitive she knew she would fly apart the instant he did it again.

Except that he didn't. He left her breasts and moved his big hands down her abdomen, over the faded marks she'd earned carrying her baby. He paused only momentarily there, and it made her heart ache. What was he thinking?

But then he moved on and she couldn't remember what she'd been wondering. He slid one broad hand around to cup her bottom, kneading her buttocks. And then he turned her in his arms until she was facing away from him, until her back pressed into him—and the evidence of his arousal made her gasp.

"Already?"

"I am a man of many talents," he murmured in her ear. "And you have much to answer for."

Caroline shivered in response as he sucked her earlobe into his hot mouth. And then he parted her, his fingers slid-

ing against her, around the sensitive nub she most wanted him
to touch. He traced her shape—slowly, deliberately—while
his penis pushed insistently against the small of her back.

"Roman," she gasped when his thumb skated over her clitoris. Her entire body clenched in response, aching, wanting, needing.

"All in good time, *angel moy*," he said. "All in good time."

His mouth was on her throat, her shoulder, his tongue hot
and wet against her flesh, his lips firm. His teeth nibbled here
and there until she was panting with frustration.

"Are you planning to actually touch me? Or are you too
spent and just pretending?"

His laugh was not what she expected. "So demanding,
Caroline. I remember this about you. It turns me on."

In response to her frustrated growl, he slid a finger into her
body. His thumb skated over her again. And then again, his
touch growing firmer each time. Caroline panted and writhed
against him, wanting more. It had been too long, far too long,
and he was going to kill her before she ever reached the peak.

"Roman, I'm begging you," she finally choked out, when
he skated over her clitoris again.

"I like it when you beg."

"Please," she said. "Please. I'll do anything."

He inserted another finger inside her. And then his fingers set up a rhythm, while his thumb moved against her.
Her body, already so sensitive, coiled tight, tighter than
she'd thought possible—and then she shattered into a million pieces, sobbing his name, her body breaking apart in a
way it hadn't in five long years.

He held her while she shook, held her when her body went
limp against him, kept her standing when she would have
fallen to her knees the way he had done.

She realized he was speaking in Russian, saying things in
her ear that sounded so beautiful, but she had no idea what
any of it meant.

"Gorgeous," he said, switching to English. His accent was thicker now, and she shuddered with the way the heavy vowels dripped down her spine. So elegant, so mesmerizing.

"I think I should say thank you," she said, when she could speak again. "I needed that very much."

He turned her in his arms and reached for the tap at the same time. The water ceased flowing and they stood there staring at each other in the glow of the wall lamps.

"Don't thank me yet," he told her. "Because this is far from over."

They dried off quickly, and then he swept her up and carried her into the bedroom, despite her protests that she could walk the short distance herself. She pressed her cheek to his shoulder, her face against his neck, and smiled to herself. *Caveman,* she wanted to say.

And yet she loved it. Loved the tenderness and care he showed, as if she were a precious and fragile thing that needed his strength.

When he laid her on the bed and came down on top of her, the fire spinning up in her belly danced out of control again. She reached for him, arched off the bed to press her mouth to his skin, but he pushed her back with a firm hand.

"Not this time," he told her.

He was too quick for her grasping hands, slipping down her body and spreading her thighs apart, his mouth leaving a hot, wet trail along her torso that made her shiver with delight. She knew what he was doing, knew how this would begin, and she didn't think she would survive the sensual torture he intended to mete out.

When he settled between her thighs, she shuddered. He looked up, his eyes meeting hers for a long, intense minute. "You've been wanting this," he said. "Needing it."

She managed to nod.

He dipped to taste her, his tongue sliding along her cleft, making her cry out. She thought she would fly apart. His tongue—his clever, amazing tongue—began to lick into her with the consummate skill of a man who knew how to drive a woman mad. He knew exactly how much pressure to apply, exactly where to press the point of his tongue, and for exactly how long.

He knew when she was close, and he moved his attention away just long enough for the pressure to subside. And then he would return, building the pressure again and again, until she nearly sobbed.

Caroline writhed on the bed, tormented by pleasure, by the need for release—and the certain knowledge that she'd never feel this way with anyone else ever again.

"Roman," she gasped as the spring inside her tightened yet again—

And then she flew free, gasping his name, her back arching off the bed, her hips pressing against that clever, clever tongue.

When she came back to herself, he'd moved until he loomed over her, until she could feel him pressing at her entrance. She drew her legs up high, and then he hooked an arm under one knee and spread her wider, his body now insistently pressing forward.

She tilted her hips, urging him faster, but he swore softly. "I am trying to be gentle," he told her.

"I don't want gentle." She sounded almost petulant, and so very needy.

"I think you need gentle, at least to begin with."

"Roman—"

"Shh, my darling. Just feel. Feel what we do to each other."

Caroline ran her hands down his sides and gripped his buttocks, pulling him toward her as she lifted her hips. His breath hissed in, and she laughed, thrilled to know he wasn't as precisely controlled as he claimed.

"You play with fire," he growled.

"Now," she said in his ear. *"Right now."*

He lifted her toward him and sank the rest of the way into her body with a groan. Caroline cried out at the sensation of having him fully inside her again. He was big and hard, and yes, her body wasn't quite as prepared for his invasion as she'd thought after five long years.

"Are you okay?" he asked thickly.

"I will be."

He swore and started to withdraw, but she clamped her legs around him and held on tight.

"Don't you dare, Roman."

"For God's sake, stop moving," he ground out.

Rebelliously, Caroline shifted against him again, sensation streaking through her as she pressed his hardness deep within her.

"Caroline, I can't—"

She moved again, more desperately this time—and his control snapped. Suddenly, he was everywhere, slamming into her body again and again, harder and deeper and more intensely with every thrust.

Caroline cried out, but not with pain. The pleasure was too much, too intense, too hot and raw and bold. Roman gripped her hips and held her hard against him, his body riding hers, overwhelming hers—and being commanded by hers, as well.

Their naked bodies pressed into each other, their flesh slapping together with the powerful rhythm they set. Nothing existed outside this bed, nothing but the two of them and the feelings they called up in each other.

Ecstasy was so close, just within reach. Caroline was straining toward it, ready to soar over the edge—when Roman stopped moving. And then a light switched on. It was dim, but she turned her head away from the source, squinting against the sharp intrusion.

"I want to see you," he said roughly. "I want to see your face when you come."

It made her heart beat hard when he said that. It was as if

he wanted too much, wanted not only her surrender but also her soul. She had no barriers left at this moment, nothing she could throw up between them to protect herself. She was exposed, raw, her body a creature of pleasure. Addicted to him.

If he sensed her turmoil, he didn't show it. Instead, he dipped his head to hers again, kissing her softly, his tongue sliding into her mouth so sweetly she could have wept.

And then he started moving, more slowly, more deliberately, stoking the fires within them both until control was again impossible. This time, she could see the pleasure on his face, feel it rising in her belly, tightening everything within her, building to unbearable levels.

She flung her head back as her orgasm slammed into her. It clawed into her belly, her brain, her limbs. It tore her apart and left her writhing on the edge of madness, wanting more of the same, feeling she would never be whole again.

Roman followed her over the edge with a hoarse groan, her name on his lips, Russian words tumbling from him as his release slammed into him. Caroline turned her head against the pillow and sucked in a shaky breath as her entire world seemed to shift beneath her.

Soon, Roman rolled to the side, taking his weight off her. His body was still inside hers, still hard, and she moaned a little at the sensations that rolled through her simply from that connection.

He nuzzled her throat, his lips gliding along her skin, his damp hair against her cheek. She was spent, and yet she could feel new tension beginning to fuse into a ball of panic in her belly. What had she done? What kind of insanity was this, sleeping with the man who'd fathered her child, who was in her life again to take her stores away from her, and who had only ever caused her heartache?

Roman lifted his head to gaze down at her. There was a line between his eyebrows as he frowned.

"What is the matter, Caroline?"

She licked suddenly dry lips. "I should go back to my own bed," she began.

"Nyet." His voice was harsh. Commanding.

"I don't want Blake to know—"

Roman swore and pushed himself away from her. Her body felt cold once the heat of him was gone, and she wanted to call him back to her. But she couldn't.

She sat up and pulled the sheet up to cover her breasts. "I don't know what this is between us, Roman. How can I explain it to Blake if I can't even explain it to myself?"

He raked a hand through his hair. "Why would you need to explain this to your nanny? He is paid to take care of your child, nothing more."

"He's a friend. A-and he was Jon's friend."

Roman's eyes were cold. "This is about your husband? About what his friend will think? My God, Caroline, the man has been dead for over a year. I don't think anyone can fault you for moving on with your life!"

She brought her knees up to her chest and put her forehead on them. "I don't understand any of this, Roman," she said. "I don't know why I'm here with you. Why I can't seem to resist you, though I know I should. There's too much between us, too much pain and anger, and I feel like this can only end badly for me. For us."

He came to her and pulled her into his arms. She went willingly—too willingly—and wrapped her arms around his torso, burying her head against his chest. She felt him sigh, and she closed her eyes, breathing in the clean scent of his skin.

"Maybe it won't end badly," he said. "Maybe this time will be different."

CHAPTER NINE

*Kazarov Leaves a Trail of Broken Hearts in His Wake;
Caro Needs to Beware*

ROMAN WOKE WITH a start sometime before dawn. He'd barely
slept at all, and now he wasn't sure what had awakened him.
A dream, maybe. He threw his arm over his head and stared
up at the ceiling. Beside him, Caroline slept, her soft breaths
whispering in and out regularly. She'd curled in a ball—away
from him, he noted.

But she was still here. He remembered what he'd said to
her right before they fell asleep. That maybe it wouldn't end
badly this time.

He had no idea where that had come from. No, he didn't
intend for it to end badly for him—but he did intend for it to
end. How it ended for her ought not to concern him.

Except, for a brief moment when he'd been holding her
close and feeling her soft body next to his, trusting him, he'd
never wanted it to end. He'd wanted to stay just like that,
holding her and protecting her always.

Insane.

How could he feel any sort of tenderness toward this
woman after what she'd put him through? He'd given her
his heart—asked her to marry him—and she'd laughed at

him. Pitied him, no doubt. Because he hadn't been worthy of the great Sullivan blood.

For some reason, that hadn't seemed to matter to him when he'd been buried inside her, feeling her excitement, giving her pleasure. Like a trained monkey, he'd wanted only to give her more of the same. More, so that she smiled at him and told him how good he was. So that she kept coming to him for her fix.

Wanting a woman this much was dangerous. He had never made that mistake with any other woman but this one. What was it about him that made him want to throw himself against the same wall again and again in the hopes the result would be different this time? A flaw inherited from his waste of space of a father, no doubt.

That thought made Roman shudder. He was nothing like his father. Nothing at all.

And yet here he was, with the same woman who'd ripped his guts out once before, and nothing was going the way he'd imagined it might. He didn't feel as in control as he'd wanted to feel. He didn't feel as if he was the victor here at all.

He imagined her married to Jon, imagined Jon doing the things to her that he'd done, and it made his inner beast coil and writhe. He could hardly look at their child without wanting to howl. For some reason, the kid hurt most of all.

And Roman had to get over it, because the boy wasn't going away.

He sat up, intending to get out of bed and do some work before it was time to get dressed and go back to Sullivan's. His empire was global, so it was the middle of the workday in some locations. Not that he personally supervised every single company, but he could check in with the managers of those territories and get reports, at least.

And he still needed a plan for the Sullivan Group. He'd bought the loans, and while he intended to honor the terms of their original agreement, he didn't expect they'd make the payment on time. When he foreclosed, he needed the players in place to do what was necessary to recoup his investment.

"What time is it?" Caroline asked, her voice rough with sleep.

"Nearly six," he said.

She reached out and put a hand on his naked back. Roman felt as if she'd touched him with a brand. "Do we have to get up just yet?"

He turned back to her. "You can sleep, *solnyshko*. There's time yet."

"I wasn't thinking of sleep," she said, and he hardened instantly. It was almost painful how much he wanted this woman.

"What were you thinking?"

Her hand slid over his torso, down his abdomen, and then she hissed when she felt the size of his erection. "That's pretty much what I was thinking," she said.

Soon he was lost inside her, his body driving into hers fiercely, her cries in his ear, her fingers digging into the muscles of his back. He didn't know where she ended, where he began—or how he'd lived the past five years without her.

Something was different now that they'd had sex. Caroline bit back a yawn as they sat in a meeting with the general manager of the L.A. store and his team. She needed to be paying attention to what the man was saying, but all she could think about was Roman. About the way he'd mastered her body last night, and again this morning, giving her the kind of pleasure she'd begun to believe she would never experience again.

He sat across from her at the table, consulting his computer from time to time, asking pointed questions. She should be angry that they were even here, doing this—but she wasn't. He'd been right that she needed to get out in the field and see what was going on. This store was doing fabulously. Part of that was the location, and part was the training and retention program for employees. People here were valued team members, and it showed. Happy employees tended to customer needs, and customers bought in response. They could spend their dollars elsewhere, but they chose Sullivan's based on the level of service they could expect.

Caroline made a note to look into employee practices company-wide. She glanced up again, her gaze sliding over to Roman. He was watching her, his eyes searing into hers, reminding her of all they'd done to each other last night.

All she wanted to do again.

This morning, after he'd taken her to heaven and back at least twice, she'd slipped from his bed and returned to her own room, showering and dressing for the day before Blake and Ryan were up. When she'd joined them for breakfast, Blake seemed none the wiser about her nocturnal activities. Not that she expected he would care, but she still felt a tad awkward about it.

She'd hoped Roman would join them, but he didn't. Instead, he'd passed through the kitchen, said good morning, grabbed a cup of coffee and went to the study. He didn't emerge again until it was time to leave. This time, instead of the sports car, they took a limo to the store.

Now, the manager finished his presentation and the room fell silent. Caroline shook herself, realizing it was up to her to speak. "Thank you, Mr. Garcia," she said. "I appreciate you taking time out for us today. Your store is a model for Sullivan's, and I'll be taking some of your ideas back to the board."

Caroline shook hands with everyone, thanking them for the good job they were doing. And then she and Roman spent a bit more time at the store, touring all the departments before heading back to the bungalow in the limo.

She put her hand over her stomach. It was tight—with worry, with apprehension, with this desperate need she still felt for the man beside her. One night had done nothing to lessen the ache. Not that she'd expected it would, but she certainly hadn't expected to feel even more jittery than before.

"I think that went well," she said as the limo moved through traffic. She had to speak, or burst with the emotions churning through her.

Roman turned. He'd been staring out the window, deep in thought, perhaps, but now he was looking at her with those eyes so like his son's that it made her want to weep. Her heart squeezed tight in her chest. She was going to have to tell him the truth. She knew that now.

Some way, somehow, someday—she had to figure it out. And then she had to be prepared for the fallout. Caroline shuddered deep inside. That was what frightened her most of all.

"It's one store, Caroline."

She toyed with the narrow snakeskin belt she'd put on over her tunic dress. "I know that."

He let out a sigh. "I don't want you to get your hopes up, *angel moy*. Sullivan's is still in trouble."

Her stomach flipped even as she chided herself for it. One night of sex wasn't going to make him merciful, now was it? He still owned the loans, and she still needed the money to pay him so he couldn't foreclose. Besides, she wanted to beat him at his own game, not get special treatment because she'd slept with him.

"I'm aware, Roman. But I'm encouraged." She let out a forceful breath. "We'll make that payment. I guarantee it."

"Let's not talk about business," he said, surprising her with the sudden vehemence of the words.

It melted her reserve. She scooted over on the seat until she was beside him, until she could lean against him and put her cheek to his chest. He put his arms around her, his chin resting on her hair. "We've spent the entire morning and part of the afternoon talking about business," he said, as if offering an explanation.

She ran her fingers along the smooth fabric of his custom suit, breathing in his vanilla-and-spice scent. So handsome. So dynamic. And, for now, hers.

"Maybe not the *entire* morning."

His laugh was soft. "No, not the entire morning. I exaggerate."

He tilted her chin up and kissed her. It was a gentle kiss, the kind of kiss between lovers long familiar with each other. And yet there was that tiny tingle of desire coming to life in her core.

He must have felt it, too, because he suddenly ended the kiss. "We have all night together," he said. "I intend for it to be a long and pleasurable one."

"I look forward to it," she sighed.

He pushed her upright so he could see her face. "Do you? Last night, you seemed uncertain about the prospect of continuing."

Caroline shrugged self-consciously. "I can't say this doesn't confuse me, Roman. But it's time I got on with my life, as you said."

His blue eyes seemed troubled for a moment. "I'm sorry you lost your husband. It cannot have been easy for you."

She lowered her lashes to hide the confusion and guilt he would surely see if she kept looking at him. "It wasn't. Jon was a good man. A good friend."

"I remember him," Roman said, and she looked up again, searching his gaze. "I hardly knew him, but I liked him well enough the few times we met."

"We weren't right for each other," she said, surprising herself that she'd admitted that much. "But we tried."

"For the sake of your child."

She dropped her gaze, nodding. Guilt was a living thing inside her, twisting and churning, making her feel sick to her stomach.

"My parents tried, too. It was a disaster."

She reached for his hand, squeezed it. "I'm sorry."

It was his turn to shrug. "My father was an alcoholic. I doubt that either you or Jon Wells had this problem."

"No." Once more, her heart ached for the little boy Roman had been. He had never shared anything about his childhood when they were together before. She didn't know why he did so now, but she was glad that he did.

He turned his head to look out the window at the traffic. "For him, children were a burden. And a tool to use against my mother. We would have all been better off if she'd just left him. But she didn't."

"Are they still together?"

"In a manner of speaking," he said. And then he turned back to her. "They are both dead."

"Oh, Roman, I'm so sorry."

"This is life. There is nothing to be done about it."

She thought of her parents in their big house in Southampton, of her father slowly forgetting everything and everyone he'd ever known, and wanted to weep. Her mother was handling it bravely, stoically, but it took a toll on her. Her smile, once so genuine and instant, was pasted on now, brittle. As if she needed to cry but couldn't. As if she had to turn a happy face to the world no matter what.

"I've found that life can be very cruel sometimes," Caroline said. "Even when you think you have everything, it finds a way to flatten you."

"Da," he replied. "This is unfortunately true."

He turned his gaze back to the window and they finished the ride in silence. The driver took them through a private entrance so they could avoid the throng of paparazzi that lurked nearby, and for that she was grateful. She didn't think she could take them on, with her heart churning and everything she felt written on her face.

What would they see if they looked at her? A confused woman? A woman who'd never really gotten over the first man she'd ever loved? A guilty woman with a secret she needed to share but hadn't yet figured out how to?

When she and Roman stepped inside the bungalow, she could hear the splash of water, and Ryan's giggles and shouts as he played. Roman stopped in the middle of the great room, hands shoved in his pockets—and her heart pinched tight.

Outside, Ryan was climbing from the pool and Blake was sitting on the edge, watching him. "Want to come outside with me and see what they've been up to?" she asked.

Roman's gaze slid past her. He was frowning. "No. You go ahead. I have work to do."

Caroline sighed. Eventually, she would need to deal with Roman's reluctance to get near Ryan. He wasn't comfortable around kids, but she wanted him to be comfortable with Ryan before she told him the truth.

She went over and slid the door open, and Ryan looked up from where he stood on the pool deck.

"Mommy! Watch what I can do!"

"No running," Blake commanded, as Ryan started for the end of the pool. He stopped running, but his little legs moved fast as he headed to where he wanted to be.

"Watch, Mommy!"

Caroline's heart filled with love as her son screwed up his little face and then jumped into the water with as much concentration as if he'd been performing an Olympic dive. He was wearing arm floaties, so she wasn't especially worried about him trying to swim across the pool. Nevertheless, Blake sat on the edge, ready to spring into motion should Ryan need help.

"Perfect!" Caroline cried as he paddled his way over to where she stood next to Blake. "What a big boy you're turning into. I'm so proud of you!"

Ryan's little face lit up. "I can do it backward, too!" he said. "Uncle Blake taught me."

Blake shrugged when she looked at him. "He did it himself," he told her, sotto voce. "I had nothing to do with it." Then he turned back to Ryan. "Why don't you get out of the pool now, sweetie? Mommy's home and it'll soon be time to eat."

Caroline expected an argument, since Ryan hated to be stopped when he was enjoying something. But he paddled to the edge even faster. "Can we have pizza? Please?"

"I think we can manage that," Caroline said.

Blake lifted him out of the pool and grabbed a towel. "I'll do it," Caroline told him, taking the towel and wrapping her baby up.

Ryan chattered endlessly while she dried him off. But then he stopped talking abruptly and she realized that Roman had come outside. For a moment, she was heartened by the effort. But then she realized he was standing there with his brows drawn down, staring at them.

Staring at Ryan. Caroline's heart skipped several beats. "What were you saying, sweetheart?" she asked Ryan.

He began to talk again, quietly, his gaze darting to Roman more than once. And Roman had still not moved.

"There, I think that's finished," she said, wrapping Ryan in the towel again and standing. "Why don't you go and get dressed so we can have that pizza?"

"Okay!" He took off running, skidding to a halt when Blake yelled at him to walk. Blake trailed after him and they went inside together.

Roman was still standing there. Still staring at her. A premonition of fear slid down her spine as she met his gaze. His hot, hard gaze that was filled with something far different than the lust she'd seen there earlier. His face was a thundercloud.

The gathering storm was about to break, and nothing would be the same when it did.

Roman turned and slid the door closed—very slowly, very deliberately—and cut off her only escape. Then they faced each other across the length of the patio. Caroline's pulse thrummed hard. The plants behind Roman began to shimmer. She forced herself to focus on him, forced the blood to keep pumping into her heart, her brain. She would not pass out. She refused to pass out.

"Tell me," Roman said very precisely, "that what I'm thinking cannot be correct."

She tried for cool. "I don't know what you're thinking, Roman."

His eyes blazed as he took a step toward her, his hands clenched into fists at his sides. She sensed that he was on the edge of his control. It was such a far cry from the man he'd been only moments ago in the limousine. She wanted to weep and yell and throw things.

"I have two brothers," he said, his voice diamond hard. "Dmitry and Nikolai. We used to go swimming together when we were children, in the water park in Moscow. It was our summer ritual, our escape." He shook himself, as if he were going deeper into the memory than he intended. "Just now, I would have sworn I was watching one of my brothers. There is something in that child's way of moving, in his expression—"

"He is not *that* child, Roman," she snapped, fury blazing. "His name is Ryan."

"He is your son with Jon Wells." Roman said it as if he expected her to agree, to tell him that the evidence of his eyes was flawed.

The lump in her throat was huge, choking her. There was no way out. No way she could deny the truth now. It wasn't how she'd wanted to do this. Hell, until just recently she hadn't envisioned telling him at all. There were repercussions to telling him, repercussions for more than just the two of them.

"Jon was gay," she said softly, her throat hurting.

Roman looked as if she'd hit him. His face drained of color, except for two red spots over his cheeks. It took him a long minute to speak. And when he did, his voice was harder and colder than she'd ever heard it. Lethal.

"What, precisely, are you telling me, Caroline? Say it clearly so there can be no misunderstanding."

She sucked in a shaky breath. But she stood her ground, even though what she most wanted was to sink to the pool deck and sob. "You already know."

"Yet I want you to say it." His jaw was hard as he worked to contain the strong emotions gripping him. "Tell me," he ordered, his voice razor-edged.

Caroline flinched. But she didn't shrink from the task. That wasn't her style. No, she delivered the words, knowing she was ripping his carefully ordered world in two as she did so. Knowing this time the rift between them would never be healed.

"I'm saying that I was already pregnant when Jon and I married. Ryan is your son, not Jon's."

CHAPTER TEN

*The Thrill Is Gone? Caro and Kazarov Not Speaking—
Photos from LAX*

ROMAN COULDN'T BREATHE. It took every effort of will he possessed to make the air move in and out of his lungs the way it was supposed to do. Every effort of will not to walk over to the woman who'd lied to him all these years, and shake her.

Violence rose in waves inside him. Sick, choking, overwhelming urges to wrap his hands around her neck and squeeze. He shook his head and stood stiffly, staring at her wide hazel eyes brimming with tears.

"I didn't know until after you were gone," she said, as a tear spilled free, sliding down her pale cheek. "You returned to Russia without leaving me any way to contact you."

Rage was a living thing inside him. He'd spent years conquering that rage, years learning not to be the man his father had been—but right now, he was on the edge of feelings he'd never before felt. He would conquer them, however, because he *was* the better man.

"As if you would have tried," he said sharply. "Do you expect me to believe that?"

She shook her head, and another tear spilled down her cheek. He hardened his heart against the pinprick of agony that caused.

"Of course I don't."

Inside, he was a mess of violent, swirling emotions. Outside, he had to be cool. He had to shut it all down and deal with her like the traitor she was. The traitor she'd always been. He didn't care that she looked miserable—it was because she'd been caught, nothing else.

"I left," he growled, "because I had no choice. Because your father fired me and managed to get my work visa yanked."

She bowed her head for a moment. And then she was looking at him again, her clear hazel eyes spearing into him. "I had no idea. I'm sorry that happened."

Sorry? He clenched his fists at his sides, fighting the urge to howl with rage.

His voice was tight with fury. "I lost everything, Caroline. My job, my home. You. I went back to Russia with nothing. Less than nothing." He swallowed the bile rising in his throat. "It was a...very difficult time."

She spread her hands in supplication. "I didn't want to leave you, Roman. But I *had* to marry Jon." She took a step toward him, her beautiful face etched with pain. "It was the only way to save Sullivan's. His parents owned majority shares at that time, and they were threatening to sell to a competitor if we didn't get married."

Roman stared at her for a long moment, his gut roiling with emotion. And then he laughed. A rusty, bitter laugh. A disbelieving laugh.

"Sullivan's. Of course. It is the only thing that has ever mattered to you."

Her skin flushed. "People were going to lose their jobs. My family was going to lose their heritage. I couldn't allow that to happen."

"Did you sleep with me now, thinking that I would soften and let you keep your precious stores? Because *that* will never happen, Caroline," he finished viciously.

She seemed to deflate just a little. And then her chin came up. Her eyes blazed. "I did *not* sleep with you for Sullivan's. God knows I'm fully aware that you are too ruthless for that. I've watched you circling closer and closer for the past two years. I've known you were coming for us, Roman. I've always known."

He stiffened. "I buy troubled companies. This is no mystery."

"No, it's not. But you would have come for Sullivan's anyway."

He felt the truth of that statement like the crack of a whip. Yes, he had been angling for Sullivan's for a long time. From the very beginning, he'd wanted to own the company that had nearly ruined his life and made his mother's last days so dreadful. "I'm a businessman. I don't take unnecessary risks."

"But you would have done so to get back at me."

He took a halting step toward her, raw fury breaking through the tight lid he'd snapped onto his composure. She was unbelievable. He was reeling over the fact that he had a child with her, a child she'd kept hidden from him, and she was babbling about her precious stores.

She folded her arms and turned her head away from him. Her profile was so achingly lovely. The sudden curl of tenderness weaving into his psyche made him angry. He had no room for tenderness for her. No room for anything but disgust.

"You've known where I was for two years at least," he said tightly, "when I took Kazarov Industries global. Why did you not tell me about the child sooner?"

She fixed eyes shimmering with tears on him. "How would I have done that? Jon and Ryan and I were a family then. Not only that, but Jon's leukemia took a turn for the worse soon after you emerged on the scene. I was a bit preoccupied."

Roman didn't want to feel the wisp of sympathy for her

rolling through him like smoke. "At least now I know why you lied about your address that night."

She dipped her chin again. "I was going to tell you," she said quietly. "I wasn't sure how or when, but I was going to. Not that you'll believe that, of course."

"I'd say the same thing in your place." He bit out the words. "But it doesn't make it true."

There was a sound behind him. He spun to see Ryan pressing up against the glass, his hands flat on the pane, his eyes on his mother. Roman felt as if someone had punched him in the gut all over again. How had he missed it before? Now that he knew, he could see the kid was a Kazarov. He had the same eyes, the same nose.

But he also had Caroline's features. Roman had noticed that immediately. The narrow chin, the jaw, the blond hair. He'd looked at the boy's picture several times and never seen anything but Caroline. And when he'd seen the kid in person for the first time, he still hadn't seen anything but Caroline and what he assumed to be Jon Wells.

His own flesh and blood, and he hadn't even realized it. What did that say about him?

Ryan looked up at him then, his big blue eyes wide with fear, and Roman's gut clenched. He had a son. And his son was afraid of him. It hurt in ways he hadn't imagined.

He spun back to Caroline. "Why is he so damn scared of everything?"

She moved toward him, smiling, and he realized she was doing it to make Ryan think nothing was wrong. That she wasn't upset. When she stood in front of Roman, blocked from the little eyes at the glass door, she wiped away her tears with the back of her hand. For some reason, her tears hurt.

And that angered him further. Why should he care that she was upset? Why, when she'd stolen his happiness five years ago—and his child, as it turned out?

"He's always been a bit shy," she said. "It's his personality."

Roman closed his eyes and concentrated on breathing in air thick with chlorine and the perfume of plumeria bushes. "Do you have any idea how much this hurts? You telling me about his personality, me needing to ask why he's this way?"

She nodded, and a fresh wave of tears spilled down her cheeks. "I know it does. I'm sorry."

He swore. Violently. The most vulgar words he could think of, the kind of words no good Russian would say without a sense of horror. His mother, if she were alive, would have washed his mouth out with soap. "Sorry doesn't fix a goddamn thing, does it?"

She shook her head. "No."

"There is no excuse for this," he told her, his voice whipping like a lash. He was boiling inside—hurt, anger, fear, all coming together, churning in his gut like acid. "No excuse."

She sniffled, and the sound tore at him. He hated that it did. He despised her. Behind him, the door slid open on its track, and Ryan shot between them, running headlong to his mother and hugging her legs tight.

She put a hand on his still damp hair, stroking it. "It's okay, baby," she said softly. "Everything is okay."

Roman stood there, an outsider, watching the tableau before him. Caroline dropped to her haunches, hugged her little boy to her until he started to squirm. "Are you ready for that pizza?" she asked brightly.

Ryan nodded.

"Then we'll go. Why don't we ask Mr. Kazarov to come with us? Would you like that?"

Ryan only buried his head against her and didn't speak. Roman felt the strength of that rejection as if it were a nuclear detonation inside his head.

"I have work to do," he said, his heart a solid ball of lead in his chest. "Go without me."

She looked uncertain. No, she looked pitying. And that he couldn't take. Roman turned and went inside, blindly finding his way to the study, where he locked the door and then sat in his chair with a thud.

Outside, the world continued the way it always had. But his world had changed. Irrevocably. Now he had to figure out what to do about it.

"We're leaving."

Caroline looked up from where she was going over some reports on the couch, while Ryan and Blake played a game at the table in the dining room. They'd gone out for pizza, but they hadn't stayed away long. The minute the pack of paparazzi swarming around the restaurant figured out who she was, they'd descended, pelting her with questions about her and Roman.

Ryan had started to cry, and Caroline had lost her temper. Roman's driver intervened before she could say anything truly stupid. Then they'd gotten their pizza to go, and hustled into the limo and back to the hotel.

Out of the corner of her eye, she could see Blake look up from the game, but she kept her focus on Roman. She couldn't tell what he was thinking from his expression. He'd managed to hide the raw emotion from earlier behind his usual cool veneer.

She wanted to hold him, but that was out of the question now. "When?"

"In about two hours."

He looked so cold, so closed off, and her heart ached. The truce between them certainly hadn't lasted long. She'd even thought, laughably now, that they might grow closer with time.

He'd never before opened up to her the way he had in the limo this afternoon, and briefly on the plane, when he'd told her about his parents.

Not that she'd ever asked. She'd been young, selfish, concerned with her own drama. She'd been so overwhelmed with love for him, so greedy for his attention, that she'd never asked him any searching questions. She'd thought they would have all the time in the world, back then. She'd only wanted to know how badly he wanted her, how much he worshipped her body. She'd spent every encounter with him thinking of *her* feelings and how to keep him forever.

How terribly naive she'd been.

"Is that necessary?" she said. "It's rather late for Ryan. His bedtime is in another hour."

The coldness in Roman's eyes could have frozen Niagara Falls. "We are traveling on a private plane, not coach class. He can sleep."

She wanted to argue, but she wouldn't. In the scheme of things, disrupting Ryan's schedule by an hour wasn't worth fussing over. And she sensed that arguing with Roman right now was not in her best interests.

"Which location are we going to next?"

She had to have something to focus on, something to prepare for, or she would go insane thinking about all the ways this could have turned out differently.

"We aren't going to any stores," he said.

"I thought that was the point of the exercise." She didn't like the note of panic that crept into her voice.

"That was before." He glanced over at the table, turned back to her with a stony face. "I think things have changed, Caroline. Don't you?"

"I still need to oversee the company," she said. "We have obligations to meet."

His expression grew hard. "You never had a chance, don't you understand that? You can't make the payment, Caroline."

"We still have a little over a week," she said evenly. "And I'm not giving up simply because you say I should."

"You can work from anywhere in the world. You have a

computer, a cell phone, video conferencing. I suggest you use them, because we are not going back to New York just yet."

Her heart was a hot flame in her chest. "You can't force me to go with you wherever you like, Roman. This isn't a dictatorship. I have responsibilities. Ryan and Blake have a schedule to maintain—"

He leaned toward her suddenly, his face twisted in rage. "Really, Caroline? You would throw the fact that our son has a schedule I am not aware of in my face?"

Chaotic emotions charged through her, shaking the landscape she'd always stood upon.

Nothing would ever be the same again, she realized. She had a son with Roman Kazarov, and there was no going back to the way things had been only hours ago.

"I'm not throwing it in your face. I'm just pointing out that you cannot uproot a child's life like this."

He looked utterly bleak in that moment, and her heart twisted in sympathy.

"You've uprooted mine," he said, his voice like chips of ice. "We are going in two hours. I suggest you get ready."

CHAPTER ELEVEN

Kazarov and Caro—Will They or Won't They?

CAROLINE DIDN'T KNOW what she'd expected, but the bright blue ocean beneath the plane's wings had not been it. They'd flown through the night and now dawn was breaking and the landscape below was blue. Endlessly blue.

She shook with some terrible emotion, some horrible feeling that he was taking them to Russia and that he would separate her from Ryan. She hadn't considered that possibility when she'd boarded the plane, the idea that he would take her somewhere foreign, where birth certificates and parental rights didn't stack up against the might of a very rich man.

But the ocean below was dotted with green islands, she soon realized. Not the vast reaches of the Pacific then, or at least not the Pacific as it caressed the shores of China and Russia. And soon she comprehended that it wasn't the Pacific at all, but the Caribbean, when she logged on to the onboard Wi-Fi and tracked their flight.

The very real relief that coursed through her was short-lived, however, when she realized that she still didn't know his aim. *Where,* precisely, was he taking them? And what was his purpose in doing so?

When they landed less than an hour later, a van waited to take them to what turned out to be a sprawling private estate.

They'd ridden from the tiny airport along empty roads that were lush with tropical foliage, until they came to a complex built on the beach.

"Yours?" she asked Roman as they climbed out of the van. It was the first word she'd dared speak to him since they'd left L.A. so many hours ago.

The house was on one level, but it spanned at least a large city block. A profusion of bougainvillea grew along the front veranda, along with potted geraniums and beds of bird of paradise and flowering hibiscus. Palm trees shaded the yard, and a hammock was tied between two trees where the grass gave way to the white sand of the beach.

"It is," Roman said. She hadn't been certain he would answer her. It wasn't a warm answer, or even a very friendly one. But at least he'd spoken to her.

"Which island is this, then?" she asked. The airport had been small, with only Roman's jet and a single island hopper that had been boarding when they'd landed.

"Mine."

Caroline blinked. "The whole island?"

His face was dark. "This is an exclusive resort where utter privacy is guaranteed. There will be no more paparazzi harassing you and Ryan." She hadn't realized he'd known about the incident at the pizza parlor, but she should have guessed that he did. "We host movie stars, politicians, heads of state, tycoons. Anyone who can afford the price can stay in one of the villas on the island. This, however, is my house."

She thought she understood now. By bringing them here, he was guaranteeing they wouldn't be hounded by paparazzi seeking a story. They were free to behave as they wished without fear of prying cameras or microphones. No one had to put on a brave face for the press when they were quietly coming apart inside.

"I had no idea," she said, turning to look at the vast stretch of white beach and turquoise water that fronted the house.

Palm trees swayed in the breeze, and the tropical sounds of bamboo wind chimes tinkled with each gust.

"I want to go to the beach, Mommy, but Uncle Blake says no."

Ryan tugged at her skirt, his little face screwed up in a pout. Until precisely twenty minutes ago, the child hadn't even known what a beach was.

"Ryan Nicholas Wells," she said firmly, "you know better than to ask me if you can do something when Uncle Blake tells you no, don't you?"

Ryan's expression fell. His lower lip protruded. "Yes, ma'am."

"Now go with your uncle Blake and do as he says."

Ryan kicked his feet in the grass. She expected a tantrum, but a large black woman in a colorful tropical dress came outside just then and invited them in. She carried a tray of brightly colored drinks with umbrellas.

"Banana smoothies," she said. "To welcome you to Isla San Jacinto."

Blake took a drink and handed it to Ryan. Beach suddenly forgotten, he disappeared inside the house with Blake, sucking his drink nonstop through the straw. Caroline started to follow, but stopped when she glanced at Roman standing so silently, his eyes hard as he looked at her.

Her heart took a nosedive into the floor at the intensity on his face.

"His name should be Kazarov," he said shortly.

"It wasn't an option," she replied, heat throbbing to life inside her. "You were gone, remember?"

If anything, he looked more furious. "I did not precisely have a choice, Caroline. I lost my visa."

She turned to look at the whitecaps breaking near the beach. A tropical breeze ruffled her hair, bringing with it the scent of flowering trees. "But I didn't know that back then."

He snorted. "And yet you were marrying Jon for your precious stores. I somehow doubt you would have told me the truth if it would have jeopardized that arrangement."

She met his gaze evenly. Because she knew he was right. She wouldn't have jeopardized the arrangement, but she would have figured something out. *Something.* "I did what I had to do, Roman."

"And I will do what I have to do," he said. "You've taken too much from me. I expect to be a part of my child's life from now on. And I expect him to be a Kazarov."

Her heart thumped. "Jon's name is on the birth certificate."

Roman still looked so hard and angry. He took a step toward her, and a trickle of sweat slid between her breasts. It was hot and muggy in the Caribbean, but she wasn't entirely certain that was the cause of the perspiration rising on her body.

"We *are* going to fix this, Caroline. We are going to give Ryan my name the old-fashioned way."

"What's that supposed to mean?" But she knew.

"Don't play dumb with me. It does you no credit."

She tilted her chin up. The breeze ruffled the ends of her hair and, thankfully, cooled the sweat beginning to glisten on her body. "You can't mean to marry me, Roman. You are the notorious playboy, the man who will never settle down. This is not how you want your life to be."

"How would you know what I want? You have never known." He shoved his hands in the pockets of the khaki shorts he wore. His dark hair lifted in the breeze, his icy blue eyes cutting into her. Chilling her.

"We can work this out," she said. "It will take time, but we'll figure it out. You can be a part of his life. I won't deny you that."

Because how could she marry him? How could she be his wife now, after everything that had happened? He loathed her. He would probably always loathe her.

"Right. The way you didn't deny me for the past two years." His nostrils flared, as if he was suppressing strong emotions. "Do you have any idea how much I despise you right now? How much you took away from me?"

She felt his words like a physical blow. "Then why marry me? It can't be good for either one of us."

His smile wasn't meant to be friendly. "You mean it can't be good for you. Poor Caroline Sullivan, forced to marry the Russian peasant, after all. Won't your parents be proud?"

Without thinking, she closed the distance between them and shoved him as hard as she could. He stepped back, surprised—but then he was in front of her again, as solid and as unmovable as a mountain.

She was filled to bursting with the injustice of it all, with everything that she'd sacrificed five years ago when she'd cut him from her life. She'd lied to him then, but she wouldn't lie any longer.

"I loved you, you idiot! I did what I had to do for my family, but I loved you—and I would have defied them to be with you if the price hadn't been so high. If it had just been *me* who would have been affected by the loss of Sullivan's." She was breathing hard now, anger rolling over her in seismic, life-altering waves.

Roman looked stunned. And then his expression hardened by degrees, until she knew he'd convinced himself she wasn't telling the truth.

"Yes, very pretty of you to say. But we know the truth, don't we? Your precious stores will always win, no matter how you try to dress it up in ribbons and bows."

His gaze slid over her, down the open neck of her T-shirt and beyond, to the denim mini she'd donned this morning. She was surprised to see a flare of heat in his eyes—and just as surprised at the answering surge in her feminine core.

After everything.

"You're wrong," she said tightly. "And I *won't* marry you."

His smile made her shiver in spite of the heat. "We shall see."

He had no idea what he was doing.

Roman watched Caroline and Blake play on the beach with Ryan, and felt like an outsider. He'd told her she would marry him, told her he was doing it to claim his child—and the truth was he had no idea how to be a father. No idea if he even could. He'd had such a lousy example in his own father that he had no idea where to begin.

Bitterness flooded his throat. If he'd been there from the beginning, if he'd watched Caroline grow big with his child, if he'd changed diapers and held the boy at night when he wouldn't sleep, then perhaps he would know what to do now.

He wouldn't be standing here in the shadows of the covered veranda, feeling like an idiot, a stranger to his own child.

Which, he acknowledged, he truly was. The boy seemed terrified of him. Worse, Roman was terrified in return. Not that he would ever admit it. And certainly not to Caroline. She could help him, he knew that, but how could he ask her?

She laughed at something Blake said, and Roman's heart squeezed. He used to love to make her laugh. She had such an intoxicating laugh, the kind that made you want to laugh as well. She must not have laughed much over the last couple of years.

He frowned at the thought of her taking care of her dying husband, a man who had only been only a friend instead of a lover. Had she been lonely? Frightened? Angry?

Roman shook off any feelings of sympathy. She'd lied to him. Kept his child from him. And she would have done so no matter what.

I loved you, you idiot.

He didn't believe it. Not for a minute. She would say whatever it took to make him merciful now. Whatever it took to keep him from destroying her world.

She looked up then, as if she sensed him standing there. He didn't shrink from her gaze. Her eyes met his across the distance. She said something to Blake, and then she was striding across the sand toward the steps leading up to the veranda where he stood.

She walked with an innate grace that had always been, to him, one of the hallmarks of her class. She moved like a woman who'd had every advantage—money, position, power—from an early age. She took it for granted that she belonged, that she was wanted. She didn't think of how people might perceive her. She just *was*.

She was wearing a red bikini with a white shirt tied at her waist, and a straw hat that covered her face. Her skin was one shade this side of golden, yet she wore it better than many of the bronzed women he'd seen on the beaches of his island. She was more beautiful than any of them, including the starlets and models.

Unwelcome heat slid into his groin as she moved toward him, loose-hipped and elegant. It surprised him that he could want her after what she'd done. And yet, when he'd been buried inside her two nights ago, he'd thought there was nowhere else he'd rather be.

"Won't you join us?" she said as she came closer. "We're playing tag."

"Tag." He said it as if the word was foreign, but he knew what it meant. What she was asking.

She nodded. "Ryan enjoys it." She put a hand over the brim of her hat as the trade winds gusted. "It would be a good way to get to know him a little better."

"He's too scared," Roman said coolly. "Of everything."

She shrugged, though he could tell the criticism hurt her. "I told you, it's his personality. He could grow out of it, but you standing here and brooding isn't likely to help. Come play with him. Act like someone fun to know."

He wanted to do it, and yet he couldn't seem to make that first move. What if he failed? What if he proved that he wasn't meant to be a father, after all? If he got down there and the kid shied away from him, what would he do? How would he deal with it?

"I have work to do," he said. "Another time."

She put a hand on her hip. "He'll be in high school before you cease being busy, Roman."

"A multinational conglomerate does not run itself," he said stiffly. Because she was right, and because he was seeking an excuse to avoid making a fool of himself. She knew it as well as he did.

Sadness clouded her pretty eyes. "You have to start sometime. It won't get any easier the longer you delay." She took the steps up to the veranda, coming over to where he stood, and stopping before him. He could see the soft curves of her breasts where the white shirt gapped, the luminescence of her skin, and he wanted to bend and place his mouth just there, where the valley of her breasts started. Then he wanted to lick the curves, slide her bikini top aside and curl his tongue around a tight nipple.

He closed his eyes. No matter how many times he told himself it was wrong to want her, wrong to even consider taking her to his bed again after what she'd done to him, his body refused to get the message. He'd never had a problem quitting a woman—except this one.

Always this one.

She looked up at him then, her blond hair streaming wild and golden over her shoulders. She wasn't the heiress now so much as the bohemian beach girl—albeit a rather pale beach girl.

"Please come, Roman. Ryan is a good kid, but he needs

your patience. Within a few days, he'll think you're pretty
fabulous. You just have to start somewhere. Why not now?"

He didn't say anything for the space of several heartbeats.
And then, because he suddenly couldn't bear the idea of being
alone with his thoughts for another minute while she and
Ryan and Blake played in the surf, shutting him out, he felt
his reluctance evaporate like mist.

"Yes," he said. "I will come."

The days that followed were as close to perfect as they could
be, considering the circumstances. Caroline had decided, that
afternoon on the beach when she'd known Roman was watching, that she needed to help him know their child. Roman
was uncertain, anguished, and though she might be angry
with him for his high-handedness, his arrogance, she owed
it to her son at the very least to make sure he had a good relationship with the man who'd fathered him.

She thought of her own father and dark emotion filled her.
They hadn't always agreed with each other, but she would
give anything to have him back, whole in his mind, and
disagreeing with her now. She missed him. How could she
deny her son the opportunity to forge that kind of relationship with his father?

She couldn't, and so she'd determined to help Roman navi-
gate the uncertain waters of becoming a parent. For her son,
she told herself.

Caroline felt a pang of sharp emotion every time she
watched Ryan and Roman together. Ryan had warmed up
pretty quickly, but Roman was still uncertain, still walking
on eggshells much of the time.

Oh, sometimes he let himself go and just acted naturally—
like when he'd taken them all out on his yacht and let Ryan
drive the boat, while he'd stood behind the captain's chair,
his hands over Ryan's little ones, steering while his son asked
a million questions.

Everything about that day had seemed perfect. The sun had reflected like diamonds on the sparkling water, and Caroline had felt as if her heart would burst with delight. Blake had given her an I-told-you-so look, and she'd smiled back at him with genuine happiness, feeling joyful in the moment and wishing it would always be that way.

But, of course, there were too many raw feelings still to be dealt with, too much reality intruding on their lives. Not that anyone had violated their privacy out here. No, that wasn't possible, as Roman had promised.

Reality, however, was always there, in the back of her mind, preying on her thoughts. It was reality that had caused her to pick up the phone and call her mother only minutes before.

"You must return to the city, Caroline," her mother said firmly. "The newspapers are simply filled with gossip about you and that horrid man. I've had to hide them from your father. It would kill him to think that Roman Kazarov might soon be running his stores."

Caroline closed her eyes and pressed two fingers to her temples. As if her father would even remember who Roman was. "Mother, the reality is that Daddy made some poor decisions and we're in pretty deep. I'm trying to fix it, but it's not easy."

They had only days left, and she had all her people working overtime. Even she was putting in overtime, spending long hours with her spreadsheets and her telephone when she wasn't helping Roman get to know his son. The numbers were still dismal—and she was tired and numb and ready to give up.

Except that every time she thought that, she got angry with herself. She was *not* giving up. Her father wouldn't if he were here. Jon wouldn't have, either. A few more days. They'd need a miracle, but anything was possible. She'd been calling everyone she could think of, searching for investors. She'd found few.

Her mother sniffed in that aristocratic way she had. Jessica Hartshorne Sullivan came from a very old and venerable New York family, and though some in her set had considered her to have married down when she'd chosen a businessman like Frank Sullivan, she'd never once given the slightest indication she agreed with them.

Considering her reaction to Roman, it was, in many ways, pure irony. Not that Caroline planned to point it out to her.

"Some days, he wants to go into the office."

Caroline could hear the wistfulness in her mother's voice, and sadness clawed at her. Her father, once so vibrant, was a shell of himself now. It wasn't fair.

"That's not possible, Mother, and you know it."

She heard her mother sniff again, only this time it was due to a far more identifiable emotion. "It's been…difficult," she said, her voice becoming thready. "Even with the nurse. It's happening far more quickly than I would have believed, Caroline. Just yesterday, he looked at me like I was a stranger. He forgets my name more often now…."

Caroline put her head in her free hand as her eyes filled with tears. "I'm sorry, Mother. All we can do is make sure he's taken care of, that he's safe and happy."

They spoke for a few more minutes, and then Caroline ended the call. She felt so bleak inside, so ravaged. There was nothing she could do to fix this. She felt she should be there at her mother's side, and yet it wouldn't change a thing if she were. When she'd suggested she should come to Southampton, her mother had waved the thought away as if it was nonsense. She wanted Caroline in New York, away from Roman Kazarov and the tabloids, not in Southampton.

Caroline grabbed a tissue and wiped her eyes. When she looked up, Roman was there. A dark frown rode his handsome face. His gaze grew sharper as their eyes met. She wondered how long he'd been standing in the entry.

"What is wrong, Caroline? Has something happened to your father?"

She started to shake her head, denial coming automatically—but she couldn't seem to complete the movement. Instead, to her horror, she burst into tears.

CHAPTER TWELVE

Has the Billionaire Playboy Been Tamed at Last?

THAT HE came to her side and pulled her into his arms should have comforted her. And it did, except that it also made her sob all the harder. It wasn't just for her father she cried. It was for Roman, for her and their child, for Jon and Blake. For everything that had been lost over the years—and everything yet to be lost.

"I—I'm sorry," she said, her face against his chest, her fingers clutching his dark shirt. He was so warm and solid, so *there* when the rest of the world seemed to be doing its damnedest to work against her at that precise moment.

His fingers traced a slow, sensual path up her spine. Not that he meant the touch to be anything other than comforting, she was certain, but her body reacted anyway. Her nipples tightened, and her feminine core flooded with heat and moisture and the kind of need that only he could call up within her.

Blindly, she tilted her head back and went up on her tiptoes to kiss him. He stiffened—and then he groaned and she was in his arms, really in his arms, and he was kissing her as if he'd been dying without her.

His big hands shaped her waist, traveled along her ribs and up to cup the swells of her breasts. When his thumbs flicked across her nipples, she moaned and arched herself into his hands.

So quickly she became his to command, his to do with as he wanted. It had been over a week since they'd made love in L.A., and she was dying for him as if it had been a century. She'd thought he would never want to touch her again. But he did, he was, and she was filled with a fierce joy that he still desired her.

She had to have him inside her again. Now. Her fingers went to the waistband of his board shorts. He made a sound in his throat—and then he set her away from him.

"Stop," he told her hoarsely.

She staggered backward until her butt was against the edge of the desk she'd been sitting at only moments before. She could only gape up at him with wide, wounded eyes.

"Chert poberi," he said, dragging a hand through his hair. "I want you, God help me, but not like this. Not when you are crying and upset."

Caroline pulled in a shaky breath as her brain focused on those three little words. He wanted her. He *still* wanted her. She dropped her gaze. Inside, she was a churning, roiling mess of conflicting emotions. Something was breaking inside her, something monumental. Something she was afraid to examine.

And it had to do with this man. With the knowledge that it wasn't quite as ruined between them as she'd thought.

He put his hands on her shoulders, squeezed, and she nearly broke down once more.

"Can you tell me what is wrong?" His voice was almost tender.

She hesitated. If she let the words out, then what? But he knew something was wrong, and if she didn't say anything, he'd only grow suspicious. "M-my father is sick." That much was true.

Roman tipped her chin up with a finger. "Then you must go to his side."

Her eyes filled again. The concern she saw in his gaze would be her undoing. She was still scrambling to protect her family, and he wanted to help her in spite of everything the Sullivans had done to him.

"It's not necessary." She bit her lip. How could she explain without giving it all away? "It's chronic, and while he won't get better, it won't kill him either. He most likely has many years left. It's just…hard."

"This is why he retired?"

She nodded. "He had to. There is no way he could continue working."

Roman looked troubled. "I'm sorry, Caroline."

She was tired of beating her head against the wall, tired of fighting and working and getting nowhere fast. "You're right that he made bad decisions at Sullivan's, but we didn't know he was ill. I've been trying to put it back together. But soon it won't matter, right?" She smiled, though her mouth trembled at the corners. "You will do what you usually do, and Sullivan's will be finished."

He looked fierce for a moment. And then he dragged her into his arms again. She slipped her arms around his waist and just stood with her head against him, breathing in his scent. He smelled like salt water and sun, alive and vibrant and delicious.

He was solid, and here, and she was suddenly glad of it.

"It's not like you to give up so easily," he said after a while. "What happened to that fierce determination to beat me at my own game?"

She sighed. It wasn't that she didn't want to save her family legacy. She just wanted it to be simpler, to not hurt so much or exact such a price. Who was she doing it for, anyway? She'd always thought it was for her family, for herself. And now for Ryan. But if it went away, what had she really lost? Compared to a father, a husband, the man she'd once lived for as if he were the entire world?

So long as she had Ryan, she had everything she needed. Maybe it was time to break from the chains of the past and let life roll along unfettered for a while.

"I'm tired, Roman," she said. "Sullivan's has cost me too much over the years. Maybe it's time for someone else to take the responsibility. Rather than breaking it up, maybe you could absorb it into your company and keep some of the better stores open."

He was silent for so long she began to wonder if he'd heard her. But then he spoke. "You're only saying this because you are upset. Another hour, and you'll be fighting again. Sullivan's is in your blood."

"I wish it wasn't," she said fiercely, because on some level she knew he was right.

But she meant it. For once, she truly wanted free of the burden. She'd done so much, fought so hard—and the mountain only seemed to grow taller. She felt like Sisyphus, condemned to roll the same damn rock up the same damn mountain, only to watch it roll back down again once she'd reached the pinnacle.

There had to be something better in life, right? Something more important? She could feel Roman's heart beating beneath her ear, the rhythmic pulse strong and steady, and she knew with a certainly what that something was.

Love. Family. Joy.

She knew then what this fierce restlessness was: she still loved him. It was a jubilant realization—and a sobering one. She loved this man, had always loved him—and yet she'd betrayed him. Betrayed them both.

She'd taken what he'd felt for her and shattered it like a piece of fine crystal dropped from a great height.

Fear curled around her heart then. How could you ever

reassemble something so broken? So completely and utterly demolished? How could she fix what she'd done?

He wanted her physically, but that was no longer enough for her. She wanted what she should have had in the first place. Roman, Ryan, a life together filled with love and happiness.

Was it possible? Would it *ever* be possible?

She could feel the change in him as they stood there in silence for too long, the slight stiffening of his body, the sudden urge to disconnect from her. She dropped her arms first, because she couldn't bear to cling to him and have him push her away.

He took a step back, his handsome face carefully blank, as if he'd erased every emotion. Caroline's world felt as if it had been turned inside out.

"You don't mean that, Caroline," he said, and she wondered for a moment what he was talking about. And then she remembered—she'd said she wished Sullivan's wasn't in her blood.

"What if I do?" Her heart felt as if it, too, had been turned inside out. She wondered if he could see everything she felt, as if the truth shone bright and hard from beneath the cracks in the veneer she'd been showing to the world for too long. "What if I want to go back and start again? Make a different choice this time?"

He didn't pretend not to know what she was talking about. She could see it in the rigid line of his jaw, the flashing of his blue eyes.

"Don't," he told her, his voice hard again. "You made your choice. Anything we might have had was destroyed when you walked away and took our child with you."

They had dinner on the veranda. Shrimp, jerk chicken, grilled vegetables, spicy rice and beans, and fried plantains. There was cool, crisp white wine, and coffee. Caroline ate in silence, listening to Ryan chatter about his day at the beach. Her gaze kept straying to Roman, who looked both uptight and relaxed at once.

He seemed to realize how critical it was to engage with Ryan when his son spoke to him. Though he appeared surprised by the continual questions being directed at him, he answered them admirably. Even confidently, as if he was beginning to understand that all he need do to be involved was make Ryan comfortable with him.

When the meal was over, Blake announced it was time for Ryan's bath. Ryan started to whine in protest.

"No arguments, young man," Blake said. "It's time."

Ryan turned to his mother. "I want Mr. Roman to go with me," he said, and her heart squeezed tight. Her gaze met Roman's over the table for the first time since he'd walked away from her that afternoon.

His eyes burned hot, searing into hers. She tore her gaze away, her heart skipping crazily. "You need to ask him," she told Ryan.

The boy turned to his father. She knew the effort it took for him to overcome his innate shyness. He was growing accustomed to Roman, that was clear, but they hadn't known each other very long yet. This request was a far bigger deal than perhaps Roman realized. She prayed that he would, however, and that he'd agree.

"Would you take me for my bath, Mr. Roman?" he asked, his little voice quieter than it had been, his eyes downcast.

For a painful heartbeat, Roman didn't speak. Then he met her gaze over Ryan's head, and while she wasn't certain what she saw there, she knew he understood the import.

Roman pushed back from the table and stood without a word. She almost held her breath, but she knew he was going to accept, knew that he was overcome by whatever chaotic emotions were whirling inside him, and that speech was beyond him at this second.

He held out his hand to Ryan. The little boy slipped from his chair and put his small hand in his father's much larger one. They stood that way for a moment, Roman looking hard at her. She couldn't tell what was behind that enigmatic stare—hatred? Rage? Resentment?

Probably some combination of them all. And then he looked away, and she felt bereft suddenly, as if she'd been standing in full sunlight and was then plunged into an arctic pool.

"You will have to tell me what this bath involves," Roman said, turning his full attention to Ryan. The two of them disappeared into the house, Ryan talking excitedly. They were gone for a handful of heartbeats before Caroline turned to look at Blake, her eyes shimmering with tears she couldn't hide.

"Oh, honey," Blake said, coming over and squeezing her shoulder. "It'll all work itself out. You'll see. He just needs time."

Caroline swallowed hard a few times before she could manage to speak. "I'm not sure it will. I ruined whatever he felt for me a long time ago."

Blake only smiled. "I doubt that, sweetie. I seriously do." He patted her shoulder before returning to his seat. "You'll see. Trust me."

Dear, sweet Blake. She laughed in spite of herself. "You're nearly as arrogant as he is, you know that?"

He looked smug as he speared a chunk of mango with his fork. "I know what I know."

Roman found her on the beach. He hadn't gone looking for her so much as he'd needed to get out and clear his head with a long walk in the tropical dusk. Apparently, she'd needed the same.

His heart twisted in his chest, as it often seemed to do these days, at the sight of her standing there with her golden hair streaming down her back, her shoes dangling from one hand, her long legs bare to midthigh, where the hem of her casual dress lay.

It hit him with a visceral punch to the gut just how much he hated her and wanted her.

Except he couldn't quite lie to himself anymore. He *didn't* hate her. He never had. He'd hated what she'd done to him, hated what her betrayal had cost him, but he didn't hate the woman. How could he? Especially now that he knew she was the mother of his child?

She'd been young and, he remembered, eager to please her father. Of course she would have done whatever Frank Sullivan asked her to do. Roman felt a bubble of anger well inside him at the thought of the man who'd cut him off so thoroughly. Yet even that didn't last long when he thought of the other man wasting away with illness.

He'd blamed the Sullivans for years for what had happened to his mother, but the truth was that his father had caused her condition. If Andrei Kazarov hadn't been a brute and a bully, she would have never needed the kind of care that had cost so much more than Roman could afford.

As he looked at Caroline now, he realized that what he felt for her was a giant tangle of things he'd never solve. It was like being caught in a labyrinth with a thousand possible threads to follow toward freedom. He suspected, however, that he was never getting free.

The waves broke close to shore tonight, and then rushed high up on the sand. Caroline stood with her back to him and let the water flood around her ankles before it rolled out to sea again.

He didn't make a sound, but somehow she heard him. She turned at his approach and stood there with the shoes dangling and one arm wrapped around her middle. Her eyes were huge in her pale face. For a minute, he wanted to go to her and drag her into his arms. But then he remembered his son calling him "Mr. Roman" and his heart throbbed with hurt.

She didn't say anything at all, just watched him with those eyes that held a world of pain, and he grew angry with himself for wanting to take that pain away. *He* was supposed to be the one in pain, not her.

He thought of his little boy tonight, of all the ways he'd felt so awkward and out of sorts, trying to help with a bath and bedtime. How could he ever forgive her for that?

"I'm sorry, Roman," she finally said. "For everything."

She made him feel rough inside, as if he'd been scraped against the rocks again and again.

"I don't believe apologies are enough."

She dropped her chin to her chest. "I know that. But it's all I have."

Roman moved closer, until he was standing beside her and gazing out to sea. She turned until they were both facing the same direction again. Neither of them spoke for the longest time. They simply listened to the waves crashing, crashing, crashing against the beach.

"When I went back to Russia, I had no money. I had no job." He swallowed, unable to believe what he was about to say to her. And yet he had to. He felt it in his bones. If he didn't let out the rage, he might never figure out how to move beyond it. "My mother had been in a nursing home. I sent money to care for her when I worked for your father. When I returned, I couldn't pay for her to stay there anymore."

Beside him, he could hear Caroline gasp. "Oh, Roman—"

He held up a hand to silence her. "*Nyet.* I had to move her into a cheap apartment in Moscow. My brothers and I took turns doing what we could. We hired a nurse to come as often as we could afford. Without the specialized care in the nursing home, she died sooner than we expected."

Fresh tears rolled down Caroline's face. He felt the guilt of it pierce him to the core. It wasn't her fault. If he'd kept working for the Sullivan Group, his mother still would have died. She just would have done so in a better environment.

"She was going to die, anyway," he said softly. "Her mind was already gone. Had been for years."

"What happened to her, Roman?"

He closed his eyes against the memories, the pain. "My father was a very violent man, *solnyshko*. We will leave it at that."

She closed the distance between them, wrapped her arms around his waist and held him tight, burying her head against his chest. For a moment he didn't move. And then, almost without thought, his arms went around her body and held her tight.

CHAPTER THIRTEEN

Rumblings of Leadership Changes at Sullivan's

CAROLINE FELT SO many things in that moment. Love, sadness, worry, sorrow, fear—and maybe a zillion other emotions she would never identify. "You never told me your mother was ill," she said against the warm hardness of his chest.

"We were too busy talking about other things," he said, his voice a rumble in her ear. "Whenever we did talk."

She pushed back to look up at him. There was sadness etched on his features. Pain. It made her heart ache. They had more in common than only a child, it would seem.

"I wish I'd known."

He shrugged. "There was nothing to be done. She was being taken care of."

Caroline squeezed his arms. "I'm so sorry. I understand what it's like to lose someone you love, and to feel utterly helpless to prevent it."

He pushed a lock of her hair that had blown free behind her ear. She shivered with the sensations that rolled through her at that simple gesture. "You were very much affected by Jon's death."

"He was my best friend." She pulled in a breath, determined to go on. "He was a good father to Ryan. He loved him as if Ryan were his own."

Roman didn't say anything for a long moment. "I am glad then. Since I could not be there."

Caroline swallowed. "You should have been. I should have found a way to tell you, once I knew where you were."

He blew out a breath. "I am beginning to think nothing is as simple as it seems, in retrospect. We both made mistakes."

Her breath caught. "Did we?"

He looked so serious. "*Da.* I believed you too readily when you told me you didn't love me. I should have fought harder."

"It wouldn't have mattered," she said, her throat aching with the weight of her words. "I still had to marry Jon in order to save the stores. I couldn't let people suffer when it was in my power to prevent it. And I couldn't see my heritage destroyed."

He took her hand in his, threaded his fingers through hers. "And this is why you fight so hard now. Why you refuse to give up."

"It's Ryan's heritage, too. I can't let you break it up."

"He is my son, Caroline. He will inherit all I have built. If this includes Sullivan's, it will still go to Ryan."

Her heart skipped a beat. "I thought you wanted to demolish it."

He shrugged. "I am a business man, *solnyshko.* I will do what is best for the company, and for my bottom line."

So many feelings welled within her then—relief, love, gratitude. She'd thought he would destroy the stores simply to get back at her. She was used to her life falling apart just when she thought everything was going well.

But perhaps he wouldn't destroy anything. Perhaps they could build something good out of the ashes of the past. Perhaps, this time, it would all work out the way she wished.

"Sullivan's shouldn't be in this position," she said. "But it all went wrong when we didn't realize—" She swallowed hard. Her father's illness was something they'd kept from be-

coming public knowledge simply to prevent the media spec-
tacle the news would bring.

"Didn't realize what, Caroline?"

Her chest ached. "We didn't realize that my father was in
the beginning stages of Alzheimer's. That he was losing his
sense of self, and had become easy prey to those who wanted
to profit from his mistakes."

Roman looked stunned. "I can hardly believe it. Your father was always larger than life. Just five years ago…"

"I know. But it's true. He doesn't remember much of anything anymore. He doesn't know me at all. Or Ryan."

"Solnyshko moya, I'm sorry."

She looked away from him suddenly, fighting the tears
that wanted to keep coming until there was nothing left, until
she was an empty husk. Life was so different now than it had
been five years ago. Two years ago.

Even one year ago.

It was lonelier and harder, and she was tired of it. Tired of
putting on a brave face and pretending everything was okay.
Tired of being strong when she felt anything but. When she
wanted to howl and wail and gnash her teeth against the un-
fairness of it all.

"Caroline," he said, and she turned to look at him. "You
don't have to be strong every moment of every day."

"I can't help it," she whispered. "It's all I know."

He cursed then, and dragged her against him.

She clung to him, to the warmth and hardness of his body
in the tropical dusk. This was where she wanted to be. Where
she'd always wanted to be.

In this man's arms, in his life. He was murmuring to her
in Russian. She didn't know what he said, but it sounded
beautiful to her ears.

And then he tilted her head back and fused his mouth to
hers. It was a hot, wet, sensual kiss that sizzled into her like
lightning. Her body was on fire. Needy.

His mouth slanted over hers, taking everything she gave him. They fell onto the wet sand as the sky turned purple and stars dotted the fabric of the night. His big body hovered over hers, pressing her into the surf.

When the tide rolled in again, she gasped with the rush of water over her body, but she didn't care that she was soaked. The sea was warm, but the breeze cooled her. Her nipples responded, beading tight against the thin cotton of her dress. Roman lifted himself away from her as she shuddered, concern in his gaze.

Whatever he might have said was lost, however, as his gaze slid over her. The dress clung to every curve, every dent and hollow of her body. His gaze fastened on her nipples. And then he was cursing softly, unbuttoning her dress and peeling it aside so he could fasten his warm mouth on her cold flesh.

Caroline arched her back, gasping when he curled his tongue around her nipple. This was what she wanted, what she'd missed for far too long. She'd had a taste of it that one glorious night they'd spent together in L.A., but it had been over so quickly.

Now, however, she reacted like a madwoman. Moaning and writhing and urging him onward. Before he changed his mind. Before something happened to break this magical spell between them.

She tilted her hips up, arching into him, glorying in the answering hardness pressing back into her.

"I want you," she gasped when he sucked hard on her sensitive nipple, sending a spike of pleasure into her femininity. "Please, Roman."

He lifted his head then, and they stared at each other for several heartbeats. And then he dropped his head with a groan and kissed her. Caroline wrapped her arms around his neck, pulling her body into his as if she feared he would change his mind.

One hand slid down her form, over her hip, and then inward. He angled his body away to finish unbuttoning her dress before he peeled it open, revealing her to the night air and his hot eyes.

"Caroline," he said, his voice a growl against her skin. "How I want you."

Her heart soared at the need in his voice. This thing between them was like the tide—inevitable, relentless, timeless. It simply was, regardless of everything that should have killed it.

She trailed her fingers to the hem of his T-shirt. "Take me," she told him, her voice a choked whisper. "I'm yours."

With a growl, he took the shirt from her grasp and ripped it up and off his body. A moment later, her fingers were tangling with his as they both went for the ties to his board shorts. He made quick work of the thong beneath her dress, and then he was lifting her hips, his body finding hers and entering her with one long, hard plunge.

Their joining was intense, overwhelming, beautiful. They rose and fell like the tide, their bodies glorying in each other. Caroline reached the peak much too quickly, tumbling over the other side in a long, hard fall to the bottom. Roman followed her, his body stiffening suddenly, his hoarse cry echoing against the night and the whoosh of the waves.

She held him to her, suddenly afraid that he would leave before she'd even managed to pick up the pieces of her soul again. His breathing was harsh in her ear, as if he'd run a great distance. He rolled off her, but she clung to him as he turned, until they were both on their side, facing each other.

He lifted a hand, and then he was pushing her wet hair off her cheeks and throat, tucking it behind her ears. The gesture was unrelentingly tender, and her heart felt as if someone had put it in a vise. She ached with everything she felt, with everything she wanted to say, and yet she remained silent. Afraid.

"You slay me," he said softly. "In so many ways."

Her throat hurt. "I don't mean to."

"You have never meant to. And yet you do."

She slid her palm against his cheek. "I think it's mutual, Roman. I've never stopped thinking about you."

He captured her hand and pressed it to his mouth.

"I want you and our son in my life," he growled. "I want to figure this out, Caroline."

"We will," she said. "Somehow, we will."

Much later they lay in bed together, with nothing but the sound of the waves and bamboo wind chimes echoing in through the sliding doors that were open to the night. When they'd come inside from the beach, Caroline had almost expected to go their separate ways in spite of the way they'd clung to each other. This feeling between them was still so raw, so fragile, and she hadn't thought that Roman would want her in his bed.

But he'd had other ideas.

He'd tugged her toward his room, where they'd showered to remove the sand from their bodies, and then they'd fallen into the plush bed with the filmy mosquito net surrounding it and made soft, sweet love that tore her heart open and made it impossible to hide her feelings from him.

"I love you," she'd cried as she'd exploded beneath him. He hadn't said the words back, though her name had been on his lips as he'd followed her into oblivion.

Caroline couldn't sleep, so she climbed from the bed and went out onto the veranda, where she found a lounge chair and curled up in it. She was wearing one of Roman's T-shirts and she bent to inhale his scent from the fabric.

Then she lay back against the cushions and stared out at the whitecaps breaking against the shore. The moon was high now, its glow painting the sea with a glittery brush. She curled her toes into the chair and wrapped her arms around her body to ward off a chill.

"What are you doing out here?" Roman's voice was gravelly with sleep. She turned to him, her heart lurching at the sight of his bare chest—and barer thighs. He'd come outside in nothing but his own glorious skin, and she shivered anew—though not from cold.

"I couldn't sleep."

He sat on the lounge beside her and folded her into his embrace. His body was warm and she snuggled closer to him, wrapping an arm around his torso.

"Do you wish to talk about it?"

She closed her eyes and pressed her lips to his skin. "There's nothing to talk about," she said.

He tipped her chin up and stared into her eyes. Her heart skipped as she imagined him loving her, really loving her, the way he once had. Was it possible? Would it *ever* be possible again? Or was she deluding herself, setting herself up for an even bigger fall?

"There must be something," he said, his voice low and deep and sexy.

She dropped her gaze from his. "I'm worried about a great many things, Roman. None of which I want to waste time talking about tonight."

"What do you wish to talk about then?"

She looked up again. His eyes were twin flames in the night and she shuddered at all she knew lay behind that enigmatic gaze. "What if I don't want to talk at all? What if I only want to feel?"

His smile curled her toes. "This can be arranged, *solnyshko*. But I'd prefer if you'd talk to me first."

She sighed. How could she ever voice everything she was feeling? "What's there to talk about, Roman? You already know everything."

His smile faltered, and her heart flipped. "Not everything, Caroline. In fact, I'd say I have missed much."

She squeezed him tight. She'd been talking about her father, about Sullivan's, but she knew what he meant without hearing him say it. Knew what that veil of sadness alluded to. "I have baby books, and videos. I know they aren't the same, but I want to show them to you when we get back to New York."

His gaze dropped, and she wanted to cry out. Everything was still so fragile between them that she kept expecting it to crack and fall apart. But he looked up again, his eyes glistening in the night. "Yes. I want to see these."

She turned her head away as tears pricked her own eyes. "I don't blame you for hating me."

He didn't say anything for a long moment. "I don't hate you, Caroline."

She looked at him, disbelief rumbling through her like a storm. "Why not? You lost a lot because of me. Because you got involved with me."

"I gained something, too," he said. "I gained a son."

She curled her fingers into a fist as hot emotion flooded her. "I'm angry with my father. Angry that he sent you away like he did, angry that he made poor decisions at Sullivan's, and angry that he doesn't even know me anymore—"

She broke off and bit down on her lower lip. Roman turned her chin toward him. "We cannot change the past. And for your father, we cannot change the future, either. But we can do something about *our* future."

Her breath caught. "Do you mean that?"

He looked so serious. "I do. Marry me, *lyubimaya moya*. Let us have the life we should have had together in the first place."

A week ago, she'd refused to consider marrying him. But so much had changed since then. Her feelings for him were raw, overwhelming. And it was so very tempting to agree this time.

But if she said yes, if she took this slice of happiness,

would it last? Or would the fall to the bottom be even longer and harder than it had the first time?

"I'm scared, Roman. What if it doesn't work out?"

He sighed. "Then we will deal with that if the moment comes."

She shivered. That was something she didn't want to think about it. She pulled him down to her, until she was pressed full length to his amazing body. Until she could feel the heat and hardness of him, feel her blood stirring hot in her veins in answer.

"I don't want to talk anymore," she said, as dread threatened to crush the dreams she'd barely begun to have. "Kiss me, Roman."

His body responded, growing impossibly harder against her flesh. His breath hitched inward. "This conversation is not over, Caroline," he said, his lips only a whisper away.

She arched against him, desire a heavy drumbeat in her veins. Roman held himself still as the ocean washed against the beach and the bamboo chimes tinkled in the breeze—and then he cursed softly and took her mouth with his.

CHAPTER FOURTEEN

Is Carol Pregnant? Rumors of an Island Wedding...

THE PRIMARY LESSON Roman had learned about love was that it didn't last. In his experience, it wasn't strong enough to overcome adversity. Yet here he lay, beside the woman he'd once loved more than the world, and his insides were twisted into knots at what he was feeling.

He'd held her in his arms and called her his love. Not that she knew what he'd said, but he did. The words—*lyubimaya moya*—had slipped out before he'd realized they were even there. Hovering like a tiger waiting to pounce, they'd caught him by surprise and torn shreds into his heart.

How could he mean them? How could he let himself be that vulnerable again?

How could he possibly love her?

He didn't know, but feared that he did. He also feared, on some level, a repeat performance of five years ago. She'd said tonight she loved him—but did she mean it? Did she want him only in order to rescue her stores? Was that what this was all about?

He didn't know. But then he thought back on the last few days together, on the way she tried to ease his relationship with Ryan, and every instinct Roman had told him the answer was no.

Yet the questions swam in his head anyway. The past was like a serpent, coiled and waiting to strike.

Roman shoved a hand through his hair and forced out a breath. *Chert poberi,* this was supposed to be simple. His plan had been to return to New York and rip Sullivan's out from under the high and mighty Sullivan family. To make them pay for all the heartache they'd caused him.

Except he'd realized that wasn't the solution, no matter that he'd carried that very thought with him, let it drive him for years now.

Caroline had been as much a victim of the situation as he had. Her parents had forced her to leave him, and then forced him out of the country to prevent her from going back on her word.

As if she would. He looked down at her, curled beside him, and felt a pang of pride and desire. She was fierce and she did what she thought was right for those she loved. Even at the expense of herself. Would he have acted any differently than she had if faced with the destruction of so many lives?

He knew the answer was no. He would have done whatever it took. Just as she had.

He ran his fingers over the satin of her skin, smiled when she sighed and snuggled closer to him.

This felt right. Being with her. Being with Ryan. Roman wasn't betraying his mother's memory by giving up the idea of ruining Sullivan's. He knew she wouldn't have wanted him to do such a thing anyway. She'd been a gentle soul. Too gentle. It had been her greatest weakness and her ultimate destruction.

He grieved for her, but he couldn't blame anyone else for the consequences of her choices. He had to let it go. He had to move forward and embrace his future.

He turned on his side and tucked Caroline against his body, curving himself around her. She wriggled her hips against him and his body reacted, hardening instantly. She came awake—or perhaps she'd been awake—her hips moving more deliberately now, tormenting him.

"Are you planning to use that?" she asked almost breathlessly.

His mouth found the place where her neck joined her shoulder. "Would you like me to?"

In answer, she moved a leg forward, exposing her sex for him. He entered her from behind, filling her until they both gasped.

It was some time later when they collapsed into sleep, bodies curled around each other as if they feared being parted during the night.

Caroline sat in the office overlooking the beach and tried to focus on the phone calls she'd been making since 6:00 a.m. Outside, she could see Ryan playing on the sand. Blake sat in a chair beneath an umbrella, a cool drink beside him and a book in his hand.

She hadn't seen Roman since early this morning, when he'd woken her with kisses and caresses as the sun rose in the sky over the Caribbean. He'd told her he had business to take care of at the resort and that he'd be back later today. She glanced at her watch, realized it was after three in the afternoon, and wondered when he would return.

God, she was so pitiful, wanting him so much even as she worked harder than she'd ever worked in her life to keep her company from defaulting, and him from winning what he'd come to take away from her in the first place.

Not that she believed he would destroy Sullivan's now. No, she knew he was smart. He hadn't built a huge, multibillion dollar conglomerate out of nothing by being stupid. He would not demolish her stores just to satisfy a thirst for revenge if it wasn't smart business to do so.

Caroline sighed. She felt as if they were gaining an understanding of one another, as if the past was not so fearsome or unconquerable as she'd believed.

Oh, it still frightened her, definitely. She'd watched her life fall apart so many times in the last few years that it was hard to suppose it wouldn't again. Especially when happiness seemed to be within her grasp.

She closed her eyes a moment, swallowed. It would be all right. She firmly believed she and Roman could be reasonable and work through their issues like adults. They had a child together. If nothing else, they had to think of Ryan first.

Today, she honestly believed they could do that. A week ago, not so much.

Caroline set her cell phone on the desk. The spreadsheets open before her showed a better picture than they had just two weeks ago, but it wasn't enough. It wasn't going to *be* enough. She had to admit that now. She'd found investors, squeezed profits, but it simply wasn't enough to make the payment due.

They were going to default.

It hurt, but she had to accept the truth. Tomorrow, barring a miracle, Sullivan's would belong to Kazarov Industries. She still wasn't quite sure how she felt about that. Sad, scared, angry—a host of emotions boiled inside her at the thought of her family legacy passing into hands other than her own.

Her mother would be devastated. Her father wouldn't even know. Caroline watched Ryan upend a bucket of sand on the beach and Blake get up and go help him build a sand castle. She pushed back from the desk, determined to join them for a few moments in the hopes it would help her stress levels. Her phone rang before she reached the door.

She turned and went back to get it. It was her CFO. "What's up, Rob?"

"You aren't going to believe this," he said, his voice sounding as if someone had just told him he'd won the lottery, "but we have another investor. We've done it."

Her heart began to pound. "What are you telling me?"

"We'll have the money, Caroline. Kazarov won't win."

She sat back in her chair as her body went numb. "You're sure?" It didn't seem possible, and yet…

Sudden joy suffused her. But sadness followed hard on joy's heels. Which was stunning.

My God, she was actually sad that Roman was going to lose! She blinked at the incongruity of her feelings while Rob filled her in on their last minute savior.

"European investment group," he was saying. "Looking to expand their holdings in the States…"

The rest trailed into a buzzing in her ears as she tried to process everything. Sullivan's was going to continue. Under *her* leadership. Roman wasn't absorbing anything, breaking anything, selling anything.

She shook herself, forced herself to get her head back in the game, and began to grill Rob about the details. By the time the call was finished, she wanted to shout with joy. She wished that Roman was here so she could tell him.

How odd was that? The person she'd just defeated was the one person she most wanted to share this news with.

She shot up from her chair, her nerves suddenly on edge from the rush of adrenaline. Pacing, she punched in Roman's number and waited. He answered on the third ring.

"Roman," she said, when his beautiful voice filled her ears.

"Yes, my angel?" he replied, his voice full of warmth that tugged at her and made her want to wrap her arms around him.

She clutched the phone tight, wanting to say the words, but realizing she couldn't. She couldn't tell him like this. It had to be in person. "I was just wondering when you were returning."

"I'm on my way now," he said, and her limbs filled with delicious languor as she imagined their bodies entwined on silk sheets. "Is everything okay?"

"Never better," she said, though her heart pounded recklessly. "But hurry. I want you."

He chuckled softly and said something that made heat pool in her belly. Ten minutes later, she heard the slam of a car door, and she rushed to the front of the house. Roman came up the steps wearing a suit, which surprised her, since she didn't remember him leaving in a suit this morning. Then again, she'd been half-asleep when he'd left.

Her heart turned over with love for him as he swept her into his arms and kissed her thoroughly. Caroline wrapped her arms around his neck and arched her body into his. He made her feel gloriously alive when she'd been numb for so long.

Her nerves throbbed with tension in spite of her happiness. The last time she'd been so happy with him, everything went wrong.

She told herself there was no one here to force her to walk away this time. This time, she was in control. This time, for better or worse, it was *her* choice. And his.

She shuddered and ground her hips against him until she found what she sought.

Oh yes, he was ready for her.

"What has happened to put you in such a good mood?" he asked, kissing a trail down her neck before he took her hand and tugged her toward his room.

"I'll tell you later." She kicked the door shut behind her and turned him until he was against it. Her fingers went to his buttons, slipping them open expertly. "First, I have needs that require assuaging."

Roman laughed as she spread his shirt open and pressed her mouth to his golden skin. "Then I'm your man."

The tables turned quickly after that. He had her naked within moments. But instead of hauling her to the bed, he used the closest surface he could find, turning her until she was bent over the arm of the couch in the sitting area, her bottom high in the air, her body open to him.

He gripped her hips and slid into her while she arched her back and tried to get closer to him.

And then they were sailing into oblivion, his body hot and hard inside hers, playing her as if she were an instrument that only he knew. Caroline didn't last long. Within moments, she'd fallen over the edge of pleasure and tumbled deep into an orgasm that had her panting and gasping and begging him to make it last.

He did. And when it was done, when they were both spent, he tugged her into his arms and settled on the couch with her, brushing her hair off her damp forehead and pressing his lips to her skin.

"So tell me what put you in such a good mood, *solynshko.*"

Caroline's heart thumped. It was the moment she'd been waiting for, and now she wasn't certain what to say. Wasn't certain how he'd take the news.

Except if he took it badly, she'd know what that meant, wouldn't she? She'd know that everything between them had been false, and that he wasn't interested in her happiness so much as he was in winning. And as much as that prospect scared her, it was better to know it now rather than later.

She bit her lip and lowered her lashes. "We're making the payment," she said. "On time."

His laugh startled her and her gaze snapped to his. But he wasn't upset. This wasn't disbelieving laughter. Warmth spread through her blood, her bones. He seemed happy. Really, truly happy.

"Well done," he said, and then kissed her. "Sullivan's carries on, and the Sullivan heiress wins the day."

"You aren't upset?" she asked, even though it was a redundant question at this point.

His smile was brilliant, his blue eyes sparkling. "How

could I be? I will get my money, and the hassle of making Sullivan's profitable still falls to you. It's win-win for me."

It hit her how perfect this moment was. They were naked on the couch, clothes strewn across the furniture and floors, and they were talking business. A bubble of happiness welled within her. This was what she wanted. A life with Roman. A life where she felt she was part of an equal partnership, where she was valued for her brain as much as her body or her pedigree. Her parents had had it wrong when they'd wanted to keep her from the business. Sullivan's *was* in her blood.

And so was Roman. She pushed away the tiny thread of panic that insisted on weaving through the fabric of her happiness. *It's fine. He's not upset. The bottom isn't going to fall out.*

"I was worried at how you would take the news," she said. "You seemed to want Sullivan's so badly."

He shrugged. "I can think of something else I want even more." He bent and kissed her, softly, sweetly. Desire, so freshly sated, throbbed to life inside her again. "We should marry, Caroline. For Ryan. For us."

She sighed contentedly, stretching against him. *This.* This was what she should have had all along. This blissful, joyful, incandescent happiness. It was not going to fall apart. It was real, and true.

"We should," she said. "We definitely should."

He sat up and tugged her upright. "Get dressed. There's a priest at the resort."

Caroline laughed as she slid onto his lap and wrapped her legs around his waist. "We have time, Roman."

His body hardened, his shaft rising heavy and thick between them. "Perhaps we do, *lyubimaya moya,*" he said, his accent becoming more pronounced again.

Caroline purred in approval. "You *are* a man of many talents, Roman Kazarov."

* * *

They were married at sunset, on the beach where they'd made love. It was a private ceremony with only Blake, Ryan and the household staff for company. Caroline's head was still spinning from how quickly it had happened. Once they'd made love and gotten dressed again, Roman had asked her once more if she would marry him here, today, on this island.

Her heart filled with love, she'd said yes. Finally, she and Ryan and Roman would be a family.

She kissed Roman when the priest told her to, and then turned to find Blake watching with tears in his eyes. Ryan looked so serious in his little button-down shirt and shorts, and she laughed as he broke free from Blake and ran into her arms.

"It's okay, sweetheart," she told him as she bent to catch him and realized she was crying. "Mommy is very happy."

"Is Mr. Roman my daddy now?" he asked shyly, and Caroline tried not to break down with the happy, delirious tears that threatened.

"Yes, baby," she managed to reply. "That's right."

She picked him up and held him tightly against her. He turned wide eyes to Roman, who watched them both so carefully that it made her heart ache. He was still unsure with Ryan, though he was getting better. She smiled to encourage him and he smiled back, his grin breaking wide.

Her heart felt as if it would stop then and there. Roman opened his arms, and she stepped into them. Ryan put his little arms around Roman's neck, and Roman laughed.

"I am happy to be your daddy," he said, and her heart squeezed tight.

They returned to the house and had a leisurely meal as a family, and then Blake took Ryan for his bath and bedtime. Caroline felt suddenly shy, which was ridiculous, when Roman came over and pulled her up from her seat.

"I want to make love to you," he said, his voice a soft growl that slid through her nerve endings and made her quiver with longing. "As my wife."

And then he picked her up and carried her to the bedroom, while she hid her face against his crisp white shirt. He kicked the door closed and undressed her slowly, thoroughly exploring her, as if he had all the time in the world. Even after she was naked, he took his time, tormenting her with his lips and tongue and teeth, before he finally sank deep inside her and took them both to paradise.

As her orgasm hit her, Caroline felt the words overwhelming her, rushing out of her as if they had to break free or choke her. "I love you, Roman!"

"Caroline," Roman said, holding her tightly. "My precious Caroline."

It was as close to an admission of love as he'd come, and she sighed happily before she fell asleep in his arms.

This time, it would work. Nothing would come between them ever again.

CHAPTER FIFTEEN

Kazarov Wins Again! But at What Price?

THE PHONE RANG in the middle of the night. Caroline turned over, coming awake slowly, while Roman talked to whoever had disturbed them, his voice hard and commanding even as he tried to keep it quiet.

She wished she understood Russian at that moment, because Roman did not sound happy. Another few minutes and he ended the call.

"What's wrong?" she asked, propping herself on an elbow beside him. He was sitting on the edge of the bed, raking his hands through his hair and yawning.

At the sound of her voice, he turned. "It's nothing," he said, tipping her chin up and kissing her softly. "Business."

"It didn't sound like nothing."

He sighed. "I have some things to take care of," he said shortly. "I need to return to New York. I'll be back in a day, maybe two."

Her heart fell into her toes. Two days seemed like a lifetime now. "I'll go with you," she said. "I have things to do at Sullivan's, anyway."

"This is our honeymoon, *angel moy*. You should not be working."

"Neither should you," she said, sitting up beside him and running her palms over the smooth muscle of his back.

"It cannot be helped," he said softly, turning and pushing her back onto the bed. His mouth found the hollow of her throat. "I'll be back before bedtime tonight, how's that?"

She sighed as her arms went around him. "It will have to do, I suppose. But Roman, maybe we should all go. There's too much going on right now—"

"Shh," he said. "You've won, *solnyshko*. The payment will be made on time, and you deserve a vacation after all your hard work. Worry about Sullivan's next week."

Caroline yawned and stretched. She was still so tired after a long day of phone calls, hot lovemaking and getting married. Still, she had every intention of dragging herself from the bed and going with Roman, but by the time she awoke again, he was long gone.

Caroline sat up in bed and blinked as the sun slanted through the blinds. Confusion clouded her brain, making everything fuzzy—and then she remembered last night and Roman's phone call.

Uneasiness pooled in her belly, though she didn't know why.

But she couldn't lie in bed any longer, so she showered and dressed and went to find Blake and Ryan. Blake was eating breakfast, while her son played with a toy car on the wide veranda. Beyond, the sea sparkled like diamond-tipped turquoise and the sun beat down on the white sand, though it was early yet.

Caroline sat at the table and reached for a piece of fruit. Blake was watching her, one corner of his mouth tilted up in a knowing grin.

"Stop looking at me like that," she said. "You are the nosiest nanny on the planet."

His grin got bigger. "I am. And I'm happy for you."

She was happy, too. Happy and even a little bit frightened.

She had everything she wanted, but it had all happened so fast that her head was still spinning.

"Mrs. Kazarov," the housekeeper said, and Caroline turned toward the large woman in the colorful print dress, who held up a phone. "You left this in the office. It's been buzzing for twenty minutes at least."

"Thank you," Caroline replied, a bit chagrined as she took the phone. She'd forgotten that she'd left it plugged in last night when Roman had carried her to bed. She pressed the home button and her heart skipped a beat. There were missed calls, voice messages and even texts—both from her mother and from Rob.

That tiny feeling of panic she'd had earlier blossomed into a full-blown wave churning inside her.

With shaking fingers, she punched the first message and listened to it. She listened to three more, all some version of "Call me, there's a problem," until her nerves were wound so tight she shot up and went to the other end of the veranda to make a call.

Rob's voice came over the line. "Caroline, thank God."

"What's wrong?"

She could hear the strain in his voice when he spoke. "The Europeans are pulling out of the deal," he said, and her heart plummeted right through the wooden slats of the veranda. *Too good to be true.* She'd known it, hadn't she? Felt it keenly.

Rob sucked in a breath and she knew he was dragging on a cigarette. A habit he'd given up, she'd thought. Cold determination settled in her gut. Whatever was coming next, she had to deal with it.

"What else?" she said, bracing herself for it, knowing what was coming even as she did so.

"It's your father. The press—they know."

She'd been wrong. She couldn't prepare for that kind of blow. It wasn't quite the same as when the doctors had delivered the bad news to her and Jon that day. But it was still bad. Gut-wrenching in ways that made her feel so helpless and angry.

Her entire body went numb as she sank onto the nearest chair. She wanted to howl, and she wanted to throw things. Instead, she couldn't move. She'd been flattened. Around her, the world went on as before. But everything had changed.

Again.

Getting off the island was not simple, especially when she had to book a private charter just to get to Miami. Blake was tight-lipped beside her, while Ryan complained about having to sit still instead of run and play as he had on Roman's plane.

Caroline sat with her arms folded and her head turned to stare out the window. She was completely numb. And furious with herself.

She thought back over the hours since that first phone call. Her initial thought had been to call Roman and ask for his help. But then Rob had told her that representatives from Kazarov Industries had arrived to oversee the transfer of Sullivan's, and her belly had turned to ice.

Roman had gotten a phone call in the middle of the night. And he'd told her to stay on the island, that she wasn't needed, that Sullivan's was safe. So he could steal it out from under her?

She'd refused to let herself think such a thing, though her soul had gone numb at the mere idea. After she'd hung up with Rob, she'd tried to call Roman, her fingers shaking as she punched in the number. He hadn't answered. Not entirely unexpected, since he could be in a meeting.

So she'd tried again. And again.

Then she'd left messages—countless messages.

He did not return her call. For hours, she didn't hear a word.

Finally, as the day dragged on and she heard nothing from the man she'd married, she'd had to accept the truth. Just as she'd had to accept the truth when her father had told her she needed to marry Jon to save the stores, or when Jon's doctor had told her the chemo wasn't working and he was dying, or when her father had ceased to be the vibrant, brilliant man he'd always been and become a confused, frightened individual.

The truth hurt. She hated the truth. She didn't want to believe it.

But one thing she'd learned in the last five years was that denying the truth didn't make anything better. Just like ripping a Band-Aid from her skin, it was better to do it quickly. Better to accept the cold, hard, terrible truth than to pretend it wasn't happening.

And the truth was that Roman had betrayed her. He hadn't given up his notion of revenge at all. Why would he? She'd broken his heart, taken his child from him. Her father had cost him his livelihood and his ability to take care of his dying mother. That was an awful lot to forgive in such a short time.

He hated the Sullivans, regardless that he might want her physically or that he wanted their child. The truth of that statement was like a dagger to her heart.

Had he told her he loved her? No. He'd made no promises that he ever would. She'd let her heart fill in the blanks, had let herself believe what she wanted so desperately to believe: that it was possible.

Instead, he'd taken her information, her good news, and worked to thwart it. What other explanation could there be?

Worse, he'd leaked information about her father. He'd had to know news of that sort would scare her investors in the interim. That hurt most of all.

She'd called her mother, who was holding up well, though she'd had to barricade herself and her husband in the house in order to prevent prying photographers with telephoto lenses from capturing pictures. The story of Frank Sullivan's Alzheimer's was big news, and a current image of him looking vacant-eyed or gaunt would only serve to increase circulation of that day's paper.

Caroline despised the vultures. But she despised herself even more. How could she be so gullible? So blind and stupid? How could she have let Roman into her life the way she had, knowing what he'd wanted from her in the first place? He'd never pretended to want anything different, except at the end. And she'd stupidly believed him. Stupidly trusted him.

Now she was married to him. He'd made sure of that before he'd left, hadn't he? He'd made sure, so she couldn't take Ryan from him once he'd snatched Sullivan's out from under her. She remembered him telling her to relax, telling her she'd won, telling her to stay on the island and enjoy herself.

She'd relaxed her guard, and he'd brought the knife across her throat while she wasn't looking.

Sullivan's had defaulted at noon, eastern daylight savings time. She imagined Roman striding into the corporate office, his minions in tow. How smug he must be. How utterly gleeful.

It was nearly nightfall when Caroline's small entourage finally landed at JFK. Blake flagged a taxi. Once she got him and Ryan home again, she instructed the driver to take her to the Sullivan Group headquarters. The store was still open, its shining storefront gleaming in the darkness. She walked inside and let the familiar scents wash over her. Everything smelled new, clean, luxurious. It reminded her of home, because it had always been a home to her.

And now it was no longer hers. Or Ryan's.

Caroline went to the administrative area and took the private elevator up to the corporate offices. The workday was over for the business staff, but a few desk lights remained on as people continued to work well after quitting time.

Caroline stopped to stare at the stylized *S* of the logo etched into the glass doors. What would it become in the future?

She marched toward her office—to do what, she didn't know. Roman looked up from behind her desk when she walked in, and she saw red. Of everything she'd expected, that hadn't even made the top ten. It was a shock to see him. And it hurt far more than she'd ever thought possible.

"Couldn't wait to move in, I see," she said bitterly.

He stood, his handsome face creased in a frown. "Caroline, what are you doing here?"

She knew she had to look like hell after all the travel, but she didn't care. She tugged at her sundress, trying to remove the wrinkles, and lifted her chin to stare him directly in the eye. For the barest of moments, she wanted to rush into his arms. Wanted him to hold her and tell her it was all a mistake.

Better to rip the bandage off quick.

"Did you think I would stay on the island once I found out what you were doing?"

He didn't say anything for a long moment. His expression grew dark. "And what is it you think I am doing?" he asked, his voice containing a hint of danger that slid over her nerve endings and made the hair on her neck stand up.

She ignored the question. "My father," she said finally, fighting for control over her emotions so she wouldn't break down and sob. "How could you tell them about my father?"

He looked thunderstruck. "You are accusing me of telling the press about your father's illness?"

"Who else?" she demanded, wrapping her arms around herself to ward off a sudden chill. "Who else stood to gain from it?"

She'd asked herself that question for hours now, and there was only one answer.

He came around the desk, his powerful form lethal and dark with suppressed energy. His face was a study in controlled rage. "How many people knew about your father?"

His voice was a whip in the quiet office, and she recoiled from the potency of it. But only for a moment. Her strength surged back, along with her anger, and she took a step toward him.

"There were a few, but none of them would tell."

"No health care workers, no gardeners at the estate, no secretaries or delivery people? My, how fortunate you are to control so much."

His words stung. And made her furious. "It has never been an issue until now. You are the one with the most to gain."

His eyebrows shot up. "Gain? You think I have something to gain by informing the press that my wife's father is a tragically sick man?"

Wife. How that word hurt. She shoved it aside and spread her arms wide. "This. You had all of this to gain. Is it any coincidence that my new investors decided to back out on the very same day my father's illness was leaked to the press? I may be the CEO in truth, but there are still those who believe my father is the power behind the throne."

Roman appeared ashen for just a moment—or maybe it was her imagination, because he suddenly looked very, very angry. "You believe I would do this. You truly believe it."

"Am I wrong?" she demanded. Part of her wanted him to deny it. Part of her wanted to believe those denials. But the evidence was overwhelming. They'd known each other such a short interval this time. How could she truly know what Roman Kazarov would do when he'd had five years to hate and plan?

"What do you think?" he asked, turning it back on her. A muscle ticked in his jaw. A very fine, very tiny muscle that hinted at how close he skated to the edge of control.

"I think you came to New York with a plan," she said, her stomach twisting and churning with hurt and anger and sadness. "And I believe you were willing to do whatever it took to see that plan through."

"I see," he said tightly.

Her breath hitched in suddenly, and she worked to control it. If he'd stabbed her through the heart with the letter opener lying on her desk, it couldn't have hurt worse. "You aren't denying anything."

He shoved his hands in his pockets. For the first time, she noted that he looked a bit disheveled. His jacket and tie were gone, thrown over a chair, and his hair was mussed. His eyes, she noted, were bloodshot.

She felt a pang of sympathy, but she hardened her heart against it. She would never feel sympathetic to him again. He probably looked haggard because he was working so hard to enjoy his triumph. No doubt he was already fielding offers for the real estate sitting beneath her stores, and counting his money gleefully.

"Why should I?" he said in answer to her accusation. "You have already made up your mind."

How did he make her feel badly, when he was the one in her store? In her office? He held the smoking gun, and yet she felt as if someone had fed her a glass omelet. Her stomach was torn to shreds, along with her nerves.

She felt so tired all of a sudden. Drained, and not because of the long day of travel. "Why are you here?"

He shrugged. "You defaulted today. I am here to claim my prize." His voice was so cold, so hard. He wasn't the man she'd made love with last night. The man she'd stood on the beach with, the one who'd opened his arms and held both her and Ryan close, as if he cherished them. She felt as if she would be physically ill.

"I don't know why you're angry," she said, her throat aching as she forced the words out. "I called you a dozen times. I left messages. You never replied. And now you are here, in *my* office, with my company arrayed before you. How could there possibly be any other explanation except the one that seems so obvious to us both?"

He turned and went back to the chair, sank down on it. His eyes glittered with heat and unspoken anger. Such deep,

deep anger. She shivered—and refused to feel anything other than anger of her own.

"There isn't, of course. Because you know everything, Caroline."

Her eyes filled with tears. One spilled down her cheek. Her heart was breaking in two and he didn't care. "I loved you, you idiot," she said. And then she laughed. "Or maybe I'm the one who's an idiot. An idiot for believing in you."

His hands were fists on the desk. *Her* desk. His eyes were bleak, harsh. "Yes, some belief. It lasted all of a few days, I think."

She felt a pinprick of guilt—and that angered her. "How dare you try to turn this around on me? I denied it when Rob told me your people were coming to oversee the transfer, and I denied all day that you would do this to me, until it was obvious you weren't going to call me back and tell me I was wrong."

"So long? I am impressed."

He sounded cold, and it hurt that he could after they'd been so hot together only hours before. Caroline closed her eyes, searching for strength. She just wanted it all to go away. She wanted to rewind the clock and have this go much differently.

"You've won, Roman. Congratulations."

He stood again and she took a step backward. Then she whirled and strode from her office as regally as she could manage. She made it to the elevator without him stopping her, and jumped behind the doors just as they started closed. She absolutely refused to break down until she was safely on her way to the ground floor.

But even then, she was too numb to do so.

He was an ass. An incredible, stupid ass for allowing that to happen. Roman sank onto the chair and watched her go, his pride too wounded for him to follow as he should.

What was the matter with him? He raked a hand through his hair and slumped in his chair. *Her* chair.

He knew it looked bad, and yet he'd foolishly thought something fundamental had changed between them on the island. That she would believe in him because she loved him, and that she would wait for him to explain what was going on.

Instead, she'd jumped to every rotten conclusion she could in the space of a few minutes. He told himself that he should have expected it, but foolishly he'd anticipated a different reaction from her.

She'd said she loved him. She'd said she wanted to be a family. He'd thought that meant something. But instead of choosing him, choosing to believe in him, she'd chosen her family—the Sullivan family—once again. If something bad was happening to the Sullivans, and Roman Kazarov was around, then he must be the one to blame.

Roman blew out a breath. He'd never expected her to leave the island and come here. He should have. He should have expected exactly that, because Caroline was too stubborn, too driven, to ever sit quietly while something was happening to her precious company.

She believed the worst of him. She believed that he'd married her, made love to her, claimed her as his again and again, with the sole intention of duping her out of her legacy.

Once, he might have done so. Once, before he'd realized he still loved her. That he'd always loved her, and that she was his soul mate. Not that he'd ever believed in such ridiculous crap, but he knew it was true with Caroline. She was the only woman he'd ever loved, the only one he'd ever felt this inexplicable kinship with. Even now, in spite of the hurt and rage, he wanted her.

But she did not want him. That thought made the breath seize in his chest. Could that truly happen? Could she deny him?

A chill skated over him then. She could. She had done so before.

His inner beast wanted to smash things, but he refused to let it out. He still had work to do, papers to sign, and then he would go home and collapse on his couch with a shot of vodka.

Alone. The thought made him want to howl.

Go after her. Go now.

Roman shook his head to rid himself of the voice. He had to give her time to think, time to cool down. And he had to give himself time to cool down, too.

Because he was murderously angry, and that was no way to feel when he faced Caroline again. There was too much at stake, too many hurtful things that could be said. He wanted to face her rationally, calmly.

And then he wanted to drag her into his arms and never let her go. Except, he acknowledged, he might very well have to.

CHAPTER SIXTEEN

A Happy Ending for Caro and Kazarov, After All?

THIS WAS NOT how she'd thought it would end for her and Sullivan's. Caroline sat on the couch in her living room, staring at the television, though she wasn't really paying attention to what was on. It had been two days since she'd left Sullivan's, and she was still thinking about Roman, about the way he'd looked at her when she'd walked in and accused him of stealing her company out from under her.

He'd looked…disappointed. And hurt.

Or maybe that was just wishful thinking.

She couldn't stop thinking about him, about the way she'd lain in his arms their last night together, the way she said she'd loved him when he made her climax for the zillionth time. She couldn't stop thinking about how he made her feel, or how he held Ryan's little hand and went wherever their son wanted to tug him.

Roman had seemed happy on the island. Happy with them.

But, clearly, not happy enough to put a stopper in his thirst for revenge.

She'd been deluded into thinking so. Whenever she thought about his reaction when she'd told him about her new investors, it made her heart hurt. The truth was that she'd seen what she wanted to see instead of what was really behind the curtain.

And she should have known better. Life had dealt her almost nothing but heartache for five long years. Why would it suddenly hand her everything she wanted right when she most wanted it? It was simply another way of reminding her how fragile happiness was, how fleeting.

"Are you planning to sit there all day again?"

Caroline turned to look over her shoulder at Blake. He was dressed in shorts and a Willie Nelson T-shirt that would have made her laugh if she hadn't been so sad. He was holding a backpack and his sunglasses were perched on his head.

"Are you going to the park?" she asked.

"We are, just as soon as Ryan figures out which toys he wants to take. Do you want to come?"

Caroline shook her head, her long ponytail brushing her neck, reminding her that she hadn't gotten dressed since she'd come home the other night. She'd sat in her pajamas day after day, watching television.

Ryan came running down the hall then, chattering happily about the robot he was taking with him to the park. He ran to her side. "Mommy, do you want to come play with me and Uncle Blake? We're going to have ice cream, too."

Caroline ruffled her son's hair. He was so like Roman that it hurt to look at him. "Mommy's going to stay home today," she said. "But you have fun."

Ryan's face screwed up in a frown. "Where is Mr. Roman? I mean Daddy," he corrected, and her heart felt ripped in two. "I want to show him my robot."

Caroline sniffed. "He's working, sweetie, but he'll be back soon."

Blake was frowning at her, but what else could she say? She and Roman were still married, and for Ryan's sake, they were going to have to figure out what came next. He would always be a part of Ryan's life, even if he wasn't a part of hers.

The thought of him not being in her life made a fresh wave of tears press against the backs of her eyes. *Stupid.*

Ryan and Blake left after a few more minutes of making sure they had everything they needed, and then Caroline called her mother. She'd been checking in every few hours, just to see how her mom was faring. Surprisingly, after the initial shock of her father's diagnosis reaching the press, the coverage had leveled off quickly. There were a few photographers lurking outside the estate, but most of them had gone. The stories in the papers were thoughtful and serious now. The more Caroline read, the more she began to think of ways in which she could support Alzheimer's research.

There would be no cure for her father, but maybe one day others could be helped. It was a thought that buoyed her up during the conversation with her mother.

When Caroline finished the call, the house was quiet. Too quiet.

She had to get up. She had to stop moping, and figure out what to do next. She wasn't a quitter and she despised sitting around and feeling sorry for herself. That ended here and now.

After a quick shower, she tugged on jeans and a silk tee with sandals. Then she pinned her hair onto her head in a messy bun and swiped on lip gloss and mascara. She was presentable, at least. She grabbed her purse as she swept through the kitchen. Maybe she'd walk over to Milk & Cookies Bakery and get some of their fabulous homemade cookies, then go to the park and surprise Blake and Ryan.

Ryan loved chocolate chip.

Plan made, Caroline yanked open the front door—and came to a screeching halt at the sight of the man with gorgeous blue eyes staring up at her from the bottom step. She clutched the door as her heart throbbed.

"What do you want?"

Something flickered in his eyes, but then it was gone. Annoyance? Anger? Fear?

"I want to talk to you."

She swallowed. "Fine, say what you need to say and go."

One eyebrow lifted. "There is a man across the street in a blue sedan. He is a photographer, and his lens has been pointed at us since you opened the door. Do you really wish to do this here?"

She waited for the space of several heartbeats, her fingers pressing hard against the mahogany of her door. And then she stepped back and swung it open in silent invitation. Roman came up the steps and into her house. She shut the door behind him, shrinking back as he turned to face her.

The look on his face was a mixture of anguish and rage. She'd let a lion into her den and now she would pay the price.

"I have been thinking very hard, Caroline," he began, his voice as cool as silk. "And no matter how I try, my anger refuses to abate."

Shock rooted her to the spot, but only for a moment. "Your anger? *Your* anger? I'm not the one who deceived you."

"Ah, but you did," he said, his eyes flashing hotly. He took up all the space in her foyer, though it was huge. He took all the space because his presence was that big. And because he had been central to her life almost from the moment she'd met him.

He took a step closer and she ducked toward the living room, putting a couch between them. She didn't know why, but it seemed the safest course.

"I have no idea what you mean, Roman. You're talking nonsense."

"Am I? You said you loved me, Caroline. You lied."

"How dare you—"

"I dare because it is true. If you loved me, you would not believe such bad things about me. If you loved me, you would give me a chance to explain without accusing me of ruining your life."

"I did give you a chance!" she yelled. "I called and called you that day!"

For the barest moment, he looked chagrined. But then his anger was back, full force. "If you had trusted me, you would have learned the truth in good time."

"How dare you come here and say that to me?" she whispered. How dare he stand there, looking so much bigger than life, and tempt her with what she wanted most in this world—for everything to work out, for it to have all been a mistake.

Life didn't work that way.

Or it didn't for her. It never had.

Without a word, he took a folded packet of papers from his back pocket and tossed it at her. At first, she only stared at it, lying on the floor between them.

"What is that?"

"Pick it up."

It seemed to take an age, as if she were afraid of what she'd find, but she finally bent and retrieved the thick envelope, smoothing it where it had been folded. She clutched it to her chest and stared at him.

"Open it, Caroline."

She did as he said, her heart suddenly throbbing hot and quick. And then it stopped beating and she felt the color drain from her face.

Roman took an alarmed step toward her, but she put her hand out and steadied herself on the back of the couch. Confusion swirled inside her. "You don't own Sullivan's."

His nostrils flared. "*Nyet,* this is true."

"But I thought…"

"I know what you thought," he snapped. "You were wrong."

Her stomach twisted. "Why didn't you tell me before?"

"You mean when you walked in and accused me of seducing you, lying to you and stealing your heritage?"

She nodded, a lump forming in her throat.

He shoved a hand through his hair. Roman was always so cool, so controlled, and yet he looked as if he hadn't slept much in the past two days. His dark hair stood up in places. His eyes were red, as if he'd been drinking, and there were shadows under them.

"I should have," he muttered. "But I was stunned. And angry. I did not react well." He met her gaze evenly. "Besides, when you walked in, I technically did own Sullivan's. I was working to undo that."

She came around and sank down on the couch, her legs unable to hold her any longer. She could hardly believe what she was hearing. Hope was an insistent spark inside her, though she cautioned it not to grow just yet. "Why didn't you return my calls?"

"I regret that," he said softly. "But I was in meetings when you first called. By the time I knew you'd heard the Europeans had pulled out, I was working hard to fix it. They'd heard about your father and got cold feet. I was trying to talk them into investing anyway, because I wanted to give you good news when I called. I did not expect you to walk into the office."

"I wish you had just told me," she said, her heart beating double time. If he'd told her, she wouldn't have been so scared. And she wouldn't have made a fool of herself.

Or would she?

"And what would you have done, Caroline? Would you have stayed on the island and waited for me, or would you have done exactly the same thing and come running back to New York?"

She swallowed. They both knew the answer. "I wouldn't have stayed."

"Yes. This is why I did not tell you."

She sat there and stared at the papers in her hand. He'd really given her back her company. They'd defaulted, but he'd worked to undo it all. And he'd handed it back with generous conditions. Sullivan's would once again thrive, thanks to him.

A new thought occurred to her then. She remembered him on the island in his suit. He'd left early and returned after a long day away. "You were the one who found the last minute investor, weren't you?"

She'd been on the phone for days, working hard to find the money, and then someone she hadn't even talked to miraculously invested at the last minute?

Roman's gaze was steady. *"Da."*

"That same day I told you," she said. "That's why you were gone all day."

He nodded. "The chairman of a very large financial firm is a guest at the resort. I went to meet with him."

Tears filled her eyes then. "Why would you do that?"

"Because I wanted you to win." The words were simple, stark. And if she hadn't been sitting, they would have knocked her over.

Yet it was still so hard to believe. When she believed, when she let go and thought that good things were going to happen to her, life knocked her flat on her behind. "Not too long ago, you wanted me to lose. You wanted to punish me."

"Things changed."

She found herself leaning forward. Maybe she should be angry that he'd interfered, instead of letting her succeed or fail on her own, but she found she was far more riveted by what had motivated him. "What changed, Roman?"

He closed his eyes, and her heart felt as if it would stop beating in the next few seconds. She realized then that it all came down to this moment. It was as if her entire life depended on his next words.

"I realized that I love you, Caroline. That life without you is too stark, too lonely. That I would rather see you happy than sad, and that I'd lose a hundred companies if it made you so."

She bowed her head, joy suffusing her even as a terrible

feeling of dread rose inside her soul. Once more, she'd made a horrible mess of things. And, once more, how could she be certain this was real? That tomorrow wouldn't ruin everything?

"How can you possibly love me after what I said to you? After I accused you of such terrible deeds?"

She heard him sigh. "I'm still angry with you. But love doesn't stop because someone hurts you. If it does, then it's not love, is it?"

Tears fell freely down her cheeks now. She dropped the papers and stood, facing him across the room. She wanted to go to him, but was scared to do so.

"I'm sorry, Roman. I should have given you a chance. But I was just so miserable, because I love you so much and I couldn't bear the thought that you didn't love me. And then, when the news of my father came out, I thought the worst...."

His face was stark with emotion. "It seemed easier to believe I would hurt you than that I might help you because I loved you?"

She nodded, and a hot tear fell on the back of her hand. God, she was a mess. An emotional, quaking mess. "That's what happens in my life, Roman. I've lost so many people I love. You. Jon. My father." She choked back the lump in her throat. "I thought I was losing you again."

"Caroline," he said softly. And then he opened his arms. She rushed into them, squeezing him tight. "I'm sorry, *lyubimaya moya,*" he said, his lips against her hair. "I should have told you how I felt. I should have told you what I was doing. You aren't losing me."

She buried her face against the hard plane of his chest. "How can you say that, when it's my fault? I should have given you a chance to explain. I should have known you wouldn't do such a terrible thing—"

He tilted her chin up and kissed her swiftly. She melted

into his embrace, her entire body trembling with adrenaline and desire.

"We have both made mistakes," he admitted hoarsley. "Neither of us is perfect."

She laughed, the sound broken. "You could have just extended the loan in the first place, you know. That would have worked, too."

His smile was gentle. "Yes, but I wanted you to win. It seemed important to you."

"Not as important as you," she said honestly, and he squeezed her tighter. "I've longed for you every day for five years, even when I tried to pretend I didn't. If I lost Sullivan's, I wouldn't care, so long as I still had you. When I walked into my office the other night, I thought I'd lost you both. And losing you was the more frightening of the two."

He shuddered, his big body rippling from head to toe. "You didn't lose me. I love you, Caroline. And I love our son. I lost five years with you. I don't want to lose another minute."

Caroline swiped her fingers over her eyes. "I don't know why you love me after everything that's happened, but I'm glad you do."

He sank onto the chair behind him and pulled her down with him until she was sitting across his lap. Then he stroked a finger over her cheek, her lips, while she shivered and ached and realized how very much she wanted him in that moment.

"I love you because I can do nothing else. I've loved you, since the first moment I saw you so many years ago. You're strong, Caroline, and fierce. You've put yourself and your needs last while you took care of others, and you've sacrificed so much. How could I help but love someone so brave that she would do that for other people?" He kissed her cheeks, her nose. "But even were you not so brave, I would love you. You are hardwired into my DNA. I could as soon breathe underwater as I could cut you from my life. It's not possible to live without you."

Caroline put her palms on either side of his face, smiling through her tears. Her heart was full of joy for the first time in a very long time. True, real joy that she no longer feared would be snatched from her tomorrow.

"You're an amazing man. And I think you'd better take me to the bedroom now. I have much to apologize for."

"No more apologizing," he told her, his handsome face serious. "We have too much living to do."

Caroline laughed tearfully. "Then take me to bed, Roman. I have much living I want to do. *Urgent* living."

Roman kissed her until she was dizzy with need. And then he stood, still holding her, and strode toward the stairs. "I think we'd better find that bed, *solnyshko*. I have some living of my own I'd like to try…."

EPILOGUE

*Sullivan's Posts Huge Gains on Leadership of
Chief Executive Officer Caroline Sullivan Kazarov*

Expecting for Real! Caro Glowing, Kazarov Beaming

*Scandalous Kazarovs Spend One-Year Anniversary in
Restaurant, Entirely Absorbed in Each Other*

CAROLINE THUMBED THROUGH the newspapers that Blake had
saved, laughing at the ridiculousness of some of them. He
did it to tease her, she knew, but she truly enjoyed them. Or
she did these days, anyway.

She hadn't enjoyed them at all when her father had been
so prominently featured, but Roman had tracked down the
source of that story. A home health care aide that her mother
had fired for petty thievery had been behind the leak. The
man had thought he could make a quick buck. And he had,
but then he'd lost it all by gambling it away at a casino in
Atlantic City.

Divine justice, perhaps. Caroline had no sympathy for
anyone who thought he was entitled to profit from someone
else's misfortune.

She put her hand on her stomach as the baby kicked.
Roman walked in just then and found her grimacing.

"What is the matter, *solnyshko?* Is everything all right?"

"Fine," she said. "But I think this little girl is going to be a kickboxer."

"She gets it from your side of the family," he said, and she turned to gape at him.

"I beg your pardon?"

Roman laughed as he came over and sat down beside her on the veranda of their Caribbean getaway.

"You are a fighter, Caroline. I've never known anyone who fought harder for what she wanted than you have."

"Except maybe you."

He laughed again. "All right, so I fight too. Perhaps she gets it from us both."

"Then she will be formidable."

"Like her mother."

Caroline frowned. "I'm not feeling so formidable these days. I feel fat and hungry."

"You are gorgeous, my love. Would you like me to get you something from the kitchen? I believe there is some jerk chicken in the fridge."

"Mmm, that sounds good," she said. But then she held up her hand. "No, I'm not doing it. Fruit, that would be better. I'll take a banana. And some mango."

"As you wish."

Caroline watched her husband walk away, her heart swelling with so much love and happiness. They'd been married for over a year now, but she still felt as if they were on their honeymoon.

The only sadness in her life was the continuing deterioration of her father's condition, but she'd instituted a campaign in the stores where the profits from a particular line of merchandise went into Alzheimer's research. One day, maybe, there'd be a cure for those afflicted. It wouldn't come in time to help her father, of course. He was now in an assisted living facility, and her mother was learning to live life alone.

Roman returned with her fruit. "Your mother called me today," he said, as if he'd known Caroline had been thinking about her parents. He laughed at her disbelieving look. "Yes, she called *me*. I believe she's coming around. She might even like me now."

Caroline smiled up at him. "You do have a way with the ladies, Roman. I think it's the sexy Russian accent."

He winked at her. "Perhaps. Anyway, she wished to know if you were getting enough rest and taking your vitamins. I told her you were."

Caroline shook her head. "I think she wanted an excuse to talk to you. She could have asked me those questions. Did she say anything else?"

"Not really. She is planning a visit. That's about it." He shrugged. And then he nodded at the tablet Caroline was holding, and the email visible there. "How is Blake these days?"

"He's painting again," she said happily. "And he's dating. I'm pleased for him. But I miss him, too."

"I know you do. But it's good he's reentering life. It takes time when you lose someone you love," Roman said. And then he frowned. "Though I have yet to forgive him for making me hire a new nanny. This one is nowhere near as fun."

"She's a bit older than Blake," Caroline said, laughing. "Mrs. Steele isn't going to take Ryan surfing, or run down the beach with him. But she will be fabulous when little Claire wakes up in the middle of the night for the tenth night in a row, mark my words."

Roman shrugged. "As you say, my love." He settled against the cushions and took the papers from her that Blake had sent. "I would call these trash," he said after a few moments, "but damn if they don't seem to be true. We *are* ridiculously happy, are we not?"

"We definitely are."

He put the papers down and reached for her hand. They

sat beside each other, watching the waves roll into shore, until Ryan came running up the steps from the beach and dumped a load of shells at their feet. Then they oohed and aahed appropriately, while their son talked a mile a minute about each and every one.

* * * * *

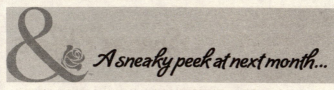

MODERN™

INTERNATIONAL AFFAIRS, SEDUCTION & PASSION GUARANTEED

My wish list for next month's titles...

In stores from 19th April 2013:

☐ A Rich Man's Whim – Lynne Graham

☐ A Touch of Notoriety – Carole Mortimer

☐ Maid for Montero – Kim Lawrence

☐ Captive in his Castle – Chantelle Shaw

☐ Heir to a Dark Inheritance – Maisey Yates

In stores from 3rd May 2013:

☐ A Price Worth Paying? – Trish Morey

☐ The Secret Casella Baby – Cathy Williams

☐ Strictly Temporary – Robyn Grady

☐ Her Deal with the Devil – Nicola Marsh

Available at WHSmith, Tesco, Asda, Eason, Amazon and Apple

Just can't wait?

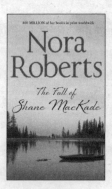